Vespera

Vespera

E.B. Haverly

DEDICATION

For my boys

Always remember that it's never too late to follow your dreams,

even though it may be scary and give you hot poops.

For my husband

(aka my editor, my brain-storming partner, my pro bono therapist,

my sugar daddy, my biggest fan, & the love of my life)

Thank you.

Table of Contents

DEDICATION i

Chapter 1: Normalcy 1

Chapter 2: Ameris 15

Chapter 3: Rogues 22

Chapter 4: The Mark.. 43

Chapter 5: Horrors.. 67

Chapter 6: Changed.. 76

Chapter 7: Rogue City 91

Chapter 8: A New Name.. 105

Chapter 9: Identity... 120

Chapter 10: Healing and Darkness.. 134

Chapter 11: The First Raid.. 152

Chapter 12: A Purpose.. 169

Chapter 13: The Next Venture 184

Chapter 14: Control... 196

Chapter 15: Complications... 212

Chapter 16: Onisk 229

Chapter 17: A Truce 246

Chapter 18: Change of Plans 262

Chapter 19: Bonded 280

Chapter 20: Caneesho 294

Chapter 21: Reunion 310

Chapter 22: The Duke 326

Chapter 23: Drowning 342

Chapter 24: The Ball 359

Chapter 25: Truths 379

Acknowledgement v

Chapter 1: Normalcy

My pulse was a roar in my ears as I gripped the staff tighter. The cold did nothing to alleviate my sweaty palms. Ignore any distractions. I took a breath and readied for the next attack. He ran at me at full speed, his staff raised overhead. My pulse quickened as I waited. I took a deep breath and my muscles tensed.

I easily side-stepped the downward slash of the attack and jammed the end of my staff into his stomach. The air fled from his lungs as he doubled over. I stepped into a spin for momentum and cracked my staff hard on his back and he collapsed onto the snow covered ground. I stood over him as he tried to catch his breath.

"Good stars, Vespera," he said with a whine, "did you have to hit me so hard?" I winced as my cousin slowly rose from all fours to kneeling in the slush. I leaned on my staff and scratched through the thick brown scarf wrapped tightly around my head. I felt my cheeks warm.

"I'm sorry, Henry. I guess I got carried away." I reached a hand to him and helped him up. I strained against his hulking size as he pulled on my hand. Once on his feet, I craned my neck to look up at him. Henry's white-blonde hair gleamed in the winter sun and his eyes shone like pieces of gold, both traits he inherited from my aunt. His size, however, was all from my uncle.

"She got you, son. My turn, girlie," a low, warm voice said. I turned to see my Uncle Fredrick grinning at us from the fence that corrals our meager livestock consisting of a cow, a goat, a pig and some chickens. They too had gathered to watch the daily familial sparring match. I wondered if the animals made bets on us. I laughed at the thought of the pig having to give the cow its slop. I felt a sharp jab in my side and winced.

"Quit your daydreaming and focus, Vespera. Distraction can cost you your life in battle," Uncle Fredrick said, jabbing the staff into my side again. I knocked it away with my own staff.

"When do you expect me to be in a battle, Uncle Fredrick?" I said, raising an eyebrow at him.

"One can never be too careful. Or would you have preferred me to not have taught you how to defend yourself? We can quit now if you like." He raised a dark but graying brow at me. I sighed.

"'One can never be too careful,'" I repeated with a sigh.

"That's my girlie. Now, blades up." Henry walked away from us quickly.

"Allow me to remove myself from the battlefield. Wouldn't want to be a civilian casualty." Henry laughed and took a seat atop the fence. I tightened my scarf and leaned down to pull a long dagger from each of my knee high boots. The weapons were thin and light weight with hilts that curved up parallel to the blade. Uncle Fredrick had recommended them to me years ago. He had said that they were a suitable weapon for my quick movements and also easier to conceal. Despite Uncle Fredrick insisting on a basic knowledge of all kinds of weapons, the unique blades were my favorite.

I took to them quickly, favoring them above swords and staffs and other knives. Uncle Fredrick had boots made with scabbards in them for me for my eighteenth birthday. He pretended that it wasn't because of his paranoia but we all knew better. Once a soldier, always a soldier.

I twirled the daggers around my fingers as he drew his great sword. His stance was statuesque, and his face was calm. My uncle was usually a lighthearted man but when there was a weapon in his hand, he became an entirely different person. Aunt Prudence said that it was because of the Devium War that he fought so long ago. He was a boy when he left and a hero when he returned. I remember Uncle Fredrick getting terribly upset with her when he found out she even said that much. We didn't talk about it anymore after that, but Henry and I always noticed the change in him when we sparred.

I barely had time to deflect his blow as the steel lunged for me.

"Focus, Vespera," my uncle said and swung again. The next time I was ready. I stepped away from him and sent a jab towards his middle. He flicked his wrist and easily batted my blade away.

"Better." With that, he stopped holding back.

I was better than usual against him that day. Much better. I even noticed a bead of sweat on his brow. I smiled and pushed a little harder. A slight ache rippled through my head but was replaced by a strange chill that crept into my eyes. A rush of energy spread through my limbs, and I thought that time moved a little slower. Uncle Fredrick began to slash at me but before I moved to parry, I noticed a slight shift in his stance. Anticipating the change in his strike, I readied a block and shot my other blade forward. His sword caught in the hilt of one of my blades while my other blade just barely touched his neck.

My eyes widened and my mouth fell open. We stood still as we both tried to take in what had just happened. Uncle Fredrick broke first.

"Very well done, Vespera. You anticipated my move and found an opening." He slowly nudged my arm away, removing the point from his neck. I cleared my throat and stepped away smiling. My body nearly went slack with exhaustion and my head swam as the chill left my eyes and took my strength with it. My shoulders slouched, struggling with the weight of my blades despite their lightness, and I swayed a bit. I took a deep breath of the frigid air to clear my head.

Uncle Fredrick patted my back, not noticing how deeply I was affected, and commended me on the fight. I glanced at Henry. His hands were knotted in his hair and his mouth was agape. Then I saw a much more frightening sight. Standing just beside Henry was a short, thin woman with long plaited white-blonde hair and piercing golden eyes. Her arms were tightly crossed over her chest and her brow was a hard line. Luckily, her fiery gaze was fixed upon my uncle.

"Fredrick, we agreed that you wouldn't push her too hard. Look at her. She is about to fall over!" Aunt Prudence rushed over to me. She grabbed the blades from my hands and tossed them to the ground near my uncle. She took my face in her hands and searched my eyes. Being nearly a head taller than my aunt did nothing to diminish her imposing demeanor. I felt like a little girl again as she looked me over. I smiled against the pounding in my head and gently pushed her away.

"I'm fine, Aunt Prudence. I'm just a little tired." Her nose wrinkled.

"'A little tired?' You look ghostly, dearie! Does your head hurt again?"

"I always look ghostly," I said looking away from her. I pulled my scarf a little lower on my forehead and rubbed my temple.

"Oh shush," she said, "You do have a headache. I knew you pushed her too hard, Fredrick. Come inside and rest a bit. I'll make you some of that tea you like so much. You boys finish up any chores you've neglected and come inside for lunch." She led me to the house while glaring at Uncle Fredrick. I winced at the throbbing in my head. Tea sounded nice.

Aunt Prudence pushed open the door of our stone house and had me sit in a chair near the hearth. She must have started a fire earlier. The heat fell on my chilled skin, and I smiled. My muscles started to loosen, and I leaned my throbbing head back. I heard my aunt moving around the kitchen and then she cursed. Willing my legs to stand, I moved to the kitchen door.

"Aunt Prudence, is everything alright?" I said, pushing the door open. She stood on her toes as she dug through a shelf of jars and vials.

"Damn, why didn't I just get more last week? She's going through it so quickly... and with Fredrick riling her up..." she said to herself and then growled.

"Aunt Prudence?" She jumped and turned to me.

"I'm sorry, dearie. I didn't hear you. I'm afraid we are out of your favorite tea." My brows moved together. She tried to look nonchalant, but my aunt's eyes told a different story. They were darting back and forth with worry. She wasn't usually so frantic. I felt an extra weight on my shoulders.

"But the jar was full earlier this week..." She straightened her apron. She smiled lightly but her eyes still wouldn't meet mine.

"Never you mind, dear. I'm sure I can make a different kind of tea that will do just the trick." Again, her voice sounded easy, but she began to pick at the callouses on her hands. A pit formed in my stomach. My headaches had been coming much more frequently lately. My eyes found my feet and my shoulders tensed. I hated the headaches. I felt like such a bother. The door opened and Uncle Fredrick and Henry strolled in.

"I'm sorry that I've used up so much of your ingredients. I know you like to stock up on things in case someone really needs it. What is it exactly? I can go get you more from the woods... or town, even." Aunt Prudence's eyes fixated on mine ferociously at the mention of town. Henry interrupted her lecture.

"I can take her to town, Mother. Really it's not a problem," Henry said as he sat at the table. Uncle Fredrick looked amused as he took a seat.

"I'm sure it isn't a problem at all, son. You wouldn't happen to be thinking about seeing a certain brown haired beauty by the name of Catherine, would you?" Henry's cheeks flushed but he didn't reply. I smiled at him. Henry had been in love with Catherine ever since he met her. I remembered how he told me all about her. He described her every detail and how lovely each one was, even the small gap between her front teeth. Aunt Prudence brought two bowls of steaming stew and sat them before the men. She seemed to have forgotten her lecture.

"Vespera, sit and eat. Henry, I'm afraid you may get too distracted and forget what I need." Henry rolled his eyes.

"Really, Mother. I assure you that I am capable of picking up some powder or plant."

"Is that so? So you won't go see Catherine if I send you on this errand?" She raised her eyebrow at him. Their golden eyes flashed at each other, but Henry broke first.

"I'm merely escorting V. I'm sure she can get you exactly what you need."

"She is unwell. She isn't going anywhere." Her response cut through the room like a knife. I sat at the table. The air in the room felt thick but I swallowed the lump in my throat and took a quick breath. I was not a burden.

"Aunt Prudence, I am fine. We can both go. Besides, I would like to visit Jeb. He doesn't get to leave the Boot much and it's been so long since I went to see him," I said but instead of answering, she just glared at me and gave me a bowl. I tried to sip the stew, if only to convince her that I was feeling better. My headache had dissipated over the conversation but now it was my chest that was in a vice. I wanted to see my friend, but I hated going to town.

"Fredrick, why don't you go? The children can stay here with me." Henry flushed and started to reply but Uncle Fredrick beat him to it.

"They aren't children, Pru. Henry is twenty-five and Vespera will be twenty tomorrow, an adult to do as she wishes. It's been long enough since she has been to town. She needs to find her own way through life eventually. Fear can't be the way forever."

"Oh, it can't, Fredrick? If you didn't have this grand idea of making her learn to fight then we probably wouldn't be in this hazardous situation," Aunt Prudence snapped. Silence filled the room and I felt myself shrink in my chair. The room felt hot, and it was hard to breathe. My headaches were something that I had always had, even as a child, but they occurred more and more often as I grew older. The past few months I went from having one a month or so to multiple in a day. The magnitude of pain was increasing too. Aunt Prudence was constantly frazzled and wanted me under lock and key while Uncle Fredrick was the opposite. The whole situation made me queasy. I stole a glance at them. The two glared at each other. Aunt Prudence looked like she was about to catch fire and Uncle Fredrick was a war general again, cold and menacing.

"Our children must be stronger than us, Prudence. That is what is best for them. I must prepare for the festival now. I leave it in your hands." Without waiting for a response, he went back outside. My aunt's nostrils flared, and she cursed, again.

"Fine, you both will go to town. But before you go, Vespera, please take off those atrocious breeches and put on a dress like a lady."

I tied the bodice of my simple gray dress and wrapped my hair again in my brown scarf. I shivered and my chest tightened as I remembered the time before we took over the orchard that we now called home. Demon, blood head, caster. The names snuck to the front of my mind from their blackened corner I tried to keep them in. I could do this. It was just a quick trip to town and back. I took a breath as I threw on my cloak and met Henry at the barn.

"I tried to saddle your horse, but you know how she is," Henry said, clearly annoyed. I patted her glossy black coat and scolded her.

"Tempest, there is no need to be mean all the time." Her head butted against mine but nuzzled me after. The tightness in my chest eased as I readied her saddle. I told myself that I had to be calm for my horse since she was always on edge. She was one of the only things that I felt really depended on me. She made feel capable. I patted her neck with a smile and then we proceeded down the path.

"So apparently Prince Aleron is supposed to come to the Dark Day Festival this year. Every girl in Ameris is going crazy," Henry said breaking the silence and winking at me.

"Really, Henry?" I rolled my eyes at him.

"What?" he said with a smirk and a glint in his eye. "The crown prince of Rokellia is the most eligible bachelor in all the kingdom and I hear he is incredibly handsome." I snorted at him. Henry was a worse gossip than an old crone.

"And did Catherine tell you that?" I pulled my cloak tighter around me as the winter wind picked up. Henry scoffed.

"I have no doubt of Catherine's love for me. A prince couldn't even break our bond."

"Still though, why would Prince Aleron make the journey from the capital? Ameris isn't the only city with a Dark Day Festival," I said, shaking my head at him. Henry shrugged.

"Maybe a change of scenery? Or trying to find a bride..." He winked at me, and I kicked his stirrup and nearly unseated him. Unfortunately, I still felt my cheeks flush.

"He's engaged to the Capilious Princess, isn't he? I'm sure marrying a merchant's daughter would be frowned upon." Henry shook his head and scoffed.

"Those are just rumors and barely that. Have you seen the darling Pearl Princess? I don't know who came up with that name, but Princess Tilteen is certainly no pearl. Who would ever marry her?"

"Have you even seen her, Henry?" He rubbed his neck and shrugged.

"Well, no but I've seen a drawing of her likeness. Not pretty at all, I say." I rolled my eyes at him.

"I don't think you're right on this one, Henry," I said smugly. Henry cut his eyes at me but grinned.

"Me wrong? I don't think so. Let's just take some bets on this 'engagement' and see who turns out right."

"Fine. If the prince and princess get married, you must do my chores for a month in addition to your own. If they don't wed, I take yours." I stuck out my hand at him and he shook. Henry looked incredibly pleased with himself.

I looked into the forest as Henry prattled on about his plans for his month of nothing. I only half listened. The Nitalla Forest had a permanent fog that clung to the tall, thick trees. With the fog and heavy canopy, the forest was dark and almost sinister. Most of the townspeople of Ameris said it was hexed or haunted. It was easy to get lost where the Nitalla was concerned, whether you were in the forest or just looking at it. There was a mystery to it that seemed to reach out. It was curious to me how we found our quaint orchard that thrived in the dark forest, but it was secluded while still being close enough to town. Just what we needed. What I needed.

Henry talked until we reached Ameris an hour or so later. Aunt Prudence had stressed that we be quick. She wanted us home before dark. There were rogues in the forest and on the road. Most reports put the rogues further in Capilious but that didn't stop Aunt Prudence from worrying.

When we reached the main entrance into the town, Henry kicked his horse forward.

"Meet back here in an hour," I said, "I will leave without you!" Henry just waved me off and rushed to see Catharine. Tempest walked to her usual grazing spot by the willow tree. I climbed off her, tied her reins to a branch, and stroked her nose. A sharp pain shot through my skull as my senses sharpened. The hairs on the back of my neck rose. I could easily hear the faint crunch of the snow under a careful boot. I breathed in the familiar scent of sweat, mead, and mint. Knowing exactly who was beside me, I pushed my face into Tempest's neck and tried to will the pain away.

"V, are you all right? Another headache?" I felt a warm hand on my shoulder. I took a few more breaths as the pain dissipated.

"I'm sorry, Jeb. I don't mean to worry you. I'm fine really." I turned and saw his bright hazel eyes filled with concern. Jeb was the son of the owners of the Blue Boot Inn and, more importantly, my best friend. He worked in the inn every day to help the family and learned all he could so he could take over one day. He always had a smile on his face, but now his mouth was set in a worried line.

"They are getting worse," he said. It wasn't a question, but I answered him anyway.

"Just today. We ran out of the tea that is supposed to help. My fault, actually." I put on a smile for him. I could tell he didn't really believe me, but he didn't mention it. Instead, he smiled brightly.

"You mean to tell me that you aren't just here for me?" He combed his fingers through his already ruffled, light brown hair and raised his eyebrows at me. I pushed his shoulder and laughed at him. Jeb had always been lighthearted and kind. It was why we were so close.

Ever since I could remember, Jeb has been my closest friend. I met him in the Blue Boot Inn when I was about six and we lived in Ameris proper. Aunt Prudence had a medicinal shop there. One day, Uncle Fredrick had business to attend to with Simon, Jeb's father, and decided to take Henry and me along. I was so excited to go somewhere besides

Aunt Prudence's shop. When we arrived at the Blue Boot, Simon called for his son to meet us. Jeb came down the stairs and just stared at me. Simon was afraid that his reaction meant he didn't care to be around a girl, but it was just the opposite.

Since that day, we were inseparable. Of course, neither of us understood that look in his eyes the first day we met. I hadn't truly understood until recently, to be honest. I'm not sure how I could have ignored it for so long. I saw it in his eyes even as he offered me his arm to escort me to the herb shop.

Chapter 2: Ameris

The streets of Ameris were full of life despite the cold. Shop owners were announcing their wares from the lower levels of the stone and wood buildings as their families hung colored fabrics and paper flowers from the windows of their home above. The brilliant blues, reds, purples, and oranges seemed ablaze against the cool gray of the winter sky. People filled the streets, scouting out shops and deals early. Dark Day brought a sense of equality to Ameris. All districts, high and low, mingled together to celebrate the mystery of the longest night of the year. The noble women flaunted their wealth with their many layered skirts of the brightest colors in the lower districts and the poor strolled freely into stores where prices were usually much too high. Today, though, most of the people around were not natives of Ameris but rather vendors looking to make a fortune or tourists looking to spend theirs.

Jeb pulled me closer to his side and stared forward. I followed his gaze and felt my stomach drop. A group of men and women our age made their way through the streets. Their bright silks and velvets declared their high status, but their hearts were blacker than a beggar's foot.

The memories replayed themselves in my mind. The first was when I was a child, still living in Ameris. Henry and I had snuck out to play but we got separated. It was them who found me. My stomach churned as I remembered their cruel smiles.

"What is that thing? It's so pale!"

"Looks like a demon to me! You see that hair? Must be washed in blood!"

"Its eyes are glowing green! It's a caster! We should turn it in!" I shook with fear as they picked up rocks. I tried to back away, but I was cornered in a dead end.

"I'm not a demon. I'm not a caster! I don't practice magic!" My pleading did not stop them. I curled into a ball on the ground as the stones pelted me. I remembered the children screaming and then someone was holding me. I glanced up and saw bright hazel eyes.

I shook the memory away and tried to breathe. That wasn't the only time Jeb saved me. After that first incident, I found myself quaking with fear around those kids. They sensed it and fed on it for years, despite me covering my dark red curls and hiding my face under a hood. Jeb was always there to stick up for me, but the damage was done. We moved to the orchard once my aunt and uncle finally learned of the cruelty. I never told them because I didn't want to unhinge our life, or leave Jeb, but it didn't matter. I still ruined it all.

I blinked away the guilt and I smiled at Jeb but he wasn't easily fooled. I knew he could still sense the vice in my chest.

"Don't worry. They won't bother you." I scowled in confusion at him and looked back at the five jackals. Of the three men, one limped severely and another had both a black eye and a fat lip.

"Jeb, what did you do?" I said, exasperated. He puffed out his chest and shrugged.

"Merely gave them a refresher lesson in manners, fair lady." I looked down at the street and chewed my lip with frustration.

"What did they did say this time?" Jeb pondered for a moment before he smiled at me.

"Oh, same things they always say. Blood head, glowy-eyes, ghost-skin... Isn't it sad that their brains haven't grown at all these past years?" I couldn't bring myself to laugh at his joke. I felt so useless today. Things had started so wonderfully. After beating Uncle Fredrick in sparring, it all crashed down. I felt like a hassle to everyone.

"You don't need creativity when you have truth," I said softly, moving away from him. I picked at one of my fingernails, trying to think about something else. My headache was starting to return. Luckily, we had passed the group and were nearing the herb shop. I was ready to go home.

"I don't agree."

I huffed at him. Why did he always try so hard to make me feel better? Was I not just a nuisance to him?

"Jeb, you don't have to try to make me feel better. I know I'm strange. I'm unsettling and unappealing but I need to get over it. I'll be twenty tomorrow. I'm not a child anymore. I need to stop being a thorn in everyone's side. I shouldn't need your help with such trivial nonsense. You're not responsible for me and I don't want your pity." I turned and saw the herb shop just around the bend. I went toward it, but Jeb grabbed my hand. He pulled me into an empty alley and pinned me against a wall.

His eyes flashed at me, and his jaw was clenched. I felt my stomach drop to my feet. I had never seen such a look from him, directed at me at least. His hands were to either side of me, preventing any kind of escape. My eyes widened and I swallowed as I stared up at him.

"I- I'm sorry," I said but Jeb cut me off.

"Vespera, stop talking." My mouth immediately closed. Jeb never called me by my name. He took a deep breath, and his shoulders relaxed a bit.

"I want you to understand that I don't pity you, V. That's not why I do what I do for you. I..." He paused and looked away. He took another breath. I could only stare at him as my heartbeat faster. Jeb was never at a loss for words. He was only this tense when he was ready to throw punches. He had also never been so close to me. I felt his breath on my face.

"So much for tomorrow..." he mumbled so quietly I barely caught it. Then he kissed me.

I was so surprised that I almost forgot to close my eyes. Was this really happening? My skin felt tingly, and my heart nearly flew out of my chest. His lips were so soft. After a moment, we parted, and he rested his forehead against mine but didn't open his eyes.

"I wanted to do all of this tomorrow for your birthday, but here we are... Vespera, from the moment I saw you, I thought you were the most beautiful treasure in the world. All I've ever wanted was to protect you and make you realize your worth. You are more than I could ever give you but still, I offer you all my heart and soul. I... I really think that I'm in love you, Vespera."

I was frozen and my brain couldn't process what just happened. Was I dreaming? I was blindsided. I felt like there was no air around me and my lungs started to burn. I closed my eyes. Aunt Prudence used to tell me to find good in every situation, but I just didn't know what to think.

"This was all too much, wasn't it?" Jeb said, with a touch of rejection in his voice. His forehead still rested on mine, but I could feel the defeat radiating from him. Guilt slowly filled my being. He just poured his heart out to me. I wasn't rejecting him. I liked the way his kiss felt. I just didn't understand.

"Why?" I whispered.

"Why what?" he whispered back.

"Why do you... think so highly of me?" Jeb finally looked at me and he smiled.

"Because I know a good thing when I see it."

Jeb was light on his feet as we walked arm and arm to the herb shop and then back through Ameris. He smiled widely and, when he wasn't smiling, he whistled. Even though my mind was still racing, a small smile was on my lips too. I wasn't sure if I was in love with Jeb. He told me that that was just fine and to take all the time I needed; he wasn't going anywhere.

As we passed the Blue Boot, just one turn from the clearing with the road to home, Simon stepped out the front door and yelled at Jeb.

"Son! I've been dying in the crowds here! Where have you-oooh." He smiled when he saw me next to Jeb. I felt Jeb's hand move around my waist.

"I escorted V to the herb shop, Pa. I didn't mean to take so long. There were thick crowds on the streets." Jeb's voice was even through his smile, but Simon glanced at his son's hand on my waist and merely raised an eyebrow.

"Twas the crowds keeping you, huh?" I felt my cheeks blaze and I cleared my throat.

"Jeb, thank you for escorting me but I must also get home before dark and I'm sure Henry is waiting for me. It was nice to see you, Simon." I bowed my head a bit and turned to go but Jeb held me still.

"Let me walk you to your horse, V," he said. I shook my head.

"It isn't that far. I'll be just fine. Like I said, Henry is probably waiting. I'll see you tomorrow." I smiled at Jeb, genuinely this time. He smiled too and kissed my forehead. My face was immediately aflame.

"See you tomorrow," Jeb said, oblivious to my embarrassment. I nodded again at Simon and nearly ran away. I felt mortified by Jeb's behavior, but I liked it at the same time. There was something different to this kind of attention that I was getting. It wasn't sympathy. He really did care for me. My chest felt light, my shoulders relaxed, and my headache was completely gone. Maybe he did love me.

Once I reached Tempest, I swung onto her and moved her to the road. Henry was nowhere to be seen. I assumed he had left without me like I had threatened to do. I really didn't care. I was too happy.

Chapter 3: Rogues

Jeb loved me. The thought just kept repeating itself. Part of me was elated. If he really did love me then he didn't just pity me. I think I was more overcome by the fact he thought I was beautiful... and that he kissed me. I felt my face burn sweetly as I smiled, and my stomach did a flip. I felt so... free.

I looked to the woods that now surrounded the road with a small smile. The shadowy trees were covered in snow and mist. The chilled air felt wonderful as it softly hit my face and snow started to fall. The Nitalla didn't seem quite so menacing as it did before. I felt so peaceful for once. I wasn't worried about anything, and my mind went to a comfortable blankness. I closed my eyes and just breathed.

I felt a rush of cold seep into my eyes, but the wind wasn't blowing. The chill moved through my face and hair and then down my limbs, tingling as it went. My hearing seemed amplified. I heard the faint footsteps of a predator chasing its prey. I smelled the prey's terror. I opened my eyes and blinked hard against the icy cold of my eyes. Was I finally going mad from the headaches? I took a deep breath and tried to relax, hoping my head wouldn't suddenly hurt.

I continued to listen to the forest, and something strange caught my attention: Stamps of irritated horses and the steps of too careful feet. I opened my eyes and stopped Tempest as my heartbeat quickened. She tensed beneath me as I looked toward the trees. I inhaled deeply and wrinkled my nose. The stench of sweat, dirt, and old blood filled my nose along with metal and leather. Tempest shifted nervously under me. She felt it too.

I heard a twig snap and spun my head in that direction. Rogues. A man on a horse appeared from behind a tall tree. He was shocked to see me staring straight at him. He believed the group of them could sneak up on me. They should have. This one had beady eyes and the bridge of his nose was crooked. He had on a dirty shirt and jacket with matching trousers and hat. Tuffs of mousy brown hair poked out from under the cap. I grimaced when I noticed darkened spots on his clothes that could only be blood. My heart raced and my stomach sank as the strange, tingly chill faded away. Pain exploded through my head so violently I gasped.

"Dear lady, are you all right? You seem a bit distressed," he said, with a dark smirk. My mouth went dry, and I swallowed hard. My head was pounding, and I squinted against it.

"Come on now, don't make such a face. Don't tell me a pretty thing like you has no pretty voice!" he said loudly.

"Just let me go," I tried to say calmly but my knuckles turned white as I gripped the reins. I should've waited for Henry or had Jeb escort me home. No, then they would probably have been hurt or killed. What was I supposed to do now?

"Let you go? Ha! I don't think so, lady."

"Hey, Smid," a very large man yelled to the leader, "She seems wealthy. Light skin, well-groomed horse." Smid smiled, revealing horrible, crooked teeth, as the rest of his men came out of the forest on horseback. I quickly counted a total of five men, and I started to sweat. I tried to breathe.

The large man, who seemed to be the eldest, had brown hair and a darker complexion with a full beard. With his every move, his muscles rippled with excitement. There was a large battle axe strapped to his back. On Smid's right were twin brothers. They had dark blonde hair with matching sun-kissed skin and blue eyes except one had a scar that went down the side of his face, temple to chin. The last of the group was an angular man with strange pale skin and silvery hair and shining yellow green eyes. His hair was very long and tied back in a braid. His skin had a gray pallor to it as if his body was carved from stone. He was eerily attractive. I didn't want to look away from him. His gaze held me in place. I felt my stomach flip and my heartbeat sounded in my ears.

"Aye, Viht my good man, she does." My fear was muddled by the increasing pain in my mind. I ground my teeth together and scowled as my vision went in and out of focus.

"I have nothing of value. Just let me pass. I'm no one," I said through gritted teeth.

"Did you hear that, Kaul?" the scarred twin said.

"Indeed, Dax. I say Beauty is a little fiery." They laughed again but without malice.

"We like fiery," they said together, clearly amused. At least I didn't sound terrified; I surely felt that way. The fifth man just looked bored.

"Oh, I'm sure you could offer us something," Smid said with another smirk. He snapped his fingers and the twins moved forward. Tempest reared at their approach and nearly flung me from her back. I gripped the reins, and she took off.

"Get her men!" Smid shouted.

Tempest was so afraid that she wouldn't listen to me. She ran blindly through the trees, and I could only hold on. Tempest jumped logs, bounded around trees, and ran through small creeks. They were still on our trail, but we had gained some ground. I could hear them moving through the woods, but I couldn't see them anymore.

We reached a clearing just as I caught my breath again. Tempest ran toward a giant tree that was flanked by overgrown shrubs. As we neared them, we both realized that the ground sloped down into a creek. Tempest turned so sharply in her mad sprinting that she sent me flying over the shrubs. I covered my head and face as I landed on the winter-hardened slope and began tumbling down. The air rushed out of my lungs from the impact. I finally came to a stop at the creek's edge with my face in the dirt. I just laid there for a moment. I tried to catch my breath as I mentally assessed any serious damage. I was sore and aching, but nothing felt broken. I had to move. The rogues weren't that far behind.

Shaking, I rose to all fours and saw that the large tree on the slope's edge was hollow. That was a better hiding place than where I currently was. I pulled myself up on the tree and slipped in the thin crack that faced the creek. I pushed myself as far back into the tree as I could and pulled my dark cloak close.

My ragged breath smoked around my face. I closed my eyes and tried to calm myself. They couldn't see me. They would chase Tempest and then give up. I caught the faint sound of the trees rustling and then horses running. I waited for them to pass but they stopped in the clearing. I tried to keep my breathing even, but panic threatened to overwhelm me. Why did they stop? I held my hand over my mouth to muffle my ragged breaths.

"Where did she go?" I heard one of the twins say.

"The horse went that way," the big man said, "but the tracks look like she might've stopped here. There's a possibility that she hid somewhere." I squeezed my eyes shut and my heart pounded.

"We'll split up. You three follow the horse tracks and we'll search this meadow," Smid said.

"Is all of this really worth it? What if she really doesn't have anything? Even if she was carrying something, it can't be much. The horse would be worth more, but we could be getting back to camp for supper."

"It's worth it if I say it is! I'm in charge here, remember, and I'm not going back to camp empty handed."

I bit my lip to keep my jaw from quaking. They were going to find me. I felt my breath turn shallow and the air around me seemed to disappear. My head ached again. My heart was hammering in my ears, and I felt like a fish out of water. They were going to find me. Tears were filling my eyes as they suddenly went cold again, so cold that I thought my tears turned to ice. The chill raced through my body. The force seemed to sense my panic and spread through my body, chilling my nerves, and soothing my terror. Not only did I feel calmer, but I felt stronger and confident. I'd be fine. My lungs remembered how to breathe, and my heart slowed its rhythm.

I heard a thud as one of the rogues dismounted his horse.

"Come out, come out, lady." Smid said as he walked. I heard his steps near the tree, pause, and then he jumped down into the bank. I raised my fists. I wouldn't be compliant, and I would strike first. I watched Smid come near the roots. When he was close enough, I threw a hard punch into his face and ran from the tree. It wasn't the best hit I could have landed but it served its purpose. I climbed up the ledge of the bank and saw that the other rogue was on the other side of the clearing with his back to me. I could run into the forest without being seen if I was quick enough. A hand wrapped around my ankle and yanked me down hard into the snow.

"Damn wench," Smid said as he pulled himself from the bank. I looked back and kicked him. I tried to stand and run but he knocked me down again. He grabbed my wrists and pinned me down on my back. I flailed my legs and saw that the other rogue was watching the scene with disinterest. A biting slap fell across my cheek and my head whipped to the side.

My mind went blank, and I felt the cold engulf me, freezing me from the inside out. My eyes felt like shards of ice but there was no pain, and all traces of my headache were gone. I looked at Smid. When our eyes met, he paused in his assault. Fear flashed in his eyes, but he snarled against it. My foot found its way to his chest, and I kicked as hard as I could. The rogue flew off me and smashed against the tree, now several feet back. How did I do that? I wasn't that strong. My mind whirled but I didn't have time to ponder. I stood and remembered I had put my blades back in my boots before leaving home.

I turned so I could see both rogues, daggers ready in hand. Smid stood up cursing and drew his sword but the other just watched from his horse with a silver brow raised.

"I don't care if you have anything or not. You're not going to see another day, wench," Smid said running at me, sword drawn. Like with

Uncle Fredrick, time slowed. I could see how poor the rogue's form was. There were openings everywhere. Despite Uncle Fredrick's motto of strike to kill, I didn't want to murder anyone. I wasn't a soldier; I just wanted to go home.

I batted away Smid's attack and hit him in the chest with the hilt of my dagger. He stumbled back in the snow and the air left his lungs. Out of the corner of my eye, I saw the other rogue turn his horse toward us, but he did not approach. He turned his head curiously. It was strange that he wouldn't help his leader. Apparently, Smid thought the same.

"Silas, get over here and help me!" Silas glanced at Smid, thought a moment, and then gracefully moved off his horse.

He was tall and older than I first thought, possibly more than thirty years. He didn't seem to belong with the rest of his troupe earlier but now it was clear. He seemed more proper, elegant even. His shoulders were held straight, and he walked with purpose, but I couldn't hear the crunch of snow beneath his feet. His long silver hair was falling out of its plait as he pulled two long thin glistening swords out of sheaths that peaked over his left shoulder. The swords looked like they were made of ice and were etched with strange symbols. He certainly wasn't just a rogue.

I stepped back to have a better view of the two of them and crouched. Whatever this cold energy was that kept me calm, I prayed that it would hold out. Smid stabbed his sword at me. I dodged out of the way and crouched in the snow as he tripped. I didn't hear Silas run up behind me, he made no sound, but I felt him coming. I quickly side-stepped and narrowly missed the swing of his swords. He was much faster than Smid, even with things moving slower for me.

Silas cocked his head to the side like a cat. I took the opportunity to study him more. He was the real threat here. He smelled like pine and metal. He had a long angular nose and a narrow face with high cheek bones. His yellow green eyes had a light of curiosity as they stared into mine. It struck me again how attractive he was. His looks were odd; unlike anyone's I had ever seen. His hair was softly blowing with the wind and each strand glistened and resembled the individual lines that made up a spider's web and through his hair I saw two thin pointed ears.

My stomach dropped and I stumbled as I caught his second attack against my blades. A devium. This was one of the creatures that Uncle Fredrick fought against for years in the Devium War. They were banished from Devtera after they finally lost the war. I had never seen one, until now.

I pushed him away and felt my chest clench with panic. Deviums were superior warriors to humans, more calculating and more agile, faster, and stronger. The main reason we won the war was because of numbers. I couldn't beat him. The cold inside me intensified, reassuring me. Then again, what choice did I have? I raised my daggers, ready for another attack, mindful of Smid circling. The devium still had a curious but knowing look. He was toying with me, surely, but I had to figure a way out of this.

Silas charged first with both swords held above his shoulder. I bent my knees and readied myself for the blow. As he slashed his swords, I ducked, twisting my blades to lay flat along my forearms. I grabbed his clothes at his shoulder and waist and flipped him over me. The motion knocked my scarf from my head. I felt my hair whirl around my face. I stared at his form lying motionless in the snow and tried to calm my beating heart. The wind picked up and blew my now loose hair around my face. A sense of freedom overcame me. I felt myself smile.

I cocked my head as I heard Smid try to sneak up on me. I waited. He tried to step lightly but I smelled him creeping closer to me. I knew that I couldn't afford to be distracted by a petty fight with Smid when there was a devium around. I waited until I heard him raise his sword over his head to slash at me. I dodged and placed my foot on the blade after it struck the ground, holding it still. He tensed his jaw and sneered at me, but his eyes were wide.

I sent my foot crashing into his face before I could think about it. I heard the nose crack and saw his blood fly. I watched a drop of blood fall to the snow. A dark haze filled my mind. It made me dizzy. If I struck with just a little more pressure, the red would pour from his body and stain the beautiful white ground. For a moment, the image looked wonderful in my head. I placed my foot back on Smid's unconscious face. I forced myself to pause. What was I doing? The chill returned, drowning out the dark, shadowy haze and then it all disappeared. A dull ache clouded my head, making it hard to concentrate. The clarity and perception I just had felt far away. My breathing grew ragged, and I stared down at him.

"What is stopping you?" I jumped and looked up and saw the devium watching me intently. I didn't hear him get up. His swords were sheathed, and his arms were folded across his chest. A small smile played on his gray-tinted lips. I quickly took a few steps away from both of the rogues. My cheeks were hot, and I was almost wincing from the pain in my head. I turned my blades toward the devium.

"It would be wrong," I said quickly. The sun was going down and it started to snow.

"Would it be wrong?" the devium repeated evenly. I didn't give myself time to think about it. He was trying to trick me.

"Yes." He turned his head to the side and smiled. He looked terrifying but he was so alluring. I could sense the power he was hiding. He was a devium. His very presence could not mean anything good.

"Who knows what he would have done to you; let alone what he has probably done to others in the past. Why should he receive mercy?" I glanced back at the unconscious rogue. The devium was right. The blood stains on his clothes, chasing me into the woods, attempting to kill me; good men don't do those things.

I jumped when I felt him take my hand and touch his forehead to the top of it from a low bow. He did not seem to mind the dagger that was still in my hand.

"Forgive me," he said, "I am Silas of Noliishilo. What is your name, mysterious maiden?" I pulled my hand away. I was so dumbfounded.

"You don't need it."

"And what if I do?" He smiled widely at me. His teeth were blindingly white.

Aunt Prudence had told me once that names were powerful things and to be careful with whom they were shared. I had the feeling that deviums fell under the list of not sharing. I swallowed.

"You don't." I took another step away and he chuckled at me. He acted coy, like he knew something he shouldn't.

"For now, perhaps," he said. He was suddenly close to me again and took a strand of my hair between his fingers, "What a lovely color." I shivered and took a step back again.

"Don't touch me," I said, setting my jaw. Cold flickered through my eyes but my headache won over, and the chill was gone. He raised a silver brow.

"Angry, are we?" he said, softly with a smirk playing his lips. It was almost like he was daring me.

"Let me go," I said quickly. I knew that I wouldn't be able to fight him again. Whatever power had possessed me, it had run out.

"Of course. I think you've earned the pass, don't you? I'm sure we will meet again soon, my dear," the devium said and bowed low. His statement made my pulse quicken. I told myself it was fear, but I wasn't entirely sure. I backed away from him and watched his bowed figure.

Was it a trick? He remained motionless. I finally turned and ran away as fast as I could.

After I knew I was far away and safe from the creature, my mind began to race. What is wrong with me? I replayed the scenes in my head. Why was I able to fight like that? Uncle Fredrick taught me the moves and how to read an opponent but the strength and speed? What was that? Smid, maybe, but the devium? He must have been toying with me. I looked at my feet and saw blood smeared on my boot. My stomach churned and I fought back the urge to vomit. I fell to one knee and scrubbed my boot in the snow. I wanted to erase everything I had done. I was gentle and timid. I was weak. I never wanted to hurt anyone. What I did and how I fought, it wasn't normal. I never felt like everyone else but... Could casters do those things? I thought they just had books of spells to cast and potions to use, at least that's what I heard. No, that wasn't it.

My thoughts raced and I felt tense as my headache returned. Despite my growing anxiety and confusion, my body felt almost giddy. My muscles twitched and my chest was light as I remembered that tingly feeling of cold energy running through me. I felt like I had woken up from a slow, sluggish dream just to be hit over the head. I rolled my shoulders, and I reached up to pull my scarf down, forgetting that I didn't have it. I ran a hand through my hair instead, the nervous habit finding a new outlet. Something was happening to me, and I just wanted to be home.

It was a long walk back home without a horse. I needed to find the road but even then, I wouldn't make it back home before dark.

"They're going to kill me," I said wrapping my arms around myself. My breath turned to smoke in the cold as I thought about Aunt Prudence and Uncle Frederick. How was I going to explain to them what happened? They'd be furious with Henry, too. I'd tell them that it was my fault. I left without him. I hoped their punishment wouldn't be too severe. My eyes widened. Surely they would still let me go to the festival. It was my birthday. And now Jeb... They wouldn't deny me that would they? I gasped.

"I can't tell them what really happened. Aunt Prudence would never let me leave the house again and Uncle Fredrick would agree," I whispered and pulled at my hair. I can't just blame Jeb; they'd be angry with him and that wouldn't explain how disheveled I looked. There had to be dirt and grime all over me. That one rogue hit me too. There is probably a mark there. Tempest did throw me, maybe...

I heard a loud groan from a nearby tree branch. I looked up quickly, thinking it was just an animal, but I saw nothing. I couldn't hear anything either. Henry loved the Nitalla and knew it well. He told me once that complete silence in the woods is never a good sign.

I stared into the trees, waiting for something to spring out of the darkness. I breathed in as a gust of air flowed passed me, pushing my hair away from my face, and I smelled a wonderful aroma: A mix of spices, old books, and something I couldn't name. Definitely not an animal or the devium.

"Who's there?" I said, leaning down and drawing my blades. I wasn't taking any chances. A cold breeze passed through and with it was the mysterious smell again. The cold rushed through me and eased away my headache instantly. I frantically turned. I saw a glimpse of a cape darting behind a tree. I ran after it with as much speed as I could muster, and I reached the tree within a blink. I jerked my head back and forth then I saw a caped figure running from me. Panic gripped me. Our house was an ideal place to raid: Stores of food, livestock, and Uncle Fredrick's old Capilious armor was extremely valuable. If the rogues knew where we lived, we would have nothing.

"Stop!" I said, chasing after the cloak. If it was a rogue, I couldn't risk him following me home. I didn't think it was any that I had encountered earlier but who knows how many were in the forest. I would have remembered that smell. I ran and ran but anytime I followed a turn, it turned again. The sun had set but a near full moon lit our chase. I thought about giving up and turning back but then I remembered I didn't have a choice. I had to be sure he wouldn't follow me. I felt that chill run through my body and down into my legs. I felt a burst of energy and started to gain on the man.

He suddenly sped faster, as if he were holding back the whole time. The gap between us increased and I watched him disappear behind an enormous tree. When I arrived, there was nothing. There weren't even tracks in the snow for me to follow. There were no low hanging branches for him to climb either. It was like he was never there. I sniffed the air. The smell was gone. I was alone. Maybe the Nitalla was haunted.

I sheathed my blades and saw a clearing up ahead. I stepped out of the trees and realized the clearing was actually the road home. The cold melted away from my eyes and I winced, waiting for the headache to return but it didn't. There was no pain or even the ghost of it. I smiled and walked home.

With weary legs, I rounded the corner and saw the lanterns shining by the front door of the house. I took a breath to calm my nerves and rehearsed my story. I neared the house and heard Aunt Prudence yelling.

"What do you mean she left without you? You should have been with her the entire time! You know how the townsfolk treat her! I can't believe this is happening... You're the eldest! You were supposed to watch out for her, Henry! If something happened to her... Oh her mother would never forgive me, gods rest her soul. Henry, how could you? I shouldn't have let her go. Why did you talk me into letting her go, Fredrick? You know about her condition, and she was unwell this afternoon! She hasn't had her tea since yesterday morning! What if the headaches overtook her? Or worse, what if they didn't?" My hand hovered on the door.

What if they didn't? What did that mean? I remembered my fight with the rogues: the headache went away and that cold took over. Time froze and my movements were so fast and strong. Such power couldn't be an illness, could it? Is that what it was: Power? I felt so alive with the cold pounding through me, but I didn't understand it. I was still trying to believe it. The more I thought about what happened, the more impossible it seemed.

"Henry, leave us," Uncle Fredrick said. After a moment, Aunt Prudence continued.

"Did you hear me? There's been too many headaches. They can only do so much, Fredrick. And she hasn't had any tea, either. How could I have run out of her tea? What if it took her over? She needs the headaches and the tea to combat it, Fredrick. What if she was overcome? Or if-"

"Prudence, enough," Uncle Fredrick said in a booming voice and cutting her off, "I'm sure that she is fine and will be home any moment." My thoughts scrambled. The tea and the headaches combatted what? The cold? Aunt Prudence started rambling again.

"Prudence, I said enough!" There was a boom that silenced the room. I waited a few minutes, but the conversation was over. I slid the latch on the door. They didn't hear me come in. Uncle Fredrick's fist was still resting on the table. His body was rigid in his seat and his eyes were bright. Aunt Prudence stood with her back to the table. Her shoulders were quivering, and her chest jerked with ragged breaths. She wrapped her arms around herself, and I knew she fought back her tears. I prepared myself for the assault and cleared my throat loudly. My aunt reacted with lightning speed.

"Vespera, where have you been? Are you all right? You made us sick with worry, Vespera. What were you thinking, leaving by yourself?" Aunt Prudence said, her voice cracking as she shrieked. I flinched at her tone and looked at my feet. I felt her arms wrap around me tightly and then she held me at arm's length. I watched her piercing eyes scan over me and they stopped on my face.

"Vespera, where is your scarf and what happened to your face?" Her brows were furrowed, and her mouth was a hard line but her eyes were softer. I thought of my cheek where the rogue had slapped me. I looked away from her and told her my story.

"I was racing Tempest through the forest, and I fell when she leapt over a ditch. I must've hit my face during the fall and lost my scarf. Tempest just kept going, you know how she is. It took some time for me to find the road. I'm sorry that I was so reckless. I'm really all right, though. I hope you weren't too hard on Henry." My cheeks were hot with the lie.

"You raced your horse through the Nitalla? Do you realize how dangerous that is?" Uncle Fredrick said from his seat, shaking his head. Henry rushed into the room as I spoke.

"Yes, Uncle Fredrick, I know it was stupid." Henry suddenly hugged me.

"Vespera, you're safe," Henry said, squeezing me. He sounded so relieved. I couldn't imagine what he was thinking and what I put him through. First not finding me in Ameris and then trying to search for me in the Nitalla only to face Aunt Prudence and Uncle Fredrick alone. I hoped he could see how sorry I was.

"Well, let's just put this behind us," Aunt Prudence said, wiping her face, "Do you have the herbs I requested, Vespera? For your headaches?" Somehow, I did have them. I felt the small pouch in the pocket of my cloak.

"I must have dropped the bag when I fell but I don't have a headache. It went away quite a while ago. I've been fine all day," I said, looking right at her. I surprised myself with how easy the lie fell from my lips. Despite everything that had happened, I never wanted to drink that tea again. Just a few hours ago, I would have drunk a whole pot but that was before being consumed by the cold energy. I was so confident and in control. I wasn't afraid anymore. I felt so empowered. Not being able to feel that way again almost made me sick. Headaches be damned.

My aunt sighed but didn't press the issue. She even smiled a little.

"Well at this point, what's one more day? I will go tomorrow during the festival. Now that both children are home and safe, let's have supper."

I took a bath that night and did my best to wash my mane of hair. The mass of curls fell down to my waist when it was wet. It was starting to get difficult to fit under the scarf. I slipped into my nightshirt after drying and went back into the main room. Uncle Fredrick and Henry had already gone to bed. They both needed to wake up early to finish preparing for the festival.

"Come here, dearie," Aunt Prudence said, placing a pillow in the floor and gesturing to me to sit in front of the fire. Sitting against her legs, I watched the fire in the hearth dance and sighed at its warm caress on my skin. Aunt Prudence picked up my damp hair and attempted to comb the knots from it.

"I thought that you might cut it, Aunt Prudence. It's very unmanageable actually," I said with a laugh and hugged my knees against my chest.

"Of course." She picked up the shears from the table next to her. I heard the metal slicing through the hair. I rested my chin on my knees and sighed. I smiled and tried to remember the last time we shared a moment like this. It was at least a year, I thought. It was at those moments that my heart panged with the knowledge that she wasn't my mother. I remembered all the things she had taught me over the years. She taught me how to read, to cook, and to sew. She taught me about herbs and the healing properties that some possessed, even though Henry took to it much better than I did. She taught me about womanhood. Most importantly, she loved me. Isn't that what a mother is?

"I took it a bit shorter this time. I hope you don't mind." I felt my hair. It now rested just passed my shoulders. It felt so much lighter. I was reminded of the headaches and sluggishness. My hair was just another weight that was lifted today.

"It's wonderful," I said smiling.

"Vespera," she said, "you're sure you're all right? Usually, your headaches linger until you're exhausted. You don't have to pretend that you are fine." I turned to look at her and I took her hands in mine.

"I'm fine. Really. To be honest, I've never felt better." My statement seemed to put her further out of ease. I wondered if I should ask her about the tea and come clean about the cold. I wouldn't say anything about the rogues. She knew more than she let on. Would she tell me the truth? Would she force more tea down me? I stared up into her eyes. She was so concerned but I could see the walls there too. I knew in my heart she wouldn't tell me. Not tonight at least.

Aunt Prudence kissed my forehead.

"I'm glad, dearie. Now get on to sleep. You have a big day ahead of you tomorrow."

Chapter 4: The Mark

I awoke in a cold sweat as images of rogues and swords flashed through my mind. I rubbed my head with a shaky hand and tried to catch my breath. My body felt rigid, and my muscles ached.

"Stupid nightmares," I said. I started to lay back down when my door slammed open.

"Happy Birthday, Vespera!" Henry cried and tackled me on my bed. "Look who's all grown up!" he yelled. He ground the knuckles of his fist into my skull, balling my curly hair into a rat's nest. "What a fine young woman you are!"

"Henry, get off me!" I laughed. Of course, he didn't listen and continued to attack my head. After a few more pleads, he finally stopped. "I swear Henry you act like a child! Now get out so I can get dressed!" I said pushing him out of my room.

"Hurry up!" he said through the closed door.

I shook my head, combing my hair with my fingers, and went to my chest of clothes and reached for a simple brown frock but I hesitated. It was my birthday, not to mention Dark Day. People wore the most extravagant costumes on Dark Day. For once, I wanted to be extravagant. I pulled out the dark green overdress of the gown that Aunt Prudence bought for me to wear today. It also required layers upon layers of petticoats and underskirts. Without them, it was fitted knee-length coat with lace-up sleeves.

I looked at all of the skirts in the trunk. I know Aunt Prudence must have spent so much on them but... I really hated dresses. They just got in the way, not to mention the hems were always so disgusting after being dragged through the muck. Instead, I pulled out fitted black breeches that were once Henry's and sheathed my daggers in my tall black boots. I donned the gold embroidered outer corset that Aunt Prudence purchased to accompany the dress and dusted some golden powder on my cheekbones and up my temples and some on my lips. I remembered seeing a high born lady wearing something similar last year. She looked beautiful. I looked in my small looking glass and examined my appearance. I smiled at the girl in the mirror.

The outfit was marvelous. It was a perfect blend of feminine and masculine. I looked strong and I liked it. I shook my wild hair, and the mane only grew. It surrounded my head like a fiery halo. It looked much livelier without the extra bulk. There were shorter pieces around my face that complimented the heart shape of my face. The spirals gleamed in the sunlight that came through my window. I also noticed that there wasn't a bruise on my face from the night before. Thank the gods.

"A river of blood..." I said, remembering the man who accused me of being a caster so long ago. I was about to pull my hair back again, but something stopped me. Instead of my usual feeling of shame when I looked at my unnatural features, I felt acceptance. I had decided to not drink the tea. If I was going to reject normal, I wasn't doing it halfway. I was going to make enough of a stir with my outfit, why not let my hair down too?

With a laugh, I flung my head upside down and ruffled my hair and flipped back. I started at my reflection, no longer afraid or ashamed. With the gleam in my eyes and tousled hair, I looked wild.

"I won't be afraid any longer," I said to myself. I looked free and independent. I was a woman now after all. What would Jeb think? I watched myself blush and I grinned and almost laughed at myself. I turned from the mirror and went to meet with the rest of my family.

"Happy Birthday, Vespera!" Uncle Fredrick said and pulled me into a hug after just a brief stare with his eyebrows raised. I laughed as he spun me around. I'm sure I felt like a feather in his arms. "That is quite a costume you've put together," he said with a laugh.

"Breeches? Loose hair? On your coming of age day? What has gotten into you, Vespera? Where are the skirts I bought you? And I think I have another scarf you can use," Aunt Prudence said.

"I thought it would be a nice change... to leave it down," I said trying to stand my ground. Her mouth turned down.

"Vespera, really. You can't go out like that. It's Dark Day so the breeches can be looked over but your hair?" I set my jaw.

"I appreciate your concern, Aunt Prudence, but I am an adult now. If I want to wear my hair down, I can make that decision." Her nostrils flared and she opened her mouth to retort, but Uncle Fredrick quickly interrupted her.

"Well, it sounds like your mind is made up. Now Vespera, part of my gift to you is no obligation to sell wares at the festival." Aunt Prudence closed her mouth in defeat and walked away to pack some more of her elixirs to sell at the festival, wringing her hands nervously.

"I don't have to help you today? It's supposed to be busier than ever this year with Rokellia's harvest falling short," I said.

"I'm sure we can manage. Perhaps you could watch the sparring tournament this year or win it," Uncle Fredrick said with a wink. My eyes went wide, and Aunt Prudence shrieked. Uncle Fredrick just laughed and turned to ready the horses outside.

"V, I made you something," Henry said from the table with a mouth full of honeyed oats and hot milk. I sat and Aunt Prudence handed me my own bowl. Henry pulled a small bundle from his pocket and handed it to me.

"Thank you, Henry. You didn't have to. I didn't get you anything for your twentieth birthday," I said. He just shrugged with a smile. Typically, we would do the other's chores for their birthday. It was an understanding between us that wrapped gifts weren't necessary.

I pulled the small string and pulled away the cloth. In my hand lay a wooden hair comb. It was painted black, and a large golden star surrounded by swirls was carved into the handle.

"Henry, this is beautiful!" I gasped.

"I remember how you loved staring at the stars all night when we were younger, and you don't have your own comb so I made it out of the toughest wood in the Nitalla Forest. I figured you'd need the strength." Tears pricked my eyes. I was too touched to acknowledge the backhanded comment. It was only a joke anyway.

"It's wonderful." I hugged him tightly and then slipped the comb into my hair.

"We don't really have time for me to give you my gift now, dearie," Aunt Prudence said lightly, "I'll give it to you tonight when we return. Hurry and eat. We must go." I nodded and quickly ate.

We reached Ameris and the noise of the vendors filled my ears. Much had changed since the day before. Stalls and booths were set up down the middle of the main streets of the city to accommodate traveling merchants. The vendors had to pay the city for the space ahead of time, but the fee was always worth it. Ameris was so close to the border and just a few hours ride to the Great River, it was always brimming with the best goods and a wide variety of buyers. Citizens from Rokellia and Capilious were piling into the city and the vendors knew to take advantage. Sellers typically stayed for a few days following the festival, trying to make as much as possible until the crowds dwindled.

I made a conscious effort to not pull up the hood on my cloak. I felt so exposed now, especially with all of the people in the streets.

"Take your horses to the Blue Boot," Uncle Fredrick said to Henry and me, "Henry, I expect you to come help us set up immediately after. V, here's some coin. Have fun today." He tossed me a pouch without slowing the cart. I thanked him and turned toward the Blue Boot. Aunt Prudence cried over her shoulder.

"You must check in with us throughout the day, Vespera!" I waved and put the pouch in my pocket. Henry and I left our horses at the Blue Boot's stable while Uncle Fredrick and Aunt Prudence drove the cart toward the arena to their reserved booth. Aunt Prudence insisted on paying the extra fee for the location. She and Uncle Fredrick sold her health remedies and elixirs to the tournament challengers that competed in the arena. Some years, she sold out before nightfall.

I took a deep breath as I left the stable. I would be fine. There were so many people with outrageous costumes on that no one would even notice me. I sighed in relief when I saw a man dressed as a red rooster walk pass, giant bright green tail feathers and all. But what would Jeb think? The confidence I felt at home faltered. If he thinks it's fine, then I'll be fine. One more deep breath and I walked into the Blue Boot Inn.

The place was packed wall to wall with all kinds of people. I could hear Simon trying to yell above the noise. Something about more mead. I saw Jeb run to the back storage room and I smiled. I tried to elbow my way to the bar. When I did get someone to notice that I was trying to get through, he would nearly trip over himself to move. My heart fell further and further. One man even stuttered only for his jaw to go slack. I just nodded at them and smiled. That was the polite thing to do, I thought. Finally, I made it to the bar. I swore I had said more to complete strangers in the last five minutes than in my lifetime. I closed my eyes and tried to calm my heartbeat. So far so good. No blood head or caster comments. I was beginning to feel proud of myself. I didn't cower once.

I turned my back to the bar and watched the patrons. I had never come in the Blue Boot on Dark Day. It was too busy for me. I was too terrified. The men and women here were noisy, but everyone was smiling and laughing. The singer in the corner did her best to project her song through the whole room but I'm not sure anyone would have been upset if they didn't hear her. Everyone had a drink in hand or wanted one. It didn't matter that it was before midday. It was Dark Day, and on Dark Day when the rules weren't bent, they were broken.

"What can I get you, miss?" I turned at sound of Jeb's voice. He was busy pouring some ale and didn't look up at me. His brow glistened with sweat and his white shirt was already stained around where the apron protected him. His sleeves were rolled up past his elbows and he occasionally tried to push them higher. Was he always so attractive? I smiled at him.

"I hear the spiced mead is good here," I said, trying not to laugh. Jeb was always boasting about his own brew. He had a right to though, it was a bestseller. He grabbed a tankard and filled it to the brim.

"Good choice! It's our..." Jeb's voice died when he finally looked at me. He was just frozen, as if time had stopped. I couldn't tell if he was pleased or not. My chest began to feel tight.

"Best seller?" I said smiling nervously and taking the drink from him. His hand fell and his eyes studied me from my hair to my eyes to my lips and back again. He must not approve, or he would have said so. I looked down and swallowed. I gripped the drink tight in my hands.

"Vespera, please, tell me that it's you," he finally said. I scowled and looked back at him.

"Of course, it's me, Jeb. What-" His mouth crashed against mine. The kiss was so much different than the first one. The day before, it was sudden but gentle. This kiss was... hungry. His hand wound itself in my hair and his thumb rested behind my jaw. I was breathless when he pulled away.

"I just had to make sure I wanted to kiss the right woman," he said with a glittering smirk. I felt my face flush as I stared at smeared golden powder on his lips. "You are breath-taking, V. I haven't seen your hair in years. It's more beautiful than I remember... and softer." He combed his finger through a section of my curls. Relief washed through me, and breathing was easier again. I tucked my hair behind my ear and smiled at him.

"I had a few revelations yesterday."

"I'm glad. It suits you," he said smiling. He took my drink from me and took a long swig.

"Excuse me, that is my drink, sir," I said reaching for it, but he pulled it away. The gold was gone.

"I assure you that I need it more than you do." He downed the rest of it, refilled it, and took one more drink before handing the tankard back to me.

"On the house," he winked.

"How kind of you." This was the Jeb I was used to. Lighthearted flirtation with a constant stream of banter. It made me happy that whatever had formed between us, he didn't really change.

"Jeb! We need more wine!" Simon yelled from somewhere in the inn. Jeb rolled his eyes before cutting them toward me.

"Finish that drink and don't move." I raised the cup in salute and took a big swallow. He grinned mischievously at me.

"That's my girl." I watched him hurry away and pour a few more drinks along the way to his father. I felt absolutely giddy. I took another gulp of the mead and shook my head as it burned its way down my throat. It was strong but it left a sweet aftertaste that made me want to drink more. I watched a few people dance to the singer's new song. Their drinks were sloshing to the floor, but they just laughed. I smiled at them and sipped the mead.

When Jeb came back, my drink was empty, and my head was light. He came to me on my side of the bar and extended his hand. He had changed too. He wore a clean blue shirt and there were a few gold-dusted braids in his usually unkept hair. There was also a line of gold down his bottom lip and chin. We matched.

"The tournament is about to start so business will slow down considerably. Pa says he won't need me until the tournament is over. So, my lady, I am yours until then," he said bowing his head to me. I took his hand and let him practically drag me out.

We went arm in arm through the marketplace, making our way to the arena. There were a few booths we stopped at along the way. We actually bought from food vendors, but we looked in almost every other kind of booth as well. It was like we traveled the world in just a few minutes. Merchants beckoned us closer and told us grand tales of their wares.

Trumpets and drums sounded in the distance. The tournament was about to start. We hurried to the arena and looked over the challenger board before finding seats on the long benches that surrounded the rectangular arena. Challengers with their family crests, names, and odds of winning littered the board like leaves on a tree-shaped pattern. Most people didn't know how to read, hence the crests, but I did.

"These two are new," Jeb whispered, pointing at a couple of crests, "What do they say, V?" It was frowned upon for women to know letters, but Aunt Prudence insisted I learn, too. I read the names to him, and he took note of the odds. Jeb didn't know how to read but he had a knack for numbers. He had to if he wanted to run the Boot someday. The trumpets sounded again, and we found seats on the south side.

A new platform had been added at the bottom of the seating to the north side of the arena, nearest the action and almost directly across from us. Black and blue pennants hung on the railings and a large black banner with the Argentus family crest, a silver wolf with blue eyes, hung in the center. Henry was right. The prince did come.

A man in the Argentus colors walked out on the field.

"All rise for his highness, Prince Aleron Argentus of Rokellia, son of King Aros Argentus of Rokellia," he said in a booming voice. We stood and cheered as a small group of people walked onto the platform. The prince led the group in all black with a silver circlet on his head. He had dark hair that was combed back, and he was tall but I couldn't see much else from the distance. I recognized the ambassador of Ameris and his family following after him.

The crier waited until the prince was seated before speaking again.

"His highness would like to extend his gratitude to Sir Nortid and the people of Ameris for their sympathies for our departed Queen Neffisiny, may her name be praised." The crowd repeated the sentiment. "Ameris, please know that your resilience in your work and as a people has helped provide for others in Rokellia who have been affected by the terrible famine of this past summer. Prince Aleron honors you on this day at this fine spectacle! The champion of the tournament shall receive a fine dagger crafted in the famed forges of Jahilta! Let the tournament begin!"

The crowd cheered again but Jeb snickered beside me.

"They were desperate so he's here to keep up appearances."

"What do you mean?" I said.

"The crown had to call in the ambassadors for food reserves this winter. After the queen died, the king just stopped everything. The capital didn't have enough food and then there was the famine that hurt the rest of the kingdom. Ameris was the biggest donator because of our trade with Capilious. Essentially, we're saving the kingdom from starvation. That capital-crafted knife must be something." I knew about the queen's death and the famine, but the rest was news to me. We didn't really talk about politics at home. My cheeks burned. Ignorance wasn't a trait I wanted. Jeb didn't seem to notice.

There was movement on the field. The tournament was a simple one. Challengers fought one on one with whatever weapons they chose. The loser was the one who yielded. The field was divided into three squares so there could be multiple matches at once. I caught myself critiquing the forms and techniques of each contestant. I analyzed their strengths and weaknesses and argued assumptions with Jeb. He didn't know that I knew how to fight. It had never come up and, truthfully, I wasn't sure how he would react. He always protected me before and took pride in it. I glanced at him and watched him cheer for his favorite challengers but still clap for the opposition and commend their abilities. I think he would accept any kind of surprise just fine.

The competition went on for hours. Jeb offered to take me to see more things around the festival, but I declined. Sitting here watching the tournament was less stressful.

The final fight was intense. The challengers seemed evenly matched but, eventually, it came to an end. The trumpets and drums played again, and Prince Aleron presented the knife. The winner bowed low and accepted the blade and the crowd stood and cheered. Prince Aleron stood with the winner and they both waved at the people and then horses were brought to them. The two proceeded to ride around the perimeter of the arena.

I clapped dutifully as the winner and prince drew near our section. The prince's eyes caught mine and I felt frozen. They were the purest blue I had ever seen and so bright they looked like they were glowing. They were mesmerizing. I blinked and he was looking elsewhere, giving someone else the chance to be entranced by him.

"Don't tell me you already have eyes for another, V," Jeb said, with mock hurt. "And the prince, no less. I can't compete with that." I rolled my eyes and playfully shoved his arm.

"Don't be so insecure. That is my job, isn't it? Shouldn't we be getting back? The sun is going down and I don't want your father upset with you for not coming back sooner."

"He'll be fine, but I should get back. Will you walk with me?" I didn't hesitate to take his extended arm.

"I think I'll walk through the marketplaces again, but I'll come to the Boot when I've finished." He kissed the top of my head, and we were on our way.

I walked through the many booths and stalls of the festival. Lively music and rich spices filled the night air. I still had the all the coins that Uncle Fredrick had given me. I was determined to buy at least one thing special. It was my birthday after all.

I stopped by a tent that displayed jewelry. I didn't own any such finery and the glittering delicate wares were too tempting to pass by. Different metals, beads, and strings cluttered the table. Two men were looking at a few rings with one consulting with the seller. I picked through a box of brooches and found a walnut-sized tarnished silver pendant on a long thin silver chain. The pendant was a crest like nothing I had ever seen before. I tried to rub some of the grime off to get a better look. At the center was a stone that looked like it was made of a rainbow. Hundreds of different colors reflected off of it in the torchlight. It was cut into multi-pointed star. Then two miniature daggers went through its center, one from the left and one from the right with the blades pointing up. Then there was a black sword between the daggers, blade pointing down. The hilts of the three blades formed a triangle around the stone. It was stunning and there was an air of mystery around it that peaked my interest.

"Excuse me, when you have a moment," I said to the vendor. He looked at me and nodded then proceeded to excuse himself from the other shoppers.

The vendor walked closer and squinted down his nose at it. After a moment, he scratched his head and had a glassy look in his eye. I reached into my purse.

"Would two silver pieces be enough?" I said. I had no idea what to offer. A loaf of bread was only a few coppers, and this necklace was small and tarnished. He thought for a moment.

"Five." I nodded and went back to my purse. As I handed the coins to the merchant, someone moved to stand beside me.

"I'll give you ten silver for it," he said. I ground my teeth in annoyance and turned toward the voice. I had to raise my head to see his face. I found bright, shining blue eyes looking down at me. All understanding of language left me and my mouth just hung slightly open. He was gorgeous. All the singers in Devtera wouldn't be able to capture his likeness. My heart was racing and I thought it would explode. He was beautiful. He had black wavy hair that just brushed his jaw. His facial features were strong and squared, perfectly sculpted. He was clean shaven, and his skin was pale. I found that I was fighting myself not to go to him and stroke his face to see if he were carved from marble. My fingers tingled at the thought of it.

"I'm sorry, sir," the vendor said, placing the necklace in my hand, "She has paid me her money." His eyes left mine to look at the vendor and I felt freed. He no longer wore his circlet or his family's colors. His clothes were simple. If I hadn't recognized his eyes, I wouldn't have known it was the prince.

"But I offered you more," he said. His voice was firm, and I couldn't understand how the vendor was not affected by him. The prince had an aura of intimidation that commanded respect. Still, the vendor shrugged and started to explain his honorable reputation. My mind was racing. If the prince was here then the Black Guard must be escorting him. If they were local soldiers, I could be in trouble. The Black Guard had labeled me as suspicious a long time ago because of my strange features. I didn't want to give them a reason to arrest me. The prince and the vendor continued to argue, and I slipped away as quietly as I could.

I quickly made my way to the Blue Boot. It was the closest and safest place for me to be at the moment. Even from outside I could easily smell smoke and vomit throughout the pub. I pushed away the urge to gag and opened the door. I pushed my way to an empty table in the back. I couldn't see Jeb well. It was just too crowded and he didn't have time to sit with me anyway. I took a deep breath and rubbed my head as a headache started to form. I growled at it. Today was going so well.

Two kisses, no headache, and no shame. I closed my eyes and sighed, rubbing my temples.

"You left in rather a hurry." My eyes snapped open to see the prince sitting across from me. I didn't even hear him sit down. He slid one of the two tankards he had to me.

"Here, I brought a peace offering: Spiced mead. Rumor is it's best drink in Ameris." His words were informal, but his tone was almost cold. His movements looked easy though. He was reclined in the chair with an ankle resting on his knee. Under his dark cloak was a gray shirt stretched across his broad shoulders and slim waist. Simple brown breeches covered his powerful legs with dark brown boots. He appeared to be all power and muscle, but his lips looked soft and had a slight fullness to them. I scolded myself as I blushed. There was a sword buckled to his belt on his left and a dagger on the right.

He glanced around the inn. I wasn't sure how to act around him. There weren't any soldier escorts, and it didn't seem anyone realized who he really was.

"Nice place. A bit rowdy but not too bad." He gestured to the card game at the table behind him. Two of the players had just slammed their knives into the table. I continued to stare in stunned silence.

"You know who I am," he said, and I nodded. I wasn't sure I was breathing; my nerves were so frazzled. I couldn't tell if he was angry or comfortable. His body language and his voice were just so different from each other. I took a giant gulp of the mead.

"I suggest we just keep that between us, no need for titles and names. So, about this necklace, how much do you want for it?"

"It's not for sale." The words flew from my mouth before I could process them. I was attached to the necklace already. It was the first thing I had ever bought for myself. The prince raised an eyebrow and took a drink.

"That's a very bold thing to say to me," he said flatly.

"Is it?" Again, the words had a mind of their own. Of all the times for me to be rash, this was probably the worst. He studied my face for a moment. I felt my heart skip a beat, or a few, and my cheeks felt warm. I took another drink.

"Would it persuade you if I said there was sentimental value in it for me?"

"No."

"Why?"

"It's sentimental for me as well so you offer a moot point." What was I doing? We held each other's gaze.

"You are interesting, Lady...?" He raised his cup as he awaited my answer. I hesitated. What was he really doing? This was the Prince of Rokellia sitting before me and actually speaking to me, a commoner, because of a necklace? Anything of sentimental value to the prince wouldn't have ended up with a random merchant. What were the odds of him happening upon an invaluable necklace that meant so much to him just as it was being bought? I had just dug it out of a box of brooches. It didn't make sense. My brow furrowed with suspicion.

"You said there was no need for titles or names." A moment passed and the smallest of smirks appeared on his lips. It disappeared as quickly as it came but not before my stomach flipped involuntarily.

"I did say that didn't I?" He leaned forward and rested his elbows on the table. He held my gaze and the air between us grew thick. I felt a chill creep into my eyes as I tried to study him to find out his true intentions. His posture was easy and relaxed but his eyes were searching too.

"What are you really after?" I said.

He didn't reply. My jaw tensed with frustration, and I inhaled deeply to calm myself. A familiar scent filled my nose: Books and spices. My eyes went wide. I didn't image it after all. I started to confront him but was interrupted.

"Everything all right here?" Jeb stood by the table and glared daggers at the prince.

"Not as well as I had hoped. Another round perhaps?" the prince said flatly. Jeb bristled and turned to me.

"Do you know this man? Is he bothering you?" I looked back at the prince, and he captured my gaze again. I knew he wasn't done talking to me, and frankly, I wasn't done talking to him either.

"I'm just fine, Jeb. Just casual conversation. We haven't even exchanged names." I smiled up at Jeb reassuringly. After a pause, he nodded.

"If you say so... I wanted to give you your present, but it can wait."

"By all means, don't let me stop you," the prince said, leaning back into his chair with a wave of his hand. Jeb's face flushed and looked at the small, wrapped bundle in his hand. Simon yelled for Jeb to come back. Jeb cleared his throat and handed the bundle to me.

"I'll just give this to you now and you can open it later. Happy birthday, V." He gave me a peck on the cheek and went back to work. My entire face went hot, and I couldn't look at the prince.

"Well, happy birthday. Is he a friend of yours?" I suddenly wanted to crawl under the table. I put the gift in my pocket quickly.

"Yes, since childhood."

"I do hope that 'V' is just a nickname." I stiffened and the chill in my eyes turned frigid.

"What's that supposed to mean?" He almost smiled again but covered it by finishing his drink.

"It's a bit simple, isn't it?" I raised an eyebrow at his condescending tone.

"I image it would seem simple to someone who stalks women in the forest at night, Princely." His eyes snapped to mine. He leaned across the table again and I tried not to move away from him. His features were so still he looked like he turned to stone. His eyes, though, showed a quiet fury so intense, his eyes seemed to glow. It was terrifying.

"Let's put an end to this charade, then, shall we? I saw what you did to those rogues in the forest."

My head started to swim. He saw me. He is going to arrest me. He must think I'm a caster. I felt the panic rising through my chest. The lingering chill surged through me, and my eyes froze over. I swung my tankard and it crashed into the prince's jaw, sending him backward. He reached out to catch himself but grabbed the card table he gestured to earlier and knocked it to its side, cards and coins going everywhere. The players roared and punches started to fly. Jeb started yelling and caught my gaze. He was at my side in an instant.

"What happened? Are you all right?" he said, frantically looking me over as the brawl grew larger.

"I'm fine but I think I'm going to go home. Too much excitement for one night, I think. Tell my family I'll see them there, please. I'll see you tomorrow." I planted a quick kiss on his cheek and then slipped into the storage room and out the back door before he could stop me.

I pulled up my hood and ran around the corner of the building to the stable. I hurried to saddle Tempest. My only objective was to get home. I was on edge. My limbs still buzzed with the cold energy, and I fumbled to buckle the straps properly. Finally, I went to swing up into the saddle, but I was flung to the ground by a strong jerk of my cloak. I landed on the ground in a heap.

"Only the guilty run," the prince said, coolly as he looked down at me. I slowly stood and felt a strong rush of energy, calming my panic again.

"And the afraid," I said, holding up my open hands. He scoffed at me and rubbed his now red jaw.

"I don't believe that for a second. I haven't seen someone as skilled in combat as you in some time. Neither has anyone been able to slip away so easily from me as you do. I know you don't serve the Black Guard. That doesn't leave many alternatives." I swallowed hard. He thought I was a spy?

"I don't serve anyone. My uncle is a retired general from the Devium War. He taught me to defend myself, that's all," I said. I took a few steps back, but he just moved forward after me. He shook his head in disbelief.

"A retired general? Really?" My back hit the wall of the stable and he kept coming.

"Yes, I'm not a soldier of any army. I swear to you. I'm no one."

"You are certainly someone and I intend to find out who." The prince's arm shot out to grab me, but I ducked under it and tried to run. His hand wrapped around my arm and yanked me back.

A terrible pain traveled up and down my arm from where his fingers touched my exposed skin. It felt as if liquid fire ran through my veins. It was excruciating. My head felt like it was splitting open, and I closed my eyes and nearly cried out. I wanted to collapse but my legs were paralyzed in place. Biting cold energy ripped through me, changing the pain and shocking my system into terrible muscles spasms. My skin was freezing over, and my eyes felt like shards of ice.

There was a blinding green light and then we were both thrown away from each other and into the hay. I panted and my skin was coated in sweat. I felt so cold, and my arm throbbed. I slowly sat up from the ground and winced from my aching muscles and head. My left arm, where the prince touched me, felt like it had been branded.

"What just happened?" the prince said and looked at his arm. His mouth fell open as his eyes went wide. Then he looked furious.

"What is this? What have you done to me? Have you cursed me, caster?" he roared at me. My mind was still muddled with pain, and I raised my hand to massage my temple. A soft green light caught my attention. I looked at my hurting arm and gasped.

On my left forearm was a glowing mark that was identical to the crest on the necklace I found. In this design, the star blazed with an eerie green light. When I looked closer, I noticed that the star was rotating slowly. The prince hoisted me up and slammed my back against the wall.

"What have you done to me?" he thundered at me. His grip was like iron. I glanced at his arm and saw the same mark but with a blue glow.

"I didn't do anything. I'm not a caster. You grabbed me and there was pain. I have a mark just like you." I stammered. His blue eyes were on fire and his teeth were barred.

"Of course, you do! The very crest as on the necklace we both wanted. Is this funny to you?"

I was so overwhelmed. I didn't know what was happening to me. I was so confused, and I was still in so much pain. My vision wouldn't stay focused, and I couldn't breathe. My heart pounded against my chest and my body started to shake. I felt a tear slide down my cheek and I struggled to keep the others at bay.

"Please, I don't know what's happening to me. I didn't do anything, I swear. I... I have to be cursed. It must be my fault. I'm so sorry. I didn't mean to do anything. I'm sorry." His grip on my arms loosened. My chest heaved as I tried to breathe, and my eyelids felt heavy. I felt him touch my face gently.

"You're burning up. Just... come with me," he said. After wrapping our marks with fabric torn from his cloak, he pulled my hood up and escorted me out with a firm grip.

Chapter 5: Horrors

It felt like we walked for hundreds of miles. By the time we reach the arena, my legs were made of lead. My head felt heavy again and my stomach pitched. I yanked away from him and vomited in an alleyway.

"I should've put you on the damn horse," he said more to himself. I leaned my head against the cool stone of the building. It eased my headache, but the relief was brief. I was covered in sweat, and I was shaking. Why was I so sick? The prince seemed fine.

"My aunt," I said softly. The prince came closer and wrapped my arm around his shoulders.

"What?" His breath was cool against my cheek.

"My aunt... has a medicinal booth. She's a healer. It should be... close by," I said, panting.

"What's her name?" he said.

"Prudence De Fortis." He paused for a moment but eventually nodded. I tried to walk with him, but he went too fast. I was so tired. He swept me into his arms and started calling my aunt's name in his thundering voice. A few people pointed and the prince took off. I closed my eyes and pressed my face onto his shoulder. I smelled spices and something else on him. I wish I knew what that other smell was. I concentrated on his scent and my panting lessened.

Finally, the prince stopped. I tried to raise my head and open my eyes, but they wouldn't listen to my commands.

"I'm looking for Prudence De Fortis."

"I'm Prudence. What's- Fredrick, come quick! Clear the table and close the booth." I heard shuffling and the prince gently laid me on a hard surface. This was all my fault. I knew my aunt and uncle would be beside themselves. I thought that I would stop being a bother, but I burdened them tenfold.

"Aunt Prudence... I'm... so sorry," I said in a harsh whisper. A cold wet cloth touched my brow.

"Don't talk now, dearie. Save your strength. I'll have you right again in a blink. Fredrick, wipe down her face and neck with this. When it's no longer cold, make another. Now you, tell me what has happened to my niece."

"I'm not sure if I can explain it, madam."

"You had best try, boy," Uncle Fredrick said in a low growl. I couldn't hear if the prince was speaking or not.

"Drink this, dearie, it'll give you strength." There was vial pressed against my lips. The smell was terrible. I wanted to gag but I managed to swallow it down. Something else was shoved into my mouth. It wasn't unpleasant but the flavor was strong.

"Suck on this root. It will calm your stomach." The elixir was already working. My breathing eased and I could almost open my eyes. A new voice spoke.

"Um, sir-"

"It can wait, Edwin." Prince Aleron's voice shook.

"It can't, milord. The Bloodied Men are attacking Ameris as we speak." My cold eyes snapped open.

"The Bloodied Men? Why are they in Rokellia?" Aunt Prudence said, pausing her grinding in her mortar.

"It was a matter of time, Pru," Uncle Fredrick said calmly, dabbing my face with a new cloth. "The kingdom is weak at the moment. Seizing Ameris, the most valuable trade center of Rokellia, would be a devasting blow. I'm sure the fanatic militia thinks it will greatly please King Karrolei. I'm surprised that they would attack on Dark Day, though. Clearly they want to send a message in hopes of finally getting the king's attention and support. They have been recruiting men all over Capilious for some time now." The older man in black armor stared in surprise at Uncle Fredrick.

"That is precisely-" The prince interrupted, bristling and he rubbed his brow.

"Edwin, are the extra forces not solving the problem?"

"Yes and no. We were not prepared for their numbers as your mission was not... successful last night."

"Yes. I don't need to be reminded, Edwin... Please, stay here and stay safe. I will be back in a moment," the prince said to us then he and the knight left the tent.

My heart stopped beating. He found me last night. The prince probably thought that I was a recruit of the Bloodied Men. There was talk of the independent militia forming in Capilious. They had been recruiting for almost a year and now they had finally acted. This was my fault. If I had just stayed home yesterday, I wouldn't have met the rogues, and the prince would have completed his mission. I raised up and swung my legs over the edge of the table. The world spun around me, and I almost vomited again.

"Vespera, lie down," Aunt Prudence said. I pushed her away.

"Did you not hear what he said? Ameris is being attacked! We have to go, now. Where's Henry?" I tried to stand but my knees buckled. Uncle Fredrick caught me and pushed me to sit on the table again.

"We have to make sure you are fit enough to travel without hurting yourself further. What happened, Vespera?" I wanted to cry again. They were risking their lives because of me. Aunt Prudence's face softened, and she held my hand gently.

"If I know what happened, I can make you better and we can leave quicker. Talk to me, dearie." I offered her my arm. She unwrapped the fabric. Her face reflected the green glow of the mark. Her eyes grew wide, and her face was overcome with horror.

"How could this have happened? It will all be undone; all for nothing. That man was..." Her grip was so strong that I thought my hand would go numb.

"What is it? What's wrong with me?" I whispered. My heartbeat thudded in my ears.

"The seal is breaking. It will take some time to fully dissipate and, unfortunately, it won't be a pleasant experience." My head started spinning and I wanted to faint.

"Seal? What does that mean? Like a spell? What was it for?" She took my hand and wrapped the mark with the cloth again.

"The seal was supposed to lock away your power but... We'll have to discuss everything later," she said with exasperation. My mind was spinning. I met the prince, Ameris was being attacked, and I had power? I thought about the rogue attack. Was that part of it?

"We need to find Henry and go home. Now," Uncle Fredrick said.

"What about Jeb? He is on the same side of town as Catherine's father's shop. Surely we can get him too," I said. My aunt waved a hand dismissively.

"If we see him, he can come but I'm sure he'll be fine. Our priority is our family." I pulled my arm from her and stood my ground.

"Jeb is my family." She turned and our eyes faced off. I wouldn't waver. I wouldn't leave him behind. I felt faint and fell back against the table. Aunt Prudence's eyes softened with tears, and she pulled me into her arms.

"Calm down, dearie. We'll find him. He'll come with us. We'll all be safe."

"Prudence, you go get Henry and go home. I'll make sure Vespera gets home safe."

"We are staying together, Fredrick," Aunt Prudence said, shoving vials, herbs, and the day's earnings in a bag.

"Pru, with Vespera's current state, you would catch up to us before we made it to the edge of the city. I know you are more than capable of taking care of yourself. I will protect our girlie. We aren't waiting for that boy to come back." Uncle Fredrick kissed my aunt deeply and then kissed her forehead. Aunt Prudence handed me another vial.

"Drink this. The other potion will wear off soon. You must stay awake until we are all together and you are safe, Vespera. Do you understand?" I nodded and quickly drank the soured liquid. Some of the weariness left my legs. She hugged me again.

"I love you, Vespera. We'll see this through, and I'll explain everything." I nodded.

"I love you, too." We slipped out of the tent.

The stalls around us were abandoned, wares and all. People were running and screaming in every direction. The once beautiful fabrics and paper flower garlands were on fire, spreading the flames to each building faster. There was smoke everywhere. How did everything happen so quickly?

Aunt Prudence went toward the carpenter's shop, where Catherine's family lived. Uncle Fredrick and I turned the other way. My legs were still shaky, and I was exhausted but at least I could move. Uncle Fredrick kept a brisk pace, mindful of me. As we passed a weapons booth, Uncle Fredrick snatched a sword and held it ready.

I hoped that Aunt Prudence would try to find Jeb. I told myself that he would be safe. He was a brawler, and he was a good runner. He thought that I went home so he wouldn't look for me. He would be all right.

We met more mayhem the further we walked. Some tents were burning, some destroyed. People were running away or stealing whatever valuables they could. I heard the clang of metal and saw a Black Guard soldier fighting what looked like a mad man. He had red war paint on his face and bare-arms and fought with such a ferocity, he didn't seem human. I had heard that the Bloodied Men sometimes forced villages and towns into supplying men for the army but never had I heard of such destruction. If there had been, King Karrolei would have moved to stop them. If what Uncle Fredrick said was right, then the Bloodied Men were now ready to march on Rokellia.

I tried not to look at the few bodies on the ground or breathe in too much of the smell of blood and burnt flesh. I kept gagging; apparently the root stopped working too. I spat out the root and stared at Uncle

Fredrick's back. I couldn't look at the city anymore. The smells were bad enough, but the sight of death made my chest hurt and my stomach fall to my feet.

Uncle Fredrick steered us through the fires and bodies, but we didn't meet any other soldiers. We were far from safe though. The sounds of clanging steel and people screaming carried in the wind and settled heavily in my ears. Smoke stung my eyes and burned my nostrils. I coughed and pain threatened to engulf me again. I stumbled and barely caught myself on the building we were walking next to. My muscles spasmed and I ground my teeth together as I started to sweat. The potion was wearing off already.

"I thought we would have more time," Uncle Fredrick muttered. He contemplated for a moment and then stuck the sword in his belt. He swept me into his arms and continued.

I felt my head bob against his chest as my vision faded in and out. I tried to force my eyelids open, but I was so tired.

Stay awake, stay awake, stay awake. I repeated it over and over in my head, but I couldn't keep my eyes open anymore. Darkness came and went as I struggled. Uncle Fredrick said something, but I couldn't make it out. I heard a grunt and then I fell to the ground. The snow was cold on my cheek, and I welcomed the feeling against my hot skin. I sighed into the ground and almost let the darkness take me. The pain was everywhere.

I heard a hard thud on the ground. I managed to open my eyes and saw that the snow had turned red. A brief moment of clarity startled me awake. I raised my head and a scream caught in my throat but there was no one around to notice; just the two of us. I scrambled to Uncle Fredrick and my hands found the gaping wound in his chest. Blood was pouring from his body. I had to stop the bleeding. I reached for my head, but my scarf wasn't there.

"No, no, no, no, no." I ripped my overdress and pressed it on the wound. "Stop the bleeding, mend the wound. Stop the bleeding, mend the wound." That's how Aunt Prudence did it. But the blood wouldn't stop.

I felt hands on my shoulders, pulling me back. My fragile calm was shattered. I jerked away and threw my fists at whoever it was that touched me. I couldn't see anything but his lifeless eyes staring through me. I felt the hands wrap around my arms. They said something to me, but I was deaf. I screamed again and again. I kicked and thrashed, never taking my eyes off him. More hands, more fighting. My view was finally obstructed, and I saw the devium standing before me.

"Apologies," he said. His fist fell and everything went black.

Chapter 6: Changed

When I awoke, I was lying on the ground near a campfire. How did I get here? I looked up and winced. My head throbbed and my limbs felt weary. It was not yet dawn. I tried to push myself up, but I couldn't. I looked at my hands and saw ropes binding them together. My feet were also bound. I was lying on a fur covered by a blanket. I looked around and saw the sleeping bodies of the rogues. Then I remembered.

Uncle Fredrick was dead.

I closed my eyes against the hot tears and my chest burned. I buried my face in fur and tried not to sob with my tears. There was so much blood. Why did I have to be so weak? I could have done something, anything. I cried until darkness took me again.

I felt a blazing heat on my face. My eyes were swollen and felt like they had sand in them. Why was it so hot? I pushed the blanket off of me and tried to get up. I groaned when I realized my hands were still tied. I kept my eyes closed. They were so cold that I was afraid that if I opened them, they would shatter like pieces of ice. My senses were so sensitive and precise. There were two men sitting near me.

"Woah, woah, keep those on, you're freezing. Boys, she's awake!" I heard movement around me. It was one of the rogue twins I met before. I remembered his voice. He walked closer and knelt next to me. I sensed him reach for the blankets.

"Don't touch them," I said, my voice catching. My throat was so dry I was surprised I even made a sound. The rogue stood and retrieved a canteen. I heard the liquid sloshing inside. I took a deep breath. I smelled the crisp water inside. My saliva was thick in my mouth as he pressed the sack to my mouth. I gulped down the water greedily.

"Slow down, slow down! There won't be... you drained it." As soon as the water hit my stomach I wanted to vomit. I rolled away from the rogue and my stomach heaved, emptying itself of the water. I coughed and tried to catch my breath. I inhaled the scent of pine, metal, and fire.

"I told you not to give her anything yet. She's been asleep for too long. How are you feeling?" the devium said.

I felt stiff and exhausted, and my senses were overwhelming me. I still didn't want to open my eyes. I was scared. I didn't know how I got there or what was happening to me. What about... I stopped the thought before I could fall into that dark pit again. I got myself on my knees and opened my cold eyes. I hissed as the light blinded me. It was so bright that I had to immediately close them again. I pressed my hands over my eyes until the stinging went away. I took a deep breath and slowly opened my eyes while my hands still covered them. I saw the lines of my hands bathed in a soft green light. Were my eyes glowing? I blinked a few times and began to open my fingers, gradually letting more and more light in. I stared at the forest in wonder. Everything was so much more vivid. The browns of the trees' trunks were richer and the greens of the evergreen leaves lusher. I looked up and sighed. The sky was a crisp blue, almost like a summer sky. My skin tingled as I took in the winter air. It wasn't as cold as I expected it to be. I swallowed and tried to speak but it was a hoarse whisper.

"Where am I?" I glanced at the twin, still kneeling next to me. He scrambled away from me so quickly, he almost went into the fire. It was the one without the scar. I could smell the sweat of fear as it appeared on his skin. His mouth opened and closed like a fish. My eyes must have been glowing. I couldn't blame him. I imagined that I looked terrifying. The other twin had a similar expression; however, the center of his face was black with two bruised eyes and a broken nose. I wondered how that happened. I looked to the devium. He just turned his head at me with a smirk on his lips and a raised eyebrow.

"You are in the Nitalla," he said. I swallowed again and stretched my neck.

"What happened to Ameris?"

"It burned to the ground," he said evenly. My heart dropped.

"The people?" I said, softly.

"Burned with the city it seems. The attack came from all sides. There were hardly any escape routes, but I assume there were a few survivors. You made it out." What about Jeb and Aunt Prudence and Henry? I had to know if they were safe, and I had to tell them about...

I struggled against the ropes around my wrists and ankles.

"There is no need for that," he said, "You won't break those." The ropes snapped and I crawled away from the three rogues.

"Now that is interesting..." the devium said, making no effort to move.

"Why did you tie me up?"

"To prevent further injury to my men." He gestured to the scarred twin I saw two days ago. I vaguely remember hitting someone after...

"I have to go back. My family needs me," I said trying to stand.

"What makes you think that they are still alive? My condolences for your... father?" he said. His tone wasn't mocking but it wasn't kind either. I narrowed my eyes at him and bared my teeth.

"Don't you dare speak of my uncle." He just smiled.

"Ah, uncle, forgive me. As I was saying, that was a terrible battle. A large and important one too given the resources Ameris provided." He slid his cat-like eyes toward me as I clung to a tree. My legs were wobbly and stiff.

"How long was I asleep?" I said wincing as flexed my muscles.

"How long has it been, Dax?" the devium said to the scarred twin. He looked up and counted his fingers.

"This is the dawn of the third day," he said finally.

"Three days?" The words were hardly whispers. My limbs became heavy again and my mind stopped working. Three days...

There was a long pause and then finally the devium spoke.

"There is nothing left of Ameris, and you have nowhere to go." He was just stating a grim fact. I didn't want to believe my family was gone, I wouldn't. Even if Ameris was nothing but ash, my home was outside the city. They would be there waiting for me. They had to be.

"You don't believe me?" the devium said quizzically. I glared up at him and I felt the cold energy swirl inside me. He raised his hands in defense.

"Hear me. As I said, the ropes were for my men's protection. You are not a prisoner here. If you don't believe my words, go see for yourself. The ruins are half a day's walk east." He pointed out the direction.

I glared at him for a moment, waiting for any sign of deceit, but he merely stared back at me. I set my jaw and tried to stand. I didn't feel weak, but my limbs were so stiff it was hard to move. Dax's brother, the twin who had given me the water, stood quickly, and reached to help me. I glared at him, and he stood still. I didn't want any of them touching me. They had taken me away from my family. They ripped me away from the only father I ever knew and left him there in the bloodied snow.

With my feet finally beneath me, I stretched to get the blood back into my muscles. My joints popped loudly. I looked back at the rogues and walked east.

As I walked I thought about my strange, heightened senses. The forest was so alive now. I could hear the slightest movement of the hairs on a bug if I concentrated hard enough. I could smell the venom of a poisonous plant and the scent of a snapped twig. The small stream I walked by sounded like a roaring river. I thought for a moment that I was going crazy with sorrow and just imagining that I could do all these things. Perhaps I was dreaming. I hoped that I was still sleeping in my room and that my birthday hadn't happened yet. I wanted to start again. My birthday had begun so well. I wanted to take Jeb away from his work and make him kiss me. I wanted Aunt Prudence to scold me again and maybe wear those skirts after all. I wanted to gossip with Henry. I wanted to hold Uncle Fredrick and tell him that I loved him.

My eyes were so cold they ached. I gently rubbed them and when I started to pull my hand away, I saw a green light shining on my palm from my eyes again. I went to the stream and gasped at my reflection. My eyes were glowing like two green torches. What was happening to me? I washed my face in the stream. I had to get to Ameris.

I broke through the tree line onto familiar road, and I felt like I was punched in the stomach. In the distance were black nubs of burnt buildings and... nothing. No sounds, no movement, nothing. Ameris really was gone.

"Oh please, no," I gasped, and my hand covered my mouth. I wanted to cry but the tears wouldn't come. My eyes were too cold and too dry.

There's no way that anyone survived. How could they? The city was decimated. The Bloodied Men wouldn't have let people live. They were sending a message. I saw the faces of my family flash through my mind: Jeb, Henry, Aunt Prudence, and a bloody Uncle Fredrick.

My knees became weak, and I caught myself on a tree.

"He didn't have to die. It should have been me. It's my fault..." Heavy tears finally fell from my eyes, and I slid down the tree in a heap. I held my face in my hands and sobbed frigid tears. I wrapped my arms around myself to try to fill the gaping hole that was in my chest. Why was this happening to me? These things I could do were so inhuman, and I didn't understand. No one was here to save me now. It was all so wrong. I just wanted to go home.

My head shot up. How could I be so stupid? The farm. Our house. It was well hidden and far enough away. They could be there, waiting. I stood, wiping my face, and turned in the direction of home. The devium stepped from the trees into my path. I guess I wasn't free to go after all.

"Leave me alone, devium," I said, staring at him with every bit of hatred I had.

"I thought that humans typically longed for companionship in times of despair. Isn't that correct? I'm merely here to lend a shoulder, or at the very least, an ear," he said as he leaned on a tree and outstretched his arms.

"That's not why you are here." He dropped his arms and looked into my glowing eyes with a small smile.

"No, it isn't... Tell me are your eyes truly glowing or is that just from the tears?" The dagger left my hand before I realized I unsheathed it from my boot. It whizzed through the air at blinding speed and planted itself into a tree after catching the devium's coat, pinning him in place. Silas turned his head with a quizzical face, but his eyes were alight.

"That was the wrong thing to say. Apologies. So, what is your plan now that you have no home?" he asked nonchalantly.

I stood and walked over to him. I yanked my blade free as I walked past him. If I stopped moving I thought I would kill him. His eyes lit with amusement at my venom.

"And where are you off to in such a rush, Fairest?" he said curiously. It was hard to tell if he was just toying with my emotions or if he really was only curious. It was probably both.

"I have an idea," the devium said walking beside me, "Join my band. You need not fear the rogues, obviously, and I would like to have you in battle. Having a capable fighter such as yourself would be an asset on the road." He glanced at the blade in my hand that had pinned him to the tree.

"No."

"But you haven't heard all of the details of my proposal. You see, we rogues get a bad name but that's only because we are a perfect scapegoat for the royals' shortcomings, the Bloodied Men for instance." I cut my eyes to him but said nothing. He continued.

"The monarchs say that we pillage and rape and murder when in reality, we just steal from the fortunate along the Kings' Road. It's heavily trafficked with important people with little protection. You'll be surprised at our number. We turn none away who wish to be a part of us. We only ask that you pull your own weight."

"My answer is no. I have to find my family." He was not deterred.

"Still hopeful? Perhaps you've thought of a place of sanctuary in which they may be hiding." Could deviums read minds? I'm sure that I would've heard about that, even as a rumor.

"As you wish," he said, "Go to this safe place and see what is there. When you find nothing, remember my offer. Tomorrow at midday, I'll wait for you on the road where we first met. See you then, Fairest." He swiftly disappeared into the forest.

I wasn't sure if a day would be enough time to walk home and back but it wouldn't matter. I wouldn't accept his offer. My family would be there.

The stars shone brightly in the sky when I saw the house appear in the distance. It seemed whole and untouched by enemy hands. My legs were shaky, but I refused to stop. I wouldn't rest until I was home.

The lanterns near the door were dark and there were no lights in the windows. It was late, they must have been in bed. I walked up to the door and pulled the latch. The hinges creaked as it swung inward. Aunt Prudence just forgot to lock the door again. There wasn't a fire going in the main room and the silence was suffocating. I took a quick glance around. Nothing seemed out of place. It was late. Maybe they were sleeping. I closed the door.

"Hello? Aunt Prudence, Henry, I'm home! I'm all right!" Nothing. I ran to Henry's room and then Aunt Prudence's, but both were empty. They weren't here. My heart shattered and my stomach heaved. I fell on Aunt Prudence and Uncle Fredrick's bed as my knees gave out.

I felt numb. I couldn't think straight. Why weren't they here? We were supposed to meet here. Where are they? I felt a tear fall down my cheek.

"They're gone." I held my face in my hands and the tears flooded from me again. I sobbed until my back ached and I couldn't breathe. I fell back on the bed and held Aunt Prudence's pillow to my face. It smelled of rosewater and sage, of her. I curled tightly into the pillow. I wanted to hide from the pain, but it found me no matter the shape I contorted into. I thought I had felt alone before, but I was so wrong.

I awoke to the sun streaming in through the open window. The rooster crowed from the yard. I opened my eyes but didn't move. I didn't have any delusions of hope when I woke. The truth had turned to chains on my body, keeping me rooted to the bed. What was I supposed to do now? A thousand thoughts bombarded my mind at once: My family's faces flashed, Jeb's smile shone, the fires flared, the blood flew. I buried my face into the pillow, trying to soothe the ache away. Dirt flaked off my skin. A bath crossed my mind, but I didn't move. What did it matter? I knew it didn't matter but part of me wanted a mindless job to do. Coldness surged through me, and I suddenly had too much energy to do nothing. I went to the kitchen and fetched the bath basin. I pulled it near the hearth. I started a fire and then drew some water from our well. It was indeed mindless work. I wanted to think as little as possible.

After my bath, I sat next to the fire to speed the drying of my hair, but I don't remember feeling its warmth. But I wasn't cold either. I dressed in a shirt, corset, and breeches. I slipped my boots back on. I glanced at the table at the purse full of coins. It had somehow managed to not get stolen. At least I didn't have to worry about funds but where would I go? I shook my head, and I went back to my aunt and uncle's room. I crawled into bed and stared at the wall. I didn't want to think. I wanted to just fade away. I closed my eyes, hoping to find the black void of sleep again.

There was a light shining in my eyes, keeping sleep away from me. The sunlight came through the window and was reflected by something in the wardrobe across the room. I stared at it and, finally, stood up. I pushed my now dry hair out of my face and opened the wardrobe door. There was a bundle of cloth with a small note with my name on it. It was Aunt Prudence's handwriting.

I picked up the note. It read: "I didn't want to give these to you yet, but your uncle insisted. These were your mother's. She would have wanted you to have them. I am not ready to talk about it now so just give me some time. Happy birthday, I love you."

I wanted to cry again but my body had no more tears to shed. Maybe it would be later. I unfolded the cloth and saw two long daggers glittering at me. I forgot how to breathe for a moment. The blades were beautiful. They were the same shape as the ones currently in my boots, but these were feathery light, and the blades were made from a strange stone. The stone was smooth and the color of mist and flecked with a thousand rainbows. The silver hilts curved up along each side of the thin blades. Down each blunt side of the blades were strange, swirled markings that shown in the sun that streamed through the window. I'd never seen anything like them.

I twirled the blades around my fingers, and they sang as they moved. I would have thought that they were just ceremonial if they weren't so sharp. My mother was a warrior. The thought almost brought a smile to my face. Aunt Prudence had refused to tell me about her, and she had never even mentioned my father. Holding the blades in my hands was both the greatest and worst gift: I now knew something about my mother, but they were just a reminder that I would never really know anything else.

I tried not to think about it anymore. I had more pressing matters. What was I supposed to do now? I couldn't just lay in bed and waste away. I replaced the old daggers in my boots with my mother's. I could travel to another town, there were maps in the house. I shook my head. I had some skills with healing, and I could cook and clean but who would hire me? I naturally put people off and without someone to speak on my abilities, no one would hire me, especially now.

I looked at my arm. The crest was still there, the star still turning. There was the prince... but I squashed the thought. I wouldn't seek refuge in Jahilta. The Rokellia capital was a long journey, weeks by carriage. The distance wasn't what dissuaded me. The prince thought I was a caster that cursed him. I was sure that he survived the battle. It just didn't sound right that he would fall to a random zealot. A thought occurred to me then. What if he came looking for me? I knew in my core he wouldn't just let it go. If I still had the mark, so did he and I knew that he would think the same. He would come to find me.

My thoughts turned to the devium's proposal. He wanted to use me. I knew it and he was aware of that. He had said so when making the offer. At least he meant for me to fight men, not submit myself to them. The worst part was that I had no choice. The rogues had never been apprehended by the Black Guard or Aurelian Army. It was probably the safest place for me. I squared my shoulders. It was a start, and I could always leave if something else came along. I nodded to myself and began packing.

After forcing some dried meat and stale bread into my stomach, I walked out to the yard to open all of the pens. It didn't feel right to let the animals eventually starve. As I pulled open the gate to the corral, I heard a huff behind me. I turned and nearly cried again.

"Tempest!" I threw my arms around her neck and buried my face in her shoulder. I hadn't lost everyone. She was still saddled and looked fine. I took off her saddle and checked her over for sores, then poured some grain into the trough and brought her fresh water. I looked at the sun while she ate. With a horse, I now had plenty of time to meet the devium and I could even pack more supplies. I took the saddle bags, and I went inside to do just that.

I reached the spot on the road just before midday. Leaving the house nearly killed me. Part of me wanted to set it on fire, to give it a burial of its own since I couldn't bury my family, but I just couldn't bring myself to do it. Part of me still hoped. I had even left a note.

I saw the devium sitting on his horse, eating a strip of dried meat. He turned to me and bowed his head.

"My condolences once again." I set my mouth in a hard line.

"I have conditions to your proposal." He raised an eyebrow and a smile formed on his lips.

"I'm listening."

"I want privacy, my own livings quarters away from others, and the freedom to do as I please, so long as I pull my own weight." He laughed.

"That's all? Granted. Now let's return to camp. Dax and Kaul will be expecting us." I tried not to look so surprised. I didn't expect him to be so accommodating. Then again, I didn't know what to expect. I straightened my shoulders and followed the devium.

Chapter 7: Rogue City

As we rode together, the devium talked freely despite my silence. I couldn't bring myself to be friendly with him. I didn't trust him and the thought of talking, laughing, or even smiling felt like a betrayal to my family. I'm not sure that he really needed someone else around for him to talk.

"You know, in winter the Nitalla reminds me of my home, except there are no mountains here, of course." I watched him while he spoke. He looked so polished and refined. Maybe that was the way of the devium. He now seemed more open with me than before, like he trusted me now, though I was sure that that was not the case. He was harder to read than anyone I had ever met. He certainly had not earned my trust.

"Ah, it is beautiful in winter there, and in all other seasons for that matter." His teeth shown like pearls as he smiled. He looked at me, prompting a reply. I gave none. I was not in any mood to talk, especially to him.

"It would be nice if you told me your name. And you can call me 'Silas,'" he said trying at conversation again. I pondered his question. The only people who used my name were my family and they were gone. Maybe my name was dead too.

"Call me what you like, devium," I said. Amusement crossed his features.

"Fairest?" I grimaced.

"Not that." He laughed loudly.

"I shall think on it then. Here we are," he said and moved his horse through some branches.

The campsite had been dismantled. There was not even a trace of a fire. The twins, Dax, and Kaul, were arguing.

"Your face doesn't look so bad, really," Kaul said. Dax gently pushed on his nose and winced.

"I just don't want my nose to be crooked. I already have the damn scar! It's your turn to have something wrong with your face!"

"I don't think so. We've got to keep my face perfect so everyone can see what yours is supposed to look like." Dax scrunched up his face into a laugh only to wince again.

"Are you two done?" Silas said, dismounting his horse. The twins turned quickly. Dax even started to pull his sword from his side. When they realized that it was Silas, Kaul grabbed his chest dramatically.

"Silas, you have got to at least try to rustle some bushes or-"

"Break a twig or-" Dax said.

"Something," they said together. Silas merely shrugged. At that moment, the twins finally noticed me. They seemed to have gotten over their fear of me.

"You got her to come back!" Kaul said, smiling.

"Wonderful. Please, don't hit me again," Dax said, raising his hands jokingly. I just looked at him. How were they so cheerful? I suddenly felt exhausted. I wasn't used to such grief. It felt like a thick fog was trying to suffocate me.

"Is everything packed?" Silas said. The twins nodded. "Good. We will arrive well past dark so let's get moving."

The trip was full of conversation, mostly provided by Dax and Kaul. There wasn't a moment of silence. The twins began chatting and singing. They reminded me so much of Henry I couldn't bear it. My chest hurt and it was starting to get hard to breathe. I looked up into the canopy.

"Stop," I said, closing my eyes. The brothers turned to me, looking confused.

"Stop what?" Kaul said.

"Making noise," I growled. My harsh tone wasn't intentional, and I felt guilty even though it was effective. Kaul swallowed and looked at his brother. They nodded to each other and didn't say another word for the rest of the trip.

Long after night fell, I could see torches in the distance and I smelled meat cooking on the breeze. Silas nudged his horse through the brush, and we followed. A large wooden wall rose into the air and stretched wide in either direction. I stared in wonder at the wall, amazed by how it could have been constructed so deep in the forest. I saw a watch station positioned at the top of the wall that was lit by hanging torches. Over the wall was a village. I could hear women and children there mingling with men's voices. My brows furrowed together as I tried to make sense of it.

"Welcome to Rogue City," Silas said smugly.

When we approached the gate, we saw men running about the watchtower.

"Friend or foe?" a voice called from the top.

"Friend: It is Silas!" the devium called back, "And what did I tell you about so many torches? Do you want us found?" The torches immediately went out.

"Yes, sir! Sorry, sir! Open the gate!" the voice cried. The two large doors swung open. Silas walked forward and we followed him through the gates. The heavy wooden doors slammed behind us. I hoped I made the right decision. There was no backing out now.

We stood in a small square. There was a well directly in the center. Small wooden buildings surrounded the square and people were walking in and out of them. There weren't just men - there were women and children too, just as I had thought. The structures were made of wood and thatch. Most of the buildings were small but every now and then a larger house struck through the air. It amazed me that this place hadn't been discovered yet. The dark city was beautiful during the night. People were snuffing out small lanterns outside and children were hurrying inside. Darkness must have been a key to their survival here.

"Dax, Kaul, you are free to do as you please this evening. Report to your usual duties tomorrow," Silas said and dismounted.

The twins nodded and left.

"Silas! You are back!" said a small boy. He looked about seven years old. He ran up to the devium and smiled. His dirt-brown hair was tousled but his golden eyes were bright as he stared at the pale devium. I turned my head finding his eyes strikingly familiar. My heart panged as Aunt Prudence and Henry flashed through my mind.

"Hello, Eriak," Silas said. Eriak turned his gaze to me, and his eyes widened.

"She's here," he said with a smile, "I told you so, Silas." Silas's face became stern.

"Eriak, go home." The boy wasn't bothered by Silas's tone. He just turned his head at me, and his eyes glazed over. Then he smiled.

"I will see you soon," he said then ran away.

I watched the boy go as Silas turned a corner. I went to ask the devium about him, but he spoke first.

"He was abandoned when he was younger, and I took him in. Now, let me show you where you will stay." I furrowed my brow at how dismissive he was about the boy, but I didn't say anything more.

As we walked the streets, I saw that there was a carpenter, a blacksmith, and a tavern. In the distance, I saw a large open area. It was a training yard. Large haystacks lined the edge of the field against the wall for archery. Silas explained he would show me every place the next day. The further we walked, the fewer houses started to appear. We were nearing the training field that was pushed back against the wall. Silas turned to the right, away from the field, and I saw a large tree. It wasn't too tall, but it was very wide. I noticed there was a small stable to the side of it. Tempest neighed at the sight. I climbed off of her and took off her saddle and harness and the saddle bags.

With the weight gone, she ran excitedly to the stable. I turned to Silas. He was staring at me with a curious expression. I realized I still held the saddle single-handedly and without strain. My cheeks flushed. I didn't know what to make of the strength either. Before the devium could ask me about it, I started to follow my horse. I heard Silas follow me, but he said nothing. I set the saddle down in the stable and slung the saddlebags over my shoulder.

"I'll show you your home," Silas said from behind me. Hearing that word was like a knife in my chest. Was that another crack at me? I turned to Silas to see his expression, but he was already walking away.

He went back outside toward the tree. A small house rested on the thick, sturdy branches. The house was quaint from what I could see. There was a railed balcony encircling the whole dark wooden building. We were a few feet away and Silas ran and leapt upon the high balcony. I stood under the tree staring up at him. He smirked again.

"Allow me to get the ladder," he said and gestured to a roped ladder from the ledge and pushed it over. It was like he was testing me. I ignored the absurd challenge and climbed up the ladder instead. His expression didn't change as he opened the door with a bow. Silas stepped in behind me and shut the door.

"Let me light the lamps," he said and moved around me. My muscles tensed as I watched him. It was different being around him in an enclosed space. Outside there was room to run or defend myself. In here, I was forced to allow him more trust.

As Silas lit the lamps, I tried to ignore him and examine the room. It was larger than it appeared from the ground. A section of the floor dropped down and stairs led down to a small sitting area. Cushions were placed on the forms, implying that they were seats. In the center, there was a large bowl made of stone fit for fires. The rest of the room was spacious and shelves full of scrolls and books lined the walls. Near the pit was a large table with chairs. To my right was a smaller cooking area. In the left corner of the back wall was a door.

Silas finished lighting the lamps and sat in the pit. He lit a fire then yawned and stretched his long arms, folding them behind his head. It unnerved me to see how comfortable he was despite that this was my space now. I had to remember to keep my guard up. I walked over to one of the shelves. He spoke and answered my unspoken question.

"We robbed a wagon of scholars heading to Caneesho. We didn't think King Karrolei needed any more reading material, but then again, the others didn't think we needed them either. I wanted them and put them in this house along with the others. Unfortunately, I didn't have any more room in my own house." I scanned the titles of the books. Writing of all sorts littered the shelves: Mathematics, legends, lore, star study, and even a romance or two.

"Rogue City has been a refuge since the Devium War. People fled the old rulers and the new and made a place of their own. We will occasionally find new people to join the ranks. Those that are not satisfied with their current lives and those that are running from something. Everyone has a role to play. Play your role and you have a safe place."

I didn't look at him as he spoke more of the rogues' role in the world. He was worse than a traveling merchant hawking wares. I was there. I had already agreed to stay there. What more did he want from me?

"You can read," Silas said when I started skimming one of the lore books. It wasn't a question. I nodded and put the book back. "You know most don't know how to read, especially women," he said lightly.

"Women aren't supposed to wear trousers either." He broke into a laugh despite the bite in my tone.

In the firelight, his features looked cat-like again. His teeth sparkled and his eyes almost looked yellow. His hair was left long, passing his shoulders to his chest, and glittered like a river of silver. His laugh rang through the air. It occurred to me again that he was very attractive. Guilt swept over me.

"You have wit, I will give you that!" he said as his laughs receded. I just looked at him. After another pause, he spoke again. "Such a beautiful house, don't you agree? I could not discover how it was built or who could have built it. I know of no devium building their homes in trees. We prefer our homes closer to the earth. I like sleeping on the ground more than a bed so I wouldn't be happy in a place like this. The devium are drawn to earth and its core, however, we do love the mountains... It's possible it belonged to a caster. They need much room for their spells and potions and whatnot. Few humans like the Nitalla or seclusion so I doubt it is of human build. The other people here say there is a dark aura around this place. They say it's like it tells them they don't belong. I feel something like that, but I believe it is because the house is in the air." My eyes narrowed at him. He must have loved the sound of his own voice; he never stopped talking. I kept my distance from the pit. Perhaps my silence would tell him that I wanted to be alone.

"It's just another puzzle I have yet to solve. I like puzzles..." he murmured.

His expression changed. His head was cocked again. He appeared to be looking up at me and he had a luring look in his eyes. A small smile played on his lips. If he was trying to be tempting he was failing.

"I would like to rest," I said. Silas pursed his lips in annoyance, but it disappeared quickly.

He smiled and said, "You are right, and I am quite sure you are tired. If you wish to wash there are a few large buckets in that room for water. There is a bedroom back there. I will be on the training fields tomorrow. Many of the rogues practice in the morning," he said walking to the door. I stood and watched him go to the entryway. "Oh," he said turning back around on the balcony, "you will be required to attend training tomorrow. I would be obliged if you brought your blades to the training grounds. It could prove to be entertaining. Goodnight." He quickly took my hand and touched my knuckles to his forehead before I could stop him.

"What do you mean 'required?'" He smiled up at me, but his grip tightened around my hand.

"We discussed that should you stay here; you must provide service to the rogues. I want you as a fighter, unless you have something else in mind," he said with a smirk. I yanked my hand from his as my neck grew hot.

"I'll be there," I said quickly. A devilish grin spread across his lips.

"See you tomorrow," he said and leapt from the balcony.

I closed the door quickly and slumped against it. Exhaustion threatened to overwhelm me. I reached into one of my bags and ate some bread and dried meat. I really wanted a hot meal. I thought of Aunt Prudence and my shoulders fell. I helped her make every evening meal. Uncle Fredrick called it our "girlie bonding." Only once a year, on her birthday, did Uncle Fredrick and Henry cook. It was always a disaster. I smiled at the memory while a piece of my heart chipped away.

I grabbed my bags to put away my things in the bedchamber. There was a bed against one wall in the room. When I looked opposite the bed, I saw the whole wall was covered with curtains. Beyond the bed was a chest. I walked over and placed the bags on the floor and turned to the trunk. I kneeled before it and slowly opened the lid.

"Empty? Well, what did I expect?" I said tartly. I stood and started to empty my bags.

I threw my cloak at the chest and a small bundle of cloth fell out of the pocket. My heart stopped. Jeb's gift. I slowly picked it up and sat on the bed. I felt the tears readying themselves. I took a deep breath and opened the package. It was a bracelet made out of thin black leather strips. The strips were delicately knotted like a spider's web. There were small beads scattered through the knots that resembled raindrops of color. I knew in my heart that he made it himself.

"It must have taken so much time to finish." I set my jaw, and a tear escaped my eye. "I just want more time with you." I held the gift to my chest and my body shook. I would not cry again but I couldn't look at the bracelet anymore. I wrapped it up and placed it in the chest. It reminded me of another birthday gift that I had forgotten. I reached into my cloak pocket and found my coin pouch. I pulled out the crest necklace and just stared at it. I wasn't sure how to feel about it. Part of me blamed that necklace for everything. If I hadn't stopped to buy it, then Prince Aleron wouldn't have talked to me. I knew that was wrong though. He was following me before. I knew the necklace was just an excuse to talk to me. I rubbed my thumb over the pendant. The better question was why was this crest on my arm and the prince's? It had to hold some sort of meaning, or maybe it was just cursed. It didn't feel cursed but what did I know? I pulled the chain over my head and the pendant landed near my heart. I would find out what it all meant.

The sun woke me. I sat up and squinted at the curtained wall. There was a parting in the center of the curtains where the sun poured through. Rubbing my eyes, I went to pull back the drape. Behind the fabric was a wall of glass. I placed my hand against it and felt its cool surface. I didn't know that glass could be used as wall. It didn't seem practical or safe and it must have cost a treasury of gold. Beyond the wall was another balcony. Interesting... I looked down the wall and saw a thin line in the glass. Completely mesmerized, I pushed on it. It was a door. I pulled the glass to the side and the door slid into a pocket in the wall that I couldn't even see. Instead of sharp, flat edges on the door, they were rounded.

"So, you won't cut yourself..." I said slowly. I stepped outside and discovered that the wall looked over the wooden fence, so no one within the town could see it. A river ran along the wall only a short distance away and it was surrounded by white snow. The morning rays reflected off the cold water in a multitude of colors.

With a sigh, I drew the curtains then made the bed from habit. Making a tidy room was always the first of my chores to be completed. As I pulled the blanket tight across the hay mattress, I felt like Henry would burst in and ruffle the bed laughing. I could almost hear Aunt Prudence chastising him and Uncle Fredrick laughing. My heart fell and I turned away. I slipped on my trousers then tightened the string that ran down the front of my shirt and tied the corset over it. I slipped into my boots, threw on my cloak, and walked to the front door in need of a distraction.

"'To the training fields,' the devium said..." I said and looked at the rope ladder. I thought back to the devium's challenge. I peered over the balcony. The fall wasn't that far. I stood on the ledge. I gathered my courage and stepped off. The feeling of free-fall sent a blissful tingling through my skin and I smiled. The wind blew through my hair and, after having it hidden for so long, it was a wonderful feeling. As I neared the ground, I started to slow, and I landed softly on the dirt. I wasn't sure how to feel about these abilities. I didn't know where they ended, and I was apprehensive about testing them. I looked at the training fields with a sigh. One step at a time.

Chapter 8: A New Name

The field was arranged into sections: One for archery, one for close combat weapons, and then one for hand to hand combat. I heard shouts as men battled one another. There was a large group of people circling around a fight. I went closer and wasn't surprised to see Silas with his twin swords flashing in the morning sun. Silas parried a blow from a very muscular man who towered over everyone. I stood close but clear of the fighting. I looked around, surveying the crowd. There were no other women on the field. I guess I shouldn't have been surprised. I was painfully reminded that I was the strange one.

I turned back again to watch Silas and rubbed at the pendant. It was apparent to me that he was hardly trying. His movements were elaborate and flashy, but he looked at ease. The man receiving the blows, on the other hand, was coated in sweat and was struggling to keep up with the inhuman movements. Silas was dancing circles around this large, dark man. The devium was, like he did to me the day we fought, playing with his opponent.

Soon more men stopped to observe. They started cheering the human.

"Keep going, Buwlo! You've almost bested 'em!" one man cried.

The rogues were too preoccupied by the fight to notice me watching. In one small moment, I noticed Silas's mouth form only a hint of a dark smirk. Buwlo's sword went flying from his hand into the air. Moans of disappointment went through the crowd as they stared up at the sword. It curved through the air, coming straight toward me.

I stared at the sword and the world slowed. I stepped to the side and caught the hilt easily.

A hush fell upon the men and many of them took a step away. Their faces had the all too familiar looks of disgust and fear as they looked at me. Instead of cowering, I wanted to roll my eyes. Some things would never change. I examined the sword. It was very long and wide with a piece of red silk attached to the hilt. It should have been enormously heavy, but it wasn't to me.

Silas sheathed his swords with a small smirk. He was unaffected by the long spar he had just participated in. His breath was even, and his tone was dry.

"Buwlo, I do believe the lady has your weapon." The men stared at me with mesmerized looks until they parted so the large man could start toward me. Buwlo was very tall and broad with very dark skin. His eyes were a gray-green, a stark contrast to his skin, and his head was shaved. I twirled the sword in my hand still amazed at its light weight. He stopped a few feet from me. I looked up into his face and noticed traces of exhaustion.

"My sword," he rumbled. I stared at Buwlo, unaccustomed to the calmness of his sighting of me. "I am not frightened by your kind, Specter," he said, but his tone wasn't firm or distrustful. He looked at me just like another person. I held out the sword, dumbfounded and confused. What did he call me? He said the word, but it didn't sound like an insult. It was more of a title.

"Good morning, lady. I'm delighted that you decided to honor us with your presence," Silas said with a bow. Leaving my thoughts, I blinked at him. "Would you like to test your skills?" Silas asked with mischief in his cat-like eyes.

"A girl fight? Does she want to be killed?" one voice cried. I knew I could defend myself if I needed to, but this was new, uncharted territory. I was here because Silas made me, that didn't mean I would jump headfirst into fights. The power that was inside me seemed to be instinctual, but I wasn't sure if I could really rely on it. I glanced at Silas. Was that his plan? I guess this was the perfect opportunity to test my limits and perhaps find some control.

"Any volunteers want to fight the girl, then?" I said loudly, tossing my cloak to the ground. No one spoke. I turned to Buwlo. As cowardly as it was, he had just fought with Silas, and he didn't seem to hate me, so he was an ideal opponent.

"Would you like to duel... or are you too tired?" I said with a raise of my brow. He threw his head back and laughed.

"I shall beat you, Specter." There was that name again...

The men spread into a large circle, leaving Buwlo and me in the center. Silas stepped into the ring.

"What are the terms, Silas?" rumbled Buwlo. Silas tilted his head with a sly smile.

"Terms? There are none. Fight until one yields." He backed out of the ring and Buwlo turned to me.

"Where is your weapon?" I swallowed. If I was going to test myself, I wanted to test hand-to-hand first.

"I will use weapons when they're needed. By all means, don't hesitate with yours." It was all false bravado. My blood was pulsing with nervous anticipation. He merely nodded.

"I will not."

We stared at one another until I heard someone yell above the crowd.

"What are you waiting for, Buwlo? Destroy her!" I waited and tried to tap into that coldness within me. It was actually easy to find and draw from, almost like an ember that waited to be stoked.

The cold swept through me like a winter breeze, strengthening all of my senses again and taking away my weariness. I smelled the sweat of his body and felt the ground tremble from Buwlo's thundering steps. Buwlo slashed at me, but I easily slipped sideways and avoided his sword. He turned with confusion on his face and the men jeered. Buwlo ran at me again and slashed across. I jumped over the blade, placing my hands on his broad shoulders, and propelled myself over his head. I somersaulted through the air and slid my daggers out of their places. I landed on my feet as lightly as a cat and faced my opponent. I heard shouts from the men:

"She disappeared!"

"How did she do that?"

"Are those weapons?"

I couldn't help but smirk to myself and my chest felt light. It felt good to be awed, or was it feared? I wasn't sure if I cared at the moment. What mattered was that I wasn't being ridiculed. I quickly turned and blocked an attack with the hilt of my dagger. A hush fell over the men.

"Her blades form from air!" a voice cried in shock. Buwlo recovered his composure and started a series of attacks. I was content with blocking and dodging. I tried to get a feel of the energy rushing through me. I felt like a leaf floating and swirling in a lazy creek. He, on the other hand, looked like he was moving through deep water. Not even halfway through with his attack, I would already be waiting to parry. Each time his sword roughly connected with one of my stone blades a sliver of metal flew from his weapon.

The fight was distracting. My grief fell away as cold, and pride consumed me. I concentrated on it and pushed it further. I started to unleash my own set of attacks. I had to remind myself to go slow when Buwlo struggled to parry and deflect my jabs. I had backed him to the rim of the circle when he blindly sliced his sword through the air. I ducked and avoided the blade's edge. I twirled the daggers around my fingers and felt a smirk form on my lips.

With a cry of rage, he ran at me. I twisted my weapons and rested the blades along my forearms. As he swung, I grabbed his wrist and rolled him through the air above me, twisting his hand. There was a loud snap as his wrist broke between the handles. Something inside of me stirred happily at the sound and the crest on my arm twitched. I furrowed my brow and shook my arm but dismissed it. Buwlo let go of the sword and it clattered on the ground. He landed in a heap as a hush fell upon the crowd.

The dark man growled in pain, and he cradled his wrist. The cold shrank away leaving my limbs heavy as I approached Buwlo.

"Do you yield?" I asked kneeling beside him and sliding my daggers in their places.

"Aye, I yield, Specter."

"My, my," Silas said through the men's shocked silence, "I am impressed. It seems you do favor breaking bones." I hoisted Buwlo up.

"Thank ye. Anyone who can throw me, disarm me, and injure me in one move and then aid me to my feet deserves my friendship... despite you having specter blood," he added with a smile and held out his good hand. I shook it.

"What do you mean, 'specter blood?'" I asked. He raised an eyebrow and went to reply but Silas spoke instead.

"Buwlo, you should see the healer as soon as possible. If the bones are not properly set they will not heal correctly. It would be a hinderance to your blacksmithing, I'm sure." Buwlo nodded and took his sword from the devium with his good hand and walked away quickly. I moved to follow him, but Silas stepped in front of me.

"I would enjoy a rematch, Fairest," the devium said with a clever glint in his eyes. I wanted to know what Buwlo knew much more than I wanted to oblige a devium. I turned from him and went to follow Buwlo. I sensed Silas move in front of me before I saw him there.

"It was not a request," he said. His tone was light but yellowed eyes peered down at me expectedly.

"Not now," I said, staring back. His face was deadly calm, but I saw a shift in his eyes. He was not used to being defied. I didn't think he cared for it much either. His thin nostrils flared slightly but he smiled.

"If you are too tired after one fight, then I will not push you further. I hadn't realized that you were so fragile. Forgive me."

I knew somewhere in my mind that he was only goading me, but I would not stand to be called fragile. Fragile was what got Uncle Fredrick killed. The weak girl was gone, and she would never come back. I wouldn't allow it. I couldn't.

I punched him.

Silas staggered and fell. After he regained his posture, he spat silver blood to the ground.

"I am not fragile," I said. The devium smiled, wiping the silver from his mouth.

"Prove it."

My will faltered. I quickly drew my daggers and twirled them through my fingers. A wave of shouts flew from the men:

"She can't beat Silas!"

"Silas is a devium!"

"She got lucky!" Silas drew his swords, and we circled each other. He would randomly reach his sword out and clang it against my blade. I sneered, feeling ice course through my veins.

"Don't play with me, devium." He smirked and winked at me.

"Too late," he said. I charged.

I knocked away his parry and launched my other arm at his waist. He spun away and then swung at my legs. I jumped into the air and kicked his chest. The blow landed. He staggered, winded, but quickly recovered. A flurry of attacks sped at me and all of them I dodged or blocked. A shadow crossed my mind. I heard something whisper, "Kill him. End him. Now."

I struck out and cut a long gash across his chest. A small pain surged from the crest on my arm. The pain was gone once my mind cleared. I blinked and shook my head, bringing my attention back to the devium.

He looked at his torso and a smile appeared on his face. I stared at his chest as his white shirt turned a glittering silver. A hush fell over the men.

"I do not yield just yet," the devium said and lunged at me. Our assault continued.

At one point he tried to trick me by lowering his shoulder for a low attack then changing it to a downward slash. I crossed my blades and caught his swords. Still pressing with all his strength against me, he closed the space between us.

"You know," he whispered, "you are remarkably beautiful when you battle... You are so... powerful... It makes you extremely... tempting." I narrowed my eyes as something quivered in my chest and I felt disgusted with myself.

"And did you decide that before or after I carved into you?" I sneered and I pushed with all my power. He flew off me onto the ground. His grip on his swords faltered and they went clattering to the side. I walked to him and kicked his swords away. I stepped around him until I was above his head. I squatted down and placed a blade across his neck.

"Yield," I said, taking in his defenseless state. His eyes glittered in the sun but not in anger. He almost seemed... satisfied, like he had been the victor. He smiled and I felt angry.

"I yield." Silas stood up and told everyone to go back to training. He retrieved his swords and sheathed them. As he did, he winced.

"The cut needs to be sewn back together. The gash is deeper than I thought," Silas said, opening his shirt completely. I forced myself to look at his face, trying not to turn red.

All the men stared at me in suspicious fear as they passed. Finally, I saw some familiar faces. Viht, Dax, Kaul, and Smid approached us. I scowled at Smid and forced myself not to take a step back. He too glared at me, but the twins were grinning ear to ear.

Kaul said, "I don't think we-"

"-properly introduced ourselves," finished Dax. "I'm Dax and-"

"-I'm Kaul."

"We are honored to meet you," they said in unison with a small bow.

"We just now worked out the soreness you done us the other night," Kaul said rolling his shoulder.

"Right. Don't worry about my nose. Viht pushed it back," Dax said with a big smile. Thankful for the distraction, I looked between the two.

"Do you always talk like this?"

"Yes," they replied grinning. They were so much like Henry. My heart ached. There were too many emotions fighting in my head. I took a deep breath.

"You are indeed a talented fighter. You have beaten Silas twice now. That is astounding," Viht said with a serious expression.

"Told you it wasn't luck, Smid," Kaul said with a smug expression.

"You owe us a round at Lily's," Dax added. My stare turned to the man in question. He just glared back. Silas chuckled as blood slowly rolled down to his belt. Was he not going to do something about that?

"Not so wise to bet against her, Smid," he said. My ears perked at the forced measure of his voice, but the others were oblivious to it. Smid grumbled.

"I owe the lady a tour of the city. We shall meet you at Lily's tonight," Silas said. The four nodded and strolled off, unaffected by Silas' wound. I assumed that blood and injuries were a common occurrence in this kind of life. I shivered at the thought.

Silas stretched his arms and hissed. Instinctively, I reached out. I immediately regretted it.

"Are you concerned for me, Fairest?" Silas said with a smirk. I scowled at him. The truth was that I felt guilty. I didn't have to lash out and cut him open, however shallow the wound was. He had offered me a place to stay and privacy too.

"Don't call me that. You need to get that stitched and bandaged. I can do it," I said, remembering that Buwlo had gone to the healer. He didn't argue. Instead, he just smirked and turned his head at me. I walked toward the house, and I heard him follow.

Silas began to stumble not even halfway there. I scowled at him again. He wasn't losing too much blood so he shouldn't have felt so weak. I slung his arm around my shoulders and had to jump both of us to the balcony, which wasn't nearly as hard as it sounded. Once inside, I helped him to the pit and lit a fire.

"Stay here," I said. I fetched a bucket from the kitchen and went to my bedroom. I left the door open and drew the curtains away from the glass wall. I pulled open the door and jumped off the balcony to gather water from the river.

What was I doing? The devium could fend for himself. I did owe him though. He did offer me a place to live, and it was me that put that gash into him. Sewing him back up was the least I could do.

When I turned back, I saw Silas standing on the balcony.

"What are you doing? I told you to stay where you were," I said, jumping up. I felt the toll of pulling at the energy. I was overexerting myself. I wasn't used to this kind of strain. Weariness flooded through me.

"I've been here for quite some time, but I never thought to completely explore the house. I've never seen anything like it... I never would have guessed such a thing was possible here," he murmured. His yellow-green eyes were glassy and dull. He looked terrible.

I tried to lead him to the pit again, but he staggered and nearly fell.

"I'm not sure why you're so weak. The cut wasn't that serious, and you haven't lost too much blood," I said, feeling as weak as he looked.

"Your weapons must be enchanted," he said, "They are quite beautiful. Stone blades are a strange thing to see..." I agreed but I wasn't going to discuss my mother's weapons with him. I shrugged and tried to drag him to the pit. He collapsed down on the cushion and grunted. I grabbed a cloth and handed it to Silas.

"Hold that on the wound."

I went back to the bedroom to dig through the chest for the supplies. Silas was so dazed. Perhaps I could use his predicament to my advantage. Such a creature had to have knowledge that I didn't. I walked back to the pit.

"You said that you've been here for a long time?" I asked recalling what he had said on the balcony. He had a dazed look on his face, but he only nodded.

"Why are you here? Why did you leave your home?" I said, sitting beside him. I landed harder than I intended. My limbs felt weighted. He flicked his eyes at me and smiled slowly.

"Reasons," he said. I narrowed my eyes at him. I had misjudged the situation. He was not as dull as I had hoped. Or I was just too obvious.

"You need to pull up your shirt," I said, looking away, "It will be in the way." He nodded faintly, threw the rag toward the bucket, and tried to pull away his shirt. He was failing miserably. He winced as he raised his arms and the shirt bunched around his chest. I reached out and tugged off the shirt, careful not to linger. My face was getting hot.

I turned back to examine the wound I had inflicted and started to clean it. Unwillingly, my thoughts began to wander to where I didn't want them to go again. Silas was beautiful. He was slender and agile. It was easy to see that his muscles were perfectly toned. His skin was surprisingly warm despite his pale, gray-tinged skin. My hand paused above his chest absorbing that warmth through my icy fingers.

"Aren't you supposed to be mending that cut?" Silas asked, flinching away from my touch. I felt my face flush again and I looked away.

"It would be easier if you lay down. Your muscles are tensed sitting up." He smirked and complied. He rested his hands on his stomach and stared at the ceiling. I knelt on the floor beside him. I took the string and threaded the needle. I heated the needle over the flame I had lit.

"This will sting," I said, steeling myself. I pinched the skin together, readying it for the needle. Silas shivered and grabbed my wrist.

"What?" I asked. He shook his head slowly.

"Your skin is so very cold. It feels..." His breathing became raspy. He gave me a look that made my stomach flip. I pulled my hand from his.

"I must stitch this," I said, trying to fight the tremor in my voice. I cursed myself. I hated that I was attracted to him. I had just lost my family, lost Jeb. I felt sick. He held my gaze, clenching his jaw but then looked back at the ceiling.

I closed my eyes and tried to focus. I tried to make quick work of the stitches, but I was so tired. Loop and pull, loop and pull. I only concentrated on those two movements; I didn't have the capacity to think of anything else. I bit the thread near the knot and inhaled the fresh pine that lingered on his skin.

"All finished," I whispered but Silas was asleep. I closed my eyes and felt my will breaking. My body felt like dead weight and all I wanted to do was sleep. The room began to spin. I lowered my head in an attempt to still the room. I hadn't realized that I was resting my head on the devium's torso. I really didn't care at the moment. I just wanted to rest.

Chapter 9: Identity

I felt fingers combing through my hair as I awoke. I didn't open my eyes, but I smiled. I remembered Aunt Prudence combing and cutting my hair and imagined it was her fingers in my hair again, but I knew it wasn't. But whose fingers were they? I opened my eyes and Silas smirked at me.

"Sleep well?" I leapt away from him and almost yelped. My face was on fire, and I pushed my hair away from my face.

"You have some nerve," I said, trying to catch my breath. The devium chuckled and put his hand behind is head, closing his eyes.

"You were the one who fell asleep on me, Fairest." I furrowed my brow and set my jaw, trying to ignore my embarrassment.

"I told you not to call me that." He opened one eye and smirked at me.

"But I really like how you react when I do." I felt my face heat up again. I ground my teeth at myself and stood up.

"How long was I asleep?" I washed my face with water from the bucket. Thankfully, it was clean since we didn't put the bloody rag in it. The cool water helped soothe my flushed face.

"It's just past midday, I believe." His hands dipped into the water beside mine and I jumped away from him. I was so flustered that I didn't hear him move. He didn't acknowledge me. He patted the water on his neck and ran his wet hand through his hair. My heart thudded as I watched him. My stomach flipped and I looked away. I grabbed my cloak and made for the door.

"I must check on Tempest. I'm sure you need more rest."

"You're quite right. A beautiful woman lying on my chest was very distracting," he said. I could hear the smirk in his voice. I covered my face to hide my embarrassment and slammed the door.

Tempest was content in her new home. There was fresh hay for her bedding and the trough was full of grain. Silas must have had someone look after her. I rubbed her nose, and she nuzzled me fondly.

"Tempest, I'm a terrible person," I whispered. She snorted at me.

"My entire family died five days ago and I'm worrying about inhuman powers and I'm ogling a devium. How could I have forgotten them so quickly? I keep telling myself that they wouldn't want me to wallow with grief, but I know that I'm just trying to make myself feel better. I didn't even go to Ameris to make sure they got a proper burial.

This is all my fault. And what am I doing about it? Nothing. I am disgraceful." I covered my face with my hands, but I couldn't cry. I was at such a loss. I was completely aimless.

"Have you finished yet?" Silas said, leaning against the entryway. He looked bored. I glared at him and crossed my arms.

"Is grief not a custom where you come from?" I snapped.

"Yes, it is but in our culture, when a loved one dies like yours have, we take revenge. Blood for blood," he said simply.

"You're suggesting that I take revenge against the Bloodied Men?" I said. He had to be joking but he didn't waver. I gaped at him.

"The Bloodied Men are an army! I may be... different but I can't destroy an entire army." He shrugged.

"Maybe not now. You don't know what you can do."

"Why do you care so much about what I can and can't do, devium? What importance is it to you?" He approached me with blinding speed. All I could see was the green-yellow of his eyes and our noses nearly touched.

"I have an interest in you, and I mean to make you my asset. Simple." He ran a finger down my jaw as I clenched it. He smirked and stepped away.

"Just think about it. At the very least, trying to thwart the Bloodied Men would help other people affected by them as well as give you a place to start your healing... In the meantime, how about that tour?" He gestured toward the town and then started walking away.

He was insufferable... but he had a point. I wanted to figure out this power, avenge my family, and make myself useful. Fighting against the Bloodied Men satisfied all of those things. I rubbed the crest on my arm as I caught up to Silas. Prince Aleron may also be hunting the zealot army but what were the odds that we would cross paths again? I had a sinking feeling in my stomach that it was very likely.

Rogue City was much, much smaller than Ameris but was still like any other village. There were wide streets for carts and horses and then there were back alleys for shortcuts. Small children zigzagged through the few crowds of people who watched them with smiles. It was easy to forget that these people may have been murderous thieves. A girl a few years younger than me was tugging on a rope that was tied around the neck of a goat. It bleated in anger but trotted along after a threat about a butcher's knife.

Silas talked the whole way through the tour. He would occasionally pause to tell someone hello and merely introduced me as a new recruit.

By the end of Silas' extensive tour, it was nearly sunset. Silas excused himself to check in with Eriak and a few other jobs that needed to be done. He instructed me to meet him at Lily's, the small tavern. I nodded but first I decided to walk alone for a while. I wanted some peace and quiet before suffering through drinking with rogues.

I strolled on a wide street and found a small corral of horses being fed by a small, round man with thinning gray hair. I stopped to watch. I was intrigued by how normal this all was. Just an old man taking care of his horses. My life had become so bizarre. I rubbed my head to relieve the tension. It didn't work.

A group of children stopped a few feet from me and whispered loudly among each other.

"Look! Do you see that girl with blood-hair? Does she have fire eyes? That must be Specter!" one tall girl said. I turned my head to catch more of their chatter.

"All the fighters have been talking about her! I dare you to talk to her!" a black-haired boy said elbowing another girl next to him.

"Nuh-uh! She'll carve me into a twig! You heard, Jako!" she said. A very small boy, probably five years old, with blond hair nodded.

"Y-yeah, she-she made knives from no-nothing!"

"They said she sliced up Silas!" the black-haired boy said.

I wasn't sure how to feel about the little gossipers. I didn't really like to be around children. I just felt uncomfortable around them since I usually terrified them. Being ridiculed by my peers as a child didn't help matters either. I watched a brown colt jump and kick his legs into the air, playing with an imaginary being.

"You have a beautiful lot of horses," I said to the short man. The owner turned and jumped at sighting me.

"Uh-uh... um, thank you," he stammered. The colt scampered away with his ears up. He reared and walked forward on his back legs.

"Quite a show-off, isn't he?" I tried to say in a friendly manner. It mustn't have come out as I intended. The man still fidgeted.

"Indeed, he is. Was kickin' when I pulled 'em from his mother, even." We watched the colt scamper about. Watching the animals was relaxing.

"What is your name, sir?" I asked. He flushed and made a small bow.

"They call me Horis." I tried not to laugh at the irony. His name was so close to 'horse' it made me wonder if he chose the name himself.

"Was it you that took care of my horse this morning? Her trough was full." Horis nodded and smiled widely. The tension completely left him as he leaned against his pitchfork.

"Yes, miss, and it was a pleasure too. What a fine creature she is! What do you call her?" I smiled back at him.

"Tempest." He laughed. His happiness was almost contagious.

"Very fitting! She did try to bite me when I went to pet her. She'll warm up to me. Don't you worry."

"Of that I have no doubt, Horis." He studied me for a moment.

"I think you're all right, Specter. Not quite as scary as people say... well maybe at first glance." I smiled with him.

My skin prickled and I turned to find the blond boy behind me. He stood still with a hand raised, caught in the act of attempting to pull my cloak. My entire body tensed as my mind flashed back to my childhood. When I really looked at this boy, though, he looked as terrified as I once felt. I swallowed.

"Hello. What is your name?" I said. His dark eyes were filled with fright. He looked like he was about to mess himself.

"The lady asked you a question, boy," Horis said lightly and propped up on the fence. The boy's eyes darted to the older man and then back to me.

"I-I-I, uh... Isaac." I took a deep breath and crouched to his level.

"Am I really that scary, Isaac?" I asked him quietly. When he didn't answer, I smiled sadly. "I promise I won't carve you into a twig," I said. He still shivered. I remembered a game that Henry used to play with the children in town. It always worked for him. Maybe that would help make me seem friendly. I patted my purse and legs.

"Uh-oh... I seemed to have lost a silver coin... Have you seen it?" His shivering paused and he shook his head. I continued to pat myself frantically. "I know I had that coin this morning. Wait, I think I see it," I said, looking to him. His eyes widened and he felt through his clothes.

"Where?" he said. I reached up by the boy's head and pretended to pull a coin from his ear.

"Right here! How did it get in your ear, I wonder?" I said. Isaac's hand covered his ear and a look of wonder spread across his face. He grinned at me. "Did you put that in there? That seems a silly place to hide a coin!" I said. The boy giggled. He was precious.

"No, I didn't!" I smiled at him.

"How about we make a deal, Isaac?" His smile disappeared and he shook his head quickly.

"Mama said to never make a bargain with a ghost. She said the dead is not to be fooled with." I couldn't keep the frown off my face.

"I promise I'm not a ghost and I am definitely not dead. You can't touch a ghost, can you?" I asked, holding my hand out. Isaac slowly poked my hand and smiled.

"I'll give you this coin if you do one thing for me." Isaac thought for a moment and then nodded. I smiled. "You see, everyone thinks I'm mean and scary, just like you did. So, it's hard for me to make friends... I'll give you this silver coin if you promise to be my friend." He smiled widely and nodded fiercely. I handed him the coin.

"My sister Gori told me if I talked to you, she would do my chores for a week... That'll show her!" he said with pride.

"I think you are very brave, Isaac. Do you really want to fool your sister?" I asked, grinning. He nodded. Horis chuckled at us.

"I'll leave you two to it. It's dinner time. Have a good evening, miss." He gave a small wave and went toward his house. After waving at Horis, I turned back to Isaac.

"All right, this is what we'll do..." I whispered a plan into his ear.

"You foul child!" I growled in mock rage standing and pointing at Isaac, "What did you say to me?" The other children, who were hiding around the corner of a building, gasped.

"You heard!" Isaac yelled and stuck his tongue out at me.

"Why you little..." I seethed. He turned and ran to the building where the others waited for him. I smiled when I heard a group of shrieks as they all ran away.

"This is an interesting side to you, Fairest. I didn't expect you to get along with children." I turned and found Silas standing not too far behind me. He had on a new shirt covered by a green cloak and his hair was pulled half back, leaving his ears in full view. The smile waned from my lips as I greeted him.

"I usually don't," I said truthfully.

"You know, I do think that boy will be very big-headed for some time." I nodded in agreement and looked back to where the children were.

"Indeed."

"Come," he said, "I believe we were supposed to be at Lily's."

We walked to the tavern and Silas pushed through the door. There was a bar toward the back and tables were scattered from wall to wall. In the back corner were a few music players playing a cheerful song. Most of the people in the place were men.

"Ey! Get off my bar!" a very stout woman behind the counter screamed at a rough man who had appeared to have fallen asleep on the bar.

"Lily!" the devium called and made his way to her. I followed, doing my best to ignore the stares of the people. The lady behind the counter,

Lily, was a curvy woman in her thirties with dark golden hair that was in a long plait.

"Hello, Silas! I heard something today and- Oh my..." she said laying her eyes on me. I looked away awkwardly. The stares and reactions of everyone were wearing me thin. I couldn't decide if being a spectacle was worse than being an outcast, or was it the same thing?

"I thought the boys were merely jesting about this morning... I never dreamed... So eerie..." she said.

"Lily," Silas said, stopping her babbling, "This is... well..." His words trailed away, and he glanced at me.

"Call me Specter," I said with a nod. I felt a weight lift from my chest. Claiming the name almost made me feel empowered. I smiled to myself. "Specter" was a lot better than "Blood head" or "Demon."

I turned my head slightly when my sensitive ears heard familiar sounds.

"I believe your friends have arrived," I said. Silas and Lily looked confused. At that moment, the door burst open and in walked Dax, Kaul, Viht, and Smid. Dax called across the room.

"Lily! I do think that-"

"-the first round is on Smid!" finished Kaul. They laughed loudly and went to the back of the room and sat at a large table. Silas and I left the counter and a shocked Lily. When we reached the table, the twins quickly stood.

"Allow me to get your chair," the twins said together, causing glares to be exchanged between them.

I was curious about the twins' change of heart towards me. Dax's now straight nose was still swollen though the purple was not so dark. I sat as they pulled the chair out together, since both refused to let go. This kind of attention made me feel more out of place than the frightened stares and name calling. I wasn't sure who to thank so I said nothing. I expected Silas to sit beside me, but Kaul and Dax took the chairs to each of my sides. Viht shook his curly head.

"Love-struck boys," he said. The tanned twins' cheeks turned red and Smid scoffed. I looked at him and remembered when he had slapped me. I know that I had gotten even in the end but the animosity between us was still there, and it was obvious.

Silas had taken the seat directly in front of me with Viht to his right then Dax, me, Kaul, and finally Smid. When I met Silas's eyes, he winked at me. I glared back at him.

When Lily had brought each of us some ale and wine, the questions started.

"So," Kaul said, "how do you just make you swords appear?"

"And how did you get Buwlo to flip over you like that?" Dax asked.

"I wish to know where you learned your technique," Viht said.

The combat questions didn't stop. I would answer one and they would have two more waiting. Silas seemed to enjoy watching me flounder under the interrogation.

We sat in the tavern until everyone had left. Silas and I had barely drunk anything, but it seemed to be a contest between Viht, Dax, and Kaul to see who could drink most between their questions. Smid also had many drinks but was quiet. It appeared that Viht, who was in the lead, lost nearly all his composure when he had had too much ale.

"Well, Miss Sssssspecter," he slurred, "You are downright pretty! And twins, you better watch it! The old man is moving in!" For a moment, I was mortified. Dax and Kaul thought his statement was hilarious. Both spilled their drinks on the table and nearly choked on their own laughter. Kaul even laughed so hard, he tipped his chair backwards and tumbled to the floor. I muffled my laugh under my hand. I felt eyes on me and looked at Silas. He was just observing me, and our eyes met. He smirked as I looked away, blushing. I noticed that Smid was not partaking in the merriment.

"Smid," Silas said turning to him, "is there something on your mind?"

At first, he just looked at his drink. Then finally Smid spoke.

"I wanna know who and what the hell she is! Girls can't fight like she does and if they could, they wouldn't go riding along in the middle of nowhere without a reason. What she does isn't natural and I think we should steer clear of her!" he finished with a shout and slammed his fist on the table.

The group went silent as we all stared at him. He was leaning toward me in a menacing way and hatred filled his eyes. The fun had been drained from the table and a serious silence had replaced it. I stared into his muddy eyes and realized he was smarter than he looked. His words made sense. Hadn't Prince Aleron said the same? Maybe all I did was bring about misery. When I wasn't miserable, it found new targets. I stood and stared down at him as my moment of happiness vanished.

"I don't know what I am or why I can do the things I can do. Maybe I am cursed, but if I am, I wish I would have known long ago. If I did, maybe a lot of people would still be alive right now. Excuse me." I turned, cold and hard as stone, and left.

I walked out of the tavern and into the crisp night air. I took a deep breath and looked up as I ambled down the deserted street. A sky full of stars looked back at me.

"I wish you could give me answers..." I whispered to them. They twinkled in the night but had no words. I shook my head and sighed. I looked at the windows of the small cottages and shops. All were dark and I could imagine the people sleeping within. I thought of how they survived, how they stole from others to sustain themselves.

The people in Rogue City lived in peace and freedom in the Nitalla; they had no king. From what I saw that day, they didn't seem like rogues, like murdering thieves. I knew that some of them probably were. Smid came to mind but most of them weren't even fighters. They were families. It didn't seem right. Even when they tried to rob me, they thought that I was wealthy. Only Smid really wanted to hurt me. And

Silas said they robbed books from King Karrolei. I couldn't make myself believe they would rob someone who was in need but perhaps I just wanted to see it that way. According to Silas, these people were refugees. It dawned on me that I was much, much worse. I stole Jeb's love, Aunt Prudence's nerves, Henry's time, and Uncle Fredrick's life. I was the cruelest rogue of all.

Chapter 10: Healing and Darkness

I had made a routine in the weeks that followed. When I woke each day, I went to the training fields where I sparred with the men. It was only Viht, Dax, Kaul, and Silas that fought with me though. I never saw much of Smid. When I did, he was on the other side of the field. I was glad that he and the other rogues stayed away from me. Most days I preferred complete solitude after training but if I were alone too long, I felt an ache in my bones that I just couldn't shake. Memories of my family would attack my thoughts until I found a distraction. Eventually, my grief would move away from the forefront of my mind. It was always there like an ominous cloud in my head just waiting for a moment of weakness.

I spent most of my time training. Fighting consumed my mind and left room for no other thought. I also practiced tapping into the cold reservoir of power at my core. It took me over a week to get through a whole day of training without needing to nap. By the third week, though,

I hardly had to think about calling on the cold. It was like it could sense my intention before I did, and it was there. After that, only Silas would spar with me. I had mixed feelings about it. I did need the challenge and I think he realized it too, but I hated how my heart pounded in my chest and my stomach turned flips when he was too close. Between his smoldering eyes and dark smirk, I wanted to drop my guard and just... melt. I hated it or at least, I wanted to hate it.

I kept some variety in my evenings. Some days I would go to Lily's others I would go back to my house and read. My favorite days were when I found Isaac. There was something about his adorable face and his big brown eyes that made everything else disappear. He told me that his mother didn't want him anywhere near me, but he didn't mind. He knew I wasn't a ghost. I had shown him so, he said. He told me about his chores and how his sister was so much nicer to him now that we were friends. I marveled at how proud he was of being my friend. All I wanted was to prove that I was worthy of his pride and admiration.

During the fourth week, Silas asked me to train some of the fighters.

"You're joking," I said, lowering my cup back to the table. We sat alone at a table at Lily's. The others of our group were engaged in an arm wrestling contest with some other rogues across the room.

"Not at all," he said, flatly.

"I don't think it's a good idea," I said taking a large gulp of ale. The devium leaned back in his chair.

"Please elaborate." He fixed his curious gaze on me, and I felt my breath quicken. My skin felt hot, and I swallowed.

"They don't care for me."

"And that matters?" I set my jaw.

"They don't respect me." Silas smirked.

"Oh, but they do. They fear you, Specter. They know that you are a force to be reckoned with. It would benefit them and, in turn, all of Rogue City if they would learn only a few things from you." I looked down into my cup and bit my lip. His praise made me feel warm, but I was still unsure. My fingers found the pendant in my anxiety.

"I do wish you could see yourself the way I see you, Specter. You have such potential; it would be a shame for you to squander it and lose out on what you could achieve... and what you have." My eyes shot up to meet his. A small smile was on his lips, but the threat was evident. He told me before that I would have to be useful to the rogues for a right to stay.

"Very well," I said and looked away from him.

"Excellent. You may start tomorrow." I could hear the smirk in his voice.

I was a jumble of nerves that first morning. I had enough trouble speaking to one stranger and now Silas expected me to instruct more than twenty. To my relief, I counted only ten men who wanted my instruction, including Viht, Dax, and Kaul, of course. The twins could hardly contain their excitement. I taught them the same way Uncle Fredrick taught me. Hand to hand combat was most important since a weapon may not always be available.

"Show me your defensive stances," I said. Most of them didn't even know what I meant even though I did my best to explain. Uncle Fredrick had been so good at instruction, but his words weren't the same coming from me. I discovered that showing the rogues what I meant was much more efficient... when they let me touch them. I tried not to feel too upset about it, but their fear and disgust made me ache. I would have quit if Viht, Dax, and Kaul weren't there to be my examples. It was a long day.

The following days were better. I requested the men spar one another and critiqued their forms as they moved. They were much more receptive to me when they could immediately see the effects. Teaching patience was the most difficult. It was as if "attack first" was ingrained in each of their minds but eventually, the concept of studying the opponent began to dawn on them. That was when I had them spar with those who did not want my instruction. My intention was to test the group's improvement. The next week, I had many more students.

Another two weeks passed and training the rogues was almost enjoyable. I felt a sense of pride at their progress. They weren't up to

Uncle Fredrick's standards, but I thought that that he would at least admit the potential. As the training became easier, I had more time to notice things about myself, or more specifically, the mark. The glow of the star had faded considerably in the time I had been in Rogue City, even the black lines had faded but one day, there was a tingling sensation seeping from it. The feeling had persisted enough that I left training early to investigate. I removed the wrap from my arm. The mark was glowing again, so soft it was barely visible in the daylight. Then the tingling turned into an itching feeling that quickly turned into a burning. The mark began to glow ferociously, and I thought my arm was on fire.

"Stop! Stop!" I said, fanning my arm with my hand. The energy responded and snuffed out the fire. Before the glow dimmed away, there was a sensation across the crest, like an invisible finger ran along the sword's edge. I shivered as my skin erupted in gooseflesh. Then the glow was gone as was the feeling. I narrowed my eyes and waited for something else to happen, but it didn't.

"How strange... What could that have been?" Maybe the prince had tried ridding himself of the mark finally. Was that his finger that I felt? I shook my head at the improbability. If that were the case then we were much more connected than I realized. Was the mark even doing anything to him? From what Aunt Prudence said, it meant that a seal was broken for me, and my power appeared, whatever that meant. What did that have to do with Prince Aleron, though? Whatever it was or wasn't doing to him, I hoped he was trying to remove the mark.

Hopefully, mine would disappear too. But would I need to be with him to remove it? That would be my next step: Can't destroy one without the other. My hands suddenly felt clammy. What would he do to me? He probably still thought that I had put the mark on us. If he couldn't remove it himself, he would certainly come to find me. His piercing blue eyes flashed through my mind, and I shivered.

I shook my head at the thought of him bringing his armies into Rogue City. How would he react to a hidden village in the Nitalla? Were we even in Rokellia? Or were we across the border and in Capilious? I shook my head. Either way, the prince finding this place would be bad. In my time here, I learned that the rogues only wanted to live in peace. Stealing wasn't even always necessary. The people were established enough to trade their goods in villages. Isaac had even told me so. These people just wanted to live without fear of famine or war. At least that is what they lead me to believe.

The sun was setting, and I had been walking down a street when I saw Buwlo at the blacksmith's forge pointing with his good hand. Until that moment, I had not seen him since the day I broke his wrist. I walked to him and realized he was barking out orders.

"More heat! No, no; not that kind of hammer! Ey! Stop it!" I cleared my throat loudly as I stood in the forge entrance. The broad man turned to me and he smiled. His white teeth gleamed in contrast to his umber skin.

"Specter! How nice it is you are here!"

"Buwlo," I said. His friendliness caught me off guard.

"I have heard so many stories about you, Specter! How funny it is to hear of your own injury! Blades of ice, eyes of fire that freeze one's movements, poisonous nails; the stories are growing as they spread." He laughed in his deep voice.

"I'm glad you are in good spirits," I said. He bent and looked me in the eyes.

"You are never in good spirits. You look like a ghost floating around this place." I frowned. No one had mentioned that to me. I thought I was fine...

"My name is Specter, Buwlo. I recall you giving me that name... How is your wrist?" He held up his left hand. There were bandages wrapped around it for some support.

"The healer took the board off last week and now I only have wraps. I am much better! I have never had an injury! It is a strengthening thing!" he said, "Do not worry! I will be fine, Specter." I nodded. I didn't know how to start this conversation. I bit my lip.

"I actually wanted to ask you some things," I said, "I wanted to come sooner but..." He looked at me expectantly and motioned for me to continue. "When we dueled, you said you were familiar with my kind.

What exactly did you mean by that?" His eyebrow rose like it did on the training fields.

"You do not know?" I felt my cheeks burn as I remained silent. Buwlo continued.

"My people have many legends, Specter. One story tells of a people, more creature than man in ability. The most distinguishing feature is their fire eyes." My heart skipped a beat.

"What were these creatures?" He twisted a rod in the forge.

"As I have said, we called them specters."

"What else can you tell me about them?" I tried my best to not sound desperate, but I felt like I was finally getting answers. I knew it was a long shot but, with my current predicament, it was something at least.

"They came to my home, Sudoesten, looking for a home and tried to conquer my people. They were fierce warriors with strange magic but our elders, what you call casters here, were able to withstand them and we fought back. When they saw that they would not win, they vanished. That was generations ago. I assumed any remains of them would be gone but, alas, I was mistaken."

"What kinds of things could they do?" I said.

"As I said, these stories are from long ago. Some things change each time they are told. Some things are nearly impossible to believe: Controlling the weather, making things that were not there, creating fire from nothing. Some versions even say that the specters could fly. How believable is that? Now go! I must fix the chaos that has found its way into my forge!"

I walked away and my chest fell a little. I had hoped that what Buwlo knew could be proven and traced back so I could find more answers. It hurt to discover that what knowledge I had found was most likely fiction.

"Fiction..." I said to myself, "the kings would have extensive libraries on all neighboring lands, whether it be fact or fiction. Surely I could find more information there." I decided to check my personal library first. It was stolen from Karrolei after all, and I wasn't sure how to get into a royal library anyway. I didn't remember reading about specters or similar beings, but a second look wouldn't hurt.

I went down the streets of Rogue City intending on going home to read until I saw a boy running towards me. I stopped when I saw that it was Eriak. I was about to panic because he was running with such haste, but I relaxed after seeing the smile on his face and his golden eyes shining.

"Good day, Eriak," I said.

"Good day, Specter. Silas asked me to bring you to our home. We wish for you to share a meal with us. I already know you will say yes so follow me." He turned and started walking away. I was, in fact, not going to say yes but I quickly followed him in a state of confusion as he led me toward the west wall.

"I know you are confused about your family." I stopped walking, shocked at his words.

"My family?"

"About where you really come from," I held my breath and tried to find words.

"How do you know about that?" I said slowly. Did Silas have this boy follow me? Eriak stopped too and he wore a sad smile on his face.

"I just see things sometimes... Your Aunt Prudence would hate to see you so worked up. Right? You should quit your fussing and have some tea." I felt the air rush out of me.

"How do you know that?" My voice cracked. He smiled again and took my hand.

"You will make it, Specter, but you have to try..." His golden eyes glazed over, and he turned his head for a moment. "Who has blue eyes? They are so bright and cold and... Come, Silas is almost finished cooking. I'm not supposed to talk about these things, though. Silas would be angry." His voice dipped and he gave a small shudder, but he walked on. He must have been talking about Prince Aleron. How does he know any of this?

I kept asking him questions, but he refused to answer. We reached the front door of his house before I stopped my interrogation. The house was identical to any other house in the city except the door was painted red. The dark-headed boy pushed open the door.

"Silas! She came!" Eriak exclaimed. The first level was one room but very large. There was a cooking area at the back and then a short table with large sitting cushions around it and a large fireplace to the far left with more pillows near it. To the right was a staircase.

"Hello, Specter. Thank you for joining us," Silas said. I wanted to grab Eriak and force more information from him but part of me knew that he wouldn't say another word. His whole demeanor changed when he saw Silas. Eriak was silent and rigid, all traces of anything child-like gone. I turned my head at him and felt the tension in the air.

"My pleasure," I said, watching Eriak. The boy took my cloak then showed me to the table. He was very mannerly. He was almost more servant than boy. Eriak hung up my cloak and then helped Silas with the food. When the table was set, dinner was awkwardly silent.

"Eriak," Silas said finally, "did you finish the book I gave you today?" Eriak nodded and stirred the food on his plate. Silas turned his gaze from his plate to Eriak. His look was hard. He pursed his lips and his brow furrowed. "And what did you think of it?"

"It was difficult to read," the boy said. He took a deep breath but said nothing else. The air felt heavier. I looked at Silas and wanted to shrink. He had a smile, but his stare was so hard. I spoke up, hoping to save Eriak from the devium.

"What was the book about?" I said gently. They both looked at me, surprised that I had spoken. "I like to hear stories. I didn't have many books to read growing up."

"It was about the Devium War," Eriak whispered. I furrowed my brow. Weren't there better things for a boy his age to read?

"Tell us about it, Eriak," Silas said. His tone was far from gentle.

"The Devium War began thirty years ago when a faction of deviums declared war on the two kings. Battles commenced-"

"Why did the deviums declare war?" Silas interrupted. The air was oppressive. Eriak held his hands in his lap and glanced nervously at Silas.

"The deviums were once the leaders of this country. They ruled over all races and were just, but the now royals usurped the throne. They divided the country in half and built their own capitals, Caneesho to the west and Jahilta to the east.

"The gilded king of Caneesho began requiring more and more men, human, caster, and devium, to join his army despite the peace. Taxes grew higher and higher to support the army. The black king then followed suit, cautious of King Karrolei's actions. More was expected from the deviums and casters because of their heightened abilities but no one knew of any war coming. Any being who refused service was executed as a threat to others.

"Soon, resentment spread among the troops. Deviums and casters were treated more like animals and only valued for their abilities. Humans, on the other hand, were given positions of power in the armies. The deviums revolted. The casters mostly went into hiding since it was easier for them to blend in with the humans. The races battled for three years until the humans finally won out." Eriak's shoulders slumped after his summary. I had never heard the history of how the

Devium War started. Uncle Fredrick never wanted to discuss his past as general in the army and the people of Ameris didn't want to talk about anything with me. My options were limited to say the least.

"Very good and you studied the battles that followed?" When Eriak said that he had, Silas nodded at the boy in approval.

"Eriak, how old are you?" I said. It seemed that Eriak was too young to read about such serious things. It occurred to me then that I had never seen Eriak out playing with other children his age. In fact, I had only seen him twice since I came to Rogue City.

"I'm nine years. Plenty old enough to learn about history," he said. His words sounded rehearsed. I studied him but his eyes wouldn't meet mine. I looked at Silas. The devium seemed oblivious to the conversation as he ate his dinner.

"Do you only read history books?" I said. Eriak's eyes lit up, but his face remained solemn.

"I read all kinds of books. I really like legends and adventures. Sometimes when I think hard enough-"

"That's enough, Eriak. I think it is time to clean up, don't you?" Silas said smoothly. Eriak's eyes dimmed but he nodded and with a forced smile, grabbed my plate. I offered to help but the boys walked away saying that guests were guests. When they were finished, Silas sent Eriak to bed. The devium handed me a cup of wine and sat at the table again. He took a slow sip and cut his eyes toward me. The fire made his eyes look yellow and I felt my heart jump.

"The men have seemed to improve under your teaching," he said. I felt a blush creep into my cheeks. I took a drink.

"They have."

"I am a bit disappointed, though." I felt my chest fall. He couldn't have expected the men to fight just like me. I trained for years, and I had this power.

"How so?" I said. His eyes pierced mine and he leaned closer to me.

"I no longer see get to see the fire within you firsthand. You did spoil me with our matches. As much as I hate the needle, part of me hoped that you would need to stitch me again. I often think of how your touch felt against my skin." His fingers ran across my knuckles as his eyes locked with mine. They were fierce. My breath caught in my throat. My skin quivered under his touch. Why couldn't I move?

"I wonder if it's still there..." he said, softly.

"What's still there?" I said. My voice was a raspy whisper.

"That ravenous, beautiful blaze within you. I was beginning to think it had gone."

He raised his hand and touched my face. Fire burned the skin that he touched but it also sent shivers down my spine.

He traced his fingers down my cheek to my neck.

"There is a mountain near my home in Noliishilo where at its summit, there is a pit of liquid fire. The force that lays dormant there... I had always believed that it would be the most beautiful thing in this world until I saw you in the forest that day. Do you remember?" I liked the sound of his words, but I didn't know what he meant. I swallowed and stared at him. His eyes reflected the soft green light radiating from my own. I shook my head, mesmerized by him.

"I watched you change from a frightened little girl into living fire. I saw it the moment you held Smid's life in your hands." I remembered back and felt a shadow seep into my mind. It clouded my thoughts in a thick haze. My hand went to his chest and found his heartbeat. Silas hummed and smirked. He knotted his fingers in my hair and pulled me closer. I felt his lips graze my neck and my heart hammered. I closed my eyes and tried to breathe.

"Remember how it felt, Specter. Remember how his body crumpled under your blows. He was at your mercy. You were in complete control. Tell me, Specter. Do you wonder what it would have felt like, if you had ended him? How would you want to feel?" he whispered against my skin. The shadow darkened as the images flashed in my mind. I smiled at the memory of the power and began to fantasize the life fading from him.

"I'd feel... alive."

His lips forcefully met mine. For a moment, I felt a shadow run through my veins. My hands knotted in his shirt, pulling him closer. He bit my lip, and my heart began to race. I couldn't think. There was only an incredible heat and darkness dominating my senses. There was no sadness, no grief, no guilt. I felt invincible and strong. Could this fill the hole in my soul?

Pain surged through me like shocks of lightning coursing through my body. With a cry, I fell to the floor. My body started to shake uncontrollably. My arm hurt so bad I wanted to cut it off with my nails. Silas stared at me in shock while I convulsed in pain.

"Specter? What's happening?" he said. He touched my face. I screamed as his touch was no longer a blissful fire.

"Don't touch me!" I screamed as I writhed. I heard footsteps coming down the stairs.

"Eriak, go back to bed!" Silas yelled.

"Silas, you have to get away from her!" Eriak said running to me.

"What? Why?" Silas asked, angry, as Eriak pushed him away from me. I felt a hand on my forehead, but no pain appeared. I panted as sweat poured from my body.

"Silas, get some cold water. She's too hot," Eriak said calmly.

As I heard Silas leave, the pain receded.

"It's going away, Eriak. The pain is leaving..." I said. He brushed my hair from my face.

"You'll be just fine, Specter." I heard Silas return, and then there was a cold rag on my face.

"She needs to be outside," Eriak said, "No Silas, you can't touch her! It'll make her pain worse. Get that blanket and take her out." I felt myself being lifted and then it became colder.

"Put her in the snow, Silas." I felt the ice sink into my skin, and I heard sizzling.

"Go inside. We'll be there in a moment."

I lay on the ground and Eriak pushed my hair away from my sweaty face.

"Think of blue eyes, Specter," he said with glassy eyes. Blue eyes? Prince Aleron? Immediately the pain lessened. I wasn't sure how it helped but I brought back the memory of his shocking eyes and held on to it. Soon the pain dwindled to a small throb in my arm. I sat up shakily and rested my elbows on my knees, soaked from the melted snow.

"Do you feel all right now, Specter?" Eriak asked politely. I nodded slowly.

"What happened?" I muttered to myself, but Eriak answered with a blush.

"Well... basically, when Silas kissed you, that thing didn't agree with it." He pointed to my hidden mark. I stared at him. What did he know about the mark? Did he know more about the prince too?

"Eriak, how do you know all of this? You have to tell me what you know." He sighed.

"I... I am a caster. I can see things... sometimes. I don't know everything. I can only see bits and pieces. I'm just nine. I know that how you're feeling has to do with something on your arm. I know that it has to do with your future, and it's not supposed to be what Silas wants." I rubbed my temples. First a devium and now a caster. And a child caster at that. How long has Eriak been seeing things about me? Was it before

Silas even met me? Was that why they stopped me in the forest that day?

"Does Silas know any of this?"

"That I'm a caster? Of course. He makes me study very hard, and I do. I want to make him proud."

"About me, Eriak," I said softly. He shrugged.

"I tried to warn him. I don't think he understood. That or he didn't care." I sighed and rubbed my aching temples some more.

"What exactly do you know?" I felt him put a hand on my shoulder.

"I can't put what I've seen into words. Sometimes, it's more like feelings and colors: dark bad things, warm good things, gray nothingness. Sometimes short pictures. Sometimes words. Just be careful. What was it I heard? 'One can never be too careful.' If you are not careful, there is darkness, Specter. That's what I see most." I stared at my boots, repeating his borrowed words again and again. I had forgotten his words so easily. Somehow, when Eriak said them, they carried much more weight. One can never be too careful. I felt the hole widen in my chest. So much for healing.

Chapter 11: The First Raid

I avoided everyone for the following few days. Instead of training, I read. I combed through every book of fiction, lore, legend, and history that was in my house, but I found nothing. There wasn't even a mention of a being with the abilities I had except a devium, let alone what Buwlo described. The little breadcrumbs I had found in Rogue City led nowhere. What did I expect? I was tired and my eyes were sore. I was also torn. I thought that I was going to avenge my family and help the country with the Bloodied Men, but it seemed more farfetched now than it did when Silas first advised it. I was never one for revenge anyway. Jeb always took that step for me. My heart fell. They were gone and I had done nothing. What did it matter if I discovered the truth about myself if I had this tormenting guilt eating away at me?

I also felt like Prince Aleron's eyes haunted me. Any time the crest was uncovered I felt like he could see me. I always glanced around expecting to see him in the room watching me. The most frustrating part was I wasn't sure how I felt about it. I should have been afraid of the feeling, but I wasn't. I just couldn't stop thinking about it. It made my research all the more difficult.

I tossed the book on the shelf and went to the stable. I hadn't ridden Tempest in weeks. I saw her every day but part of me was sure that she would throw me as soon as I mounted her just for spite. Fortunately, she wasn't that annoyed, but she did nip at me as I tightened the straps of the saddle.

We walked down the main street, and I noticed a large crowd was growing in the square around the well. I stopped Tempest at the edge of the crowd and saw there was a man conversing with Silas. Silas nodded and climbed onto the ledge of the well, facing the crowd.

"Friends!" he said, "We have reports that there is a party of soldiers laden with supplies making its way through the Nitalla. The scouts have reported that this could be the last raid for this winter should we choose to pursue it." The crowd murmured at the information. I watched with my brow furrowed. Why would Silas even tell everyone about the raid? Doesn't he make the decisions on who to rob? Silas glanced at me. I stiffened and my breathing stopped. My mind was flooded with thoughts of the other night. My neck felt hot, and I swallowed. For a moment, I thought the devium was about to smirk. He continued to address the people.

"As I said, it is heavily guarded with twenty men. We are unsure what army escorts the supply train and so we are presented with a potential gamble. We have enough supplies to last us another week or two, given that our trading success continues or... we gather some men and take this supply train. I want a majority agreement on this as some lives will most likely be lost. In a gamble such as this, we decide together. Let us all meet back here at midday. We will decide." My mouth dropped open as he leapt from the well. What kind of leadership is this? He wants the people to vote? I had never heard of such tactics. Silas didn't seem like the kind of person to let go of control like this. My suspicion grew and I nudged Tempest forward.

"Devium," I said as I neared him. He stopped and raised an eyebrow at me.

"I have told you many times to call me 'Silas.'" I ignored his comment. In truth, I couldn't bring myself to use his name. Calling him devium helped to remind me that I really didn't know him. He was an enigma that I wasn't sure that I should solve.

"This vote that you have requested. Is it something that you always do?" He turned his head at me and smiled.

"Why do you ask?" I narrowed my eyes at him.

"It seems uncharacteristic of you." Silas chuckled and stepped closer to me. I steadied Tempest as she tensed.

"I'm afraid that you do not know me as... intimately as I'd like, Specter." His gaze was unwavering. My breath caught as his stare sent me back to that night. I blinked and cleared my throat.

"Apparently not," I said and quickly steered Tempest back to the treehouse.

All of Rogue City gathered around the well for the vote. Silas stood on the well again and instructed those in favor of the raid stand to one side and those opposed stand to the other. I didn't feel that I should take part in the vote. I hadn't been there long enough or done enough for my opinion to matter. I honestly wasn't sure what I would do.

The people were counted, and Silas announced the decision.

"A raid it is. We will leave in an hour. Only the bravest and fiercest rogues will go on this mission. I will take twenty men. Are there any volunteers?" Men began shouting their names. When a rogue volunteered for a raid, they received a bigger cut of the spoils for risking their lives. It was a smart way to always have willing men but all I could think about was that some of them may not come back. The decision seemed so stupid to me. Why risk lives on a gamble? Perhaps I didn't understand the struggles of the people in Rogue City but were they difficult enough that their own people may need to die for them? Silas' voice interrupted my thoughts.

"Specter, will you take this opportunity and volunteer to serve Rogue City?" My body went rigid as I felt the multitude of eyes on me. My chest tightened as I glanced at all of them. The judgment poured out of them, and I felt guilty. I could almost hear their thoughts: Ungrateful, freeloader, leech. Did I even have an option? I looked at the devium and felt rage bubble inside me. He was smirking.

I was stuffing my pack with the last bit of my supplies when I heard a single knock on my door. When I opened it, no one was there. Suddenly, a rock flew over the railing. I deftly caught it and peered down. I smiled when I saw Isaac.

"Hello there, dear sir!" I called, "To what do I owe this pleasure?" The little boy looked at his feet and I saw a blush creep to his cheeks.

"I wanted to give you something before you left, Miss Specter." I leapt over the railing and kneeled before him.

"What do you have for me?" I asked grinning. He twisted his foot in the snow.

"Something so you won't forget me on your mission." He reached into his pocket and pulled out a flat rock that was the size of my hand. I took the rock and saw that Isaac had painted a black horse rearing and a person with long red hair streaming in the wind with two weapons raised for battle. On the person's head was a big crown.

"Oh, Isaac, is that Tempest?" He nodded and pointed to the rider.

"And that's you." I smiled and my heart lifted.

"I see. Why do I have a crown?" He grinned.

"'Cause you're gonna be Queen of the Rogues!"

"Oh, I am?" I laughed. What would the prince say about that? I scolded myself for the thought.

"Uh-huh!" he said, "And you will be the kindest, best queen to ever rule Devtera!" He put his fists on his hips proudly. He was so confident that I couldn't bear to tell him that I had no intention of being a queen of anything. He had such faith in me.

"Isaac, I think this is one of the best presents I have ever received." His face reddened again.

"It wasn't nothing, Miss Specter."

"Well, I love it," I said and hugged him, "I'll try my best to get you something just as special sometime, all right? Run home now, Isaac. Don't want your mother worried." I nudged him toward town. He grinned and ran home.

I went back up to my room and set the rock on the table in my bedroom. I slung the packs over my shoulder and started out. After readying Tempest, we went to the square. There were still some men missing when I made it to the well, so I went to Lily's to wait. As I walked through the door, all conversation halted. My shoulders tensed and I quickly made my way to the bar.

"Ey! What's with the death act? She's been here long enough! Get over it! Good morning, Specter," Lily said. The men shifted and quickly began chatting again.

"Good morning, Lily," I said, trying not to smile. It was hard not to like Lily. She cared about everyone so deeply even if she was a bit rough around the edges.

"Want some mead before you go? It'll warm you up." I shook my head.

"I don't need warming up. Do you know who is going on the mission? Anyone I know?" She nodded.

"Only Silas, Viht, Dax, Kaul, and Smid. Then again, that's nearly everyone you know. The men are still skittish about you, Specter, they respect you, but they're skittish. You aren't exactly the friendliest rogue," she said. I shrugged and pulled at my necklace. I didn't expect to be friends with everyone. I only had my family and Jeb before. I couldn't image that I would suddenly become more outgoing especially given everything else that happened...

She smiled and patted my arm, bringing me out of my thoughts. The action reminded me of Aunt Prudence.

"You take care of yourself, little miss," Lily said. I swallowed the grief and nodded.

"Have some wine waiting for me," I said as I walked out of the door.

Silas assembled the men who were to take part in the raid. I stood among them and waited for instructions.

"Men, we are to ride a day into the forest, and we will set camp a half day's walk from the path we suspect the carriage will take. Three men will stay at camp to keep watch. They are also expected to report back here if we do not return by that nightfall. We will discuss everything else when we set up camp. Is this understood?" All the men nodded or murmured in agreement. Silas nodded.

"Good. Grab your weapons and let us take our victory!" Silas cried with a fierce look on his face, and he threw his fist in the air. The rest of the men raised their fists with battle cries.

Silas appointed Viht to lead the way as he stayed at the gate watching the men file out. I mounted Tempest and moved toward the gate. Silas steered his horse to block my path. I looked blankly at him.

"Hello, Specter," he said.

"Devium." I tried to move around him, but he blocked me again. We stared at each other as the air grew thick with tension. Finally, he spoke, and his face showed mild surprise.

"You are angry with me."

"Very perceptive of you." He smiled which only irritated me further.

"What have I done to anger you so, Specter?" My teeth ground together.

"Did you not think I was capable of volunteering on my own?"

"I know that you are capable, but it seems that you need to be pushed to a decision quite often." His words caught me off guard.

"How do you mean?" He smiled and raised his hand but lowered it again.

"I only mean to help guide you, Specter. You have been lost for some time and staying so guarded will only keep you stranded... Come. We are falling behind."

His words struck a chord within me. Lost was the perfect description. I didn't know where to go or what to do about anything. Silas knew it. I had been so suspicious of him but maybe he was just trying to help. I looked after the devium. I wouldn't let my guard down so easily but maybe I could lower it a bit.

The journey was more of a hunt. We were like foxes stalking our prey; silence was our most loyal friend. After making camp and resting for a few hours, Silas assembled the group for instructions. He named three of the men to stay behind to watch the camp and horses. They kicked the dirt and muttered but did as they were told. Watching horses meant less pay.

"Men... and lady," Silas said, "We will be doing things a bit differently this time..." He shared his plan and we set out. My skin tingled with nervous energy and my breathing was sporadic. This would be the first real fight for me. Silas' plan seemed simple but I felt like I was marching into war. Silas ordered us to sleep until dawn, but I just lay on my blankets, wide awake with a pounding heart.

I perched high in a tree and watched the road. I stayed hidden behind the thick needles of the evergreen. The air was thick with snow. I closed my frozen eyes and listened. I heard the slight fidgets of the rogues below me. The archers thumbed their bow strings. I smelled the metal of swords and the leather of boots through the scarf that covered half of my face. I felt the bitter cold wind on my face and wished I could feel it run through my hair, but it was stuffed under the scarf and big hat Silas gave me. The red was too visible, especially in the winter. I felt the panic building my chest and took a deep breath. Everything would be fine.

I smelled the stink of overworked horses and heard the squeak of wagon wheels. I looked down and signaled to the archer below me. I watched him signal the next man. I heard the nocking of arrows and the unsheathing of swords. The other rogues were ready.

It was hard not to see the entourage. There were two large wagons piled high with crates and barrels and another cart carrying ten men. A single man drove each cart. The train was surrounded by eight men on horseback. A full twenty. I had hoped that the scouts were wrong. A pit formed in my stomach. There would be so much death today.

The rogues let their arrows fly from every direction. Five of the horsemen fell to the ground dead. The first carriage driver was hit in the arm by an arrow and the second driver was killed. The injured driver ran into the woods while the horses scattered.

The smell of blood filled my nose and my head reeled. I took a few breaths through my mouth and my heartbeat was in my ears. It was my turn. I didn't know if I could do this. I steeled myself as the cold flooded through me. If I did my part right, no one else would have to die.

"Leave the supplies and you will be spared from the Specter," Viht said from the trees. None of them replied but they began to draw their weapons.

I yanked away the hat and scarf around my hair and leapt from the branch, tackling a soldier from his horse. Before the others could see, I dragged him into the forest screaming. He stared at me with wide eyes as I knocked his helmed head into a tree. He crumpled to the ground unconscious.

I stayed in the forest as I was told. The soldiers nervously looked around them trying to find their comrade.

One of the men let out a battle cry and raised his shield. A single dripping red slash went across the shield. My blood went cold. The Bloodied Men.

The rogues ran out of the woods and into battle. The Bloodied Men fought like they were mad just as they did in Ameris. I watched the fighting reeling with emotion, but it wasn't fear and panic I felt. The cold energy was consumed by darkness and all I wanted was to kill them all.

My senses were almost animalistic. I inhaled the metallic smell of blood with delight and my mouth almost salivated. My palms itched to feel the snap of bones and I wanted to hear their screams. They would all pay.

I heard a cry and saw a rogue lying on the ground holding his leg. Despite his attempts, blood was staining the snow beneath him. My eyes fixated on it until I saw the red slashed shirt of the man walking toward the rogue. The fanatic raised his sword above his head with his back to me. Without hesitation, I leapt forward.

Everything seemed to slow down. I felt my eyes grow cold and I smiled to myself. Then my eyes met with the rogues,' and I could have sworn I saw fear in them, not fear of the knight, but fear of me. I smiled wider.

As I was landing, I took the soldier's raised sword and shoved it between his shoulder blades. The sword passed easily through his body under my strength, and it protruded out of his chest. The man collapsed and turned to face me. I looked into his eyes with anticipation. I watched the life fade from his eyes and the darkness swirled inside my head. I closed my eyes and inhaled slowly. It wasn't enough. His was the first life I had taken, and it felt exhilarating. I scanned for another, and I heard the rogue gasp in pain. I looked at him and for a brief moment, my mind cleared.

I took the rogue by the arms and drug him away from the battle. His face was already pale from blood loss. I crouched to examine his wound. It was a clean deep cut in his thigh, but it would be simple to stitch and heal after the battle. I tore his shirt and tied the fabric around the gash. I didn't think to be gentle; I wanted to fight and inflict more pain.

"Stay here and try not to move." He merely gritted his teeth and nodded.

I turned back to the battle. There were nine Bloodied Men still standing. The rogues were taking too long. The filth needed to die. The darkness clawed at me, and I drew my blades. I ran ahead with blinding speed. I slashed and stabbed at the Bloodied Men, barely aware enough to avoid the rogues. Silas caught my eye as he was easily dueling with two of the soldiers. He glanced at the carnage behind me, and his eyes changed. He took a small step back from his fight and that was all the invitation I needed. I ran at the two soldiers and plunged a blade into each of their necks. Hot blood gushed from the wounds as they fell to the ground.

I sheathed my blades and looked over at Viht as he dueled with the last soldier. I jumped on top of the carriage just as Viht pushed the soldier back.

"Ah! Specter, how lovely it is for you to join us! I hope you didn't make too much of a mess of that man." The man swiveled his head as I stepped off the carriage. My curls unfurled in the wind as I landed.

"What is this?" the zealot said, "You now have women fight your battles? How pathetic." I felt that darkness sweep over me and walked closer. The man began to laugh.

"You want to fight me? You are a worthless peasant girl. You are a waste of my time and a waste of our lord and provider, eternal King Karrolei." I stopped within arm's reach of him as he continued his preaching.

"I serve the mighty King Karrolei, wench. He is divine and all powerful. If I must exterminate a few pests, I will gladly do-" My hand wrapped around his throat and I raised him into the air. A calm fury possessed me. I turned my head at the extremist.

"I have seen the effects of your 'extermination.' I watched as you bigots murdered innocents and burned their homes to the ground. How would you feel, sir, if you watched someone you love die?" I said, my voice calm but filled with venom. The man clawed at my hand, sputtering.

"And for what? Some land? Power?" My voice lowered to a hard, menacing whisper. I felt my arms and hands tingle and I could hear the crackle of lightning.

"I don't think you know what true power is." The man's mouth gaped.

"It-it can't be... Who are you?" he said. I smiled and turned my head at him.

"I am Specter, and I will destroy you all," I said. I let the darkness that had been ripping at me free. Tiny bolts of green sparks flew down my arm, around my fingers, and up the man's neck. He screamed and shook as the sparks pulsed through him. Smoke drifted from his skin and carried the smell of burning flesh into my nose. Steaming blood fell from his eyes and his face turned red. The darkness surged with joy at the spectacle. Then the man stopped screaming and his body went limp in my grasp. I dropped the corpse and took in its gruesome sight. His skin had turned to a putrid gray with bright green still pulsing through his veins. How divine... I covered my mouth, stifling a giggle. I was dizzy with the rush. A shock of pain tore through me from my arm.

I staggered back and felt arms wrap around my waist. I looked up and Silas watched me with a dark hunger in his eyes. The darkness snuffed out the pain as I looked at him. I wanted to kiss his lips and feel his skin on mine. I ran my finger along his jaw. He leaned closer but then stopped. Instead, he helped steady me and stepped away. I smirked at him and then looked at the others. Dax, Kaul, and Viht stood with their mouths open.

I heard the snow crunch in the forest line, and I saw the carriage driver holding a small crossbow. He was shaking badly but it seemed he was aiming at me. The men ducked for cover as a bolt embedded itself into the wagon.

"I'll take care of it," I said with a grin. I sped to the driver. I appeared silently behind him and whispered into his ear.

"Feeling brave? We can't have that..." He shivered and spun quickly but I was faster.

"Who was that?" he said, staring into the forest. I moved behind him again before he saw me. I giggled softly, menacingly.

"The Specter." I grabbed him by the shoulders and slammed him into a tree. He dropped the crossbow and started shaking.

"Please, don't kill me, Specter. Please, don't kill me," he repeated over and over. He was a short soldier. He was middle-aged and was balding. His fear was intoxicating. I took a deep breath but snarled when I smelled him soil himself.

"What is your name?" I asked softly as green lightning crackled down my arms and around my fingers. He looked at me in terror and dropped the crossbow. "Deg."

"What did you see, Deg?" I asked. I felt like I was playing a game. A dark, lovely, twisted game.

"I saw everything," he stammered. I smiled, feeling light and dizzy again. The crest on my arm started to throb and my mind cleared a bit.

"Good. I want you to take this filth to King Karrolei. Tell him that he will put an end these Bloodied Men fanatics or I will put an end to him. Do you understand, Deg?" He nodded quickly and went back atop the cart that now held the dead and wounded Bloodied Men. He lashed out the reins and sped off without looking back.

I picked up the crossbow and tossed it to Dax when I neared the group. All but Silas took a small step away from me, but I wasn't bothered. Their eyes were still a bit wide as they stared.

"What happened exactly? Lightning leapt from your fingers, Specter," Viht said cautiously. I smirked, savoring the feeling of the fire. Again my arm began to ache.

"I woke up." I looked at Silas. I wished we were alone. I wanted to feel the fire between us again. The pain from the mark intensified but I ignored it. I was too enthralled with the power, but it was fading. Silas met my eyes, and I could see how tense he was. His body shook with effort. I enjoyed how I affected him. That in itself was intoxicating. I smirked at him, and he glowered at me.

"Maybe we should talk about this another time. We need to get these supplies to camp," Silas said quickly. Sweat glistened on his brow. The others may have thought it was from the fight, but I knew better.

Chapter 12: A Purpose

When we arrived at camp, the rogues sorted the spoils in the fading light. There was mostly dried food, bandages, blankets, and clothing. What little bit of gold that was found was put into a bag to be counted later. No rogue was lost during the raid, and it gave me some peace, but I still paced around the site. My head was clear, but I could feel the remnants of the tingling energy making my skin shiver. In the moment, the power was intoxicating but now I just felt uneasy. I ran my hands through my hair and inhaled a few deep breaths. The rogues recoiled from me as I passed them. I couldn't blame them. I was afraid too.

"Silas! There are some letters here!" My head quickly turned toward the rogue. Letters? I watched Silas retrieve the letters and rip them open. His eyes scanned through them. A hint of a smile played on his lips. He folded the letters and slipped them inside his coat while nodding to Viht.

"Pack it up and get some rest, men! We leave for home at first light!" Viht said in a bellowing tone. The rogues had divided into small groups the previous night. Each group gathered around their own fire and readied for bed. The cold didn't bother me anymore but, at the twins' insistence, I had put my blankets near their fire with Viht. Silas had not been with us the previous night, but the twins quickly made room for the devium when he walked to our area. He scanned the clearing until his eyes met mine. He motioned for me to join them as he sat by the fire. I swallowed and made my way to them.

"Specter!" Dax said as I approached.

"So, what happened today?" Kaul said cautiously. Their identical grins flashed in the firelight. I felt my stomach sink as the images raced through my mind: Blood, gore, death. And all at my hands. I killed people today. I killed ten people. My hands turned to fists so they wouldn't shake, and I swallowed down the bile in my throat. I wasn't ready for their questions. I still couldn't wrap my head around it either. The more time that passed, the more repulsed I felt. I killed people.

I jumped when a warm heavy hand fell on my shoulder. Viht looked at me with concern. He reminded me of Uncle Fredrick then.

"The first time sits with you. At least you can find solace in that they were wicked men. They have killed many times over and they would have killed you too, Specter." My mouth was too dry to speak but I managed to nod. I stared into the fire, but it only reminded me of the strange unyielding force inside me. I realized then that I wasn't sure what unnerved me more. The fact that I killed ten men or that I enjoyed it.

After a sleepless night, the day's ride through the forest was thankfully uneventful. When we arrived home the next evening, Rogue City was waiting for us. Silas had sent one of the rogues with news of victory the night before. The people gathered around and clapped and cheered.

Silas ordered that the supplies to be delivered to the loft of the barn to be further divided the next day. He then instructed that the troupe ready ourselves for a party in the same barn. I kicked Tempest toward the house once we were dismissed. I had no intention of celebrating anything. My limbs felt like lead weights, and I just wanted to sleep away the past two days. I didn't want to think about the lifeless eyes of the soldiers I killed but they haunted me. I could still smell the lightning scorched skin and my stomach churned again. I squeezed my eyes shut. They were evil men. They were evil.

I hung Tempest's saddle on the railing of her stall once we reached the stable. I brushed her coat, then hung the brush on a hook and looked at my open hand. My legs gave out and I crumbled to my knees.

Red-brown stains spotted my skin. How had I not noticed earlier? I scrambled to the water trough and scrubbed my hands violently. Tears pooled in my eyes, and I ground my teeth.

My hands still felt stained even though they were clean. They squeezed into fists under the green light of my eyes. This was the Bloodied Men's fault. They started this whole chain of events. They killed my family, made me turn rogue, and now I was turning into a monster. They had to be stopped.

"The letters," I said, remembering Silas putting them in his pocket. Surely they had some type of battle plans or at least a correspondence with superiors. Those letters were an opportunity that I wouldn't let go. I would get them from Silas at the party whether he wanted to share or not.

I poured the steaming water into a basin, forcing my mind to stop spinning in circles. I shook my head and stripped. Doing a mindless task helped me before; I hoped it would have the same effect. It felt amazing to free my skin of the dirt and grime of the raid. I washed my long hair and just sat in the tub as I combed it. I tried to clear my mind as I worked the knots from my hair. Doing such a simple task was welcomed. The crest caught my eye. The spinning star shone at me. Had it been that bright before? The black design seemed darker now too. Was the crest just getting more prominent because of my growing power or did it mean something else? My thoughts turned back to Prince Aleron again. Did he still have his mark? I was sure that he did. I hope he still did...

"What am I thinking?" I said with disbelief. I was not going to become one of those girls who were infatuated with the prince. It didn't matter that he was beautiful and strong.

"And cursed and probably wants to kill me," I reminded myself. I bit my lip. Ever since Eriak suggested thinking of Prince Aleron, I couldn't keep him from my thoughts for long. It was ridiculous but when I thought of him, I felt more at peace. I took a deep breath, and I rubbed my head. I needed to focus on matters at hand. I had to stop avoiding everything that had and was happening to me. Once I avenged my family, I would find the meaning behind this mark and then find out what I am. It was time to stop hiding.

I dried and put on the only dress I packed. It was also the only clean garment I had at the moment. It was a simple blue dress with a fitted bodice and loose skirt. I purposefully avoided comparing the hue to Aleron's eyes. The dress had room for more layers of skirts, but I didn't have any. Such a show of status didn't matter here anyway. In the chest I saw a few of the scarves Aunt Prudence had made me to cover my hair. I took a blue one with green leaves embroidered on the edge. Nostalgia crept through me and looped it around my neck.

After putting on my boots, I leapt from my house and went toward town.

The building looked more like a grand hall than a storage barn. A long table covered with food was pushed against a wall and barrels of wine and ale sat at the end. There was loud cheerful music playing and people were dancing around a large bonfire in the center of the room. The people had dressed up. Everyone was in bright colors, and a few had even painted or powdered their faces. It reminded me of my birthday...

I felt a pull at my arm and found Lily at its source. I almost didn't recognize her. Her eyes were lined in black, and her lips were a dark red. She had on a nice dress, but the true marvel was her hair. It was in a long, complicated plait and she had placed jewels in every knot. A rainbow of colors glittered in the light. I started to greet her, but she interrupted me.

"Specter, I'm a bit disappointed in you. With the looks you've got; it wouldn't take much to fix up and you didn't do a damn thing... Well, at least you wore a dress." I felt my face flush. Her expression was so fierce that I forgot what I was there to do.

"I- I'm sorry, Lily. I didn't know." She rolled her eyes but patted my arm.

"I'm sure you didn't. Those rogues didn't say a thing to you, I'd bet on it. Come with me, I can at least do up your hair." She pulled me to a chair and pushed me into it. She pulled and cursed at my curls, but she made quick time. I felt my hair to have an idea of what she did. It was half back and knotted into a multitude of braids. They felt so intricate that I was amazed that she did them on her own and so quickly.

"Hold still," she said, stepping in front of me. She held a small jar of what looked like red clay. She smeared the substance on my lips, let it set for a few moments, and then wiped it away. She looked me over and nodded.

"That'll do. I'd really love to spend some time with you the next party we have. I used to be a handmaid before I came here. Dressing up those girls was my favorite..." Her eyes drifted away briefly. I had never heard Lily talk about her life before Rogue City. I didn't think I had heard anyone talk about their old lives. It was an unspoken rule here and it was one everyone respected. I smiled softly at her.

"I'd like that, Lily. Thank you." She blinked a few times and nodded curtly at me.

"Well... get going, missy. You're the guest of honor!" She grabbed a cup of wine and shoved it into my hands.

"Guest of honor?" I scowled at her.

"If it weren't for you taking down so many men, we would have surely lost some rogues during this raid. All of the men are talking about it. You saved them, Specter." She pushed me into the center of the room, right in front of the fire. All I wanted was some letters, not to be put up for a spectacle.

"Rogues, stop your feet and hold your tongues!" Lily said over the music. The band stopped playing. Everyone in the room turned to look at me. I knew I shouldn't have been terrified, but I was. My skin crawled under the weight of so many stares. Lily must have had too much to drink. She was confused.

"Raise your cups to Specter, the Terror of the Nitalla!" Lily said and raised her cup into the air. I held my breath and looked at the crowd of people. They looked back at me with respect and admiration, but there was a little bit of fear there too. I swallowed and sweat beaded my brow. Slowly, cups rose, and the people's voices filled the air.

"To Specter!"

My neck and face flushed, and my chest tightened but there was a warmth that spread throughout my body. For once, I felt welcomed. Was this what acceptance felt like? But at what cost? I raised my cup and drank but it didn't make the pit in my stomach go away. I needed those letters. My cup was empty when I looked around again. Buwlo and Silas stood next to Lily.

Buwlo wore a red tunic with orange embroidery and lace around the cuffs. It wasn't what I expected from him given his mountain-like physique and rough blacksmithing hands, but yet it suited him. Silas stood next to him in a white shirt and dark blue vest with a high collar that made his eyes look much more yellow. Would he still have the letters with him even though he changed clothes? Probably not. Maybe

I should have just broken into his house... I started to ask Silas for a moment of privacy, but Buwlo spoke first.

"Lookee there! Specter went and dressed up too! I have been waiting for you all night! My wrist has healed, and I wish for a dance!" My eyebrows rose and I was caught off guard again. I had never danced before.

"A dance?" He grinned at my evident surprise and sat down his drink.

"Yes! I am a wonderful dancer. You must be as well. All great fighters are!" I shook my head, and my words came out in a stammer.

"What? No-no. I don't dance. I need to speak to Silas." Buwlo took my hand ignoring my protests. He laughed.

"Not to worry, Specter. I think my feet are stronger than my wrists!" I looked back at Silas for help. He just looked at me and took my cup as we walked away. That dark look was back in his eye, but Buwlo had already swept me away.

I tried a few times to excuse myself from Buwlo but there was no escaping him. Surely one dance would be enough. I wasn't really good at it at first and the struggle to learn distracted me. When I lost step Buwlo would pick me up and spin around and somehow managed to get us back on track. It was so freeing. I caught myself smiling as I moved with Buwlo to the music. I realized that I liked dancing. When I finally was dancing without needing instructions from Buwlo, I felt a tug on my dress. Buwlo and I stopped and saw Isaac waiting patiently.

"Miss Specter, may I dance with you?" he said like a proper gentleman. I smiled as my heart melted. His blond hair was combed back, and his shirt was tucked into his trousers.

"Of course, you may," I said and held out my hand.

"It seems I have been outdone," the big man laughed and went to find a new partner. He didn't have any trouble, either; there was a line of girls waiting to dance with Buwlo.

"You look pretty. I like your scarf," Isaac said, shifting from side to side. I smiled widely at him.

"Thank you, Isaac. My aunt made it for me a long time ago... Shall we dance?"

Dancing with Isaac was more fun than dancing with Buwlo. Every once in a while, I would twirl him around and he buried his face in my scarf as he laughed. My heart lifted with each of his giggles. But eventually, his mother called to him and Isaac hugged my legs.

"Thank you for dancing with me, Miss Specter." I kneeled and kissed his forehead. He shivered from my cold touch and giggled.

"Anytime, Isaac." I watched him leave with his family and my chest fell just a bit. They reminded me of home. My thoughts spiraled. What would they say to me about what I had done? Would they be able to look at me? My stomach turned and I scolded myself. Where was Silas?

"Specter!" I turned and saw Lily waving to me by the food. I walked to her and grabbed another cup of wine.

"Are you having a good time, Specter?" she said with a smile. I nodded and took a drink. I scanned the faces of the people but couldn't spot the devium.

"And what about you, Lily? Have you danced this evening?" She moved to look at my face and narrowed her eyes. I tensed but she didn't comment on it.

"I don't need to dance to have a good time. Food and wine is all I need." We watched the dancers. I glanced over at her. Her shoulders and hips swayed with the music and her foot tapped every now and then. I smiled and waved at Buwlo in the crowd.

"Buwlo! Lily'd like a dance!" I called. Lily went stiff as Buwlo lumbered over to us, forgetting about the girl he was currently dancing with.

"Oh, gods help me..." Lily said under her breath. He stopped and smiled down at her, holding out his hand. I could almost see the tension between them and hid my smile. What did I stumble upon? Lily looked at him through her lashes and a small smile was on her lips. He smiled widely and pulled her away.

I watched them dance until they disappeared into the crowd. I wonder if that admiration between them had been there long. I thought about that look Silas gave me before Buwlo swept me away. My stomach flipped and I bit my lip. My thoughts were so scattered. Where was the devium? I looked around again, but I didn't see him. Dax and Kaul appeared on either side of me.

"Specter, would you care," Dax started.

"To take a bout," Kaul interjected.

"Around the dance floor with me," they said, glaring at each other.

"Well, I was looking for the devium..." I said. They both smiled, not dissuaded.

"He's busy," they said.

"So, you can," Kaul said.

"Dance with me," said Dax grabbing my hand before Kaul had the chance. I finished the cup of wine and tossed it to the table as Dax drug me away. Kaul was right behind, though. It was a strange dance the three of us were in. I was passed back and forth between Dax and Kaul so much that I was almost dizzy from all the turns. As fun as it was, I still looked at the faces around me. I was searching for cat-like yellow green eyes. I was in the middle of a spin when I felt hands wrap around my waist, stopping me suddenly. My back was pressed against his chest and the smell of pine lingered in the air.

"Looking for someone?" I heard a velvety voice say.

"Thank gods," I said. Silas turned me to face him. His brow raised as he wrapped his arm around my waist and took my hand. His hand was hot, and his thumb rubbed my knuckle. My mouth went dry, and I tried to swallow. His eyes were mesmerizing.

"'Thank gods?' Did you miss me, Specter?" His voice was low as he pulled me closer.

"No, devium, but I need to speak with you," I said. Silas turned his head at me and smirked.

"I'm sure it can wait. You look lovely tonight, Fairest." I scowled at him, and he pushed me into a twirl. He pulled me back hard and I crashed into his chest. The top of his vest and shirt was undone and my hand landed on the silver scar I had given him. My heart skipped and I quickly moved my hand.

"This is important. I've wasted enough time this evening," I said and tried to plant my feet. Silas dipped me without pause.

"I fought hard for a dance with you, and I am seeing it through. You can interrogate me later." He brought me upright and his nose almost touched mine. My pulse pounded in my ears as his eyes bore into mine.

"Just one song," I whispered. He smirked and twirled me again.

Thankfully, the song didn't last much longer. My skin felt hot were he touched, and I kept finding myself staring at his lips. The music stopped and I quickly moved away from him. The air was suddenly oppressive.

"Now, I need to speak with you," I said firmly. My face was hot, and I couldn't look him in the eye. He bowed and his arm gestured toward the door. I sped outside and welcomed the cold air on my skin.

"Your hair is exquisite, Specter," Silas said. I felt him run a finger through a curl. I took a step away and he smirked. He always smirked.

"Are you feeling all right? Too much wine, perhaps?" the devium asked as he turned his head at me. I narrowed my eyes at him.

"I'm fine. I need to see the letters from the raid." Silas raised his eyebrows and leaned against the wall of the barn.

"All this fuss over some letters?" I squared my shoulders and nodded.

"Yes."

"Do you think that they even have worthwhile information?" His tone filled me with doubt. They must be important, or Silas wouldn't have kept them. He was playing with me.

"Don't they?" I said flatly. He shrugged and picked at his nails. My nostrils flared and my jaw tensed. I felt the energy spread through me. He was infuriating. He had me wound up and flustered with his flirtations and now he just wanted me to be angry. I hated how he could just toy with my emotions so easily.

"Just give me the letters, devium." He cut his eyes at me and then inclined his head.

"Why?" I ground my teeth together.

"Because I'm tired of doing nothing! I've hidden in the forest like a coward for long enough. I want to avenge my family and I want to know what I am, and I want to know what this thing-" I cut myself short before mentioning the mark, but the damage was done. The devium turned his head at me and took a step forward.

"What else do you want to know?" I swallowed but stood my ground, crossing my arms across my chest.

"It doesn't matter. I need those letters. I know that they have important information, or you wouldn't have reacted as you did when you read them." Silas stood before me, so close we almost touched. He ran a finger down my jaw and smiled with dark eyes. I didn't move. He would not intimidate me. My heart pounded in spite of my mind. His voice was a rough whisper.

"Oh, but it does matter, Specter. It is no secret that you fascinate me, and you just hinted at a new piece of the puzzle. Now I must know what it is." His finger followed the curve of my neck and my breath caught. He smirked at my reaction.

"Let's make another deal, shall we? You share your secret with me and start calling me by my name then I will give you the letters. I will also aid you with all that you need in your pursuits of revenge and discovery. It seems fair enough to me." I searched his eyes for any sign of deceit, but I couldn't find any. Honestly, I had no idea how I was supposed to take down the Bloodied Men, especially alone. And after, how was I to figure out what I was? The deal was more than good for me. How was this good for him?

"You hardly have any gain in this deal."

"I wouldn't have offered it if I wasn't satisfied with the terms. Do you accept?" He held out his hand. His tone was level but there was anticipation and excitement in his eyes. I knew there was more to it just like my deal with staying in Rogue City. Doing my part ended up with me killing people. But what choice did I have.

Chapter 13: The Next Venture

I laid my washed clothes on the stone steps near the firepit to dry as I waited for Silas to return. We agreed that my house offered the most privacy. I didn't want anyone to know about the mark just as he didn't want anyone to know the letters' contents. I heard him walk across the balcony and then knock on the door.

We both sat near the firepit. My face flushed when I thought of the last time we sat here. His shirtless torso flashed through my mind and my ears went hot. I blinked hard and pushed the thoughts away. The one time I gave in to those impulses lead to severe pain. I didn't want to risk that again.

He removed his coat and I noticed that he no longer wore his vest. He took the letters from his coat pocket and laid them to the side, away from me. He noticed me eyeing them.

"You get the letters after I know your secret, Fairest." I was too nervous to be annoyed with him. I had been so careful to keep the mark, and my past, hidden away. Part of me didn't want any of it to come to light. If it were out in the open, it would be all the more real. But I needed the help and Silas wouldn't help me for nothing.

I removed the fabric from my arm. I felt so exposed in the green light of the spinning star. I couldn't look at Silas as I felt his hands pull my arm closer. Dread consumed me. I shouldn't be telling him. He shouldn't see it. I felt like I was being watched again but I didn't look around. I knew there were no blue eyes here.

"And what is the story behind this?" he said, curiosity evident in his voice.

"I'm not entirely sure..."

I explained the story as best that I could. I was careful not to mention Prince Aleron by name or that he had the mark too. I wasn't sure why. Maybe it was the absurdity of it, the prince and I being linked. Maybe I just wanted to keep him to myself.

I said that he was a soldier with the Black Guard and that he thought I was a caster turned spy. After witnessing the fight, I had with the rogues, he followed me during the festival to question me. When he grabbed me to take me to his superiors, the crest appeared. I then became ill, so he took me to my aunt. The man left once the Bloodied Men attacked. My voice trailed off as my mind went back there. Silas didn't prod me further. He didn't say anything for a long time. His brow was deeply furrowed, and his eyes had a far-away look to them.

"If the seal was broken, why did a mark appear? One would think that when a seal is made then a mark would appear. Since that is not the case, what does this mark do? An enchanted symbol such as this must have a purpose... Since it appeared, have you noticed it do anything?" he said, finally. I felt my face start to burn.

"The night I had dinner with you and you... kissed me... The pain I felt came from the mark." His silver eyebrow rose, and he chuckled.

"Now that is interesting..." His grip softened and I pulled my arm away.

"I fulfilled my end of the deal. Now give me the letters." The devium picked up the letters and offered them to me. I quickly scanned the pages. A few were recruitment reports and supply inventories and requests. One letter, though, requested immediate travel to Caneesho, the capital of Capilious. The only detail provided was that troops were to arrive within two weeks' time for specific orders.

"Are they going to attack the capital? Why would they do that? Don't they idolize King Karrolei?" I said. Silas shrugged.

"Perhaps they are tired of not having their deeds recognized by the king. It is hard to predict the thoughts of mad men." I reread the letter hoping to find more information from the words.

"Do you know of anything happening at the capital in two weeks?"

"The princess's birthday celebration," Silas said flatly.

"But wasn't her birthday weeks ago?"

"Yes but the celebration was postponed. The Rokellia royalty could not attend due to the attack on Ameris. King Karrolei insisted on their attendance and gave them time to sort out the problem." I shook my head at him in disbelief.

"How do you know all of this?" Silas chuckled.

"I have scouts in many places. Their job is to report on major events that may disrupt our flow of revenue, if you will. The postponement affected Rogue City immensely. We were holding out for the wealthy that would travel through for the celebration. Hence the importance of yesterday's raid." His explanation made sense. I hadn't thought about how Rogue City survived. It would be foolish to trust the lives of almost one hundred people to chance.

Now that I had the information I wanted, what was my plan? I told myself that I would track down the Bloodied Men and put a stop to them. I took a deep breath and ran a hand through my hair.

"I'm going to Caneesho," I said under my breath. It was more to convince myself, but Silas replied.

"I suppose I must accompany you then. It has been sometime since I was in the capital."

"Accompany me?" He smirked at me.

"That was part of my end of the bargain, was it not?" I shook my head at him. He knocked me off guard. Silas took the letters from me and placed them back into his coat.

"Yes, but-" He didn't let me finish.

"Then I will go with you. I will inform Lily tomorrow that we will be leaving for some time."

"Lily?"

"Yes, she is in charge when I'm not here." He left a woman in charge? He could tell what I was thinking. He rolled his eyes and stood. He began to put on his coat as he spoke.

"It amazes me how you humans believe that women are so inferior to men. I have met an equal number of capable men and women as I have incapable. Everyone has a different potential. Their body parts make no difference. As I was saying... I will inform Lily tomorrow. I will also speak to Viht, Kaul, and Dax. I have a feeling that they would enjoy this excursion. We may have to travel separately of course. Such a large group could draw suspicion."

"Silas, stop," I said sharply. His movements abruptly ceased, and he cut his eyes to me. I motioned for him to sit, and he did. He was eerily silent. It unnerved me.

"What is it?" I said.

"You said my name... I hadn't imagined that it would have such a profound effect on me." He was so serious that for a moment I thought he was angry, but his eyes told me otherwise. My chest tensed and I glanced away from him.

"I know that you agreed to help me avenge my family, but I don't want you to abandon Rogue City on what could be a fool-hearty adventure. For all we know, this is suicide. You have more important things to attend to and the others... I don't want their lives on my conscience."

"That is their decision isn't it? We can't force them to do or not do anything. And what about me? You don't care about my life on your conscience?" I scoffed at him.

"I don't doubt that you can handle yourself." He chuckled and then there was silence. I looked over the devium. He looked into the flames, deep in thought. The scene reminded me of my first night in Rogue City. The glow of the firelight made Silas look golden from his skin to his hair and his eyes were shining yellow. He was otherworldly and so attractive. I wanted to feel his smooth warm skin and run my hands through his silken hair. Suddenly his eyes met mine and I flushed. I felt vulnerable and exposed under his intense gaze.

"Tell me, Specter. Why do the Bloodied Men take precedence over discovering the truth of the mark? And yes, I understand that you want to avenge your family, but you said yourself that this venture could be suicide. There must be more to it. Why avoid learning who you are?" His question rocked me to my core. I felt an immense pressure in my chest and dread seeped into my bones. It was a question I had avoided but I knew the answer. Silas did too; it was in his face and yellow eyes. My mouth went dry.

"Because I'm afraid," I said in a whisper. He turned his head at me quizzically, but he wasn't the least bit puzzled.

"Of?" He knew what I meant but he wanted me to say it. I looked down at my hands and remembered the blood that had stained them just a few hours before. I shook my head and the air felt thick.

"I made a man's blood boil. I made his flesh melt and... I liked it." My stomach turned and I shook. Silas lifted my chin to face him. His touch was so soft and gentle. He had never touched me like that. My heart thudded against my chest. He was so close.

"Even the bloodiest of hands are flawless when it is justice they deliver. There is no shame in the power you have. It is a beautiful fire within you, and I refuse to let you snuff it out." His voice was soft but there was an edge to it. His eyes were full of conviction and awe without a trace of fear. My body tensed under his gaze. He was too close.

"But what if it consumes me?" I said, my voice barely a whisper. He ran his warm finger along my jaw, and he looked at my lips. My heart leapt to my throat, and I held my breath.

"Then let it consume us both." He closed the gap between us and kissed me. Maybe he was right. Maybe I shouldn't be so afraid. The darkness stirred again. I grabbed his shirt and pulled him closer. He chuckled against my mouth and slid his arm around my waist, pressing me against his chest. My hand slipped into the gap of his shirt and my fingers traced the knotted skin of his scar. The darkness danced as I remembered cutting into him. The mark started to burn as Silas shivered under my touch and moved to pull me closer.

His hand landed on the mark and a searing jolt of pain ran up my arm. I jumped away from him with a yelp. I looked down at the crest as it shone brightly.

"What happened?" Silas said. I tried to catch my breath and I rubbed the mark, even though the pain was gone.

"There was a pain when you touched the mark." He looked intrigued.

"Only when I touched it? Not when I kissed you?" My face grew hot, and I looked away from him. The mark started to burn during the kiss, but the real pain was when he touched the mark. I shook my head, not sure of how to answer.

"When you touched it." He narrowed his eyes at my arm.

"Interesting, indeed..." How was he not bothered by the whole situation? I couldn't decide if I was angry and annoyed or thankful for the interruption. I couldn't understand how I let myself be so attracted to Silas when I couldn't trust him. I felt so awkward and confused.

I stood and wrapped the fabric around the mark. Silas stood too.

"You should go home," I said, crossing my arms over my chest.

"I think you should reconsider not removing this mark first. Just my opinion," he said with a smirk and brushed his knuckles across my cheek. I batted his hand away lightly.

"Go home," I said firmly. He held up his hands with a smile.

"Alright. I'm leaving. Please come to my house tomorrow at midday. We will have a meeting with the others about leaving for the capital. I would like you to explain. Until then, I hope you sleep well." He bowed low and was gone before I could reply.

I wasn't the first to arrive at Silas' house the following day. I was thankful for that. I still felt a bit of embarrassment from the night before. Silas, Lily, Dax, Kaul, and Viht were casually standing in the room talking about last night's party. Silas didn't act differently when he noticed me. There wasn't even a knowing look on his face.

"Specter, thank you for joining us," Silas said. His tone was even, as it usually was. I nodded at him. He gestured to the table. "Everyone, please sit."

I could see the confusion on their faces. Silas hadn't told them anything yet. I sat between Lily and Viht. I didn't think I could handle sitting close to Silas. I was uncomfortable enough as it was. Silas sat across from me and looked at me expectantly. I huffed and steeled myself.

"Thank you all for coming. Silas called this meeting on my behalf so I will explain why we're here. During the raid, there was some correspondence found with the Bloodied Men. One of the letters contained orders for an attack on Caneesho in two weeks. Given my circumstances, I want to try to stop them so I will be leaving Rogue City, at least for a while."

"You can't just leave!" the twins said.

"You are quite the warrior but I'm not sure you could face an entire army, Specter," Viht said cautiously.

Dax and Kaul continued to voice their outrage. Lily touched my hand softly.

"Are you ready to leave?" she said gently. I was nearly overwhelmed by her concern. I squeezed her hand quickly.

"I can't hide here forever."

"And she won't be alone, nor will she have to face an army," Silas said. The twins stopped their ranting.

"You're going with her," Lily said. It wasn't a question, but Silas nodded anyway.

"I ask that you take charge while we are gone, Lily, if you would. As for you three, you have the opportunity to join us. You are under no pressure to go especially since this is not necessarily for the gain of Rogue City or even yourselves. Specter actually didn't want any of you to take the risk, but you can make your own decisions. If you don't go, I ask that you not speak of this to anyone else here. The mere idea of the Bloodied Men attacking the capital is enough to send the people into panic, however far away the capital is. What say you?"

The three rogues sat for a moment. Viht stroked his beard while the twins stared at each other with strange expressions. Finally, Viht spoke.

"You have a plan?" He glanced at me and then Silas. I remained silent. I didn't have any kind of plan, but Silas nodded confidently.

"Of course."

"We're in," the twins said happily. Viht shook his head at them.

"You haven't even heard the plan." They shrugged.

"We'd go even without a plan," Kaul said.

"We can't just abandon Specter," Dax said.

"She's one of us now," they said looking to me. I smiled at them and felt warm.

"So, you coming or not, old man," Dax said to Viht. Viht pinched the bridge of his nose and sighed.

"When do we leave?" Relief flooded through me, and I let go of the breath I was holding. I didn't realize how much I wanted them to go. It was ironic to think that these were the same men who tried to rob me once. Now they were willing to leave the safety of their homes for me without any other benefit. I didn't think I would ever be so fortunate to have so many people to care for me that wasn't my family. But then again, I guess we had become family after all.

We were to leave before dawn the next morning. We met at the tavern where Lily had prepared us a quick breakfast as well as food for our journey. Silas didn't want to make a show of our leaving. He said that a formal announcement would bring about too many questions. It was all so sudden that I didn't have the chance to tell Isaac goodbye. I decided to leave him a gift. My heart hurt at the idea of him being upset with me.

"Lily, would you please give this to Isaac? He's the little boy that talks with me," I said and handed her my blue scarf that I wore during the party. She smiled and nodded.

"Of course, Specter."

"Thank you... And tell him that I'm sorry that I had to leave without saying goodbye. And that I have my rock with me for luck." She stifled a laugh and nodded again.

"I'm sure he will understand." I just smiled and thanked her again then ate quickly.

Silas signaled us to leave, and I stood with the others to go. Lily hugged me tightly. I just stood still for a moment.

"Be careful, you unfriendly ghoul. You come back here in one piece... And I expect some of the capital's best wine. Two bottles would be better," she said. I smiled and hugged her back.

"Yes, ma'am."

"Now get out of here. You're losing daylight." She shooed us out of the tavern, and we mounted our horses.

Chapter 14: Control

We rode through the forest for almost two days. Viht led the way to the Kings' Road followed by Silas, then me, and then the twins. It was unusually quiet the morning of the third day. I preferred quiet but it was never quiet with Dax and Kaul around. It was a bit unnerving since they weren't making any noise. I peered behind me. They were both dead asleep on their horses. Dax still sat upright, and his chin slumped against his chest while Kaul rested his cheek on his horse's neck. I snorted out a laugh. Silas slowed his pace until he was on my left.

"It's a talent, I must say," he said with a smile.

"They finally fall asleep riding?" Viht said over his shoulder and then shook his head. I raised an eyebrow.

"Is this a typical thing?"

"It is. I think they trained their horses to follow the lead horse just so they can sleep more. If they exerted as much dedication to more important things, they would be quite amazing," Silas said flatly. I looked back at them and laughed again.

"How are you?" Silas said. He looked at my covered arm. I cleared my throat.

"I'm just fine." Silas just stared at me. It looked like he wanted to say more but Viht spoke.

"We are near the road. You two should cover up," Viht said. We agreed that it would be best for me to cover my hair. We didn't want to draw attention to ourselves. I was already wearing a skirt over my pants.

I knotted my hair into a braid and spiraled it on the back of my head. I didn't have a hairpin, but a stick worked to hold the mass together all the same. I tied a brown scarf around my head and pulled up my hood. I felt strange being so covered after nearly two months of freedom. Silas was just as uncomfortable. He pulled and itched at the knit cap he donned to cover his ears.

We neared the Kings' Road and Viht went ahead to make sure it was clear. He waved to us an affirmative. Silas woke the twins, and we moved forward. The Kings' Road ran along the southern edge of the Nitalla. It was the most prominent trade route on land and the most heavily trafficked. Travelling to Caneesho this way would allow us to all travel together. I looked the opposite way, to the east. That way led to Ameris and my house, both now barren. Beyond Ameris, the path eventually led to Jahilta. Was Prince Aleron there? Or was he travelling this very road on his way to the same destination? I shifted in my saddle and twirled my necklace as my nerves got the better of me. I had grown accustomed to the safety of Rogue City and the forest.

"We'll ride on to Feldan. It's a quiet town and there's a decent inn there. We should arrive after nightfall but have enough time to rest. Then on to Onisk," Silas said. His tone was sure even though he didn't consult a map.

"You seem to know the way well." Silas cut his eyes to me.

"I know this country incredibly well." He kicked his horse and moved ahead. Silas had lost most of his flirtatious actions since leaving Rogue City. Part of me was relieved but another part almost... missed it.

When the forest was no longer in view, we had reached what Silas called the Flower Fields. There were rolling hills covered with dark purple flowers sprouting from the snow but not a tree in sight. The blooms were shaped into a many-pointed star. At their center, they were a rich red but quickly faded outward into the purple petals that I had first seen. The stems were thick and thistle-like and the thorns were long and black. The flowers were dark and haunting but still beautiful.

"What are these?" I said. Viht's voice answered.

"They are called Illiums. They only bloom in the winter. When spring comes, they die and dozens of different wildflowers bloom in their stead. The Illiums persevere in the winter and leave enough nourishment in the soil so that the more delicate flowers can grow and flourish in the spring and summer. Illiums are also very poisonous once consumed. All the beasts know not to eat them. The thorns help too," he said just as we heard a yelp. We looked back and saw Kaul sucking on his finger while Dax snickered at him.

We arrived at the town after nightfall like Silas had predicted. However, it wasn't as small as he made it seem. It was smaller than Ameris and the buildings were mostly made from brick and clay. There were hardly any wooden houses. That would make sense; with the Flower Fields so close trees were hard to come by.

We soon found an inn and Viht went inside to secure us some rooms. After leaving our horses to be attended to at the inn's stable, we went inside. The inn was fuller than I expected but we still had a few large tables to choose from. I sat on the bench and shifted uncomfortably. I was sore from so much riding. I stretched my back and my bones popped. The others seemed fine. Silas sat beside me and casually looked around the bar. Dax ordered some food and a pitcher of ale for the table from a barmaid. He threw in a wink at the end and the girl blushed deeply. Her hips swayed as she walked away. Kaul whistled low as Dax elbowed his brother and they exchanged some crude remarks. I raised my brow and stared blankly at them. They met my gaze and immediately turned sheepish.

"Sorry, Specter," they said. Shaking my head, I rolled my eyes and Viht sat down.

"We have rooms. Is there food coming? I'm starving." The food came soon after. I'm sure it was just from eating dried meat and stale bread for two days, but the inn's food tasted heavenly. We ate quickly and silently, too enamored with the wonderful food.

When the food and ale were mostly gone, Viht stretched out and sighed happily.

"Now I'm ready for a good night's rest. Oh, Silas here's the key to your room." It was made of iron with a blue ribbon tied to it. Blue eyes flashed through my mind. I blinked hard and looked expectedly at Viht.

"And my room?" I said. Viht looked from me to Silas and rubbed his neck.

"Uh, you said you discussed our roles, Silas..." he said, awkwardly avoiding my gaze.

"What roles?" I said turning to Silas. The devium ignored me. The twins shrank in their seats and stared intently at us.

"I discussed them with the twins, yes," Silas said with a smirk. He was up to something. I felt a heat in my stomach and my nostrils flared. Viht sighed and stood.

"I don't want to be here for the carnage. The twins and I are going. Goodnight." He grabbed the brothers by their collars and hoisted them up the stairs.

"Care to explain?" I said. My jaw tensed and my eyes narrowed at Silas. He slowly finished his ale and stood. He paid the barmaid what we owed and then turned to me.

"I think we should discuss this when we have a little more privacy. Shall we?" He offered his hand to me. I ignored his hand and stood, glowering at him. He shrugged and went up the stairs.

Silas went to a door that had a blue stripe painted on it and unlocked it with the key. He extended his arm, and I went in, throwing my bags into a corner. The room was small. There was a chair by the window that overlooked a single bed pushed against the adjacent wall. I heard Silas slide the bolt to lock the door.

"Now will you please explain what 'roles' Viht referred to?" I said turning on the devium. He smiled at me.

"When we venture out of the forest, we can't have people knowing that we are rogues. We would be arrested immediately. So, we invent roles to play. It is quite simple really," he said haughtily. I set my jaw.

"I grasp the concept. So what is the role I'm playing? I feel that I should be enlightened of it." He grinned at me, and I had a sinking feeling in my stomach.

"You are Viht's daughter and Dax and Kaul's sister. You are a family travelling to the capital to scatter your mother's ashes at sea. It's a teary tale, I must say." I rolled my eyes.

"It's exceedingly melodramatic. And who are you in this charade?" Silas smirked devilishly.

"Why, I'm your husband, of course." My eyebrows rose at him.

"My husband?" His grinned widened.

"I couldn't be your brother. We look nothing alike." I scoffed at him and threw my arm in the air.

"I look nothing like the twins! Or even Viht! Was all of this your idea so we would be alone together?"

"Yes." I was shocked into silence by his bluntness. I hadn't expected him to admit it. My heartbeat skipped and I swallowed.

"And what were you expecting out of this arrangement?" I said carefully. He walked passed me and moved the chair from the wall. He positioned it directly in front of the bed. Silas motioned for me to sit in the chair. His face was so serious that I was afraid to decline. I lowered myself into the chair and he sat on the bed across from me.

"I would like you to practice what you did at the raid." My mouth fell open and I searched his face. There was no emotion in his features. He wore the face of the rogue leader. It wasn't a request that he made. It was a demand.

"What do you mean?" I said softly. He scowled at me.

"You know exactly what I mean. You have had plenty of time to overcome the shock of it. You created lightning in your hand, Specter. This is not something you can ignore." I looked away from him. His gaze was too intense, but he was right. I had been ignoring it.

"It's not at the top of my list at the moment..." He snorted.

"Your list be damned, Specter. You must learn to control it. Now." His tone shook me. I scowled back at him.

"And who are you to instruct me on this? You don't know any more about it than I do," I said sharply. We held each other's harsh glares for some time. Silas spoke first.

"That may be true, however, I am not the one who is afraid. Your fear is limiting you."

"My fear could be protecting me," I said. My tone was firm. There were too many unknown factors to just fall blindly into that power again. I was consumed by bloodlust when the energy manifested in my hand. I didn't want to go that far again. What if I hurt someone again? Someone who really didn't deserve it? Silas turned his head at me and furrowed his brow.

"Protecting you from what? Death? Power? What you have is a gift, Specter! And we don't even know what else you can do. Think of the things you could do if you had control of this! Think of the people you could help; of families you could save." My spine stiffened and I frowned at him. How could he say that to me? I searched his eyes. They twinkled with anticipation. He knew what his words meant to me. I stood and went to the door.

"Where are you going?" Silas said firmly as he stood. I jerked the hood back over my head.

"I need some air."

The streets were nearly deserted in the darkness. I passed by the brick buildings but didn't really look at them as I twisted the pendant. I knew that Silas was right. I needed to try to have some sort of control over the lightning but I didn't want to be overcome again. Dead bodies flooded my thoughts, and I could almost smell the burnt flesh again. I closed my eyes and tried to breath the images away. I paused my walk and looked up. The moon was nowhere to be found but the stars shone brightly in its absence. The stars used to fill me with wonder but at the moment, they just made me feel small.

"Excuse me, miss. Are you all right?" Did I know that voice? I turned and almost jumped. I had never been so thankful for the scarf around my head in all my life. His black armor made his form hard to see in the night, but his face was exposed.

Edwin.

I quickly glanced around and swallowed. I didn't see him anywhere. Maybe the prince wasn't here. My chest fell a bit. I looked back at Edwin.

"Um, yes. Yes, I'm fine. I-I couldn't sleep so I decided to take a walk." The knight held his helm under his arm. There was a sword belted around his waist and a dagger around his thigh. Stress lines framed his face around his eyes and on his forehead. I assumed there were more lines around his mouth, but his neat gray beard hid them. His wary eyes looked me over.

"The hour is very late, miss. You shouldn't be out alone. Please allow me to escort you home." My chest constricted.

"That really isn't necessary, sir. I'm staying at the inn. It isn't too far and I'm sure I can make it back on my own." I was amazed that I didn't stutter. I began to walk passed the knight, but he stepped further into my path.

"What a coincidence. I, too, am staying at the inn. We shall walk together." Clearly losing the argument, I nodded, and we headed back to the inn.

We didn't speak for some time. My thoughts were running mad in my head and worry filled my entire being. One thing kept pushing to the forefront of my mind, though: Prince Aleron. My mouth opened before I could stop it.

"What brings you to Capilious, if I may ask? Isn't your armor that of the Black Guard?" His dark eyes cut to me and examined me for a moment. It was as if he was trying to find something that made me a threat. Suspicion oozed from him.

"I am heading to the capital for her majesty's birthday celebration. I am to ensure that all is safe for the prince's arrival." My lungs released the breath I was unintentionally holding. He isn't here. I was relieved but my hand still gravitated to the mark, and I thought of blue eyes.

"And you, miss? Where are you traveling?"

"Hmm? Oh, I am also travelling to the capital. My mother passed and we are taking her ashes to the sea." I was so thankful for the stupid story. I would have to remember to thank Silas for it later.

"We?" Edwin said.

"My father, two brothers, and my husband." His eyebrow rose. It was the first change in expression he made.

"You're married?" I wanted to roll my eyes. Men.

"Yes. It was recent." Edwin seemed satisfied with my answer, and he nodded.

"Congratulations on your marriage and my condolences for your mother. Losing a mother can be... overwhelming." He had a far-away look in his eyes and I knew he wasn't really talking about me. Blue eyes flashed in my head then disappeared just as quickly.

"Thank you, sir," I said as we walked to the entrance of the inn. The knight held the door open for me and I nodded my thanks. I stepped inside and saw Silas sitting at one of the tables. His hands were clasped together with his elbows resting on his knees. His eyes were burning a hole through me but when the knight entered the room, the devium's expression quickly changed. The anger fell away and was replaced by worry. He almost fooled me. He stood quickly and rushed toward us. I narrowed my eyes at him.

"My dear! Thanks gods you're safe!" He swept me into his arms and then looked me over with convincing, however false, concern.

"This is your husband, I presume," Edwin said, straightening his shoulders. His heavy armor clinked as he moved.

"Yes, I am. Darling, where did you go? I awoke and you were gone. The innkeeper said that you left." Silas seemed unaffected by the knight's presence, but I knew that wasn't the case.

"And you did not think to go looking for your wife? It is your duty as husband to do so. She could have been seriously hurt and is fortunate that I found her first." Irritation flickered across Silas' face, but he masked it quickly. I looked down and bit my lip to avoid smiling. Silas pulled me closer to him.

"Yes, of course, you are right, sir. I was so overcome with worry that I didn't know what to do. I am grateful that you brought her back to me. I hope you will excuse us. It's been a stressful evening, and we must get some rest." His tone was civil but still a bit frazzled. He was putting on quite the show. The knight nodded.

"Of course, I wish you good evening and a safe journey to the capital."

"You as well," I said. Silas stiffened beside me but nodded. He quickly steered me back to our room and I glanced back at Edwin. Suspicion covered his features, but he said nothing as we turned the corner at the top of the stairs.

"Did you get enough air?" Silas said as he bolted the door. His tone was flat, but I sensed the edge in it. I removed my cloak and scarf, shaking my hair free of its tight coil.

"No," I said, removing the skirt that covered my breaches. I was still upset with him despite that he had a point. I wasn't ready to see the smug smirk that would ultimately follow my acknowledgement of that. I sat on the bed with my back to Silas and took off my boots. I heard Silas' boots fall to the floor as I rubbed my temples. I jumped up as the other side of mattress sank.

"What are you doing?" I said turning toward him. Silas merely stretched out on the bed and brushed his hair behind his head, leaving his pointed ears in full view. I looked at the rest of him and my cheeks flushed. His bare chest glimmered in the candlelight.

"Trying to go to sleep," he said closing his eyes. I looked up at the ceiling to keep from staring at his slender, toned form.

"Could you put on a shirt?" I said turning away.

"I couldn't." I ground my teeth together. I knew he was smirking at me. I snatched the blanket and a pillow from the bed and made a pallet for myself on the floor. I heard the bed shift.

"What are you doing?" he said. I looked over my shoulder at him. He lay on his side propped up on an elbow and his head rested in his hand. Amusement glittered in his eyes.

"Trying to go to sleep," I said sharply.

"The bed is more comfortable."

"I'm sure it is."

"There is plenty of space for the both of us," he said lightly. I snickered and straightened the blanket on the floor.

"I'm not so sure of that."

"Allow me to show you." I felt his arm snake around me and yank me up onto the bed. I tried to scramble up, but his arm was around my waist, holding me down.

"Let go of me! You're being ridiculous!" I hissed at him. He grabbed my wrists and pinned them down as he pressed his weight on top of me. I went very still, and my heart hammered. His face was smug in the green light of my eyes as he looked down at me.

"What exactly do you think are my intentions? I only wish for you to be comfortable. It seems that you are the one being ridiculous." I scowled at him and pushed against him, but he didn't budge.

"We both know that your intentions are never so straight-forward. Now let me up." He leaned his head to the side and raised a brow.

"You should be more than capable of letting yourself up, Specter. Perhaps you are exactly where you want to be." I narrowed my eyes at him but my face flushed in spite of me.

"I won't fall for your antics, devium. I won't let you bait me. Let me up."

"It's Silas, remember? Is it because you are still upset with me about our conversation earlier? Is that why you are not in a better mood?" The green light illuminating his face brightened as I scowled at him, and he grinned.

"Ah, I see. That is a shame. I have no reason to apologize especially when it is your fear and your pride that is the problem." I scoffed at him and reeled.

"My fear and my pride?" My voice raised slightly. Silas was even more amused.

"Yes. You're too afraid of the unknown and you're too proud to admit that I'm right." My mouth made a hard line, and I huffed out the air in my chest. He was right. I knew that but I hated how smug he was about it and how he used words to purposefully try to manipulate me. I hated how he made my body feel and I hated that I couldn't do anything about it. I hated that he was pinning me to a bed, and I was helpless. The anger rushed through me, and I felt the energy quickly follow it.

"Get. Off. Of. Me." Silas merely grinned at me. My nostrils flared and I pushed against him. His body raised a bit, but he straddled my waist and pushed down harder. He watched me intently. It was maddening. I ground my teeth and pushed again but he didn't move.

"Surely you can do better than that," he said smirking. Why did he do this to me? He loved to see me so riled up and I just couldn't stop myself from letting him do it. I was as angry with myself as I was with him. I just wanted to get his arrogant face away from me. There was another rush of power, and my hands began to tingle. Silas glanced at my hands and a cautious excitement filled his voice.

"Just a little more, Specter," he whispered. I felt stupid and angry. I was just some puzzle to him. A toy that had many tricks he had yet to discover. I was just a spectacle. I wanted to leave. Now.

Unlike the raid, my head was clear of the mind-hazing darkness. I concentrated on the power in my veins and followed it to its source. From the tips of my fingers and toes, through my arms and legs, and into my torso. It felt like a cold star at the center of my chest, but it was deeper than that. It was a part of my soul. It pulsed with life and radiated power. I called on it and, after a moment, it answered tentatively.

Crackling energy pooled in my hands, and I fought to keep it there. Silas looked overjoyed.

"Beautiful..." he said breathlessly. I glowered at him and pushed him away while he was distracted. He fell beside me on the bed. I quickly got up and looked at my hands. The green lightning cast an eerie glow over the room. My hands shook with exertion and my brow creased. My strength gave out and the energy faded away. I panted and tried to keep myself standing. I looked at Silas, who now stood, and almost sneered at his awestruck demeanor.

"Happy now?" I said.

"Yes... for now." My hands became fists, but I just shrugged passed him and crawled into bed. I pulled the blanket from the floor over me as exhaustion hit me. I sensed Silas move back toward the bed.

"You touch this bed, and I will burn you alive." Silas just chuckled as he lay on the floor.

Chapter 15: Complications

Silas woke me when it was nearly midday. He informed me that we were leaving soon since they had gathered up supplies that morning. He left saying that they would wait for me downstairs for one last meal before starting out again.

My body was sluggish and still wanted sleep, but I managed to get up. I stretched my arms high and then ran my hands through my hair. I used the lightning last night... without killing anyone. The thought made me smile despite my weariness. I felt so proud and, more importantly, hopeful. I looked at my hands and took a deep breath. I closed my eyes and began to reach down but my stomach roared instead. I winced. Maybe some food first...

I wrapped the skirt around my waist then coiled and covered my hair. After grabbing my bags, I opened the door and froze. Spice and books lingered in air. I forced my lungs to breathe, causing the aroma to make me dizzy. Why was he here? Didn't Edwin imply that he wasn't?

I focused on the sounds, movements, and smells of the hallway and downstairs. I felt the chill rush through me as my senses heightened. The rogues were at a table near the staircase. I concentrated harder and tried to feel out Edwin and the prince by their voices and their smells. They weren't upstairs; I caught the strange spice smell coming from downstairs, but I couldn't pinpoint the source. It was lost among the vast number of people that filled the inn. I took a moment to steel myself. It was crowded downstairs, and the prince was bound to be surrounded by guards. He wouldn't notice me. I paused. What would the prince be doing staying in a crowded inn with the common people? He should have stayed with the ambassador of Feldan, or at the very least a nobleman... My brows raised. He had disguised himself in Ameris. Maybe he did that now.

I couldn't hide in the room forever. I pulled my hood low and tried to seem as insignificant as possible as I descended the stairs. I slumped my shoulders and stared at the floor. I found the rogues without looking up. I sat by Silas and across from the twins with Viht at the head of the table. I kept my eyes on the gnarled wood. I didn't want to risk meeting the prince's gaze. I wasn't sure what I would do if I did.

"Bout time, sis," Kaul said. He wore a mischievous smile.

"I was about to eat your portion, sister!" Dax said and winked. He slid a bowl of soup and a chunk of bread toward me. I nodded absently. My senses strained as I tried to find Prince Aleron through the din of the patrons. My hunger had vanished, so I pushed the soup around with my spoon. The rogues casually chatted but I didn't pay attention to them. My ears perked and my heart jumped when I finally heard Edwin's hushed tone.

"We should leave soon, sire. We have lost enough daylight as it is." His voice was careful but there was a hint of a reprimand in it.

"Prepare the horses," Prince Aleron said. His voice was as stern as I remembered. It still had that frightful edge to it, but it wasn't as terrifying as I remembered it. My eyes darted in their direction before I could stop them. I peered between Dax's and Kaul's shoulders to a table in the back corner of the inn. There were two other men with the prince and knight that rose from the table at the order. Edwin was again in his full metal armor, but the prince was dressed simply in a Black Guard uniform like the other two men. There was dark stubble on his square jaw. His black hair was pulled back with thin braids running away from each of his temples, a warrior's style, leaving his piercing eyes in full view. I shivered. They were just as I remembered them. He looked so ruggedly handsome that my breath caught just a bit.

"I was drawn here, Edwin. I've told you that it's hard to explain..." Aleron's voice had lost most of its authority. It took me by surprise. He almost sounded... vulnerable.

"And I've told you that you shouldn't listen to those feelings. More often than not, the outcome is not good. Use your head." I nearly smiled. He sounded just like Aunt Prudence. The prince shook his head and pulled his sleeve back. He looked at his mark.

"You're probably right... I just... I can't get her out of my mind." His tone wasn't angry but more dumbfounded. I bit my lip to hide my smile. I told myself I was glad because he wasn't infuriated and that maybe meant he didn't want me executed. Did it really matter why my heart fluttered at his words?

"Because she cursed you, sire." Aleron shook his head slowly.

"I don't believe she did." He ran his thumb over his mark, and it was like he touched my own. I shivered violently and felt Silas turn to me.

"Just a chill," I said. As soon as the words left my mouth, Prince Aleron stiffened.

"What is it?" Edwin said reaching for his sword. I looked down into my bowl of soup and tried to eat again. I could feel Aleron searching the room. My heart raced in my ears, and I tried to keep my breathing even. Silas reached his arm around me.

"Is that better?" I nodded at the table and tried to casually eat soup. It was hard to swallow around the lump in my throat. What would I do if he found me? I couldn't surrender but I didn't want to put Viht, Dax, Kaul, and Silas in jeopardy. Did I have time to run? But I didn't know where I was going and what could I do alone really? Protect myself, yes, but function in society?

"She's here, Edwin."

My heart pounded in my ears and the air left the room. My hands turned to fists as I chanted to myself: Stay calm. Stay calm. Stay calm. I felt the cold whirling like a storm within me. My hands shook lightly as

I held back the lightning. I felt a hot hand lay over my fist, covering up the beginnings of the soft green glow.

"I think it is time we go," Silas said coolly. The rogues stood and Silas hoisted me up with them. Dax and Kaul unknowingly stood between me and the prince. I could feel the tension radiating from him. How did he know I was there? Did he really hear me? Silas wrapped his arm around me and steered me to the exit.

"Calm down," he whispered. I stared at the floor and focused on breathing. I could still feel Aleron searching, and it made me shudder again. I just have to get outside. I'll be better once I'm outside. I forced myself not to look back as we made for the door.

"Care to explain what happened, Specter?" Silas said once Feldan was out of sight. Aleron and his men hadn't followed, and we had no issue leaving the city. Silas had forced us into a quick pace until the place was long gone.

My mind scrambled as I twirled my pendant. I couldn't tell them about Prince Aleron. The very thought made my stomach turn.

"I've been on edge since last night," I said. The twins elbowed each other.

"'Last night?'" Dax said smirking.

"What happened last night?" the brothers said together. Viht rolled his eyes at them as I did.

"She accessed the sparks without provocation. Or at least without bloody provocation," Silas said. His eyes cut to mine slyly, but his tone was even.

"Perhaps you've a leak in the barrel," Viht said. The statement made me pause.

"What do you mean?" I said.

"Forcing a barrel open will sometimes damage it and then cause a leak. Perhaps without the right reasons for using your power and forcing it, you caused some damage and have, well, a leak." I understood what he meant but it didn't really sound right, despite that, the power wasn't trying to flow out of me. It just seemed more willing now that I had reached out to it, like it wanted to let me control it.

I held out my hand and gently pulled at the force inside. It did take some concentration, but it wasn't nearly as strenuous as the previous night. I scowled at my palm and finally small sparks appeared.

"I'm not sure that a leak would stop and go on command," I said, letting the sparks fizzle out.

"Just be sure to have a better handle on the 'stop and go' by the time we get to Onisk. It is a large city, second to Caneesho. There may be more people to hide among but there are many more soldiers. I would hate to see you arrested as a caster. It would certainly be inconvenient," Silas said with a smirk. I cut my eyes at him but said nothing.

I looked at my hands again as the lightning came easier this time. It rippled up and danced through my fingers. My pride was dampened. I should have done this on my own, but I was too afraid. I narrowed my eyes. I said that I would no longer be afraid. The lightning cracked as it circled my hands. I didn't have a reason to be afraid anymore, right?

The next three days went by without mishap. I practiced manipulating the lightning when we were alone on the road, which grew more difficult the closer we got to Onisk. Silas always watched me intently but never critiqued or teased me. I assumed he took my threat in Feldan to heart, but I could feel his high expectations like a weight on my chest.

Thankfully, the twins were much more light-hearted. They joked and talked about humorous scenarios like what if the sky was green and grass was blue. They would also sing. Some songs were better than others and most of them were quite crude. When the twins weren't singing, Viht told strange stories about the sea. Before he was a rogue, he was a sailor on the western coast. He told of spider-like creatures clad in armor that he would catch and boil for dinner. My nose wrinkled.

"You ate spiders?" I said cringing. Viht's shoulders shook as he laughed. We sat around a small fire to camp for the night. Viht told of how beautiful the ocean was from the smell to the colors. It could be terrible too. The lovely shades of blue and white could quickly turn purple and black and ravenous. There were ships that could hold one hundred men that were swallowed by waves and were never seen again. I couldn't wrap my head around the concept of how large it really was.

"No one knows how far it goes, neither deep nor wide. It is truly a sight to see. It will be hard to leave it again." Viht sighed as he stoked the fire.

"We will see it?" I said. Silas answered.

"Yes. Caneesho is bordered by the ocean. It should be warm enough to swim in by the time we get there." I looked at Silas intently.

"How did you come to be here?" I said softly. There was a brief pause around the fire. I broke the rogues' unspoken rule: Don't pry into another's past. Silas stared into the fire, but it was Viht who answered me.

"A sickness told hold of my village. It was strange. The weather was so mild that any illness was rare but this one swept through so quickly and violently; we were blindsided... Half of the people perished, including my wife and two daughters... After they were buried, I left. My girls loved the ocean so much that I never wanted to see the crystal waters again." My heart ached for him, and I felt terrible for being the cause of remembering such awful memories.

"Viht, I'm so sorry," I said softly. He gave me a small smile and sighed.

"It was a long time ago. I have grown older and wiser too, I hope. I think seeing the sea will do my soul good."

"Maybe you'll feel them there," Kaul said hopefully.

"Our grandmother always said that," Dax said.

"The spirit lingers where love is," they finished. I hadn't seen them so sincere since they day I awoke tied up at their camp. Viht smiled warmly at them and began to settle into his bedroll.

"I hope so, boys."

Silence fell on us as we all retreated to our own thoughts. I had been so consumed by my own grief and my own problems that I never considered what they had gone through. Silas had told me that all the people of Rogue City had fled their normal lives for some reason. I never once wondered what reasons those were. I looked at Viht in a new light. It made so much more sense how he took the twins under his wing and how naturally fatherly he was. It was painful to know that he had been a father once but wasn't any longer. His story made me wonder what had happened to the twins. How had they come to Rogue City? I wanted to ask but there was enough sadness in the air for one evening.

"When will we arrive in Onisk?" I said breaking the silence.

"If we leave at first light, we should arrive before the city gates close for the evening. If not, we will have to sleep in the dirt another night," Silas said sharply. We all took the hint.

Dax doused the fire and the rogues turned in while I sat up to take the first watch.

I looked at my hands as the sparks appeared on my palms before I could really think about them. The power was buzzing coldly in my limbs. The feeling had intensified the more I summoned the sparks. It was suspiciously simple too, almost like it was just waiting for me to accept it. Truthfully, I wasn't afraid of the lightning I created anymore. At least, I wasn't afraid of the small dancing sparks in my palms. The green glowing energy was beautiful, and it twirled and crackled in the night. I still wasn't sure about the stronger violent kind that charred skin and took lives. I took a deep breath and held the orb of light close. Small steps and then I could control it. Small steps.

We left at dawn and saw the gates of Onisk just before evening. A towering stone wall stretched around the entire city, and I was awed by it. I had never seen such giant walls. Two tall wooden doors stood open but there were two guards attending them. They may have been the only ones on the ground but there were teams of soldiers atop the walls with crossbows waiting for the smallest sign of trouble. The number of soldiers surprised me. Silas said that there would be more soldiers here, but he didn't prepare us for this.

Kaul let out a low whistle.

"Remember your roles," Silas said quietly as Viht took the lead. I pulled my hood lower and tried not to meet any of the guards' eyes.

"Good evening," Viht called to the soldiers as we neared them.

"State your business," one of them said as he raised a hand at us. We stopped our horses, and they looked us over. A slight strain was in Viht's voice.

"My children and I are traveling to the coast to scatter my wife's ashes at sea." My heart fell a little as I wondered just how much of the tension in his voice was an act.

"These are all your children?" the guard said skeptically. Viht nodded and pointed us out.

"My two sons and my daughter and her husband. We only wish to rest for a night or two and gather supplies." I could feel the guards studying us. Were we really so suspicious?

"Show me the ashes." My heart stopped once the confusion faded away. Why wouldn't they believe us? I sensed the rogues stiffen.

"Excuse me?" Viht said. The sharpness of his voice hid any panic that he may have felt. The guard stepped forward.

"You want access to the city; you'll show me the ashes. Can't be too careful nowadays." What kind of a city is this? It had to be a military base. Why would Silas have us come here?

"You insult us!" Kaul said.

"Disrespecting our mother like that!" Dax said. The guard moved his hand to the sword at his hip.

"Then move along." My shoulders sagged. I was looking forward to a bed again. My legs and rear were weary from so much riding, enhanced strength or not.

"Father," Silas said, "we need true rest. And Mother wouldn't have missed the opportunity to prove someone wrong." We all glanced at the devium. I narrowed my eyes at him. What was he playing at? He and Viht shared a look and Viht eventually nodded.

"No, she wouldn't have. Go on." Silas reached into his bag and withdrew a simple corked jar. He held it out to the guard, but he shook his head and scowled back at Silas.

"I'm not taking anything from you. You've got some look in your eye... Give it to the woman to bring to me." Silas just shrugged and extended the jar toward me. I stared at it, trying to understand what he was doing. Finally, I took a deep breath and dismounted, jar in hand. Stay calm. Stay calm. Stay calm. All I could do was trust him.

I walked to the guard with my head down. I prayed that whatever was really in this jar would pacify the skeptical soldiers. I pulled away the cork and the guard peered in. I couldn't help but glance at the contents too.

Ashes?

"Now that wasn't so hard was it?" the guard said. He raised his arm and the archers relaxed. I returned the jar to Silas. Viht tried to look annoyed, but his chest fell in relief.

"Hmm. Could you point us to the nearest inn? A hospitable one would be preferable." The guard's brow creased but he tilted his head back.

"The Horsetail is just at the end of the main street. Can't miss it. City curfew is at nightfall. Best hurry, you're running out of time. Violators of curfew are arrested."

Viht glared at him as we rode through the gates but none of the rogues said anything more.

"What exactly was in that jar, Silas?" Viht asked once we were out of earshot of the guards. Silas shrugged.

"Ashes from our campfires. It was probable that someone would want proof of our story at some point. It would have been foolish to think otherwise." I rolled my eyes at his arrogant tone. The others just nodded in agreement.

The guard wasn't exaggerating when he said we couldn't miss the Horsetail. The inn was twice as big as the Blue Boot. Viht and the twins took the horses to the stable and Silas and I went in. The inside was just as surprising. There were much more gambling tables and scantily clad women walked the floor or sat on the laps of very surly men. One of the underdressed women approached us with swaying hips. She looked over Silas but then turned to me.

"And how may I help you, sweet? We don't see many... dignified people in here." I felt my heart skip under her gaze. Silas just looked her over with mild curiosity.

"Just two rooms, if you please," I said. Her dark kohl-lined eyes seem to peer into my soul.

"Two? And I was hoping the three of us could have some fun..."

My eyes went wide, and I was at a complete loss for words. Silas chuckled at my shock and his arm slid around my waist.

"As interesting as your proposition sounds, my wife is a bit... reserved. One room for my wife and I and I suppose you'll have to ask the others if they need separate rooms." I looked between them with disbelief. The woman shrugged lightly.

"I'll get you some rooms. In the meantime, find a table and I'll bring you some food." After looking over me again with a smile, she turned away and went to the bar. Silas guided me to a table large enough for all of us and sat.

"We can't stay here," I whispered harshly. Silas lifted a brow and leaned back in his chair.

"Why is that?" I scowled at his smirk and felt my face go hot.

"This is not funny, Silas." His eyes twinkled at the sound of his name, and he stretched his arms behind his head.

"Oh, but it truly is."

"This place is perfect," the twins said with beaming smiles as the three rogues walked in. I gaped at them and looked to Viht for support. I shook my head in disbelief when I saw his gaze lingering on some of the pretty ladies in the room. I rolled my eyes at them. Cold food and warm ale arrived shortly after and, however underwhelming, it was a welcomed distraction from my friends.

I found myself looking around the inn as I ate. The inn itself was grand or was at one time at least. The walls were lined with ornately designed paper but there were tears in some places that looked fresh. The furniture was made of glossy wood and some pieces were even embellished with silver and gold leaf but some of that was missing too. Our cups were goblets, and the plates were metal instead of wood. The patrons clearly didn't belong here. Nearly every man wore some sort of armor and carried a weapon. This was a warrior's den with the gambling, women, and plenty of ale. It made sense now why the guard at the gate directed us here. I mumbled a curse. There was something wrong here. There were so many soldiers around the wall and then the strict curfew and now there's an extravagant inn full of dastardly warriors. Onisk couldn't be a military fortress. Aside from the inn, there were businesses lining both sides of the street we rode down. Bakeries, dress makers, and jewelers weren't found in forts. I would speak to Silas about it later. He must have noticed too.

"The keys to your rooms, my dears." The woman from earlier appeared at the end of the table. She threw her lush brown hair over her shoulder and tilted her head to expose even more tanned skin. She drifted around the table like a dark ghostly vision. She was beautiful, with a curvy body and full dark lips. She had a look in her light eyes that held a forbidden invitation. Her hand slid across the twins' shoulders and then stopped on Viht's, slipping a key into his breast pocket. The twins stared at her with glossy eyes and Viht's face flushed. I even felt heat rush to my cheeks. She caught my gaze and gave me a small smile. My face was on fire, but I couldn't look away. She leaned over the table between Viht and Kaul and slowly slid the other key to me. The neck of her shirt dipped low, only being held up by a corset that was threatening to burst open at the top.

"If you get to feeling a bit less... reserved, my name's Jaylee." Her voice was low as her gaze bore through me. I swallowed and gingerly took the key from her. Jaylee winked at me as she stood.

"Gentlemen. Lady." She made a small curtesy and swayed away. I couldn't help but watch her go; the whole table did, with the exception of Silas. The devium studied me with an amused expression. My chest tightened and my face burned.

"She's gorgeous," Kaul said with a sigh.

"Stunning," Dax agreed and propped his chin on his fist.

"She must make a fortune," Viht said. The twins nodded absently.

"I didn't realize you enjoyed the company of women," Silas said, still looking at me. I widened my eyes at him.

"I don't," I said firmly. The twins snorted.

"You'd be crazy not to enjoy the company of that woman," Dax said as Kaul nodded. I shook my head and stood, grabbing my bags.

"I'm going to bed. Spare me any details that you may want to share in the morning."

I went up the stairs and found the room with the painted door that matched the gold ribbon on the key. Much like the main room downstairs, this room showed signs of past glamor. There was a large bed with thick blankets and pillows that had some rips and tears in them. The room also had a small table to one side with two chairs and a wardrobe and dressing screen in the corner. I put my bags in the wardrobe and readied for bed.

I sank into the feather mattress and nearly melted to sleep.

Chapter 16: Onisk

I awoke before Silas, who had slept dutifully on the floor. I snickered to myself and then my stomach rumbled. We had been travelling hard for the past few days and I really needed a hearty meal with all the practice I had been doing. After putting on my skirt, scarf, and cloak, I took my purse of coins that was my share from the raid and went downstairs.

There were a few men passed out in the main room, some on the floor and some on tables, despite it being morning. The innkeeper stood at the bar trying to clean up a spill on the counter. I cautiously stepped over an unconscious body and went over to the bar. The innkeeper was simply dressed and looked quite plain except for the flair of his full mustache.

"Excuse me, do you serve any kind of breakfast?" The man snorted without looking up.

"Not anymore. Can't afford to keep a cook all day long. Try the bakery down the street. They still open up at this hour, I think." I tried not to sound annoyed as I thanked him. I stiffened as the smell of ale fell on my cheek. I tried not to snarl at the drunkard that leaned against the bar next to me.

"I don't remember seeing you last night. Where were you hiding?" His words slurred and he swayed despite having the counter for support. I tried to turn away from him and just walk away but I sensed him reach for my shoulder. I knocked his hand away without turning.

"Don't touch me," I said but he began to reach again. I glanced at him as his face contorted to a sneer.

"You can't walk away from me, wench! Do you know who I am?"

The way he looked at me made my skin crawl and my stomach pitch. I felt my temper flare and with it came the darkness that I had almost forgotten about. The shadow raced through me and the thought of breaking his bones flashed through my mind.

"I really don't care who you are," I said.

Before I could stop myself, I spun around, batted his hand away, and slammed his head onto the counter. I felt his nose give way under the force and I smiled. He fell to the floor in a heap, matching the rest of the men in the room. My eyes caught the few spots of blood on the counter before the metallic odor made its way to my nose. My body tingled and my head felt light.

I heard a gasp from the stairs. Jaylee stood there, eyes wide with shock. Only then did I realize that my mark burned. I took a step back and tucked a stray curl back under the scarf. The innkeeper had pressed himself against the wall and watched me with wide eyes. I rubbed at my arm and felt my face start to flush. I hoped that it was from embarrassment, but I knew it was really from the darkness. My head was still light, and my arm burned more. I needed to get out of there. I felt Jaylee's gaze follow me as I sped out the door.

I roamed the streets of Onisk until my head cleared and the ache in my arm dissipated. I couldn't stop replaying the scene in my head. Why had the darkness taken over then? That man hadn't done anything to me. Why now? My mind raced and my chest felt tight. I started to think that I had overcome it, but I was clearly wrong.

I wrapped my arms around me and tried not to think. The smell of sweet bread drifted on the air, and I found myself before a bakery. Maybe this was the one that innkeeper referred to. Beautiful loaves, wreaths, and rolls of bread were displayed in a shop window, all delicately decorated with icing. Henry had always said that a good dessert could cure anything. I took a deep breath and went inside.

I watched a baker pull fresh sweet buns from the oven and my mouth watered. I purchased two and nearly inhaled them. I licked the stickiness from my fingers and the worry about the darkness faded away, at least for the moment. The bread was indeed the healing kind. The bakers were ecstatic when I bought the rest of the tray to take back to the rogues. Viht was going to love them. He had quite the spot for sweets and then I could go back to my secluded room in the inn and, more importantly, away from innocent people. I snatched another bun from the sack.

I went in the Horsetail and saw Viht and the twins sitting at a table, tankards already in their hands.

"Early start?" I said. Dax and Kaul winced and Viht rubbed his head.

"Not so loud," the twins whispered and took begrudging sips of ale. I bit my lip to hide my smile.

"Drinking the drunk away, then," I said, raising my voice. They all moaned and covered their ears. I laughed and sat the sack of rolls on the table. Viht reached for the bag first.

"You're an angel, my girl," Viht said and shoved an entire roll in his mouth. I shook my head at him but smiled. I knew he would like them.

"Where is Silas?" The twins fought the sack from Viht, and they vaguely pointed toward the door.

"Gathering supplies," Dax said.

"But we aren't leaving until tomorrow," Kaul said. I furrowed my brow. We only had five days until the attack in Caneesho. It didn't make sense to stay here for long.

"Did he say why?" The three men shifted and wouldn't meet my eyes. Finally, Kaul, red faced, elbowed Dax. Dax rolled his eyes and answered.

"He said that we needed to not be distracted in the capital, so we needed to satisfy-" I raised my hand to stop him and began to step away.

"I don't want to hear anymore. I understand. I'll be in my room." I turned to go back to the stairs but then I heard the loud sounds of the courtesans conducting business. Blushing, I turned on my heel and walked toward the door as the rogues laughed.

Even though the rogues said Silas was taking care of supplies, I went ahead and restocked my own food stash. It was quicker and simpler than I expected. The store owners seemed eager to sell to me, more so than in Ameris, but there was something forced about their actions. Their smiles were a bit too wide, and their tones were a bit too cheerful, and their eyes were uneasy. Was the baker's just as strange? I couldn't remember. I was too preoccupied to notice. The people in the streets were just as peculiar. They seemed to avoid coming anywhere near my path, an act that was common in Ameris where everyone thought I was a caster. Onisk had no reason to fear me as far as I knew. Still, their gazes would find the ground and all conversations ceased until they passed me. It was probably for the best, given what happened this morning. Then I noticed that it wasn't just directed toward me. The different groups of people did it to each other too. It was like all interactions must be avoided. How odd...

I stopped in front of a dress shop, distracted by color. A pink gown was on a mannequin in a window. Bows, ribbons, and lace adorned the gown, and its skirt was full and stiff. The corseted bodice was pulled so tightly that I couldn't imagine it fitting a living person. It was pretty but looked uncomfortable to say the least. I sensed someone approaching, but I didn't turn. Holding my necklace, I prayed that they would pass by or go into the shop. I didn't want another incident like at morning.

"Why, hello, miss." A lavishly dressed man stood next to me. His dark purple shirt and coat embroidered with gold did not distract from his rounded stomach, nor did his oversized purple hat. His voice had a confident drawl to it and his eyes looked me up and down. Darkness started to swirl within me, and I tried to focus on the growing pain in my arm. I refrained from scowling, but I couldn't just ignore him or walk away. He was obviously wealthy. Wealthy usually meant powerful and powerful meant influence. I turned to him and gave him a small curtsy.

"Hello," I said, politely. He smiled at me, but his searching eyes weren't friendly. My skin crawled under his gaze and power buzzed through my veins.

"You must be a traveler, otherwise our paths would have crossed long ago. What is your name, my dear?" My panic was a great distraction from the stirring darkness. A name? I didn't have a name to give him. My throat went dry as I scrambled for something to call myself. I said the first name that came to mind, and it seemed to calm me a bit.

"Prudence," I said. He raised a brow but took my hand and brought it to his lips.

"I do hope that name is not a fitting one, Prudence. I am Sir Goy Farth, Royal Ambassador of Onisk. It is a pleasure to meet you."

"Ambassador?" I said, genuinely surprised. I clung to the different emotion. Anything to keep me from giving in to the sinister pull. Sir Farth gave me a satisfied smile.

"Yes. Impressive, isn't it, that one as young as I should have earned such a prestigious position?"

"Quite," I said, flatly. Entitlement radiated from Sir Farth, and it was stifling. He still held my hand.

"What brings you to Onisk? I do hope you plan to stay for some time." I tried to pull my hand away, but he held firm. There was a hunger in his eyes that made my other hand clench to a fist beneath my cloak.

"I am traveling to the coast to spread my mother's ashes at sea." He frowned but there was no sympathy in it. He took the opportunity to step closer and I impulsively leaned back.

"How sad. You must have endured much suffering: The loss of your mother forcing you to travel a grueling journey across the kingdom, risking rogue attacks, vagabonds, and scoundrels and all alone." He raised a hand to brush my face, but I quickly stepped back, more for his sake than mine.

"I'm not alone. My father, brothers, and husband are with me." Sir Farth's shoulders slumped a bit and he looked annoyed. Images of him crumpled at my feet flew through my mind. Maybe just a bloody lip or a broken finger would be all right...

"Father, brothers, and husband? I must say, it is shameful for you to already have a husband when you are so young and beautiful," he said stepping closer to me again.

"I beg to differ." Silas' flat, arrogant tone usually irritated me but, at that moment, I couldn't have been more relieved. I moved away from Sir Farth and stood beside Silas, whose arm slipped around my waist as I introduced them.

"Sir Farth, this is my husband, Silas. Husband, this is the Royal Ambassador of Onisk, Sir Goy Farth." My voice was strained, and Silas glanced at me before he slightly bowed his head to Sir Farth. Somehow he still managed to look down his nose at the ambassador. Sir Farth just smiled at Silas as he straightened his purple coat over his girth.

"I meant no offense, on the contrary, I gave only a sincere compliment to Prudence." Silas raised his brow, and I could see the confusion on his face. He paused briefly before finally asking.

"Prudence?" he said.

"Yes, husband?" I stared hard at him and hoped he understood. After a moment, he smirked at me.

"You really must stop bewitching people, Prudence. It taxes me beyond measure."

"I'm sorry, husband," I said, bowing my head dutifully.

"Sir Farth, if you would excuse us. We must rest before getting back to the road. We have quite the journey ahead of us." Silas turned away without waiting for Sir Farth to respond. I went to follow him, but the ambassador grabbed my elbow. I felt his breath on my cheek, and he pushed a card into my hand.

"I'm having a party at my estate this evening. I would love for you to attend, dear Prudence, but please, do not bring your husband."

I caught up with Silas and we started back to the Horsetail. He commented on my terrible luck: First the Rokellian soldier and then the Onisk ambassador. Even though he smirked at me, I could see that he was a little unnerved. Despite our efforts, I still attracted attention. I hoped that he wouldn't find out about the drunk I knocked out that morning. I also hoped he didn't notice my struggle with the ambassador. Then again, maybe I should confide in him. I may not agree with his methods, but he did help push me to control the lightning. I shook my head. No, I wouldn't tell Silas. He needed to believe that I was in control.

"Was your day productive?" I said, changing the subject.

"Quite. The people here seem strange though. Guarded. I don't remember Onisk being in such a state of disrepair, either."

"You've been here before?" Silas' face looked harder than it ever had before. Anger flashed through his eyes.

"Yes, a long time ago... Onisk was the city of the arts. It was known for its music festivals and plays and unique artisan goods. It was quite the tourist city, but it is not that anymore."

His rigid tone caught me off guard. What happened here? Just how did Silas know so much about the country? The deviums were driven out nearly thirty years ago. He would have been a small child then.

"Silas," I said, catching his attention immediately. His head turned to look at me and his pace slowed.

"Yes?" His yellow green eyes bore into mine.

"How do you know so much about the kingdom? You must have been very small when your... family left. How did you even come back? Why did you?" His expression grew darker. His steps quickened as he turned away from me.

"I don't wish to discuss my past with you. Do not ask me about it again." His cold, biting tone hit me like a blow. Not with me? What was that supposed to mean? I knew that our relationship was strange and tense sometimes, but I thought it had at least grown. He knew about my mark, my family's death, and we had shared... affections. I narrowed my eyes at his back and resentment overcame me. I guess I was right to not tell him about the darkness after all.

The sun was about to set when we arrived at the Horsetail. The inn was full of people and their loud voices rolled out into the street as we opened the door. Viht, Dax, and Kaul were already through more than a few pitchers of ale when Silas and I found them.

"Aye! You're back!" Viht said, raising his cup.

"We missed you!" the twins said. I raised my brow at them. Each brother had a woman sitting on his lap, holding a pitcher of ale to refill his cup when it was too low.

"I doubt that very much," I said, shortly. The rogues didn't notice my harsh tone, but I did. My shoulders were tense with anger and dejection. I cut my eyes at Silas, but he didn't look at me. I tightened my fists against the chill that began to creep into them. I closed my eyes and tried to calm down. My hood was suddenly pulled back and I felt a light hand unclasp my cloak.

"Allow me," Jaylee said softly into my ear. My body tensed even further as she pulled the cloak from my shoulders. I stood perfectly still and tried to measure my breathing. Stay calm. Stay calm. Stay calm. "I took the liberty of having a private bath drawn for you in your room. Good thing too... You seem on edge."

Her expression seemed sincere and a little guarded and I wondered if she referred to my current stance or to earlier that morning. I did need to relax, and baths had helped before.

"A private bath?" I said watching her closely. She smirked at me and handed me my cloak.

"Of course." She smiled again but I couldn't get a grasp on whether or not she was being truthful.

"Sit down, Silas! You have some catching up to do! Let the girl have her wash and then she can drink us under the table!" Viht clapped Silas on the back and the twins shoved their drinks in his hands. Silas glanced at me with a smirk and sat.

"I suppose you're right. We'll see you later, Fairest?" I frowned back at him and narrowed my eyes. I had no intention of drinking with them. I was agitated with Silas but some of it spilled over onto Viht and the twins too. This wasn't Lily's. We were on a mission to possibly save all of Capilious, and they wanted to waste time in an inn-turned-brothel.

"I think I'll just stay in my room for the evening. I wouldn't want to ruin all the fun. Goodnight." I turned and went up the stairs before they could stop me, if they even noticed my absence.

After washing the filth from my body and fighting with my knotted hair for what seemed like hours, I sat soaking in the tub and breathing in the smell of lavender-seeped water. My muscles relaxed and I sank lower in the tub. My mind was blissfully blank for the first time in a very long time. I was more than content to stay in the steaming water until it got cold. I closed my eyes and sighed.

"I thought you would enjoy the bath." I nearly startled out of the tub. My eyes snapped open, and my arms covered my body. Jaylee slid the bolt back to the locked position.

"By the gods! How did you get in here?" My voice was nearly a shriek. I had locked the door, so I wasn't expecting anyone to enter. She smirked and held up a key.

"A master key. It's just a precaution of the business. Can't have guests locking girls away." She leaned against the door and studied my face as she crossed her arms over her chest.

"I must say, you're not what I imagined... You going to stay in there all night?" Jaylee said. I was still dumbfounded at her presence. My knees were drawn up and my arms covered my chest. She laughed and looked away from me.

"I didn't expect you to be so modest either. Go ahead, I won't look." I waited a moment but when she didn't move, I jumped from the tub and wrapped a towel around me. I considered grabbing a dagger, but I really didn't think this woman was a threat. Not at the moment at least.

"Why are you here?" I said with as much confidence as I could muster. When she met my eyes, her composure fell. Fear and hope filled her eyes. She suddenly seemed much younger.

"You're the Specter, aren't you?" My mouth went dry. How did she know? How could she tell? My heart dropped as I remembered that morning. She saw everything. She moved closer to me but stopped short.

"Please, tell me that it's you. This morning when I saw what you did to that man and your eyes... At first I told myself that I imagined it, but I have never seen anything like them... And now your hair... Don't tell me I'm wrong." Her voice was filled with desperation. Should I tell the truth? I tried to weigh the pros and cons in my head. Hiding my appearance was just to avoid any unnecessary attention. I had never thought about being recognized as the Specter. Deg must have fulfilled my threat but why did anyone believe him? What were her reasons for believing? I searched her face again.

"Yes, I'm the Specter," I said cautiously. Her arms flew around me. I stiffened and my eyes went wide. I was only wearing a towel.

"Thank the gods! The other girls told me I was a fool to believe that story, but I knew better! I know when a man lies. You have to help us." Her words started running together in a harsh whisper into my wet hair. I pushed her away to arms-length.

"Jaylee, slow down. What are you talking about?" She looked over her shoulder even though we were alone. She took a breath and held my hand tightly.

"Onisk has been taken over by the Bloodied Men." I felt a cold darkness rush through me. Jaylee shrank away from me slightly as a green glow fell on her skin, but she still smiled.

"You really are her... A customer, one of the Bloodied Men, told me the story of the Specter. He said that she had glowing green eyes and blood red hair... But he also said that she-"

"Just tell me about how the Bloodied Men got here, Jaylee," I interrupted. I didn't need to hear a retelling of the massacre, especially with the darkness making its presence known again. I tried to keep my voice level, but my mind raced. If they really were in the city, it could be a perfect opportunity for me, however, it was extremely dangerous too. They knew about me, whether they believed or not was another matter.

Her words were rushed as she tried to explain. Onisk was always a luxurious artisan city, just as Silas had said. It prided itself on its fine crafts, music, and plays but during the previous fall, a crier appeared in the square trying to recruit for the Bloodied Men. This was before the attack on Ameris, so the city soldiers thought nothing of it; just another group of sell-swords moving through. More and more of the men appeared, some recruited from Onisk, but most were outsiders. As their numbers grew, they showed no intention of leaving.

As she spoke, I moved behind the screen to dress. All that I saw made sense now: The soldiers at that gate, the curfew, the state of the inn and its patrons, the people. How were the Bloodied Men still here? Why? The ambassador should have requested help if he couldn't force them out himself.

"What did the ambassador do about the Bloodied Men?" I said. I heard the disgust in her voice.

"Nothing. He said that they hadn't done anything wrong so he couldn't request that they leave. Then they destroyed that Rokellian town. Onisk was in a panic, but the Bloodied Men didn't attack us. They just... made themselves at home and Sir Farth let them. They rule this city now. They don't pay for goods and services anymore." Once dressed, I moved to lean against the table and crossed my arms. Fury nearly made me shake as I remembered the fat pompous man in purple.

"Sir Farth has done nothing to get them out?" I said. She shook her head.

"No. It's almost like he wants them here. He enforced the curfew and even made the people open their doors to them." Lightning threatened to leap from my hands, but I forced it back.

"Has anyone tried to leave and get help?" Jaylee went stiff and wouldn't meet my eyes.

"Some tried but they were hunted down. They brought most of the people back badly beaten but a few... they never came back. Help never came so... we know what must have happened... Very few travelers are allowed in the city and the people know that we mustn't tell but I saw you and... You must do something, Specter. Please. You're only person to have done anything about them. They are afraid of you." Her eyes met mine, hope filling them again.

I ran my hand through my hair as I tried to keep my rage in check. How many of them were here now? They could be just a room away. The darkness clawed at me, but I shoved it down. I had to keep a clear head. I had no idea what to do. I pulled out a chair and sat. I stared at the floorboards and hoped I would find an answer there. Sparks cracked around my fists as I thought about how the ambassador had failed his people so completely.

"I should have ripped Sir Farth apart when I had the chance," I said grinding my teeth. I heard Jaylee inhale sharply and I forced the lightning away. It waited, though, just under the surface. The air grew tense. After a moment, Jaylee sat in the other chair at the small table.

"You met the ambassador? He's a slimy womanizing dung beetle, isn't he?" Jaylee said finally with a snicker. She smiled at me, and I snickered too.

"I couldn't agree more. He even invited me-" My voice died as I remembered the card.

"What is it, Specter?" I turned to her with a dark smile.

"Jaylee, I need your help."

Chapter 17: A Truce

I pulled up the hem of my dress as I crept through the shadows in the alleys of Onisk, pulling Tempest along behind me. Jaylee had said that she was familiar with Sir Farth's "preferences" and tried to mold me to them as best she could before sneaking me out a hidden back door of the inn. My hair was still hidden, and I wore my pants and boots under my borrowed dress. Jaylee wanted to make the bust of the gown much lower, but I insisted otherwise. Eventually, she gave in and said my kohled eyes and dark lips should be enough distraction.

The dark blue and purple gown looked like spilt ink in the partial moonlight. I pulled the cloak tighter around me, keeping my bare pale shoulders covered, and pulled Tempest behind me. I glanced at the card, looking again at the image of a large white mansion atop a hill. Jaylee had given me directions to the estate that was supposed to look just like the image on the invitation.

I had considered telling Silas and the other rogues what I was doing but I knew that they wouldn't be in any shape to go anywhere and if they even knew, they would only try to come with me anyway. It would be simpler if I went alone, just as Sir Farth requested. I did, though, leave a note in the room for Silas. In the note, I explained that I was following a lead on the Bloodied Men, and they should continue on as planned. I promised that I would meet them in Caneesho before the celebration. I gave explicit instructions to Jaylee to not say anything to anyone about meeting me or what I was doing. I didn't want her to get hurt and she agreed wholeheartedly. She gave me a kiss on the cheek in thanks before hurrying me out.

I heard the music before I saw the house. I followed the sound and paused in the dark alley, looking at the glittering estate atop the hill. There were a few people still walking into the house. I tied Tempest to a small post hidden in the alley. I wanted to be prepared in case something went wrong and I had to run. I quickly went to the tall iron gates as the last of the guests walked through. The guards didn't question me when I ran up and showed them the card. They shrugged and let me through without a hassle. So much for the curfew...

There was an older man collecting the invitation cards at the door. He looked at me strangely when I reached the front of the line.

"Do you have an invitation?" He narrowed his eyes as he tried to recognize me. I handed him the card. He looked it over and nodded before stepping aside. As I stepped into the grand ballroom, I fought to retain my nerve. I had never done anything like this before. I didn't know the first thing about being seductive. I had only seen such actions; I didn't make them.

I needed to get Sir Farth alone and question him. The darkness swirled and hinted at my other options. I took a breath and tried to stay focused. I needed information first. If Sir Farth allowed the Bloodied Men to stay in his city, then he must know some of their plans. If he didn't, then he would have to know someone who did.

The party was well under way. At first glance, it was like the celebration in Rogue City. Dancers twirled on the dance floor and groups mingled around the food but as I moved through the groups of people, I realized there was no joy in this party. The people had smiles on their faces but there was nothing genuine about their laughs. They reminded me of the terrible wealthy children that tormented me as a child. Their critical expressions took in the party with mild detachment. It was all beneath them, less than. There was no trace of the anxiety that the common people had. I narrowed my eyes at them, and anger and darkness bubbled in my chest. They were all profiting from the Bloodied Men. I tore my gaze and my thoughts from them as best I could.

I looked at the guards that stood around the perimeter of the ballroom. They stood like statues as they silently observed the festivities. The other guests were oblivious of their presence. I scanned the room, searching for Sir Farth but I didn't spot him.

I merged with the crowd and tried to pick up any useful information from conversations. Most of the topics were of favorite fashions, foods, and music. I would stand in one group as long as I could before they grew suspicious of me. It was a pointless attempt. The wealthy were a close-knit group and they quickly picked up that I wasn't one of them. I found myself the topic of discussion.

"Who is she?"

"Where did she come from?"

"Maybe Goy's new pet. He told me he was growing tired of the last one..."

This was getting me nowhere, but their comments gave me an idea. I steeled myself as I approached a group of guests.

"Excuse me but where is Sir Farth? I'm afraid I arrived late, and I don't want him angry especially since it's my first... visit." The women peered down their noses at me and the men looked me over with a knowing smirks.

"In his study, presumably. I think I heard someone say he was finishing up some business... but I'm sure he would be delighted to see you," one of the men said after looking me over. He waved at the man who had attended the door. The older gentlemen walked over quickly and gave a small bow.

"Your lordship?"

"Escort this... woman to the ambassador's rooms. She is his entertainment for the evening, I believe." I wanted to gag as the servant lead me away. It didn't matter how I seemed to them, but it was a struggle to keep my shoulders squared as the servant led me through an open doorway and down a hall. He gestured to a door.

"The ambassador's private bedchamber. Stay here until he arrives. The ambassador is currently concluding business in his study. Do not disturb him. Good evening." His even tone wasn't rude, but it was well rehearsed. Sir Farth must have many "pets" visit his home. I clenched my fists as the darkness swirled with ideas. The servant opened the door for me and then walked away. I watched him round the corner, and I tried to prepare myself.

A hand reached from the room, grabbing me and slamming into the white stone wall. I closed my eyes against the pain when my head struck the wall. I shook the throbbing away and opened my eyes. All breath left my body as I looked into ice blue eyes.

Prince Aleron stared at me in disbelief. His presence froze me in place, making my thoughts, and the darkness, vanish. I was severely aware of how tightly his hands were wrapped around my arms and how close his body was to mine. My mark tingled and I could hear my heart hammering in my ears. The last time he was this close, I was terrified of him and in so much pain. Now, I inhaled his warm spicy scent and wanted to smile. I didn't feel that terror now... I didn't know what it was I felt. Finally, he spoke, his words a harsh whisper tinged with both anger and shock.

"What are you doing here?" His question brought me out of my trance, and I buried the strange feelings I had toward him. I was here to get information and Prince Aleron was in my way. The Bloodied Men came first and the mark and Aleron came second.

"Me? What are you doing here, Princely?" I amazed myself that I was able to speak, let alone with such bravado in my whisper. It was just like when we first met. He was just as surprised. His grip loosened on my arms slightly but not enough for me to break free. He was incredibly strong. I didn't want to force him off of me, though. Any kind of scuffle could alert Sir Farth, so I stayed still.

"Don't call me that... At the moment, I'm interrogating you," he said cautiously. My confidence seemed to put him off his guard, so I decided to stay the course. My brow raised at him.

"Well, here I am. You found me. Now, will you let me go so I can get back to what I was doing? I may have already missed my opportunity." He turned his head at me, and his grip lessened even more.

"Your opportunity?"

"To find out the Bloodied Men's next move." Prince Aleron shook his head at me and dropped his hands. He took a step back and I was able to take in his appearance. His hair was still in a braided style and his stubble was thicker. He wore simple black fitted clothes without a crest and his sword and dagger were around his waist. I took notice of another knife strapped to his calf.

"What?" he said flatly.

"I've been trying to find the Bloodied Men so I can avenge my family." He raised his hand, interrupting me, and furrowed his brow. The truth just seemed to baffle him further.

"But... what? What about the mark? You cursed me. Why? What is it doing to me?" I rubbed my forehead. I was running out of time.

"We don't have time for this right now. If you care at all about what happened to Ameris, you'll listen to me. The Bloodied Men have infiltrated Onisk and Sir Farth is harboring them." He just looked at me. His piercing eyes seemed to search my soul.

"Did you hear me? The Bloodied Men are here!" I said, waving my arm. Didn't he understand the importance of what was happening?

"I know that." It was my turn to be dumbstruck.

"You know?" He nodded.

"I've been tracking the Bloodied Men for months even before the attack in Ameris, of course I know. That's why I'm here."

"Then let's go," I said reaching for the door latch. Prince Aleron's hand slammed against the door, making it rattle on its hinges.

"You're not going anywhere." His voice had that terrifying edge to it that it had in the Blue Boot so long ago but it didn't frighten me anymore.

"I go where I please, Princely," I said just as darkly. We stared daggers at each other but Aleron was the first to back down. His expression was still hard but not quite so frigid as he extended his arm to me. His bladed crest glowed with a blue light.

"Just remove it. I'm afraid it will drive me mad," his voice lost all its edge, just for a moment. His blue eyes twinkled at me, and my heart jumped. I felt my shoulders sag.

"I didn't curse you. I don't know how to remove it. If I did, mine would have been gone long ago," I said softly. He studied me and finally pulled down his sleeve.

"You really had nothing to do with it..." Aleron rubbed the back of his neck and looked up at the ceiling. He closed his eyes and sighed. With the hard authority gone, I could see the fine lines and exhaustion on his face. Guilt made my stomach sink. I didn't know what the mark was doing to him, but it must have been more of a torment than mine was.

"How about a deal?" I said. Aleron cut his eyes at me suspiciously.

"A deal?" His voice was so sharp that I almost flinched.

"A truce then. We both want the mark gone but there are obviously more important matters we need to address first-"

"This is very important," he said. I almost rolled my eyes at him.

"Yes, it is but as Prince of Rokellia, I assume that any threat to the kingdom would be a bit higher on your list. So, we take care of the Bloodied Men and then we can figure out the rest." I extended my hand and waited. He stared at my hand in thought. As the seconds went by, I felt the air leave the room. I couldn't remember the last time I had felt so nervous. I hoped that it didn't show in my expression. What would happen if he didn't accept the terms? My heart thumped. What if he did?

I sensed movement coming down the hall and my eyes went wide.

"Hide," I whispered. Aleron looked toward the door.

"Keep him distracted," he whispered and then bolted to one of the large windows, hiding behind one of the thick floor-length curtains. I turned toward the door just as the latch slid open. Sir Farth paused in the doorway when he saw me. He wore the same dark purple ensemble, but his hat was gone. He had a tall forehead that was covered in a veil of thin oily hair. His face was red, and his eyes were glassy from drinking. He turned his head quizzically.

"I don't remember sending for a courtesan..." he said. I cleared my throat and took a step back.

"Courtesan? Why, Sir Farth, if you don't remember me, I could always go back to my husband." His eyes lit up in recognition. He stepped in the room and closed the door behind him.

"Ah! Of course not, my dear! How could I forget the beautiful Temperance?" he said with that nasty glint in his eye. I frowned.

"Prudence." He raised his brows in confusion before waving his hand at me.

"Yes, yes. Prudence, of course. I'm delighted that you decided to come. You do look ravishing. Would you like a drink?" He walked passed me to a small silver table decorated with glittering crystal bottles.

He chose one filled with a dark liquid and poured it into two goblets. He walked back and handed one to me. He clinked his goblet against mine.

"To a fruitful relationship," he said and tipped his head back. As he drank, I glanced at the curtain. Aleron's presence made me apprehensive. Sir Farth looked at me once his cup was empty and ran his finger across my shoulder. I took a step back and gestured to the ornate bedroom.

"Your home is quite lavish, Sir Farth." It wasn't an exaggeration. There were beautiful life-sized marble statues around the room and paintings all over the walls framed in silver and gold. The canopied bed was stacked high with furs and velvet pillows. I turned and walked to the largest painting, trying to get Sir Farth to turn his back to the curtain. It was a misleading portrait of Sir Farth, with a thin figure and lush dark hair.

"Oh, it is. I get a large sum of money for being a royal ambassador, not to mention a cut from Onisk's taxes. I've been thinking of raising them again. I've had to give quite a bit of gold to- uh... never mind. Why are you still in your cloak?" Sir Farth said faltering. Maybe getting information from him wouldn't be as difficult as I thought.

I tried not to shirk away as he reached around from behind me to the clasp at my throat. My cloak fell to the floor, and he ran his hand over the bare skin of my neck and shoulders. I fought the urge to punch him.

"You've had to share your riches?" I said. I felt him lean closer to me and he inhaled deeply. Power surged inside me, but I kept it back.

"Yes. Quite tragic, really, but business is business. I stand to make much more later than what I am losing now." I turned and moved to look at some of the other paintings, moving farther from where Aleron was hiding.

"This business... was that what kept you so long in your study?" I tried to keep my voice light, but my heart was hammering. Sir Farth followed close behind.

"Yes, I had a meeting regarding royal affairs." I glanced at the curtain again and met Aleron's gaze as he stepped lightly toward the door. He must have meant to go to the study. I turned back to Sir Farth to keep his attention.

"Royal affairs? Is there trouble? I heard about that army... The Bloodied Men. It isn't them is it?" Sir Farth stopped walking. He searched my eyes, but he didn't notice Aleron leave the room and close the door soundlessly behind him.

"Why would you ask about the Bloodied Men? You're asking a lot of questions..." My chest seized at the suspicion in his voice. Had I said the wrong thing? I didn't know what I was doing. I didn't know how to manipulate people.

"I-uh... I... heard about the town in Rokellia. It's terrible and frightening. I just hope they don't do the same here." I felt the panic rising in my throat as I waited for his reply. I wasn't careful enough. I should have told Silas about this. He would have taken care of it.

In my distraction, Sir Farth pulled the scarf from my head and my hair tumbled down in ringlets. I spun around and saw the tip of a knife inches from my nose. I felt the cold increase in my eyes as the energy shot down my limbs. No point in pretending now. Sir Farth's eyes widened but he held the knife steady.

"They told me to be cautious of spies, but I never expected... It can't be... You're not... The Specter isn't real..." he said.

"I assure you; I am very real." I tried to sound menacing and, judging by his expression, I succeeded. I stepped closer but he flung the knife to the floor.

"I get nothing if I tell you anything so do what you want. I'll only become a martyr in the end." I felt the sparks crackle around my hand, but it was a bluff. I couldn't hurt him, not until I had answers. He had the information I needed. Sir Farth back-pedaled until his back hit the wall. He stared at my hands with widened eyes. I appeared in front of him and slammed my crackling fist against the wall by his head. He flinched but said nothing. My nostrils flared.

"Tell me why the Bloodied Men are here," I said firmly. Sir Farth forced out a laugh.

"You're not going to do anything to me. And I heard that you were bloodthirsty! Such a waste of power and a pretty face. You're pathetic." I ground my teeth with rage, and I felt the energy surge down my hands.

I wanted to set his skin ablaze, but I needed him to tell me what he knew. I had to know what the Bloodied Men planned. He had to tell me.

I felt the power flee from my hands and it moved up my throat so suddenly it forced my mouth open. Green smoke fell from my mouth and went across Sir Farth's face. His expression relaxed and his eyes glazed over as he peered over my shoulder. I stared at him as he remained motionless. I followed his gaze, but we were the only people in the room.

"What just happened?" I said, furrowing my brow.

"I don't know," Sir Farth said softly. I turned back to him.

"Look at me," I said. Sir Farth's eyes snapped to mine. What was happening? I remembered Silas suggesting that there may have been more to my power, but I never expected this. It was like he was under a spell.

"Why are the Bloodied Men here?" I said cautiously. His tone was flat and sleepy but insist.

"Onisk is their base of operations." My eyes widened.

"What?" I said in shock. He repeated himself. I stared at him, my mind wheeling.

"Why?"

"Plentiful resources, little army protection, and they promised me more gold than I could ever imagine." I narrowed my eyes and fought the urge to set him on fire. He was the reason the Bloodied Men grew as powerful as they did. Would they have destroyed Ameris if Sir Farth hadn't had helped them? Darkness clawed at my core.

"What do you know about the attack at Caneesho?" He shook his head.

"They will be at the celebration in Caneesho and then there will either be peace or war." My heart sank.

"War?" I said in a whisper. Sir Farth shrugged.

"Gold for Goy either way." Rage engulfed me. My fist crashed into his jaw, whipping his head back. He slid to the floor, and I kicked him between his legs. My foot went back again but a cough from the doorway stopped me.

"You know, he's unconscious," Aleron said. He leaned against the door frame with his arms crossed over his broad chest. I could see the smile in his eyes despite his stony face. I kicked the motionless ambassador again as the darkness disappeared and then smoothed out my dress.

"He'll feel it when he wakes up... How long have you been there?" I didn't meet his eyes as I tied back my hair under the scarf. Did he see the sparks? Oh gods, did he see the smoke?

"Just in time to see the ambassador fall." I could have sighed in relief, but I just nodded and looked at the floor. I could feel his stare on me as silence filled the space between us. I thought back to the truce I offered. What if I was just being stupid about Aleron? Why would he not want me arrested? He had no reason to believe anything I said.

Fighting rogues in the woods, sharing a magical mark, and then disappearing? That especially couldn't have helped anything. It all pointed to guilty. He was probably trying to decide how best to torture me.

"What did you find out?" I asked, stepping away from the ambassador. I dared a glance at him. His unrelenting eyes held my gaze.

"Not enough. Something big is happening in Caneesho but no one here is privy to what it is. We will have to go to the capital to find out." My heart leapt and I bit my lip.

"We?"

"I've thought about your 'truce.' I'm inclined to accept; however, I have some conditions," he said finally. My smile was immediate, and my shoulders relaxed. I hadn't realized how much I wanted to hear him agree. He continued.

"From now on, you will not leave my sight." My smile vanished and I crossed my arms over my chest.

"No," I said firmly. He set his jaw and his eyes seemed brighter.

"Excuse me?" I met his stare confidently.

"I have people travelling with me to Caneesho. I can't abandon them."

"Then bring them along," he said quickly. I shook my head.

"They won't want to travel with you, or the Black Guards." Aleron blinked at me.

"Why? Who are they? Criminals?" When I didn't answer, his cynicism turned to disbelief. "You're travelling with criminals... Edwin will love this... So, what is your counter, then?" It was hard to meet his eyes. His gaze was so intense.

"We will travel separately and meet in Caneesho." I said. Aleron stared at me. I knew he was weighing the possibility of me disappearing again. His gaze almost made me shiver but he finally nodded.

"And then you won't leave my sight." I rolled my eyes at him then.

"Would you like to keep me roped to you as well?" He didn't smile but his tone was lighter.

"That is an excellent idea." I raised an eyebrow at him to which he shrugged.

"You've proven difficult to find." It was my turn to shrug.

"For good reason... Where will I find you?" I said.

"There's a tavern called The Sea's End. I'll be there each day at dusk."

"And we'll stop the Bloodied Men," I said. We had maintained the distance between us as we negotiated but I noticed my cloak on the floor. I moved toward it, but Aleron was quicker. He snatched the cloak from the floor and placed it around my shoulders in one graceful movement. I felt rooted in place. His fingers brushed against my collarbone with feather lightness as he fastened the clasp. My skin nearly tingled at his touch.

The smell of spices and books clouded my mind, and a sort of peace overcame me. I looked up at him as my face flushed at the strange sensation. His face had softened, and his eyes landed on a stray lock of red hair resting on my cheek. He slowly raised his hand but hesitated. It was the first time I had seen him lose his confidence. My heart pounded as I waited for his next move. He touched the curl with the same softness he had when clasping my cloak and tucked it under the scarf. His fingers lingered for a moment, and I closed my eyes, trying to commit the feeling to memory. Aleron took an abrupt step back and cleared his throat. His stoic demeanor returned and his mouth was a firm line.

"After the Bloodied Men have been dealt with, then we'll find the truth... Do you agree to this truce?" He extended his hand and waited. I hated how I always found myself getting into impossible deals. At least this time, it was my idea.

I took his hand and thought a spark flashed between us. Aleron didn't seem to notice so I set my jaw.

"Truce." Aleron tightened his grip and pulled me closer. I almost crashed against his chest as my mark buzzed. I stared up into his icy eyes.

"Don't make me regret this... V," he whispered harshly. I swallowed as my stomach turned flips and my heart pounded. I was already starting to regret it.

Then the door started to open.

Chapter 18: Change of Plans

Aleron pulled me behind him through the open window before I could process what was happening. My dress caught on the windowpane, ripping the skirt up to my thigh, but Aleron did not pause. We sprinted across the yard as the servant called for the guards to aid Sir Farth. I wasn't sure if the servant saw us, but it wouldn't take long for the soldiers to find the strip of fabric caught on the window.

Thick, tall bushes lined the interior of the high fence that surrounded the estate and Aleron ran straight for them. He slipped easily into the thicket with his sleek clothes but, once again, my large dress proved to be an obstacle. I yanked at the skirts, tearing them to shreds on the branches. The space was cramped, and I found myself pressed closer and closer to Aleron as I gathered the dress out of the open. His scent made me dizzy and every muscle that touched him went rigid. Once fully in the bushes, I stared at the destroyed dress to distract my thoughts away from him. The layers and layers of ruined fabric piled high around us were condemning. I had to get out of that dress. I glanced through the prickly leaves at the house trying to slow my breathing. The house seemed still except for Sir Farth's room. Figures moved quickly across the space and there was shouting.

"The guards are still at the gate. If we're lucky, they'll question everyone inside first and we can slip out. I doubt Farth will wake until morning so- what are you doing?" Aleron said as I began unbuttoning the front of my dress. His chest was tense against my back. My cheeks were blazing hot, and I had never been so thankful for darkness before. I forced my voice to be even.

"I'm taking this off. It's slowing me down and it will get us caught." Aleron gave a sort of grunt as a reply. I think he was as uncomfortable as I was, but he didn't move away, then again, I don't think he could have.

I unfastened the last button at my waist, leaving just my corset covering my top half. The skirt was torn along the hem, but the thick waistband was still intact; I had to cut it. I couldn't reach my daggers with all the skirts but then I remembered Aleron's small knife on his calf. I snatched the knife, quickly cut the fabric, and slipped it back into the sheath.

"I am most definitely regretting this truce..." Aleron said with a sigh. I smirked and tried shimming my arms out of the sleeves but there wasn't enough room. Aleron's hands moved under my cloak and rested softly on my arms. My movements ceased. My heart hammered as his fingers slipped under the fabric and gently pulled the sleeves down. I shivered at his cool, feather light touch. His fingers moved so slowly, like icy water drops sliding down my skin.

"The guards are moving toward the house now. Be ready." Despite facing the estate, I hadn't noticed what was happening. I blinked hard and brought my attention forward. Aleron was right. The soldiers ran toward the house just as others came out shouting. Aleron cursed under his breath as some of the guards began looking around the walls of the house. He pulled the tattered dress toward him.

"What are you doing with that?" I whispered.

"This will be our distraction. I'll throw it that way and we'll run to the gate." I scoffed.

"Throw it? Won't a ball of fabric being thrown in the air just give us away?" I glanced at him over my shoulder and my voice caught in my throat. He was so close that our noses almost touched. He stared at me for a moment before answering.

"No. Be ready. I'll be right behind you." I swallowed and turned to face the gate. I shifted until all of the dress was compressed in Aleron's hands. I stared at the gates and waited for the signal to run.

"Now," he said as he threw the dress into the air. I jumped up and ran. Once at the gate, I glanced back. Aleron had his back to me facing the group of soldiers running after the dress as it moved through the air, skirts billowing. My brows furrowed at the sight of it. The dress moved around the corner of mansion, drifting strangely in the air. Almost as if it was floating. As I watched the soldiers disappear behind the corner, Aleron grabbed my hand and ran through the gate. Forcing my thoughts to escape, I turned toward the alleyway where Tempest waited but I was yanked in the opposite direction.

"We can leave the city is this way," he said pulling again. I held firm and pointed.

"But my horse is in that alley!" He spun around without hesitation and ran to the alley. Tempest stood right where I had left her. She stamped her hoof at the sight of me. I paused so I wouldn't spook her, but Aleron swung into the saddle quickly and gracefully and extended his hand to me. It was a magnificent sight, like something out of a story: The dark handsome prince atop his powerful black steed. What I was truly amazed at was the fact that Tempest didn't buck him off.

I grabbed his hand again and, as soon as I was on, we shot off. I held on to Aleron's waist as he maneuvered us through the streets. At first I thought he had no idea where he was going as he made so many turns that seemed to go back on themselves, but I realized that we never saw another person.

Finally, we arrived at the wall at the edge of the city. Aleron pulled Tempest to the right, and he ran his hand along the stone bricks. He glanced at the buildings to our right, moved his hand lower, and shoved against the wall. A section of the wall swung away as if it was a door. I felt my mouth fall open as Aleron slid to the ground and lead us through the opening and then closed it behind us. The door blended seamlessly into the wall. He almost smirked again when he saw my face, but he quickly cleared his throat.

"Most larger cities have some type of escape route like this. Usually only the ambassador within each city knows about them."

"So how do you know about this one?" He did smirk then, but only for the briefest of moments.

"I know about all of them." Despite my questioning look, he said nothing more as he climbed into saddle and kicked Tempest into a gallop.

We didn't stop riding until morning after coming to a forest. It was only then did I remember I was just wearing my trousers and a corset under my cloak. I leapt off Tempest and snatched a shirt out of my bag. I put some distance between us as Aleron lead Tempest to a small stream. With my back to them, I hung my cloak on a branch and pulled the shirt over my head. I usually liked to wear my corset over the shirt since the corset was made out of much stiffer fabric. It wasn't comfortable but I wasn't going to switch them now. I tucked the shirt into my breeches with a small sigh and looked around.

This forest was nothing like the Nitalla. The bark of the trees was lighter and there was more space between them, allowing the sun to stream through the branches in glittering rays. The leaves above made a thin canopy that left the ground lush in spite of the frost. Birds chirped and I could hear animals moving freely. I inhaled deeply and could almost smell spring.

"Peaceful, isn't it?" Aleron said suddenly standing next to me and extending his hand. In it was half a sweet roll.

"You ate my sweet roll?" I said. He raised an eyebrow at me.

"I particularly enjoy dessert for breakfast... You're fortunate that I didn't eat all of it." I narrowed my eyes and grabbed the roll from him. He didn't smile but his eyes weren't hard either.

"I can't tell if you are joking or not," I said finally. The corner of his mouth twitched, and his eyes glanced through the open shirt at my chest.

"You still have it." My hand touched the necklace.

"Of course, I do." He stared at the necklace for a few moments before finally turning away. He looked back toward Onisk.

"We need to keep moving. It would be better if we could make it through this forest before nightfall. There's a small village on the other side where I can buy a horse and then we can push on to the capital..."

Aleron continued to lay out his plan, but I stopped listening. I was struck by the absurdity of the past few hours. How had I gotten here? Just days ago, I was running away and hiding from this man, this prince, terrified that he would torture me until the mark disappeared from his arm. Yet, here I was, talking to him like he was just another person.

I watched him as he spoke. One hand rubbed the back of his neck and the other rested on his hip in a fist. He scowled slightly at trees, making his eyes shine brighter under his dark brows. He was imposing when he was clean shaven but shadow on his jaw made him look much more intimidating. It emphasized the curve of his mouth in a lovely way.

"Are you going to eat that?" he said after turning to me. My eyes quickly darted away from his lips, and I popped the roll into my mouth. He turned his head at me but said nothing. It was painfully awkward, and I felt my face heat up. Did he notice me staring at his mouth? I swallowed roughly and he offered me a waterskin without a word. Was he holding that before? I couldn't have been that distracted... I could feel his intense stare as I drank. I handed it back and I avoided his eyes. My head threatened to sweat under the scarf. The silence stretched on but neither of us moved. I finally looked at him and was amazed to see him smirking at me.

"What is it?" I said cautiously. His small smirk grew a little wider and his eyes twinkled.

"You're nervous." I frowned at him and crossed my arms.

"Is that so surprising?"

"Given our past interactions, extremely so," he said walking back to Tempest. I followed him and started to pull at the now uncomfortable scarf.

"And you are referring to what exactly?" He placed the waterskin in the bag and faced me, crossing his strong arms across his chest.

"I have never had someone speak to me as you do. In Ameris, you knew who I was the moment I started talking to you and yet you had the gumption to just play along with the charade. Then last night, you made it seem that I was the one out of place and then, like a seasoned ambassador, struck a deal with me, who as far as you know wants to throw you in a dungeon. You also cut off your dress with my knife." My chest fell and my shoulders tensed.

"Are you going to throw me in a dungeon?" His speech wasn't calming me. He was right. I was nervous and uncomfortable once I started thinking about all the details: Who he was, who I was, the marks. I tried to decide if this was worse than being around the devium. I pulled at my scarf again.

"I haven't decided yet," he said calmly. I waited for his expression to change but it didn't. The only slightest tell was the casual look of his eyes. I took it as a good sign.

"I still can't tell if you are joking, Princely." He narrowed his eyes a bit.

"I asked you not to call me that."

"I have to call you something and I'm sure there's a law about calling you by your name," I said shrugging and began to untie the scarf. The heat was becoming too much.

"I have many titles, any of those would do." I pulled the scarf away from my hair. I closed my eyes and shook my hair free of its braid. I tilted my head back and ran my fingers over my scalp.

"But wouldn't that just expose your identity?" I waited for answer and when none came, I opened my eyes to look at the prince.

He stared intently at my hair. I felt my cheeks flush again. He saw my hair before...

"This is your true color then... I thought you had changed it for Dark Day Festival. Hair dyeing is a trend in Jahilta," Aleron said finally. I shook my head and began to coil it again.

"I don't know why anyone would choose this color." I went to wrap the scarf around my head, but Aleron's hand caught my arm. I froze and he suddenly looked sheepish, but he didn't let go.

"Don't. It suits you." My heart thumped hard in my chest. I lowered my arms and frowned as my mind flashed. I remembered the rush of people, the Blue Boot, hazel eyes, and a warm smile. Jeb had said that. There was a beat of silence and I felt myself falling into the dark hole that I had almost managed to forget.

"What happened... in Ameris?" I said softly. Aleron's face grew dark and serious.

"What do you remember?" I shook my head and looked away from him.

"Screaming, fire, death... my aunt was separated from my uncle and me as we tried to start home but... I was so sick, so weak, then he... died..." It was the first time that I said it aloud. My arms turned to lead, and my mouth went dry. Aleron waited patiently for me to continue. My mind was racing as it replayed the scenes of that night.

"I don't remember what happened after that. I woke up days later, but Ameris was gone. I couldn't find anyone. Were there any survivors?"

"Very few... None that I recognized... The rest of the army arrived after most of the damage was done... I'm very sorry for your loss." I almost snickered at his words but when I saw the immense guilt on his face, I just nodded at him.

The air was thick between us as we reflected on that night. Finally, Aleron broke the silence.

"Where did you go? I searched for you all through the city. I questioned the survivors, citizens and soldiers alike, but no one had seen you or even knew your name. You just vanished." His voice was heavy, but his eyes flashed. I couldn't tell him the truth, could I? I knew he couldn't know about Rogue City. I searched for a way to tell him the truth without openly lying.

"After my uncle fell, the rogues found me," I said cautiously.

"Rogues found you? The same rogues that you fought in the Nitalla?" His voice took on that edge again, but his expression didn't change. I nodded.

"When I woke up, they offered me a deal. Work for them for a place to stay and I accepted." The air around us went still.

"You did what?" I flinched at his biting tone and then my nostrils flared.

"I had no choice! My family died and I thought that you wanted me dead! What should I have done, Princely? I was alone and lost and they gave me a reason to keep going! How dare you judge me... You don't know what it's like to lose your entire world." I felt the tears brimming in my eyes, but I refused to let them fall. My fists shook at my sides as sparks threatened to fly. Aleron stood as rigid as ever, but his eyes gave him away. They seemed to do that often. They softened and had a far-away look for just a moment. I remembered that he had lost his mother, almost a year ago now. Maybe he did know what it was like.

My anger fell away as we stared at each other. We didn't say anything more about our families but there was a mutual understanding between us, nonetheless. I wondered if we would ever talk about them again. I hoped so and that we would have healed a little by then.

"We should be on our way," Aleron said finally. His voice was soft even though his mouth was a hard line as he turned to retrieve Tempest. He paused and glanced over his shoulder at me.

"I hope you have a dress of some sort to wear in town. A woman in trousers would be quite a scandal." I smiled at him.

"That was definitely a joke, Princely." His blue eyes twinkled in the morning sun.

The forest was peaceful, just as Aleron had said. There was a road that ran through it, but Aleron avoided it. He didn't want to risk running into any Bloodied Men or guards from Onisk. The terrain was rough with sudden ditches and thick brush, but Aleron didn't show any signs of worry. He remained silent for the journey, though, taking extreme care to guide Tempest through the possible dangers. His silence allowed my mind to drift.

I worried about the rogues that I left behind in Onisk. When I left Silas the note, I didn't really think that I wouldn't return. I scolded myself at the vagueness of the letter. Viht, Dax, and Kaul were probably sick with worry. Silas, on the other hand, would be furious. I had never seen the devium angry... I shuddered and tried not to think about it anymore. All would be well.

We saw the village from the forest's edge before nightfall. Aleron was pleased with the time that we had saved by cutting straight through the forest and impressed with Tempest.

"Most horses wouldn't have been able to move through the bramble so easily. She is proving to be a worthy mount," Aleron said patting her neck. I snorted as Tempest bobbed her head and nearly pranced in her stride. She had been so affectionate with Aleron that it was nearly sickening.

"Traitor," I said under my breath. She just snorted back at me as I dismounted. I placed the skirt over my pants and grabbed the scarf. I yawned widely as I tied it in place. When was the last time I slept? I could feel the weariness in my bones and my stomach growled. I took some dried meat from the bag to try and hold off the hunger. I reached up to pull myself on Tempest, but Aleron took my hand and practically lifted me to my seat.

"Not used to riding for so long?" Aleron said.

"Not used to staying awake for so long," I said feeling my head sway. He nudged Tempest faster.

When we reached the village, there was no gate or guards to question us. The tavern was easy to find given that the other buildings just looked like houses. All of the villagers outside paused to stare curiously at us. Aleron nodded casually at them and steered us to the tavern. There was a small railing running near the door on which Aleron tied Tempest's reins. She greedily lapped up water from the long trough. The prince was on the ground and lifting me from Tempest by my waist before I could protest. His hands lingered for a moment before quickly withdrawing them and going inside.

The tavern was very humble and completely empty of customers. The innkeeper stood behind the bar. I followed Aleron to the counter.

"Good evening. Do you have a room for rent?" I smiled at the polite frankness of the question. There was no elaborate story or role to play. It was nice to not have another husband. Then it occurred to me what he asked. Aleron walked away, key in hand, and I quickly followed after him.

"A room? I thought we were going straight to Caneesho," I whispered as he unlocked the door just feet away from the bar. He pushed the door open and looked at me expectedly. I sighed and went in. The room was small. There was a bed to one side and a small table by the head of it.

"You are too tired for us to continue now, and exhaustion is the last thing we need. Rest. We'll leave soon," Aleron said and shut the door behind him. I stood there dumbfounded, but I was too tired to try and understand Aleron. Without a thought, I took off everything but my large shirt and collapsed on the bed. I fell asleep marveling at how a hay mattress could be more comfortable than a feather one.

I remember smelling smoke and blood in the air. Buildings were on fire and people were screaming. I stood surrounded by bodies: Viht, Dax, Kaul, Lily, Aunt Prudence, Henry, Jeb. I held my daggers, both black with blood. I ran the side of the blade across my tongue. My head felt hazy as I began to laugh. Black smoke fell from my mouth and black lightning surged in my hands. I felt alive again.

I awoke with a gasp in a cold sweat. The mark felt like it was on fire and the flames were quickly engulfing me from the inside out. I screamed and turned my head into the pillow to try and muffle the sound. I hugged my arm to my chest and curled into a ball on the bed. I had never felt a pain so intense. I ground my teeth and moaned into the pillow. My muscles began to spasm. The door banged open and shut again. I glanced over and saw Aleron, blurry through my unshed tears. His blue eyes were wide, and the horror was evident on his face. He took step toward me, and I thought back to the incident at Silas' house.

"Stay away." My voice cracked as I fought back tears, but he kept coming. His arms snatched me up and held me close as he sat on the bed.

"Let me help you. I'm here. I won't be useless this time," he said harshly into my hair and his grip tightened. I breathed in his scent and the pain lessened a bit. He ran his hand through my hair and rocked me.

"Just tell me what do to. Please." I took a deep breath, taking him in, and the pain eased even more. I raised my head and met his gaze. His blue eyes were blinding in the darkness. My heart stopped for a moment. A thought danced in my mind, but I dismissed it. He scanned my face and started to lean down. I closed my eyes as his lips pressed gently against my forehead.

The pain fled from my body, leaving me weak beyond measure. I slumped against Aleron and sighed with relief.

"It's gone... Thank you." My voice was soft and raspy, and he hugged me tighter in response. We sat like that for a few minutes, and I had never felt so content. My head grew heavy with sleepiness, and I felt

Aleron begin to move away. My chest seized and I gripped his shirt with all the might I had left.

"Please don't leave me." Without hesitation, Aleron lay on the bed and pulled me close. As I tucked my head under his chin, Aleron said something, but I was already drifting into sleep.

I woke up feeling refreshed as sunlight began to lighten the room from the window. I closed my eyes again and nestled closer to Aleron. His arm tightened around my bare waist, and he sighed. My eyes snapped open.

I shrieked and shoved him. I pushed my bunched up shirt back down as Aleron tumbled out of the bed. He grunted when he hit the floor. I panted as my heartbeat slowed. His glare made me pull the blanket closer. He opened his mouth but then shut it to a grim line and swallowed hard. I could have sworn that his cheeks had started to turn red. He stood and promptly left the room.

I ran my hands through my hair. What happened? My stomach dropped when I remembered the dream... and the pain. The fabric that normally covered the crest was gone and the green star shined brightly as it turned. The lines were darker than fresh ink. I cursed at it as I quickly dressed. At least Aleron was here... The thought made me pause. Why did he make the pain disappear?

The door opened and Aleron walked through carrying a chair. He kicked the door closed behind him and planted the chair right in front of it, blocking the only escape. He showed no emotion on his face as he sat but Aleron's eyes cut through me like knives.

"Caneesho can wait. We're discussing this mark. Now."

Chapter 19: Bonded

At some point, my mind managed to forget that Aleron was a prince.

"Explain to me what happened last night," Aleron said. The air was too heavy in the room, and he was too hard to look at. He sat too straight, and his voice was too stern. He was every bit a prince then.

"It happens sometimes..." I said. I shifted as I stood in the center of the room.

"'It happens sometimes?' You'll have to be a bit more specific." I grimaced at his tone.

"There are times when the mark burns. Sometimes it's just irritating and sometimes... it's like last night."

"Why? What causes it?"

"I don't know."

"You don't know? How can you not know? Have you tried to look for a pattern?"

"I-no-"

"Did something happen? Think about it. Something must trigger such a response." He looked at me expectantly as he waited. He wasn't angry, only direct. I thought back.

"Nothing happened. I went to sleep and..." My voice trailed away.

"And?" he said. I shook as the images came back. I felt the darkness creep over me like smoke. I looked at Aleron, but I didn't see him anymore.

"I had a dream... I was surrounded by my friends and family. I slaughtered them and I... liked it." I could almost taste the blood again and my pulse began to race. My fingers twitched and I smiled. The crest began to heat up, but my mind was preoccupied with gore and fire.

Aleron placed his hands on my face, and I snapped out of the trance. I didn't notice him stand and walk to me. I tried to move back but he held firm and searched my eyes. The darkness faded.

"There you are," he whispered finally. He sat back in his chair and gestured to the bed for me to sit. I didn't.

"How often do you feel the bloodlust?" I nearly choked. He said it like he was asking about the weather.

"Excuse me?" I said.

"Bloodlust. Violence. Wrath. That could be the trigger." The evenness of his tone made me stop. Was that the trigger? I thought back to the raid and the man in the Horsetail. That was most definitely wrath and bloodlust but what about Silas? I felt my cheeks flush.

"It could be..." I twisted the pendant. I didn't want to dig too far into how Silas affected the mark. At least not now. Or with Aleron. The prince pushed on with his investigation.

"Were you particularly violent before the crest appeared?" I scoffed at him.

"Not in the slightest. As timid as a lamb." Aleron furrowed his brow and rubbed his chin.

"So, the bloodlust developed after the crest appeared, but the crest tries to divert you from the bloodlust? If you weren't violent before the mark, then why would it even appear?"

My stomach dropped. I knew why: The strength, the speed, the lightning, the smoke. The bloodlust, or the darkness as I knew it, came when my abilities did. But I could use them without bringing on bloodlust. Reveling in blood and pain was the true trigger.

"You're not telling me something." I looked up and nearly jumped. Aleron was inches away from me again. I took a step back. I couldn't tell him about my abilities. It would seal my fate as a caster in his eyes. I squared my shoulders.

"You haven't told me anything about your mark. You expect me to tell you everything about mine?" Aleron frowned and he straightened to his full height. I tried my best to match his icy gaze and I set my jaw as I looked up at him. His shoulders relaxed but only slightly.

"I can feel when your mark burns." My eyes widened and my voice was soft.

"Every time?" He nodded and rubbed the back of his neck as he lost his rigid posture.

"I don't feel pain as you apparently do. It's more of a feeling of... warning or dread. I know something wrong is happening and I'm overcome with a sense of urgency to stop it." Dejection hit me and my limbs felt heavy. Whatever, or whoever, put these marks on us must have known that I wouldn't be able to control my abilities. It knew I would hurt people... I wrapped my arms around myself as that bleak hole inside started to pull me in.

"You're the next level of defense against me..." I whispered. Aleron shook his head and opened his mouth to answer but stopped as his gaze looked over my shoulder and out the small window in the room. I turned to look, and my chest seized. Four figures on horseback began to emerge from the forest in the distance.

"Travelers don't come this way. It's too far from the main road... Friends of yours?" Aleron said. Panic gripped me and I threw on my cloak. We had to go. I wanted to see my friends but now wasn't the time.

"They can't find us. We have to leave now." Aleron nodded and went to the door.

"I completely agree. I doubt that they would be keen on me joining your party and I'm not leaving your company just yet. But we can't outrun them now, especially with one horse. Stay here and I'll hide your horse in case they come through town. I'll be right back." Aleron left and I tried to control my breathing.

What would Aleron do if he realized what Silas was? What would the rogues do if they realized who Aleron was? How was I supposed to explain everything to them? Did I want to? I knew the answer to that one: No, I didn't. How likely was it that they would just skip over this town? I knew that they were trying to catch up to me so they would most likely stop and ask some questions. A lone woman on a big black horse would be conspicuous. Would they talk to the villagers? Probably not, they didn't want to draw too much attention. My eyes went wide. They would talk to the barkeeper, though. I quickly wrapped my hair, put on the skirt, and gathered the bags.

I opened the door and peered out. The tavern was still empty save for the barkeep, who stood dutifully behind the counter. I went to him quickly. Aleron could be back any second. I took a deep breath and reached for the energy inside and pulled it to my throat.

"What is your name?" I said softly to the barkeeper. Green smoke fell on his face as he turned to me. His expression relaxed and his eyes went glassy.

"Haun," he said sleepily.

"If anyone comes looking for me, I want you to tell them that a woman on a black horse stopped here last night and got directions to Caneesho and then she left. Do you understand?" Haun nodded and went back to cleaning a cup.

"Say it," I said as more smoke fell from my mouth.

"A woman on a black horse stopped here last night and got directions to Caneesho and then she left." I nodded, satisfied, and placed some gold coins in his shirt pocket. I didn't know if he would remember that we had stayed the night, but I would. I went to the exit and Aleron opened the door just as I reached for the latch. He scowled at me.

"I told you to wait for me." I grabbed his arm and pulled him outside.

"You were taking too long."

"I should probably bribe the barkeeper," Aleron said, trying to go back in. I pulled him away again.

"No need. I took care of it. What is your plan?" Aleron turned his head at me but didn't question me further. He placed his hand on my shoulder and steered me down the dirt path to a small barn.

"We'll hide in here," Aleron said simply. I stared at the barn in disbelief.

"Are you serious? Is this not the most obvious place to hide?" Aleron shrugged.

"We have no other options. Unless you think your friends will welcome a stranger into their ranks with open arms..." I marched inside.

The barn was small with only three stalls but there was a loft. I glanced around but didn't see Tempest.

"Where is my horse?" Aleron walked around me toward the back of the barn and then gestured to a rear stall before climbing up into the loft. I looked in the stall and Tempest laying down quietly on the hay.

She blinked lazily at me. I shook my head. Aleron must have been some kind of horse whisperer. I rolled my eyes at her. As long as she stayed like that, it really didn't matter how she got that way.

I climbed the ladder into the loft. It stored stacks and stacks of hay bales and overlooked the two wide doors of the barn. A line of bales served as a barrier on the edge of the loft. At some point, Aleron had also gotten us food. Soft cheese, dried fruit, and hard bread lay on a small cloth on a hay bale with... a bottle of wine? I couldn't help but smile at the picnic and my anxiety eased. I sat beside Aleron, and he handed me some bread with the cheese and fruit on it after adding a few drops of wine on top. I raised my eyebrow at him.

"All at once?" His eyes sparkled.

"It's the best way." I shrugged and took a bite. He was right. The wine brought the dried fruit back to life while the cheese was a perfect binder on the bread. They almost tasted fresh. I smiled and nodded at him.

"You must really enjoy food," I said, taking another bite. A small smirk came and went.

"Doesn't everyone?" I cut my eyes at him and huffed. He was very talented at avoiding details. It almost reminded me of Silas, but, to my relief, Aleron was never smug.

We ate breakfast in silence. I wish I felt as peaceful as Aleron looked. The lines around his eyes had disappeared and his jaw was relaxed. Without a distraction, my thoughts quickly went back to the rogues. I kept glancing at the open window wondering if we should keep watch or close the shutters.

"What did you mean when you said that I was a defense against you?" I snapped my head to Aleron. His blue eyes were sharp and searching and I was frozen. I couldn't tell him what I could do.

I turned my head toward the door, sensing something. Aleron pushed me back into the hay and crashed on top of me. His hand covered my mouth just as I opened it. I glared at him but couldn't help but think of how handsome he looked as my heart raced. I tried not to blush as I heard the door open. We both went still. Straw crunched as the person walked inside.

"Ay! Someone in here?" My eyes went wide. It was one of the twins. Aleron saw the recognition in my eyes.

"I see the food up there! You come down or I come up! I don't mean any trouble!" Aleron pressed a finger to his lips. He untucked his shirt and ruffled his hair. Then his expression changed, and his face began to blush. I glanced at the picnic and then realized exactly what he was doing. He winked at me as he rose to his knees.

"I'm here! Don't come up!" Aleron's voice sounded a bit higher in his false panic. He raised his hands for emphasis.

"This your barn?" Aleron winced and rubbed the back of his neck.

"Well, not exactly... More hers..." He glanced down at me, winced, and then shook his head. "What do you want? I'm a bit- uh- busy here..." Aleron's eyes darted to me again. There was a low whistle. Kaul.

"Sorry to interrupt, friend. Just had a horse run off last night. A big black mare. I was hoping someone had found her and this was the only barn in town..." Aleron shook his head.

"You see a black mare here?"

"No, I don't. Well, I'll leave you to it. Thanks for the help." Aleron gave an awkward wave, and I heard the door close. Aleron's persona vanished, and he watched the door intently. After a few moments, he sat and made himself another bit of bread. I slowly rose up and then glared at him.

"Really?" I said sharply. Aleron's blue eyes gleamed at me and extended the half-eaten slice of bread to me.

"Another bite?" I ignored him and rolled my eyes. He shoved the bread in his mouth, hiding the smile that was forming on his lips.

"That was a very convincing show." He took a drink of wine before answering.

"I should hope so. We don't want him, or the others, coming back."

"We're lucky that it was just Kaul. His brother, Dax, wouldn't have been so embarrassed. Viht would have kept his distance. Silas..." I'm not sure if Silas would have believed him at all.

"He's the cautious one then?" Aleron said. How would I describe Silas? I thought for a moment.

"He's the cunning one." Aleron studied my face before giving me a curt nod.

"Anything else I should know about them?" They are expert fighters and are very protective of their own, oh, and Silas is a devium. I shook my head at myself and sighed. I felt conflicted about telling him anything more about the rogues. Aleron noticed.

"If I am to help us avoid them, I need to know a little more about them." I felt my eyes grow colder as I looked at him.

"I've already said more than I should have. They gave me a home. I won't betray them." Aleron relaxed and nodded.

"I have no intentions of arresting them or exposing them for that matter. If you traveled with them, then you obviously have similar goals in mind... At least tell me what they look like." He didn't appear to be lying. What hurt could it do?

"Kaul, the one who was here, and Dax are twins, but Dax has a scar on his face. Viht is at least twenty years older and broad and dark with curly hair."

"And Silas?" he said when I stopped speaking. I hadn't even noticed that I paused. There were so many words that ran through my mind to describe him, most of them conflicting.

"Tall and pale, with long white hair." Aleron raised a brow at my curt tone.

"Anything else?" He grunted when I shook my head but didn't question me further. Aleron stood and inched open the shutter on the window. I hated this waiting. My nerves were on edge, and I gripped my fists to keep the lightning at bay. Then cool calmness washed over me, radiating from the mark. I glanced at the prince and saw him absentmindedly rubbing his arm. Was calming me as simple as touching his mark? What else could he do? He stopped when he noticed me watching him.

"How long should we wait?" I said after a time. Aleron inclined his head and looked back out of the crack between the shutters.

"Depends on when your friends leave." I was standing by him in an instant.

"You see them?" I tried to look over his shoulder and he shifted out of my way. I could easily see the tavern from the window. Four horses and three riders waited outside. Any villager that was still outside quickly went indoors. A man and woman on a single horse may be a curiosity but four armed men was a threat. I watched as Silas ran out of the inn, mounted his horse, and took off with the other three close behind. I let out the breath I had been holding. The smoke worked.

"They are in quite a hurry to find you. I wonder, why are you not in a similar rush to be reunited with them?" His voice wasn't arrogant. He was genuinely curious and almost concerned as he looked at me. I opened my mouth, but no words came. Aleron didn't wait for my answer as he packed up what little was left of the food.

Aleron and I had agreed before that we would meet in Caneesho so I could have easily gone with the rogues now to carry out that original plan. Even though Aleron said he didn't want to be separated, I believed he would have let me go if I had wanted. Why didn't I want to? Why was I content to stay with Aleron? I looked at my arm and then his. Yes, we were bonded but the bladed crest didn't draw us together, otherwise I would have gone to Jahilta to find him long ago. Maybe it was last night's discovery. Aleron could keep the darkness in check and make the pain go away. For now, that was enough. I didn't want to think too much on how his arm had felt around my waist or his strong chest against my back.

I rubbed the pendent, refusing to look at Aleron as my face turned red.

After purchasing a horse well above its worth from a farmer, Aleron lead us out of the village just before midday. I was worried about running into the rogues along the way, but Aleron shook his head. Caneesho was barely half a day's ride and at the rate they left the village, he estimated that they were already there.

I felt anxious knowing that we were so close. I could find the Bloodied Men before nightfall. I scowled as I thought. Finding the leader was the top priority. Like in Onisk, I needed information. I wanted to know how they were organized, what their main goal was, how far their reach was. I glanced at Aleron. He scowled as he stared ahead. Was he forming a plan too? More importantly, did our plans match up? The only way to find out was to ask.

"I assume you have a plan, Princely." Aleron flinched in his saddle. It was the first time that we had spoken in hours.

"More or less. We'll need a place to stay until I am expected at the castle so we will go to The Sea's End. From there we can try to find the Bloodied Men and also meet up with our estranged parties. I think it's best that they don't meet each other, don't you?"

"I couldn't agree with you more on that point. But I do think we should find our groups first. Doing so will just speed up the search for the Bloodied Men." I glanced at Aleron for his opinion. He gave a curt nod.

"Very well. I am not to meet with Edwin until tomorrow. Any idea on where you'll find your rogues?" I bit my lip. Not in the slightest... I tried to remember if Silas had mentioned his plan for Caneesho but knew that he never had. The only thing that remained a constant detail were the roles we played. I paused.

"The sea is close to the capital, isn't it?" I said.

"The entire northwestern side of the city is bordered by the ocean." My heart felt lighter, and I smirked.

"Is there any specific place where one might spread a loved one's ashes?" Aleron raised his brows at me but nodded after a moment of thought. He gave me the names of a few places as we crested a hill.

Aleron pulled his horse to a stop once we reached the top. I forgot how to breath when I stopped at his side. What I called a hill from the east was a mountain from the west. The path twisted back and forth as it descended the mountain range that spanned both north and south. I looked straight ahead to the west and couldn't form words. In the distance was a glittering white castle with an immense tiered city spreading down and away from it. Behind the city was endless blue water. My mouth fell open as I tried to take it in.

"Don't worry. It takes everyone by surprise." I could easily hear the amusement in Aleron's voice.

"It's beautiful," I said softly.

"That it is... Come, let's get moving. We'll be there in a few hours."

I stayed motionless, though. In that moment, everything fell away: The mark, the Bloodied Men, the suffering, the death. All of it was eclipsed by the beauty of the world before me. I embraced that moment with open arms and tried to savor the feeling of peace and wonder. I didn't think that I would get another one any time soon.

Chapter 20: Caneesho

There was a sudden change in temperature on the west side of the mountains. The land that stretched around us had already found spring. A few fields had already been plowed and farmers were hard at work on others. Aleron explained that the ocean carried in warm winds and the mountains kept them from moving east so the area never really saw a winter, least of all the kind we had in Rokellia.

"Capilious has never wanted for food," Aleron said. There was something about his tone and the sternness of his brow.

"And Rokellia?" I said, thinking back to what Jeb had told me so long ago: Rokellia was starving. Aleron's eyes darted to me. Pondering over his answer, he sighed.

"There have been better years."

The couple of hours went by slowly. I was excited to see the city and the sea. I had heard stories of the glittering capital surrounded by the deep blue waters and I was fascinated by it. Now that I got a glimpse of it on the mountain, it wasn't enough.

When we finally reached the city, I was surprised to see a line of people filing through the gates. There were guards standing to each side of the door, but they didn't question any of the visitors. Aleron said that the princess's birthday was more like a holiday that went on for a week in Caneesho and all were welcome. It was similar to Dark Day in many ways.

We rode through the gates into the business district and my heart hurt. Aleron was right about it being similar to Dark Day. There were vendors booths set up in neat rows calling out to the citizens and visitors as they walked by. Paper chains, flowers, and bright fabrics hung from building to building. Large white banners with the crowned golden Capilious eagle were everywhere: On flagpoles, on top of buildings, hanging in windows, and small ones were even given out to the people. The excitement in the air was contagious. I smiled brightly as a girl handed me a flag and I tossed her a coin.

"Careful with that," Aleron said quietly.

"What do you mean?" But it was too late. People began surrounding Tempest and holding up their wares, shouting out their bargains. Tempest pranced around nervously and snorted as they closed in.

"Just keep moving forward, they'll get out of the way," Aleron said and even spurred his horse faster. I followed suit and he proved correct again. He quickly led us away from the crowds to calmer streets.

"You have to be careful in the business district, even when it's not a holiday. If the vendors don't take all your money, the pickpockets will," Aleron said.

"Are there a lot of them? Pickpockets, I mean." Aleron scoffed.

"Yes. Just assume every person you see there is a thief, and you may be able to keep your purse. Especially watch out for the children."

"Noted."

I got a better look of the city the further we moved from the gates. The stone streets were spotless. That was one of the most shocking things about the city: Its cleanliness. There were people, horses, and carts everywhere, but the roads were almost shining. The buildings we passed were three and sometimes four stories tall. The whitewashed stone walls looked as pristine as the roads. I asked Aleron if this was the noble district where the wealthy lived but he shook his head. He explained that the buildings were more like inns but working class people lived there permanently. The rooms were more like small houses. It allowed the city to continue growing without taking too much farmland and resources. He called them hive-homes.

Aleron had no problem navigating through the streets and the people. He had perfect posture as he sat on his horse, but he almost looked bored.

"How many times have you been to Caneesho?" I said.

"Five times or so." He knew his way around this large, strange city much too well. Remembering how we snuck out of Onisk, I smirked at him.

"And how many times unofficially?" He looked at me from the corner of his eye and smirked back.

"Too many to count."

"I feel like I hardly know you, Princely," I said lightly but when Aleron responded, his tone was pointed.

"At least you know my name." I felt my heart pound as his eyes looked through my soul, but I said nothing. Would it matter if he knew my name? Would it matter if anyone knew my name? I suddenly felt silly for keeping it so guarded, but my pride wouldn't let it go just yet.

"'V' is fine," I said looking forward again.

"For now..." I decided not to respond and, instead, tried to take in more of Caneesho.

We made another turn, and I could smell salt in the air. I tried to keep my excitement in check, but I couldn't keep the smile from my face. As the smell grew stronger, the sky began to dim, and the people lit lanterns outside their doors. Then I heard a rushing sound. It reminded me of wind blowing through trees, but I knew that wasn't quite right. The sound only got louder as we rode on. Aleron said that the tavern was just around the bend in the street. I would have laughed if I hadn't been so awestruck.

The Sea's End was, quite literally, at the end of the sea. The tavern sat on the edge of the shore, washed in the red-orange light of the setting sun. The ocean, which had been a clear blue earlier from the mountain, looked like it had caught fire as the sun sank. The water rushed and collapsed onto the sand in lovely waves. The warm wind from the ocean was kissed with salt as it blew softly on my face. I fell into a state of calm that almost compared to being in Aleron's arms. The thought immediately brought me back to my senses and I rode quickly after the prince.

The tavern only had one room left for rent due to the celebration. I only shrugged when Aleron glanced at me. At this point, I really should be used to it, but I had to hide my blush when I thought about his arm around my bare waist again. Aleron secured the room while I tried to find a table in the crowded bar.

There was a healthy mix of men and women in the tavern, but most were sailors. After ordering some dinner, I sat at a table as Aleron finished the transaction and listened to the bizarre sea stories around me. A weathered woman with a dark tan told an elaborate story about seeing a sea monster that morning while another man lightly chastised her saying that the beast was supposed to be purple not orange. I smiled, thinking that this place was just like Lily's.

"Aye but have you heard 'bout the Specter of the Nitalla?"

I stiffened. The young man smiled as the room hushed. He cleared his throat after taking a long drink from his tankard. His voice was hushed as if he was telling a haunting bedtime story.

"They say the Specter appears as a beautiful woman with long curling locks red as blood and shining eyes of green fire. She wields two long daggers of glittering stone that are sharper than any steel blade and holds lightning in her hands. Only a fortnight ago, a troop of men dared to travel through the Nitalla and, brandishing her blades and lightning... meant to destroy them all."

Images of that day flashed through my mind and the darkness stirred. I took a deep breath and then a long drink of ale that had been brought to the table.

"She cut the first man nearly in two and then vanished only to reappear behind another and slice his throat. The men were defenseless against her wrath, but she saved the worst of it for the leader, who was stupid enough to mock her."

My hands twitched at his every word as my mind went back to that day. I gripped the wooden cup tight. My eyes began to freeze over, and the mark began to burn.

"She took him by the throat... raised him into the air... and sent her lightning coursing through his veins."

I could smell the blood and burnt flesh as my hands shook. The darkness hummed at the memories and a haze clouded my head. A hand wrapped around my arm and jerked me up. I was pulled outside, and the salty air eased the fog in my head. I felt the wall against my back and found Aleron staring down at me. His face was stern, but his eyes were full of concern.

"Clear your mind. Listen to the ocean," he said. I nodded and closed my eyes. I tried to breath with the tide and soon the bloody memories faded away. Then a new concern came to mind. How did they know about the Specter here? The Bloodied Men must have brought the tale with them as they moved to Caneesho. How did he know the darkness was taking over? Did Aleron hear? But surely he wouldn't make the connection. It was too farfetched... I exhaled in an attempt to steady myself and opened my eyes.

"Are you all right, now?" he said. He was too close again. My face flushed and I sidestepped away from him, staring at my feet.

"Yes, I'm-" The words stuck in my mouth when I looked up. Edwin stood in an alley on the other side of the street, watching us. His black armor gleamed in the moonlight and his hand rested on his sword. He thought he was hidden but I saw him all the same. Why was Edwin here? I took a few more steps away from Aleron. The prince followed my gaze to his guard and cursed under his breath.

"Stay here," he said and walked away. I watched him go to Edwin and I moved farther back onto the sand of the beach, dazed. Aleron said that Edwin wasn't expecting him until tomorrow. How did Edwin know where we were? How did he know that we were even in Caneesho? My mind began to spiral. I never asked where the guards had gone. Did they even leave Aleron alone in the first place? I felt the energy rushing inside of me as my lungs fought for air. What about our truce?

I remember how Aleron lied so easily to Kaul in the barn. He had even staged the scene to his advantage. Had he been lying to me this whole time? This had to be a trap. The more I thought, the more things clicked together.

The rogues and I had gotten away from Feldan too easily. Would his guards really leave him alone to investigate the Bloodied Men's base? Of course not. Then Aleron even got me separated from my friends at my suggestion! That was his aim. I scoffed at myself and raised my hands to my face. I was so stupid. I was blinded by the damned mark and his beautiful eyes. Was he lying about what the mark did to him too? I thought about how he held me, took advantage of me. I ground my teeth and felt the darkness cloud my senses again. The crest started to burn, and I cursed at it.

I saw Aleron approach me, and Edwin was nowhere to be seen. I clenched my fists to hide the sparks. Aleron easily noticed my anger. He reached out to touch my arm, but I yanked it away from him.

"Don't you dare touch me," I seethed. I felt my eyes freeze over and there was a slight green glow in the darkness. Aleron took a step back and he scowled and set his jaw.

"Let me explain," he said cautiously. The shadow inside grew darker.

"No explanation necessary. I can see that I've been lied to." He studied me intently but didn't move.

"What have I lied about?" I quaked with rage at his guarded tone. It reeked of guilt.

"Don't play your games with me, your highness. Consider this truce over."

My fist collided with his face. Aleron staggered back and I kicked his chest, ripping my skirt to the thigh. I tore it from my waist as Aleron stood, spitting blood onto the sand.

"Calm down! Just let me explain," he said and marched toward me. He shot his hands forward but I was ready. I dodged and punched him in the stomach. He grunted at the impact and doubled over. The darkness swirled at his pain.

"I understand perfectly. You got me alone so you could have me arrested the moment I proved myself a caster. Guess what, sire, I'm no caster." My knee crashed into his head, and he tumbled over. He groaned as he slowly got to his feet.

"Can we just talk about this?" Blood trickled from a cut over his eye, and I smirked as it glistened in the moonlight.

"I'm done talking." I launched a series of blows, but Aleron blocked nearly all of them, surprising me and spurring the darkness. Aleron gripped my wrists in his hands and pulled me against his chest. His clear eye pleaded with me.

"Stop this, V." Rage nearly swallowed me whole.

"Don't call me that." I crashed my forehead into his jaw. He fell back into the sand as I heard someone call out from the tavern. A few people stood by the door of the tavern watching us and more began to join them. I struggled against the need to hit Aleron again and ran to the stables at the rear of the pub. I swung onto Tempest and ran away as fast as I could.

Across the city, I managed to find an inn with a vacant room, but I didn't sleep. I tossed and turned with a multitude of conflicting emotions. I was most often angry but after the rage dissipated, my stomach ached when I thought about Aleron. Part of me was guilty about not giving him the opportunity to explain but then I thought about how ashamed I was to have trusted him in the first place. Any explanation he gave me would just be another lie.

My head ached as the morning sun came in through the window. I thought about how I woke up yesterday, feeling refreshed and Aleron's arm around my waist. I rubbed my eyes and sat up. I had to stop thinking about him. I needed to focus on the original plan: Stop the Bloodied Men.

I washed my face in the basin on the small table, tied on another skirt and head scarf, and then gathered my things. I made for the door, but my hand stopped on the handle. For the first time in months, I was alone. There was no one around to guide me or make a plan for me to follow. I should have been afraid, or at the very least, apprehensive but I wasn't. I had gone through so much since my birthday. I wasn't the introverted and terrified girl I used to be. Besides, there was always the lightning. I smiled and pulled the latch.

The main room downstairs was practically empty save for the barkeeper. I took a seat at the bar and asked for some breakfast. He laid down a small platter of ham, cheese, and fruit. I paid him and looked around the near empty room.

"I thought your rooms were nearly full," I said. The thin man chuckled.

"Oh, they are. Festivities run late for her majesty's birthday. I suspect my guests are still sleeping, if they have returned at all."

"Festivities?" He turned his head quizzically at my remark.

"Are you not here for the celebration?" I shook my head and quickly defaulted back to the rogues' story.

"No. My mother passed, and her last wish was for her ashes to be scattered at sea." The man promptly poured a clear liquid into two tiny glasses and offered one to me with a sad face.

"My condolences. To your mother." He raised his glass and tossed the contents back. I thanked him and followed suit. The liquid felt like fire as it went down my throat. My eyes watered and I nearly coughed.

"Never had the gods' tears. Hits you right in the heart every time... Well, during the week of the princess's birthday, there is an event each night: Parties, tournaments, plays, games, balls. It's a lovely time to be in the capital. Today is the jousting tournament at the arena. Tomorrow will be a play of the Devium Wars at the square. And the day after is the masquerade at the castle, Princess Tilteen's favorite." My brow furrowed.

"At the castle?" His eyes lit up.

"Oh yes! Everyone is invited. That's the point of the masquerade, anyone can be anyone." Bells went off in my mind. That must be when the Bloodied Men intended to strike. They could slip into the castle without any question.

"So even I could go to the masquerade?"

"Of course! All you need is a costume and a mask, although good luck getting something good now. Most of the shops are booked up or sold out of the best costumes. Maybe try over in the south district. The best shops are there. They usually have the largest inventory." I thanked him and finished my plate. I laid some coins down on the bar.

"Hold my room for me." He nodded with a smile, and I went to the door.

Finding the dress shops wasn't as difficult as I had imagined. I walked my way south through the city. I decided to leave Tempest at the inn. I had to be as inconspicuous as possible, and she tended to stand out. I knew Aleron was looking for me. My mark itched at the thought.

I noticed a few more elaborately dressed people as I walked further through the city. I followed one of them south and found myself in a fashion district. Once there, some of the outfits seemed much more costume than everyday wear. I saw feathers for skirts and brilliantly dyed animal hides as capes, sometimes they were even worn together. There were also dresses made of metal that looked like gold, but I assumed they were just painted that color judging by how easily the women could move in them.

The oddities helped to distract me from thoughts of Aleron, but the anxiety lingered in my bones. Did he have his guards looking for me too? Every time I heard the clink of a metal dress, I imagined armed soldiers racing down the street after me.

I walked into a shop and was overwhelmed by colors. It was like stepping into a rainbow. Costumes of all types filled the room, men's on one side and women's on the other. There were costumes of animals, flowers, monsters, and even gemstones and metals, like the few I saw outside. I looked at the tall statues that displayed the outfits, afraid to touch them. I was afraid that I would ruin the beautiful works. A few customers looked through the selections but seemed dissatisfied and left without speaking to the older woman behind a counter. She sighed and looked bored but lit back up when she met my gaze.

"Hello, there! My name is Della! Welcome to my shop! Looking for a costume for the ball?" Her smile didn't reach her glass-covered eyes despite the lightness of her tone. She was miserable.

"Yes, actually. I'm not sure what I need. Could you help me, please?" I said politely. Her smile disappeared and she raised a brow.

"You're not from the capital." Her bluntness took me aback and my confidence wavered.

"No... I'm not. How can you tell?" She smiled grimly.

"You actually spoke to me." She walked around the counter with a finger on her chin. She looked me up and down through her yellow-tinted glasses and began to circle me.

"You ever been to a ball?" she said lifting my elbow away from my waist. I moved away from her with narrowed eyes.

"No, I haven't." She kept tapping her chin as she stared at my body.

"What color is your hair?" she said. My mouth went dry. When I didn't answer, her critical eyes met mine.

"You do have hair, don't you? Or is that why you wear the scarf?"

"I have hair... but I would prefer to keep it covered." She raised her brows.

"Covered? Hmm... Do you have a partner that will also need a costume?" I shook my head and she smiled. Was all of this necessary for some clothes? I tried not to flinch when she began to take my measurements.

"Very well. Any preferences, requests, or specifications?" I glanced around the shop to make sure we were alone.

"Nothing too extravagant or constricting, light weight... I also need to be able to wear pants under the skirt." She paused her measuring for a brief moment but then continued in silence. When she was finished, she went back behind her counter and flicked her hand toward the door as she began drawing on some paper.

"Come back the morning of the ball, I'll have it finished then and you can pay." I blinked at her and then glanced at the costumes surrounding me.

"Can't I have one of these?"

"No." I waited a moment for her to continue. When she didn't, I thanked her and left the shop bewildered.

I wasn't sure what to do after that. I knew I should try to find the rogues but, as I explored the city, I realized I really enjoyed my freedom. I was being hunted, yes, but at that moment, the pressure and anxiety of it all was gone. No one here knew who I was and not a single person had been afraid of me. I glanced around at the strangely dressed people again. The people in the capital had their oddities and saw plenty of them it seemed. Here, I wasn't a demon, a caster, or even the Specter. My chest felt light, and I smiled. I hadn't felt like this since my birthday, before everything turned terrible. I remembered forgoing my skirt and shaking my wild, red hair free. I felt such confidence and independence. Standing outside that dress shop in a city I didn't know, I felt like Vespera.

I went back to the business district near the gates and strolled through the booths, keeping a hand on the purse at my waist. I was relieved that the similarities to the Dark Day festival didn't make me unhappy. On the contrary, I found myself smiling as I remembered my birthday, at least parts of it. Maybe it was just my current mindset or maybe I was finally starting to heal.

I looked through some more booths before buying another skirt to replace the one I destroyed last night. The thought dampened my mood. I sighed as I put the fabric in my bag. I was wasting time. The Bloodied Men were here somewhere. I needed to find them but first, I needed to find the rogues.

I looked around the business district once more and took a deep breath, savoring that last bit of nostalgia. I turned away, expecting to become the Specter once again but something lingered, something that felt just a little more me.

Chapter 21: Reunion

I scanned the beach the following afternoon as I stood by a fishmonger's stall. I almost didn't go to the places that Aleron had told me about. It was a high risk since the prince could be waiting for me but after aimlessly wandering the city for hours the day before, it was my best option. If this didn't work, I'd have to start visiting every inn and tavern in Caneesho.

I found myself lingering at the beach, though. I thought that the ocean was beautiful at sunset but there was something miraculous and alive about it during the day.

The high sun was reflecting off the infinite water, turning into a shimmering, moving rainbow. The white foamy waves crashed on the sand relentlessly, yet there was something soothing about the rushing rhythm. The birds, gulls someone had said, were soaring through the blue of the sky only to dive into the blue of the water to catch small glistening fish between their beaks. Boats with white cloud-like sails bobbed atop the water while tan men hustled to pull in large nets filled with fish. Small children ran along the water's edge picking up shells and building castles in the sand. Their laughs echoed with the waves creating a beautiful symphony. The air, crisp with the smell of salt, wafted across my skin and caressed the scarf that covered my hair. How I wished I could have let my hair down at that moment. I imagined what a wonderful feeling that would be. I wanted to walk bare footed along the sand and feel the waves tickle my toes.

"Ay! You looking for something special? I got the best fish right here from Genma's Smile!" I turned back to the vendor with my brow furrowed.

"Genma's Smile?" The tanned willowy old man smiled.

"You must not be from around here... This bay was named Queen's Point after Queen Genma when she died in childbirth. It's the prettiest beach of all the coast. Us locals call it 'Genma's Smile.'" He grinned ear to ear and I found myself smiling too.

"You must have been fond of her," I said, glancing over the beach again.

"Oh yes! She was very kind. She liked to sneak out of the castle and come here. I even talked to her once. I didn't know it was her until later when I saw her in a parade. She was lovely. She had the prettiest eyes..." I stopped listening when I saw a tall broad figure slowly walking along the sand. I held my breath until he turned, and I smiled brightly.

I watched Viht take a jar and pour ashes into the sea. Even though I knew they were from campfires, the spectacle was convincing. The few passers-by gave him a wide berth with bowed heads. I refrained from going to him. I wasn't sure if the Black Guard, or Aleron himself, was watching.

Quite a bit of time went by before Viht turned to leave. When he did, I saw him rub his arm quickly over his face. This wasn't just playing a role to him. My heart ached for him. He took a breath and squared his shoulders before walking across the beach and back to the city. I nodded at the fisherman, who was still rattling on about the late queen, and followed after Viht.

I made sure to keep my distance from him as I periodically checked over my shoulder. I felt eyes on me at every turn, but I never noticed anything out of the ordinary. The streets were much busier now, though. I occasionally bumped shoulders with passers-by in order to keep Viht in my sights. He wasn't moving at a hurried pace, and he never looked back as he went deeper and deeper into the city.

I followed him into the Caneesho Square where he went into an inn with a golden suit of armor painted on its sign. I stopped in the square to make sure that no one else had followed.

At least that's what I said to myself. I still didn't know what I was supposed to tell the rogues. They deserved to know that the Black Guard, and maybe even the Aurelian Army now, might be after us. But then I would have to tell them all about the mark and Aleron. The thought made my stomach turn. Pulling at my necklace, I glanced around the square.

A large stage had been built on one side of the square. I remembered then that there was supposed to be a play for today's festivities. The stage was humble and more of a large platform, but its location was well-planned. The sparkling white castle in the distance served as a beautiful backdrop for the stage. The tall white spires of the palace reached into the sky like gold trimmed icicles growing up from the ground. A blinding light reflected from the walls when it caught the sun's rays, making me squint and turn away. I couldn't keep stalling. I took a deep breath and went inside the tavern.

The place was packed with people. Memories of the Blue Boot flooded my mind. I even expected to see a hazel-eyed man passing out drinks at the bar but instead, I saw Viht. He sat at the corner of the bar with a tall tankard in his hands. His gray eyes looked forward in deep thought, or deep in the past. My anxiety fled away. The seat next to him became free and I made my way to it.

"This seat taken?" I said to him with a small smile. He turned to me and dropped his tankard.

"By the gods," he said as he stood and pulled me into a hug. I felt like a bear was squeezing me, but it made my heart light after the initial shock went away.

"I missed you too," I said with a small laugh. He held me at arms-length and scowled at me.

"What were you thinking? Going off by yourself? I was frantic, the twins were kicking themselves, and Silas- um- uh... well... it doesn't matter. How did you find me? That doesn't matter either. You're all right." He pulled me in again and huffed into my hair. I hadn't realized he cared so much... I swallowed the emotion down and just squeezed him back.

I pulled away first and Viht couldn't look me in the eye. His cheeks were red as he cleared his throat. I decided not to dwell on the exchange. I think we both might have cried.

"Where are the others?" I said. He nodded to the stairs behind him.

"We were all supposed to meet upstairs. I was just having a drink first. Needed to clear my head..." His expression fell and the far-away look was back in his eyes. I hooked my arm in his and went toward the stairs.

"Let's join them shall we?"

We walked up the stairs to the third floor and went to the very end of the hall. Viht knocked on a door with a green helmet painted on it. I tried to keep my breath even. I knew Dax and Kaul would be happy to see me but judging by what Viht said about Silas... I shivered as the latch slid.

"Bout time, old man," Dax said opening the door. Viht crossed his arms over his chest with a smirk as Dax's jaw went slack. I bit my lip to stop the laugh.

"Yes, well, someone held me up." Viht pushed into the room, and I followed after. Dax slowly closed the door to the spacious room with a large bed, a wardrobe, and a table with chairs. Silas stood with his back to us, his hands resting on the windowsill as he looked at the square below. Kaul sat at a table, spinning a gold coin across the surface. Kaul looked up first and gaped at me like his brother had but he recovered quicker.

"Specter! You're here! How? What happened? Onisk was turned on its head over you! Soldiers were everywhere and talking about the Specter-"

"Enough." Silas' icy tone cut off Kaul's excited stream of questions and the chill permeated the room. He still kept his back to us, and I felt my stomach drop. He was furious. I stood awkwardly in the middle of the room while Dax and Viht took seats at the table.

"Explain yourself, Specter." Silas' hands gripped the windowsill tighter. I swallowed but my mouth stayed dry. I had rehearsed the story over and over in my head, but I still almost couldn't put it into words. I took a deep breath and tried to find the best way to start.

"Now!" The rogues flinched as his voice boomed but my nostrils flared, and I set my jaw. I could understand if Silas were upset but this level of anger was absurd.

"As I said in my note, I got a lead on the Bloodied Men while we were in Onisk and so I followed it to the ambassador. You must forgive me for not mentioning it to you directly. You were all a little busy at the

Horsetail." Even though I glared at the devium's back, I could sense Viht, and the twins shift uncomfortably. I continued before they had the opportunity to speak.

"I snuck into the mansion and questioned the ambassador. He had been harboring the Bloodied Men and they had taken Onisk as their base of operations. They didn't tell him about all of their plans but he knew that whatever is happening tomorrow could mean all-out war. Then I had some issues escaping but I got out of the city and came here. I've been trying to find you since." It was a weak story that was full of holes, I knew, but what else could I tell them? The Rokellian Prince helped me escape by secret gate since he was spying on the ambassador too? And we have this magical bond but I beat him up so the Black Guard may or may not be after me? I huffed out my breath to keep from rolling my eyes at myself.

The room was heavy with the tense silence. Finally, Silas spoke.

"That's it?" I narrowed my eyes at his cynicism and held firm.

"That's it." Silas' fingers tightened on the wood until his knuckles were white.

"Everyone out. Now." The rogues deftly stood and walked out of the room after giving me sympathetic looks. I tossed my bag to the floor and crossed my arms, waiting for him to speak again.

"What are you keeping from me, Specter?" he said finally. His voice was low and angry, which only annoyed me further.

"Does it matter? You keep things from me." He whirled around to face me. His yellow-green eyes were fierce.

"Is that what this was all about? You left on this grand lone adventure because you were sore with me for not telling you about my past? That's a bit hypocritical, isn't it?" I was surprised by all of the emotion in his voice. It was always so flat and bored that now he sounded like a different person.

"I'm not sore at you for that. My point is that I can keep things to myself just like you can. And I am more than capable of going about things alone." Silas walked toward me, chuckling and shaking his head.

"That is not how this works, Fairest." My hands dropped to my sides in fists. The energy swirled inside my core and my eyes grew colder.

"Explain to me then 'how this works.'" He looked at me for some time and then Silas' angry demeanor gradually fell away. His eyes were almost tender. I softened. Silas had never looked at me like that before. I looked him over and realized then how disheveled he looked. His usually perfectly groomed hair was haphazardly braided and there were dark gray bags under his eyes. The pride fell from my chest. He had been worried about me. Extremely so.

He slowly raised his hand and touched his knuckles to my cheek as he stared into my eyes. I swallowed. This was almost too much.

"I thought that I had lost you... There is nothing in this world that will take you away from me. Do you understand?" Take me away from him? The frustration returned. I looked into his eyes, hardened with determination, and tried to shake my head.

"Silas, I-" His lips snuffed out my words. His arms wrapped around me so tightly that I thought my ribs would break. His lips were feverish and almost desperate. This wasn't like Silas at all. I pushed him away, having to use more force than I thought would be necessary.

"You- you aren't yourself. What's wrong?" I said, stepping away from him to catch my breath. Silas snickered and ran his hand through his hair, further ruining the braid.

"You, Specter. You are what's wrong with me." Something inside of me reeled. I wouldn't fall for this again. Didn't Aleron say the same thing? Look at what he had done. I knew Silas much better than the prince. There was something off about this.

"This... isn't the right time for this. We need to focus on the Bloodied Men," I said cautiously. Silas froze and I held my breath. After a moment, he blinked, and his shoulders relaxed. The intensity faded from his eyes, and he became the Silas I knew.

"Yes, of course, you are right, Specter. We will have plenty of time to discuss... things after this revenge of yours is done. Apologies... Now that you have returned, we can all rest."

"Rest? Shouldn't we make a plan? The Bloodied Men are supposed to strike tomorrow. We are running out of time." He turned to me calmly.

"While you were away, we did some searching. There is no army amassed in the surrounding areas. That leads me to believe that they are already within the city, posing as tourists." My heart sank. If they were already in Caneesho, there would be no way to find them on our own. We would need luck and a miracle. I found the pendant around my neck and rubbed it as I thought. There had to be a way...

"I need to rest, Specter," Silas said, pulling me from my thoughts, "When my mind is clear, we will find a solution. Until then, do not leave this inn. Do you understand?" That sharp edge had crept into his voice again. I nodded and turned toward the door.

"I will not hesitate to burn this city to the ground to find you."

Dax, Kaul, Viht, and I sat at a table in the tavern of the inn drinking ale and wine. We were silent for some time, each of us lost in our own thoughts. What Silas said as I left shook me. As much as I wanted to go out into the city to try to find something of the Bloodied Men, I knew he meant what he said. He looked terrifying. I finished my cup of wine and waved at a maid for another.

"I must say... I've never seen Silas so... out of sorts," Viht said finally. I took another long drink.

"We don't have to discuss it," I said. My tone was harsher than I intended. Viht seemed relieved though, as were the twins. There was another long silence. The inn wasn't too crowded. The other patrons mentioned the play would start soon and most people were trying to find a good place to watch it from. Maybe I could find a window with a nice view...

"So, what do you think of the city?" Kaul said.

"Not much has changed since we were last here," Dax said. I furrowed my brow at them.

"You have been to Caneesho before?" They grinned.

"We grew up here," they said in unison.

"Really?" They perked up at my interest and leaned forward.

"Pretty rough. Our parents died when we were small. Don't really remember them. Our grandmother raised us," Dax said.

"We lived in a rundown hive home on the east side of the city, near the business district. She didn't make much money, so we got an early start to thieving," Kaul said.

"You were pickpockets?" Viht said. The disappointment was evident in his voice, but the twins were not deterred, instead their eyes lit up.

"The best pickpockets in Caneesho!" they said and toasted their drinks. I laughed at them.

"I feel as though I shouldn't be surprised by this," I said, raising my cup to my lips.

"You shouldn't! You should've seen us. We only got better as we got older," Kaul said.

"Rose through the ranks quick. We got up to baron," Dax said. I paused and lowered my cup back to the table.

"What do you mean 'rose through the ranks?'" Dax shrugged.

"All the pickpockets are a part of a network. There were zones that were assigned by the Duke, who gave orders to barons to give to everyone else."

"Can't have too many pickpockets in one area going for the same people. Everyone would get caught."

"And off go fingers," they said.

"How far does this network reach? The business district?" Their laughs echoed through the room.

"More like all of the capital," Dax said. My head whirled. A secret network of people that run through the entire city?

"Do you still know the Duke? Can we talk to him?" I said quickly.

"There's probably a new Duke now. It changes every year based on the baron that steals the most. Keeps everyone on their toes," Kaul said. My shoulders sagged.

"But there's a good chance that we would know him, though. It's only been a few years since Silas recruited us," Dax said. I twirled my necklace in my fingers.

"What are you thinking, Specter?" Viht said.

"I think we may have just found our miracle."

The inn door closed behind Dax and Kaul, and I wondered if Silas would approve of this plan. The other rogues thought that it was a fine idea.

"Do you think they'll be able to convince the Duke to help us?" I said to Viht. He set his jaw and sighed. After taking another swig of ale, he spoke.

"They took a lot of gold with them. I'd say this Duke may do anything for the right price."

"We just need their eyes and ears. That doesn't seem to be as risky as stealing from people," I said, more to convince myself. Viht cut his eyes at me. I could see that he had a retort, but he kept it to himself. I knew that there was a multitude of things that could cause the Duke to say no. We just had to hope he didn't.

"Where are the twins?"

My shoulders tensed when I heard his voice. Viht went rigid too. Silas sat in one of the empty chairs across from me. His movements were easy, and his body relaxed. The gray bags were gone from under his now hard green-yellow eyes. Viht and I were still on our guard. Silas was an intimidating creature when he was in control. He was nearly terrifying when he wasn't. He glanced at Viht but settled his gaze on me. I took a deep breath.

"Dax and Kaul went to see the Duke, the leader of the pickpockets, to see if they had heard anything of the Bloodied Men.

They have connections there, so they went to follow that lead." I kept my voice even and confident. Afterall, there was nothing wrong with the idea.

"On whose order?" he said, turning his head at me. I squared my shoulders.

"At my suggestion. They can decide things for themselves, if you can recall." The air was thick with tension as we stared at each other. I could feel Viht shifting uncomfortably. Finally, Silas gave me a small smirk.

"I do recall. It is as good an idea as any."

Viht melted into his chair with a sigh and drank from his cup until it was empty. Silas raised a silver brow at him.

"You being out of sorts is worse than sailing toward a hurricane. I'm glad you're better." Silas nodded and waved for a drink.

"As am I."

Silas and Viht began to chat, and I watched the crowd growing outside through a window. The play was to start at sunset, and it was quickly approaching. The sky was a beautiful orange that darkened to purple where a few stars were bright enough to shine against the last of the sun's rays.

"Did the twins say when they would return?" Silas said to me. I turned back to him.

"Late this evening. Maybe after the play is over." He nodded.

"Very well. We can discuss what they discovered tomorrow morning after a long rest." Silas held my gaze as he spoke. I fought back a frown. I knew that he expected me to stay with him and after two days of being on my own, I frankly didn't want to. I didn't want to be alone with him. I wasn't ready to discuss "things" with him yet and I knew he would question me further about Onisk. It was just a matter of time. I also remembered that Tempest was still at the other inn, and I had already paid for another evening. I also needed to pick up my costume. I knew this conversation would not go well.

"I will meet you all here in the morning then," I said and began to stand but Silas' hand grasped my arm.

"You are staying here," his voice was calm but his vice like grip told me otherwise. I sat back down and matched his intense gaze with my own icy glare.

"I have my own room elsewhere and that is where I will stay this evening." From the corner of my eye, Viht stood.

"I think I shall watch the play. I will see you both tomorrow." We did not acknowledge his departure. We were both too caught up in our glaring match.

"Your other room be damned, Specter. You will stay here." I pulled my arm from him, and my nostrils flared.

"You really have no say in the matter. I have already paid for the room and my things, and my horse are there."

"Then I will come with you," he said flatly. I refrained from rolling my eyes.

"No." His jaw tensed, and his eyes flashed.

"You will not be left on your own."

"Why? We both know that I can take care of myself."

"I can't have you disappear again!" The tables around us went silent and I sensed that we were being watched. None of that tempered my anger. My eyes froze over and my tone was low. I could feel the darkness stirring inside but I tried to push it down. I didn't want to lose control and I couldn't take the chance that Aleron could sense it.

"What difference does it make? You and the others are here on my errand. You don't have to be here. You have no right to decide what I do every second of every day. We are not in the forest anymore, Silas. You do not rule here. You do not rule me." Silas was not cowed in the least. He looked like he could strangle me. Thank the gods for the audience. I slung my bag over my shoulder and stood.

"I will see you in the morning." As I walked out of the door, I heard a loud crash. Silas had flipped the table.

Chapter 22: The Duke

I couldn't go straight to the inn. I didn't think Silas had followed me, but I honestly couldn't be sure. He was acting so strangely. He had used the word "attached." I didn't know what that meant. He didn't say that he cared for me. I wasn't confident that he cared for anyone. Respected, yes, found useful, yes, but not necessarily cared for. I was no expert on the subject, but I hoped I would know it when I felt it. But what if he did care?

The salt was thick in the air as I found myself at Genma's Smile. The sun had already been lost to the waves and the sky was dark red at the horizon. I wasn't alone on the beach. There were couples strolling along the water's edge and families ushering their children away from the sea and back home. I sat in the sand just beyond the water's reach, closed my eyes, and listened. The sound of the ocean was so calming. It washed away the anxiety, doubt, and fear. It was almost as if Aleron were holding me again. I smiled as warmth wrapped around me, radiating from the mark.

My eyes snapped open, and I looked around. Night had swallowed all light from the sun leaving only darkness around me. I couldn't see anyone on the beach, nor could I sense them. The mark said otherwise.

I grabbed my bag and made my way to the inn. The streets were surprisingly empty despite moving further into the city. Everyone must be at the play. I stayed on guard. I couldn't shake the feeling of being watched. It was similar to earlier when I was following Viht, but no one was on the streets now. I reached out, trying to sense something.

I heard soft footsteps and the subtle cling of metal armor. My chest tightened and I glanced over my shoulder. A shadow shifted in an alleyway a few streets back. I was being followed. It wasn't Silas. He wouldn't have kept his presence hidden once he was discovered. Aleron didn't wear armor as far as I knew. That only left the Black Guard.

How long had they been following me? I remember having the feeling until I reached the Gold Armor Inn, not inside it though. Did they see Viht or the others? I prayed that they didn't care about them. Would Aleron really send someone after me?

I shook my head and tried to come up with a plan. I didn't want to lead them to my inn. For now, it was my safe haven. I really didn't have a chance at losing them since the roads were empty and I didn't know my way around. My only other option was to fight. I noticed a small alley to my right and darted down it. I removed my skirt and shoved it into my bag and threw it against the wall. I stood in the center of the alley and waited for the guard's arrival, but I wasn't as prepared as I thought I was. It wasn't just a guard that rounded the corner. It was Edwin.

He seemed just as surprised when he rounded the corner and saw me standing in the moonlight. His gray brows were raised ever so slightly. My jaw was set, and my eyes were narrowed as I scanned his frame. He had the same sword and knife. He rested a hand on each of them. I wasn't naïve enough to think that he just wanted to talk.

"We meet again, miss," he said politely and bowed his head.

"What do you want, Edwin?" He furrowed his brows for a moment but dismissed it.

"His majesty requests that you come to the palace... as his guest." I scoffed at him.

"His guest in chains, I assume?" The faint sounds of light footsteps from behind me reached my ears.

"I hope that is not necessary, miss," Edwin said, holding my gaze.

"But it was expected," I said, looking over my shoulder at the two soldiers I saw in Feldan. They froze their movements. I could see the shocked look on their faces before I turned back to Edwin for an explanation.

"Let me apologize, miss, for any misconception." I crossed my arms over my chest.

"Misconception from whom? You or his highness?" Edwin's lips formed a thin line. He really had a small threshold of patience.

"Will you accompany us to the castle of your own volition, miss?" I squared my shoulders and readied myself.

"No, I will not." Edwin looked behind me and nodded to his comrades. The three of them walked toward me with their arms out in an attempt to block any escape. I was almost offended, but I remembered that they didn't know what I could do, and they obviously didn't want to kill me.

Edwin reached me first. His hand shot for my arm but I easily deflected it and punched him in the nose. I didn't strike hard, but his head whipped back, and blood trickled from his nostril. The look on his face nearly made me laugh. He was shocked, horrified, and agitated nearly all at the same time. I had to bite my lip to keep it back.

"I don't have time for games, miss," Edwin said through gritted teeth. His words sent me back to when the prince betrayed me. All he did was play games. The darkness stirred inside me, and I felt my eyes run cold.

"Neither do I."

One of the other men rushed at me from behind. I crouched under his arm and swung my leg, knocking him to the ground. The other soldier grabbed my scarf and pulled me back. The fabric tightened around my neck and made me gag. I quickly yanked at the knot and the tension fell away. I pulled on the other end of the scarf, bringing the guard down. I wrapped the fabric around his neck, meaning to incapacitate him but Edwin ran towards me. His fist swung toward my face, but I tied the rest of the scarf to his wrist. The momentum sent both men toppling to the ground, knocking out the guard. The other soldier stood and lunged at me, but I simply caught his arm, turned, and flipped him over. He landed on top of Edwin in a heap.

With the two guards unconscious and Edwin trapped under their bodies, I grabbed my bag and started to leave the alley before the darkness could get too strong.

"Miss, stop! Please! Let me explain what happened the other night," Edwin said, breathing heavy. I paused but did not turn.

"I don't need or want your explanation. Just... tell Princely to leave me alone." I walked away from the alley, taking note of the sound of little feet following after me.

I waited for some time before addressing my follower. The footsteps were so light that I had to strain to hear them. They also kept to the shadows much better than the Black Guard had. I wouldn't be able to surprise them, but I also didn't think I would need to. I stopped in the empty street and turned.

"Come out. I know you have been following me since I left my... acquaintances," I said, trying to pinpoint the stranger in moonlit street.

Nothing moved. I reached out to sense something but there was nothing to hear.

"I mean you no harm. You must be following me for a reason," I said. After few moments, a small figure stepped out from an alley. I raised my eyebrows at the young girl. He looked to be twelve or thirteen with his small slender frame. He had chin length brown hair that was the same shade as his dirty shirt and ripped trousers. He was also missing his pinky finger from his right hand. A pickpocket.

"You're the woman the twins talked about." My eyebrows went up with surprise. The pickpocket was, in fact, a girl. Her voice was soft and had a sweet melody to it. It was a startling contrast to her rough appearance.

I didn't respond. I had already been attacked once this evening and I had no intention of it happening again. She didn't wait for my response.

"The Duke wants to meet you."

She led me to a two-story building in the business district. From the outside, it looked like most of the other storefronts in the area. The girl went around the side of the building and went in a small door, leaving it open. I stopped at the entry way. She disappeared into the dark and did not turn to make sure I still followed. This could end up being a very bad idea. I sighed and stepped inside.

A single lantern hung just inside the door. I looked around the room and found that the first floor was a shop. There were tables and shelves filled with small trinkets and knickknacks for sale. The girl had gone up a flight of stairs behind the counter. Her soft footfalls were barely audible on the steps. There was a door to the left at the top of the stairs, but the pickpocket turned right into a large open room. There was a sizable table in the center of the room, similar to a grand dining table, with a motley group of young people. There were boys and girls of different ages, clothing styles, and cleanliness. I guessed that none of them were older than twenty. At the head of the table was a dark haired boy of around sixteen with a crooked nose and a flashy gold necklace around his neck. To each of his sides sat the twins, who were gagged and bound to their chairs.

"Gods help me," I muttered to myself as I rolled my eyes. The boy noticed our arrival and extended his arms.

"Look at that! Fingerless Mouse found her. Didn't expect that! Take your cut and go, Mousey." The girl dropped her head. Her cheeks turned red, and she clenched her jaw. She quickly grabbed a large sack off of the table and slipped away as a few larger boys surrounded me. They kept their distance, but it was clear that I was not free to go anytime soon.

"So, you're supposed to be this 'Specter' that I've heard so much about, huh?" The boy seemed unimpressed. The feeling was mutual. I was annoyed by the entire situation. These were children and they had

Dax and Kaul, two men that I trained, captive. I also couldn't just fight them; they were children.

"And I am to assume that you are the Duke?" He smiled smugly and placed his hands behind his head casually.

"Good to know that people still know my name! You know, you don't seem so menacing. These two have always talked a big game that got them in trouble. Obviously, a few years out on their own hasn't helped that. They come in here saying they got a big score for me if I do some spying for the Specter of the Nitalla Forest. Last I checked, this was the League of Thieves, not spies, and ghosts aren't real no matter how many people believe the stories." I remembered the sailor at the Sea's End but that was just one story. Any other stories would be fiction unless he had heard about Onisk. That meant he knew something about the Bloodied Men, whether he realized that or not.

"So, you've heard stories of the Specter?" I said. He scoffed.

"Plenty. Heard a couple of bards singing some poems yesterday even. I must say, it is a nice change from the Devium War shit." I turned my head at him. It took every part of me not to snicker or roll my eyes at his pompous attitude. It made my blood boil.

"And you don't believe any of it?" The Duke barked out a laugh. Dax and Kaul looked at each other and raised their brows. They were ready for a show.

"At first I thought that a caster was just stirring up some trouble in the woods... But a girl single-handedly escaping the Bloodied Men's fortress all on her own? That's a fairytale."

I ran across the room and held the Duke in the air by his throat in the blink of an eye. My eyes grew frigid as he clawed at my hand and the other children gasped.

"It's unfortunate that you don't believe in fairytales, Duke. It's also unfortunate that you didn't take Dax and Kaul's offer. You have wasted my time. I've had better days... Do me a favor and don't make me worsen yours." The Duke nodded and squeaked a reply that I couldn't make out. I let him go and he landed on his knees, panting.

The rest of the room was speechless, save for the twins whose eyes sparkled with glee. I untied the ropes that held the rogues, and they removed their gags.

"Thanks, Specter," they said.

"We didn't expect the meeting to go so poorly. We didn't expect Seret to be Duke either," Dax said.

"We've got some bad history, and they got the jump on us-" I held up my hand and rubbed my forehead before it began to ache. I dreaded the thought of telling the others about this. I shook my head at them.

"I don't want to discuss how you were beaten and tied up by children. Nevertheless, we'll get what we came here for. One way or another." I glanced at the Duke, Seret, as he steadied himself on his chair.

"So, Seret," I said, "Please tell me everything you know about the Bloodied Men." He glared at me, and my anger surged with darkness.

"I'm not saying nothing." I clenched my fists to keep the lightning from flying at him.

"Come on, Seret," Kaul said.

"She can make your head explode," Dax said. I shut my eyes in frustration and gripped an empty chair.

"Barons! What are you all just standing there for? Get them!" Seret said at the other league members.

"This is ridiculous! All of you children sit down!" Green smoke fell from my mouth and spread throughout the room. As it brushed across each league member's face, they came to the table and sat with glazed eyes. Kaul and Dax watched them with gaping mouths. I almost did the same. I didn't know I was capable of controlling a group, but it wasn't the time to question myself. When everyone found their places, the twins began asking questions so quickly, I could barely understand. I just raised a hand at them.

"Please, not now. I just want to get information and go. Yes?" They nodded at me and took a step back. I took a deep breath and pulled at the energy in my core and directed it to my throat.

"League members, do any of you have information on the Bloodied Men's current location or what exactly they are planning for tomorrow. A show of hands, please." The green mist floated around the room and three hands went up; one was Seret's. I asked him to explain what he knew.

"They are all over the city. They plan to go to the masquerade tomorrow."

"To do what?" I said.

"Either nothing or start a war." I sighed.

"I know that. What will dictate that decision?"

"A meeting at the palace. It will happen during the party." My heart thumped. A meeting at the palace? Maybe the Bloodied Men were finally tired of being snubbed by King Karrolei and they wanted to give him an ultimatum.

"A meeting with whom?" Seret shook his head.

"I don't know." I repeated the question to the barons, but they didn't know either. My mind was racing. I didn't know what to do. I rubbed my aching forehead again and the mist began to fade away. Seret and the rest of the members' eyes cleared but they suddenly looked pale. One of the barons grabbed his stomach and retched on the floor. Seret groaned and hunched over the table.

"I feel like horse shit..." The twins looked smug, but I felt horrified. Was this what happened to everyone I had done this too?

"Should've taken the deal, Seret," Dax said. The Duke held his head in his hands and groaned again.

"I would have if I'd known the Specter could take over my mind!"

"Well, now you know. Maybe next time you'll trust us," Kaul said. Seret looked murderous despite his slightly gray face.

"After what you two did to my older sister?" he said. The twins raised their hands in defense.

"She approached us, mate," Kaul said, and Dax smirked.

"She seemed to enjoy herself." I groaned in exasperation.

"We're leaving. Now."

"But they have our money," the twins said. I felt my eye twitch.

"They gave us the information we needed. They can keep it."

The brothers looked at me with their mouths agape and then proceeded to list the offenses Seret had committed against them. Each reason was more idiotic than the last. My blood burned and I ground my teeth. The mark burned lightly. A haze filled my head, and I heard the darkness whispering sweet malicious ideas in my head. I tried to ignore it, but it just got louder, drowning out the mark's attempts to stop them. Images of blood and gore flashed before my eyes. The room felt hotter, and the air was thick. Kill them. Kill them. Kill them.

"Silence!" Green lighting was crackling around my fists and up my arms. The sleeves of my shirt were gone, and green flames were creeping across my shoulders. Dax and Kaul were silent with wide eyes and the league had shifted away from me. I quickly brushed away the flames before they could destroy what little remained of my shirt. I looked back at the twins, but they were both looking at my arm strangely. My hand quickly covered the shining mark. I swallowed.

"We received information so they should receive payment. Both sides were a little... excessive. We are done here... Any objections?" I glanced around the room. Seret and the twins shook their heads while the barons just looked afraid. I nodded and left the room. I just wanted to be alone. The darkness was back again and stronger than ever. What scared me the most was that the mark couldn't stop it.

The streets were just as empty in the morning as they were the previous night. Despite that and the warm weather, I still pulled the hood of my winter cloak down. I lost my only scarf last night and I had nothing to hide my hair with. I nudged Tempest's flanks to a canter towards the fashion district. The seamstress would have a scarf for me to buy and maybe another shirt. Yesterday had been a bad day for my wardrobe. I just needed to get to the shop without another mishap.

Once outside Della's, I tied Tempest to a small post and went in. The shop was devoid of people, much like the streets in the early morning, and nearly devoid of costumes too. She must have been busy after I left. I went to the counter and saw a small bell. I rang it. The tiny trill sounded monstrous in the silence of the shop. A raspy voice screeched from the back room.

"I'm coming! By the gods, why would anyone come in so early? I have to get better about locking that door- Oh it's you!" she said as she emerged from the doorway. Her dark bluish black hair was unkept, but her eyes lit up behind her yellow glasses when she saw me. She waved her hand at me.

"Come in! Please come to the back and I will show you my creation! Lock that door first! This is much too early." She disappeared into the doorway. This woman was so strange. After locking the door, I followed her back.

The workshop was a large open room with more fabrics than I had ever seen, all rolled and stacked by color. There was a large worktable to the left haphazardly covered with beading, crystals, feathers, and metal pieces. Mannequins were lined along the right wall, some with clothes on them and some without. On the back wall with the fabrics was a ladder that led up to a loft where there was a small fireplace and bed.

In the center of the room on a mannequin was the most interesting dress I had ever seen. I made my way over and circled it with curiosity. The dress was partially covered by a flowing cape that clasped at the shoulder by a large clear jewel. At first it looked like a simple black fabric but, as the sun streamed through a window, tiny jewels scattered throughout the cape sparkled in the light. Under the cape, the bodice was just a low-cut corset. There were no straps or sleeves to be seen. My brows rose at the discovery. I had never seen such a design. It was risqué to say the least. The skirt, similar to the cape, looked like living shadows. The fabric of the billowing skirt was the same as the cape but layered so fully that the skirt was pitch black and opaque.

I gingerly touched the skirt, almost expecting my hand to vanish inside it. The fabric was light as a feather. The skirt shifted and I saw black trousers under the skirt. They were light with a bit of stretch to them like tights, but they weren't sheer. The costume was a work of art, maybe even magic. I looked at the seamstress with wide eyes.

"Is this mine?" I said in disbelief. She rolled her eyes at me but there was a hint of a smile on her lips.

"Of course, it is. So, you like it? Wonderful! You will be the embodiment of the night sky! Revolutionary, elegant, and discrete... with trousers! I've created the fabric myself. Lightweight, moveable, comfortable. I know it will be the start of the latest trend in Caneesho, should anyone see them, that is." I smiled and ran my hand over the bodice.

"It's beautiful." I still couldn't imagine that I would wear this dress. I hoped that I would do it justice.

"Now, what to do about that hair-" the seamstress pulled the hood from my head and lost her words as my blood red locks fell free. My stomach clenched and I winced at her slacked jawed expression. She just stared at me. She did not scream or shake or cower. She just stared.

I finally cleared my throat.

"As I said yesterday... I prefer to keep my hair covered. I'm... sorry for startling you." The silence was heavy in the air. I started to raise my hood again, feeling ashamed, but she stopped me.

"No, I am sorry. Your hair reminds me of a dear friend of mine. She passed long ago. It just... caught me by surprise... I have a net that would match the dress perfectly." She scurried away and then returned with a small package.

"Inside is your mask and the net with jeweled pins. Put your hair in two plaits and then loop them together under the net. It's very simple. I also recommended placing pins all along the hairline on your forehead if you want all of your hair hidden." I nodded and gently took the package from her.

"Thank you so much... If it isn't too much trouble, I would like to have something to cover my forearms to wear with the dress."

"Just the forearms? I can make something quickly, I think."

"Also, I lost my headscarf. If you have something similar, I would like to add it to my total... and a shirt too, if you'd please." She started to shake her head before I finished my request.

"I have nothing in this shop like those rags you wore yesterday. I will replace it with quality fabric as a gift... for reminding me of my friend."

"Oh, thank you but I couldn't-" She walked away, waving her hand in the air, and saying that I should be worrying about how I would even pay for the dress.

Chapter 23: Drowning

I pulled at my necklace as I left the stable of the Gold Armor Inn. I had forced myself to not think about last night, any of it, and I regretted the decision. I had no idea what to say to the rogues. The twins must have told the others about the mist, smoke, or whatever they decided to call it. I imagined the twins thought it was fantastic. Viht would be impressed and maybe a little concerned. Silas... I cringed.

I pushed through the entrance to the inn, bags over my shoulder and new dark purple headscarf covering my hair. Della had shown me a new way to tie the scarf that completely covered my head and neck, leaving only a conservative opening for my face. It felt so much more secure. I hoped that I would remember how to do it again.

The tavern was mostly empty. A few patrons littered the room snacking on fruit and cheese. One of those patrons was Viht. He sat alone at a small table drinking from a steaming cup. He smiled when he saw me. I almost sighed with relief. He couldn't know yet.

"Hello, girl. How is your morning?" I dropped my bags on the floor and sat in the chair across from him.

"Nothing to be upset about yet," I said with a shrug. Viht raised an eyebrow and took a drink of the black liquid. I breathed in its aroma and recognized it as coffee.

"They have coffee here?" I said. I only knew of it because a traveling vendor had come to Ameris during Dark Day trying to sell it. I was very young, but the vendor let me try a cup mixed with honey and cream. I thought it was lovely but it's effects kept me from sleeping for nearly two days.

"Yes. I used to come to Caneesho to buy the powder and brew it at home. My wife loved the smell but hated the taste. I didn't expect to miss it so much. Having this again reminds me of her," he said with a soft, bittersweet smile. I smiled too.

"Perhaps you could buy some powder before going home?"

"Perhaps... It seems that you have been shopping already. What have you there?" He nodded to the large bag that held my costume.

"Something that I'll need to discuss with everyone. Speaking of, where are they?"

"Still upstairs. The twins had something to discuss with Silas. Let us join them." My heart sank. Viht stood with his cup and strode toward the stairs after taking my bags. I tried to prepare myself for the onslaught and followed him.

Viht knocked on Silas' door and we were greeted by the devium himself. His expression was calm and a bit cold, normal. My heart pounded in my tight chest, and I scolded myself. I had no reason to fear him but there I was, jaw set to try to hide my anxiety.

"Are these all of your things?" Silas said, flatly. I narrowed my eyes.

"Yes." He nodded and stepped away from the door to allow us in. Viht cut his eyes at me but said nothing. Silas sat gracefully in one of two chairs that had been pulled away from the table near the door to under the window. The twins were both sitting on a large chest. Viht went and sat on the bed after placing my bags by the chest. Silas glanced at the chair next to him and then back to me expectedly. I closed and locked the door. I narrowed my eyes at Silas and then sat on the table, putting myself as far from him as possible. He clenched his jaw but said nothing. The room was too tense. The twins had already looked uncomfortable and now they shifted audibly on the wooden chest.

"What did you find out, boys?" Viht said finally. His words helped to alleviate the tension, but it was still there. As Dax and Kaul told the story of finding the hideout and trying to proposition the Duke, Silas stared at me. The intensity of his gaze maddened me. I couldn't decide the source of the intensity. I was sure most of it was rage but there was more to it.

"I think Specter can tell the rest of the story from here," Silas said just as Kaul was explaining how they were held captive. I felt frozen in place. I had no idea what the twins told him. I wasn't sure that I was ready to tell him, or anyone else, about the mist.

"A pickpocket found me and-"

"How did she know you were the Specter?" Silas said. I searched for a story. Why hadn't I rehearsed this?

"I lost my scarf after I left here yesterday. Perhaps she guessed from my hair." Silas just looked at me and said nothing, so I continued.

"She said the Duke wanted to meet me. She led me to the business district and inside a store where he and his barons waited with Dax and Kaul bound and gagged. The Duke didn't believe that I was the Specter. Once he realized who I was, I... persuaded him to tell us any information he had on the Bloodied Men. There will be a meet-"

"And how did you 'persuade' him exactly?" Silas said tilting his head to the side. I swallowed. He knew. I looked at the twins. Their faces were red, and they wouldn't meet my eyes. Silas most definitely knew.

"I don't see how that matters now, devium."

"It matters to me." The mark gently burned as my anger rose. He had no right to tell me what I should do about my abilities. I knew that's exactly what he wanted. It was my prerogative to take time to come to terms with my power. I did not have to abide by his timeline. I wouldn't let him manipulate me.

"The Bloodied Men are having a meeting in the castle during the ball. The results of that meeting will determine whether or not there will be a war. That is what matters right now. We must go to the ball-"

"Are you afraid of this too, Specter?" The room was suddenly hot, and my fists clenched. I was not a coward. Dark rage washed over me hard and fast, as if I fell into an ocean of it. Any sway the mark once had was washed away and I struggled to keep myself afloat. I never thought I would wish for the pain of the mark, but I did then. I ground my teeth to keep my voice down and my body began to shake.

"We are not doing this now." My skin was colder than ice, but I was melting on the inside. I could see the green light from my eyes had started to change.

"It seems that we must," Silas said with a bit of excitement in his voice.

"What's happening? Specter, are you all right? Silas, why are her eyes red? What's happening to her?" Viht said and took a step toward me. The lightning was fighting for release. I fell to my knees as I struggled against the power. I was drowning in it.

"Everyone. Get. Out." My words came out in jagged breaths. I barely noticed the struggle of the twins dragging Viht out of the room. I stared at my fists as dark red lightning sparked around my arms, setting my sleeves on fire. Panic seized me. The air disappeared from the room and my chest heaved.

"Just let go, Specter. Don't be afraid," Silas said from above me. The darkness echoed his words, but they felt so wrong. I squeezed my eyes shut and fought against the exhaustion. I couldn't do this much longer.

I opened my eyes and saw the bladed crest on my arm, still glowing a faint green. I pressed the mark against my sweaty forehead, where Aleron had kissed me. I tried to reach out to him through the mark with what strength I had left.

"Please... help me." There was a blinding flash of blue light and then all went black.

I awoke feeling like I had been stoned. My head ached and my body felt broken. Then I remembered what happened. I quickly sat up and held my hand over my eyes. A soft green light reflected off my skin. I sighed in relief and collapsed back on the bed. I took a deep breath and smelled food. I slowly sat up and saw a plate of hen and spiced potatoes with a large tankard beside it. There was also a steaming bathtub in the room but that wasn't my goal at that moment.

I stumbled when I first got out of bed, but I managed to get to the table. I collapsed into the chair and practically inhaled the food and the tankard. I thought it was wine, but it was gone so fast, I couldn't be sure. My fatigue improved immensely. There was a small note beside the plate. The handwriting was crisp and flowing. Silas. It explained that the rogues went to find costumes for the ball and would return just after midday. I went to the window and glanced out. The sun was high but still to the east. Plenty of time for a bath.

After thoroughly scrubbing my skin and hair, I just sat in the water to soak and reflect. I hugged my knees to my chest as I thought about how far I fell. My pride was gone, and I was terrified. I realized that I had taken the mark for granted. It wasn't a curse at all. This power was the curse.

I looked at the crest and sighed. Aleron had helped me. I could feel it in my bones. I just didn't understand why. Had I been wrong about him again or was this just another trick? My finger hovered over the blades. Whatever his reason, I was still thankful. I softly traced my finger down the black sword that ran through the center of the mark. The green glow intensified.

"Thank you," I whispered. There was a gentle pulse that radiated from the mark, and I smiled.

I had dressed and just finished combing my damp hair when the rogues returned. The innkeeper had already removed the tub, making the room feel more spacious again. I carefully wrapped Henry's comb and placed it back in my bag then sat on the bed. There was a weight on my chest and everyone else seemed to feel the same except for Silas. He almost looked annoyed. After they each found a seat, Viht spoke first.

"How are you feeling, Specter?" His gray eyes were full of concern and worry.

"Normal again, thank you." I gave him a small smile. There was a pause. The room felt too small. There was an oppressive cloud in the room and it made my skin crawl in the silence. Time felt like it went on for years.

"What was that?" Kaul said softly, finally breaking the silence. I swallowed. The twins had seen the mark and after what happened that morning, I guess it was time.

"This... force I have inside... I don't know why I have it or where it came from. On my twentieth birthday at the Dark Day festival, I ran into a Black Guard who had watched our fight in the woods the day before. He thought I was a spy for the Bloodied Men and wanted to arrest me. When I tried to get away, he grabbed my arm, and this appeared." I removed the cloth from my arm and showed them the glowing crest.

"Is it moving?" Dax said leaning in close. I nodded at him.

"You don't seem surprised by this, Silas. I assume you already knew?" Viht said.

"I only learned of it after the raid celebration."

"It's the same as your necklace, isn't it?" Kaul said.

"So, you know what it is?" Dax said but I shook my head.

"I had just bought the necklace that night. The two daggers reminded me of my own blades. I don't know what it means."

"Continue your tale, Specter. I'm sure there is more," Silas said flatly. I cut my eyes at him and tried not to get angry.

"After the mark appeared, I fell extremely ill. The guard took me to my aunt, a healer, but the Bloodied Men attacked. We tried to escape but... that's when you found me. Some of my abilities were there from the moment I awoke after that night: The strength, the heightened senses, my eyes. Others appeared over time like the lightning. But there is a darker side to the power. I hear a voice in my head urging me to do terrible things. It's what happened at the raid and I... enjoyed it."

I could feel my eyes sting with tears. I took a few slow breaths until they eased. The rogues were silent, but I couldn't look at them. I just stared at my hands and continued.

"The mark helped keep the darkness in check, even to the point of causing me pain when I wanted to go too far. But now it seems to have stopped." Silas shifted in his seat but said nothing.

"It doesn't stop the darkness anymore? When did it stop?" Viht said.

"I noticed last night during the meeting with the League of Thieves. I got angry so quickly and I almost lost control of the lightning. I wanted everyone in that room dead. Everyone... Then again this morning. I got angry and lost control, but it has never felt so strong. I don't know what the red meant but I know it can't be good. I'm so sorry."

Viht's hand landed on mine softly.

"I am sorry that you felt that you needed to endure this alone."

"I just don't want to hurt any of you." The twins snickered but there were smiles on their faces.

"Not like you haven't before, Specter," Kaul said.

"Just try to break Kaul's nose this time, alright?" Dax laughed as Kaul glared at his brother. Viht and I laughed at the pair.

"Now let's have everything out in the open, shall we? Please show us this new ability of yours," Silas said, casually. I turned to him with wide eyes. He stared at me intently and leaned forward, resting his elbows on his knees. I looked at the twins. Their smiles had disappeared, and they wouldn't meet my eyes.

"No. I think I've pushed my luck enough for today." Silas raised his brows and then smirked.

"But it seems unfair for us all to know except for Viht." I furrowed my brows.

"Silas, is this the best time-" Silas cut Viht off.

"It is."

"I can control people, Viht. Make them do things and make them tell me things even if they don't want to and I don't like to do it. That's how I got the Duke to tell me what he knew about the Bloodied Men. There, now that everyone knows, can we discuss what we are doing this evening?" I said pointedly at Silas. He looked smug. I wanted to punch the smirk off of his face.

"We get to this meeting. We hope that all goes well and then we have more time to learn about the Bloodied Men. If things go poorly, we try to kill the leaders after learning as much as we can from them. At least that part will be easier now."

"That's it?" I said. It just seemed too simple and, honestly, not fully thought out. Silas raised his brow at me.

"Yes. I suggest we all get some rest this afternoon. We don't know what will happen tonight and so we should be prepared for anything."

Viht and the twins agreed and left. I stood to follow but Silas stopped me. I hadn't noticed him move. His hand was gentle on my arm.

"Stay." I looked at his hand and then up at him.

"I'm not sure that I should." His lips form a smirk.

"Where else have you to go?" His tone was missing its usual condescending bite. It was light and reassuring. It confused me and I had no response for him.

"Stay, Fairest. Please. I'll bring up some lunch." He took my hand and pressed it to his forehead, bowing low, and then left.

Part of me was thankful that he wasn't trying to goad me, but the other part couldn't help but wonder why. It was suspicious, to say the least.

We finished our lunch of smoked fish at the table in relative peace. At least Silas seemed completely at ease, but I felt more anxious as time passed. He was acting too suspiciously for me to relax. I kept cutting my eyes at him, waiting for him to reveal exactly what he was after.

He took our empty plates and sat them outside the room. After closing and locking the door, he made his way to the bed, took a pillow and laid it in the floor. I had had enough.

"What are you doing?" I said. I could only see his feet from around the bed. He kicked off his boots.

"Trying to get comfortable. This was our previous arrangement, was it not?" I set my jaw. Was this a game?

"It was..." I said slowly.

"So, I am honoring that arrangement. Although, I do hope that you do use the bed. I may get upset if it goes to waste." I rolled my eyes and stood. My muscles ached from the movement. I was still tired from that morning. Silas was right. We all needed to rest. I pulled off my boots and crawled into the bed.

I closed my eyes and started to drift to sleep when Silas spoke.

"Specter, I would like to apologize." My eyes opened in surprise, and I waited a moment before answering.

"Apologize for what exactly?"

"My behavior."

"You'll have to be more specific," I said, flatly. There was a pause and then he sighed.

"My insistence this morning... as well as my exasperation yesterday." The fact that he was apologizing made my mind spin but that with his bizarre mood swings just gave me a terrible headache.

"I don't want to talk about that now. When this is over-"

"That is what you said, yes, but after having time to think about it, I do not agree. Either we die tonight, or we discover yet another destination to reach. We don't know how much farther this will go. I'm afraid I will go mad before this is over." My heart quickened in spite of me. I wanted to dismiss him and this antic as a game, but he sounded so sincere. Silas was never sincere. All of that, with the fact that he was right, made me reconsider.

"I don't know what you hope to accomplish... but fine. Say what you have to say."

"May I sit with you?" My stomach flipped and I spoke before thinking.

"Y-yes." I sat up and slid over to make room for Silas. I stared awkwardly at my hands while he sat on the bed. I was painfully aware of how close he was. I hugged my knees to my chest but becoming smaller didn't make me feel better. He scowled at the wall in front of us.

"I am much older that I look, Specter. Deviums are blessed with a much longer life than that of humans. I have travelled to many lands and experienced things I never dreamed possible. In all my years and all of my experiences, I have never felt so drawn to anything as I do to you." My cheeks flushed as my heart raced. My brain reacted differently to my body's excitement though. I was bewildered. I had no idea what to do with this confession, but Silas wasn't finished.

"I didn't hide the fact that you fascinated me. A young woman full of secrets with a fighting ability greater than my own, wielding unimaginable power, and possessing unparalleled beauty. I was a fool to think that I wouldn't become... attached. When you weren't in the room at the Horsetail, I thought you just wanted space but then the city was in an uproar. The Specter had attacked the ambassador and fled the city. It was as if something inside of me broke. I felt worry and anxiety; two things that are not common to my kind. I lost all of my composure. For nearly three days, I became something I had never believed possible: Desperate. And then you just appeared, seemingly unaffected by your absence, except you had more secrets." Silas held up a hand when I tried to speak.

"I know that you are not telling me everything that happened while you were gone. It angered me but now, I realize that it doesn't matter. At least not now. You had returned... but then you insisted on leaving again. I didn't want you out of my sight. All I could think about was what if you didn't return again. What was I to do then?" He finally looked at me and I wished he hadn't. The panic on his face was too raw and his eyes were too fierce. He looked mad. I held my breath as he touched my face.

"You must understand, Specter, that I can never lose you." I was at a loss for words. I was flattered and my heart fluttered but my head and my gut had a different reaction. He was too intense, too strange.

"I don't know what to say," I whispered finally. He moved his hand down to my neck and his thumb traced a line across my jaw. He refused to break eye contact and his voice dropped to a low, raspy whisper.

"Say my name." There wasn't enough air in the space between us and I could hear my heart in my ears.

"I think we-" He nearly sneered at me, and his eyes went dark with impatience. His hand on my neck tightened ever so slightly.

"Say my name," he ordered. My eyes went wide, and my breath caught.

"Silas." Just like the day before, he kissed me. He knotted his hand in my hair and pulled me to him. As he kissed me, I felt a haze fill my mind. He was so warm, nearly burning to the touch, and it was intoxicating. I closed my eyes and moved my mouth against his. I wrapped my arms around his neck and ran my hands through his silken hair. He bit down hard on my lip, and I gasped. He deepened the kiss, and his tongue explored my mouth. I got caught up in the frenzy of him and copied his movements. I felt him smile and he pulled me closer.

I wanted to run my hands over his bare skin. I pulled at his shirt, but he made no effort to remove it. I huffed with frustration and pulled harder, tearing the fabric. I threw the ruined shirt to the floor and Silas was spurred to go further. He pulled down on my hair sending my head back. I gasped as his lips moved to my neck just below my ear, nipping at the skin with his teeth. My hands roamed his scorching torso and he sighed into my neck as he shivered.

I pushed Silas down onto the bed and I moved my lips across his chest. He trembled under my touch. I smirked and my hand moved lower to his navel, drawing light circles around it. His muscles constricted and he shivered again. My mouth found the scar I had given him, and I kissed down its length. Silas shook violently and he groaned. He flipped us over and pinned me down with his hips as he tore apart my corset, leaving me in my undershirt. He moved the hem of my shirt and slid down to kiss my stomach. I hummed as his hot mouth touched my cold skin. I wanted to feel his burning warmth everywhere. Silas' lips moved lower, and he began to pull down my trousers.

There was a knock at the door. I jumped at the sound and Silas froze. Another knock. His head fell on my stomach, and he growled. My chest heaved as I tried to catch my breath. My heart pounded in my ears, and I ran my hands over my face. The lustful haze began to lift as there was another knock on the door.

Silas placed a soft kiss on my hip and lingered there as I pushed my hands into my hair and stared at the ceiling. Finally, he moved off the bed. What just happened? What was I thinking? Wasn't I angry at him just minutes ago? What did this mean for us now? My mind went to Aleron, but I shook my head. Why would I be worried about him? My mind wasn't working as it should.

I swung my legs out of the bed and saw Silas' shirt and my corset lying in tatters on the floor. My face flushed and I kicked them under the bed as he opened the door.

"What do you want?" Silas said, flatly. I looked toward the door and was horrified to see that Silas stood there shirtless with his trousers hanging low on his hips. I couldn't see who had knocked but I heard a familiar voice, soft and song-like.

"I need to speak to the Specter."

Chapter 24: The Ball

Silas let Mouse into the room and leaned against the door after he closed it. I stood and gestured to a chair. The girl looked me up and down, glanced at Silas, and looked back at me with a raised brow. I crossed my arms over my chest after trying to smooth my hair and tried to keep my face stoic.

"Why are you here, Mouse?" She sat in the chair and looked again at Silas. He looked more frightening than I did at the moment. His brows were furrowed, and his jaw was set. He was definitely annoyed and maybe even a little angry.

"Don't mind him. Just tell me why you are here," I said, softening my voice. She rubbed her hand where her pinky used to be, and her eyes shifted around the room.

"I have more information about the meeting." I tried not to react, but my mind was a whirl.

"What do you want for it?" She met my eyes in surprise.

"You aren't going to smoke it out of me?" I pursed my lips and sat on the end of the bed across from her.

"Not if I don't have to. You came to me with this information for something so what do you want from me?" She clenched her fists and squared her shoulders. Her courage was impressive.

"When you leave the city, I want to go with you." My brows rose and my mouth fell slightly open. I didn't expect that at all. I glanced at Silas, but he made no move.

"Why?" I said, looking back at Mouse. Her expression went flat, and she held up her hand with the missing finger.

"My life is hell and I want a new one." Silas chuckled from the door. I rolled my eyes at him.

"Well, you certainly have the right kind of humor... Do you have nowhere else to go?" She shook her head at me. Her eyes pleaded with me even though her face was firm. This girl was proud and brave. I sighed and looked at Silas. He closed his eyes and rubbed his forehead in thought.

"What good would you be to us?" he said finally. She swallowed but her voice remained confident.

"I'm quiet. I could be a good spy. I even have experience."

"Experience?" he said skeptically.

"I know more about the Bloodied Men than anybody else. After what I saw the Specter do last night, I went out and got the information she wanted. Here I am, them none the wiser. And I knew where to find you, didn't I?" I smiled at her tenacity.

"She has made fine points," I said. Silas pursed his lips and huffed.

"Indeed. I'll need to speak to the others about this."

"Dax and Kaul will speak for me. They were my barons before they left," she said quickly. Silas stared at her for some time, but she did not waver. Finally, he sighed.

"You pull your own weight from now on until you decide to leave. You will receive no pity from us. Do you understand?" She nodded. I could tell that she wanted to smile in her excitement, but she didn't.

"It's settled then. What do you know?" I said.

"The meeting will be between a few leaders of the Bloodied Men and the king. It'll happen in the king's personal study after the he dances with his daughter at the ball."

"Did they say what the meeting was about?" She shook her head, but I smiled anyway. Now we had a better chance.

Evening fell on the city as I adjusted the black bracer-like pieces that covered my forearms. The gown fit perfectly, and the hidden trousers felt like a second skin. It was strange, though, to have my shoulders completely bare. I looked at my mask lying on the table next to the hair net and jeweled pins. The mask was molded black lace, light and delicate, that was supposed to reach up to my hairline. I sighed. I still needed to finish my hair. I picked up the net. It was hard to believe that the flimsy fabric would be able to conceal the curly mane, but I trusted Della's work.

There was a knock on the door as I began to braid my hair. Silas walked in after I called saying that I was dressed. He had put on his costume with the others. We agreed that neither of us needed the distraction of the other's presence. I needed space to think. I wasn't sure how I felt about what happened. Silas also took the opportunity to explain Mouse's arrival to Viht, Dax, and Kaul. Mouse was to come back to the inn and wait for us to return from the ball.

Silas wore a dark orange shirt and dark brown fitted trousers. A fox mask rested on his forehead so I could see his face. He carried a plate of food and sat it on the table. I tensed as his arm brushed against mine. I glanced up at him, but he didn't look at me. He took my hand away from my hair and kissed my knuckles. I held my breath.

"Allow me," he said and picked up my comb. I put my hands in my lap and had to remind myself to breathe. He was so close, and it made my skin crawl. I couldn't decide if it was a good or a bad thing. The more I thought about what happened, what almost happened, I became more unsure about it. I enjoyed those moments: The haze in my mind, the rush through my body, and the heat of his lips. What I detested was how he made me feel nearly every other moment.

Silas created two neat braids in my hair, his fingers lingering on my skin as he did. He looped the braids around my head and secured the net in place with the jeweled pins. He brushed his fingertips across my shoulders and down my arms, leaving burning lines on my skin. He leaned down and I tilted my head. He kissed my neck and softly bit my ear.

"Please know that I fully intend to finish what we started. Sooner rather than later... Much sooner."

My heart leapt into my throat, and I turned to look at him. He quickly planted his hot mouth on mine. He then stood and held his hand out to me.

"Come, Fairest. The masquerade awaits."

The castle looked ghostly in the full moon light. The stars twinkled in the crisp and clear sky, just opposite the ground. People in fantastically ornate costumes covered the gardens leading up to the castle. Apparently the party started as soon as one crossed the gates. Fire dancers and acrobats littered the yard surrounded by spectators. A servant greeted us and offered us glasses of golden sparkling liquid. Only the twins accepted. They removed their full-face masks, one a sun and the other a moon, and tossed back the drinks. They shrugged, unimpressed, and put their masks back on.

"You two chose the wrong kind of masks to partake in food and drink," Viht said, shaking his head.

"There was nothing left," one twin said.

"After you took the bear mask," said the other. Viht just laughed.

"You shouldn't let girls distract you." I nearly jumped when Silas took my hand. He smirked and linked my arm through his.

"We need to get inside. Remember, we split up and try to find the leaders. If that fails, follow the king." Everyone nodded and we pushed forward toward the castle's entrance. Silas kept his hand on mine even while our arms were linked. Part of me wondered if it was just to keep me from withdrawing it.

We ascended the steps that led to the two towering golden doors of the castle. Servants stood on either side of the door. Some held golden platters with drinks and other took coats and shawls from the people entering palace. One of them approached me when we reached the top of the stairs.

"May I take your cloak, milady?" he said and bowed. I nodded after a moment of hesitation. I unclasped the large jewel, and he took the cloak as it fell from my shoulders. His brows rose as he handed me a small card with a number on it. He instructed me to give this to a servant to retrieve my cloak when I wished to leave. I nodded again and slipped the card into my waistband.

I felt so exposed without the cloak. I regretted not asking Della to add sleeves. I tried to ignore the surprised looks from women and smirks from men as we moved through the palace. I instead focused on the architecture as we followed the flow of people forward.

The floors were smooth white marble and there were matching columns trimmed in gold lining the white walls. Large paintings with ornate golden frames hung between the columns. Some were of common people, and some were landscapes but there were no portraits. Then we passed a mirror, and I froze. My hand slipped from Silas' arm, but I was too preoccupied. I hadn't seen myself in the gown yet and I was speechless. The woman in the mirror was fair and mysterious. Her form fitting gown was dark and endless save for the tiny twinkles from the jewels on the flowing skirt as they caught the firelight. The dress was woven from the night sky. The only color the woman possessed were two shining green eyes. They were eerie and striking against the black mask. She was beautiful but it didn't feel like me. Wasn't that the point of the evening, though? To become whatever one wanted to be for one night?

I set my jaw and squared my shoulders. It didn't matter what I wanted to be. I needed to be the Specter and she had a mission. I turned away from the mirror and looked around for the others, but they were already gone, swept away in the crowd of people. I took a deep breath and made my way to the ballroom.

The entryway was much closer than I expected it to be. I stepped out of the hall and was awestruck. The ballroom was gorgeous. There were two layers to it. The top floor served as a viewing area of the lower. A marble railing with golden candelabras protruding from it circled the level. Food was offered on the upper level. I could smell roast pork and beef in the air as well as spiced fish. Enormous bouquets of red roses stood by each table of food which lined the outer area of the rotunda. Instead of walls, towering windows lined the level. There was an outdoor balcony on each side. The south balcony overlooked the city below and the north had a beautiful view of the ocean.

The lower level was the dance floor but there was no music playing and no one dancing. Groups of people littered the area chatting. More golden candelabras and rose bouquets rounded the floor. A giant golden chandelier hung from the painted ceiling. It was light blue and white fluffy clouds were scattered throughout. It looked just like the sky above Caneesho. With all of the light in the room, it truly seemed like the sun was streaming through the windows.

Across from the staircase leading down onto the dance floor, were three thrones sitting atop a platform. The largest throne was in the center. It was made of marble with a golden eagle with outstretched wings carved at the top. To the left was a smaller golden throne adorned with rubies and diamonds. The final throne clashed with the entire room. It was an understated gray stone etched with silver and onyx. I caught myself smiling at it and quickly scolded myself. Just because I thought that Aleron had helped me that morning didn't mean that he didn't lie to me. His personal soldiers also attacked me. I needed to be on my guard.

I glanced around, deciding that the twins and Viht would be on the upper level. The twins wouldn't be able to resist the food and Viht wouldn't be caught dead dancing. I held up my skirts and went down the stairs. How were we supposed to find the Bloodied Men in all these people? I reached the landing and took a glass of wine from a passing servant. There were small tables around the dance floor where people stood to take breaks from dancing to drink and chat.

I slowly made my way around the room, trying to reach out my hearing for anything of interest. Most conversations were about the party itself: The food, the wine, the revels. I did discover that the dancing would start only after the king and princess led the first dance. Apparently, it was a tradition. Some spoke of the princess and the prince.

"You know the real reason why the king pushed the party back, don't you?" a bird woman said to a horse man. He shook his head. "Well, they had to have Prince Aleron here to announce the engagement!" I choked on my wine as it nearly came out my nose. The horse man turned to me and offered me a handkerchief as I hacked, and tears stung my eyes.

"My gods are you alright, milady?" he said as the bird woman patted my back. When I could finally breath, I nodded.

"The wine is much too strong for me. I do apologize." The bird woman giggled.

"You must slow down, my dear. The night is young! I say, who did your costume? It is magnificently sublime!" We exchanged a bit more small-talk before I excused myself.

My head was a mess. How could he be getting married and not bother to mention that to me? We slept in the same bed! He held me throughout the night! I grabbed another glass of wine from a servant, downed it, set it back on the tray, and grabbed another. Why was I so upset? Didn't I even bet in favor of their marriage a few months ago? Nothing had really changed for him since then. Nothing truly romantic happened between us. Besides, I'm sure I'd done more with Silas than Aleron had with Tilteen. Right?

The room started to heat up and I pressed my back against a marble column. Its smooth, cool surface helped to clear my head. I was winding myself up for no reason. None of it affected me. Trumpets sounded and silence fell upon the room. I looked up at the top of the staircase and saw two figures appear.

"Introducing, his royal highness, King Karrolei Chrysos, and his fair daughter, Princess Tilteen!" The room erupted with cheers and applause.

The king held his arm out and his daughter laid her hand on top of his. Both of them smiled but neither one reached their eyes as they descended the stairs. Karrolei wore a white silk shirt, a red vest with swirling golden stitching, and crisp white trousers. He was very broad through the shoulders and tall and looked much younger than he should at his age. His nose was long, straight, and prominent. He had thick, rich brown curling hair and his face was shrouded by a matching curling beard. He didn't smile but his head raised a bit higher, and his eyes twinkled as the people cheered. Perhaps it was the rubies on his large golden crown, but his eyes looked red.

The Pearl Princess was a surprise to me. Henry hadn't been totally right. She wasn't dumbfoundingly gorgeous, but she certainly wasn't ugly either. Her long mousy brown hair hung in thin waves around her shoulders. Her large eyes were a bright brown that matched the light freckles on her cheeks. Her costume was much more elaborate on her long and lean body. She wore a single-pointed golden crown that was covered in rubies and diamonds. The bodice of her dress was deep blue lined with green and tied with purple ribbons. The neckline and skirt were made entirely of peacock feathers.

"His royal highness of Rokellia, Prince Aleron Argentus!" Much quieter applause sounded, and I moved further back into the shadows. Aleron descended the stairs alone. His father hadn't come. I wondered why but seeing Aleron distracted me. His hair was slicked back like it had been at the Dark Day tournament and a small silver crown sat on his head. He wore black trousers and a gray coat embroidered with silver and black that stopped at his hips. His shoulders looked tense despite the calm; stoic look on his face. His blue eyes stared straight ahead. I winced when I saw the thin red line above his left brow and the greenish bruise that hid in his beard. I wasn't sure how I felt about him, but the marks reminded me that he wouldn't be happy to see me. Aleron paused at the base of the stairs as the king and princess stopped in the center of the dance floor.

The people circled around them with anticipation. I stood against the wall about thirty feet to the right of the thrones and as far from Aleron as I could be. Music began to play, and the king and his daughter danced. I scanned the room, hoping to see something, anything, strange.

On the other side of the thrones, I saw a small door-like opening appear in the wall. If I had been standing anywhere else in the room, I would have missed it. I was already starting toward it when three hooded figures went into the opening. I glanced at Aleron, praying he wouldn't see me, and ran as fast as I could. I caught the hidden door just before it closed. I peaked in and saw a secret passage leading deeper into the castle. I removed my skirt and hid it in the thin space between the column and wall just next to the door. Another deep breath and I went in.

I could easily hear the footsteps on the stone floor. I stepped as lightly as I could and raced after them. The corridor branched to the left and right as well as lead straight to a staircase. I paused and listened intently. I heard a door open and close up the stairs. I followed the sound and it led to a single door. I pulled the latch softly and the door swung toward me. A tapestry hung over the door. I waited and listened before peering around it. They didn't speak but I sensed people in the room. They weren't too close. I cautiously peered around the tapestry. The room was filled with bookshelves that were trimmed in gold. The study. My heart pounded. I found it.

The three figures gathered around a table in the center of the large room. I closed the door behind and bolted behind a tall bookcase until I could find a better hiding place. There was nothing to hide behind except more bookshelves and the tapestry. I looked up and saw large statues of strange creatures perched around the room on a ledge near the ceiling. The ledge was fairly high, but I could make the jump, I hoped anyway. I just didn't know if I could do it without being seen.

I picked up a tiny stone that was displayed on the shelf beside me and tossed it across the room. The figures quickly turned toward the sound and I leapt up onto the ledge and hid behind a statue. I could hear my heartbeat in my ears, and I tried not to breathe too loudly. The men searched the room but after finding nothing, they went back to waiting at the table. Now to wait for the king.

I didn't have to wait for long. Not even a few minutes later, King Karrolei walked through the ornate door and closed it behind him. It seemed strange that he wouldn't have knights with him. In the ballroom, he was a stern but gracious, and perhaps a bit vain, leader. Now, as I watched him from the shadows, he was someone else entirely. There was a terrifying aura around him. It commanded attention and obedience with a sinister edge. I could feel the wrath just lurking inside of him. His eyes were narrowed, and his mouth was a grim line.

"Our eternal king," the figures said and bowed deeply. The king sat in the largest chair at the head of the table, facing me. I moved a bit further behind the statue and into the dark.

"Sit." His deep voice rumbled through the room. I flinched at his tone, despite his low volume. The men sat immediately, two on the king's left and one on his right. They slowly lowered their hoods, one's hands trembled slightly. He sat immediately left to the king. I looked over their faces, but I didn't recognize them.

"Reports," the king said. I furrowed my brow. Mouse must have been wrong. These couldn't be the Bloodied Men... perhaps they were spies with the Aurelian Army.

The man on the right cleared his throat and began to speak.

"The army's number currently stands at three thousand. Our recruitment has... slowed since the... victory at the border. Criers have been sent further south to... flourish our numbers. All men have been armed. Our food supply is holding out. We should not have to ration if we gain access to another city's resources," the man said. His voice was slow, and he measured his words. Sweat beaded on his brow and he swallowed audibly. My heart pounded against my chest. The king cut his eyes to him, and he continued.

"My eternal king, there was... a... situation in Onisk... It was infiltrated. She managed to escape but we have reason to believe that the Specter-"

Karrolei struck so quickly, I almost missed it. I didn't even realize he had a weapon. A metallic tang filled the air as blood poured from the man's throat. The smell shook the darkness awake as my stomach dropped. Mouse hadn't been wrong.

"I thought it was understood that anyone that speaks her name will speak no more?" the king spoke slowly, each word dripping with malice. Karrolei knew about me? He stood and brought the dagger to his face. He closed his eyes and inhaled slowly. My heart pounded and my palms itched as the room grew hotter. Rage swirled at my core and the darkness hummed at the smell of blood. The voice began to whisper. I blinked hard as Karrolei casually moved around the table and pushed the body to the floor with the blunt of his knife. The man sitting next to the body stared at the floor, caught between horror and reverence. Karrolei stopped behind him and placed a hand on each of his shoulders. He tensed and held his breath. The king bent to his ear and spoke in a measured tone while holding the other soldier in his paralyzing gaze.

"I remember making my request clear... Explain to me how an entire city filled with my loyal followers managed to allow this... girl into the base but then also let her escape. What say you?" He traced the knife's edge along the one's face but did not cut him. The man began to stammer as his comrade's blood stained his cheek.

"M-my eternal k-king, we did-didn't think-"

"No, you didn't think... but I cannot fault you for that. I haven't asked you to think, however, I do not feel that you truly understand." Karrolei stood and walked back to his place but did not sit. My blood boiled as I watched him. I felt my eyes grow colder as he sat the bloodied knife on the table and planted his palms to either side of it.

"Let me reiterate so that the weight of my request is understood. We have had many victories: The death of the Rokellian queen, the ruin of Rokellia's harvest, the destruction of the Rokellian trade center. We have so easily proven to them what my visions have foretold for so long. Devtera will be under attack, and it is not ready. Only I can lead the forces to victory against our enemies, whenever it is they come. Rokellia has not listened, but I am merciful. They shall have one final opportunity to give me the forces I need. Should they refuse, I shall remove all that stand in my way, whether they be ghost, queen, or prince. I will be the All Powerful and nothing will take what's mine."

My body shook with rage, overtaking the mark easily once again. The king killed them. And for nothing. He murdered hundreds, if not thousands, all for nothing. There was no threat at our borders, so he created one. He took away everything I had ever known and destroyed my life. I wanted to see his skin burn under my lightning. I smiled and the darkness began to take over.

"Hail, Karrolei Chrysos, the Eternal King, the All Powerful," the men said.

I drew my daggers and leapt.

The Bloodied Men barely had time to react before I landed on the table and sliced their throats. They crumpled to the floor, and I smiled as the blood pooled on the ground. I turned to Karrolei with frigid eyes. For a very brief moment, the king looked shocked. His reddish eyes were wide, and his mouth was open, but the expression vanished almost as quickly as it appeared. I was puzzled at his reaction, but I did not stop. I kicked at his chest but instead of falling to the ground, he simply caught my foot. My chest fell and my brow creased. He smirked at my confusion and then threw me across the room.

I crashed into a bookcase and the breath was knocked out of me. For a moment, my shock and confusion snuffed out my rage. What just happened? How did he throw me like a twig? I heaved and tried to push the books and artifacts off of me. Karrolei walked around the table with his arms behind his back. His expression was smug. My anger resurfaced but not at full force. It didn't matter. He was going to die.

I raced at him and swung the dagger at his head. The king ducked and kicked my legs out from under me. I landed flat on my back, and he kicked me in the ribs. There was an audible crack and pain erupted from my side. I grunted and rolled to my hands and knees and coughed. Blood splattered on the floor.

"Come now," the king said, "they wait fifty years to send an assassin, and this is who they choose? I must say, I am offended." I scowled. I had no idea what he meant but I didn't have time to think about it. I rolled away just as Karrolei tried to kick me again. The movement was excruciating with my broken ribs. I stood and realized I had left one of my blades behind. I spit more blood from my mouth as Karrolei stooped to pick up my weapon. He held it up to the light and narrowed his eyes.

"Lovely weapons. Incredibly deadly... at least when wielded by someone who knows what they're doing." I ground my teeth and green lightning swirled around my empty hand. Karrolei raised a brow and twirled my dagger in his hand. I ran at him again to strike high with the lightning but changed at the last second, sliding across the ground and cutting a large gash on his leg. I had sprung back to my feet, expecting the king to react to his leg. I was wrong. I turned just as he threw a punch into my left cheek. I staggered but I managed to catch his wrist and sent lightning coursing up his arm. He slashed at my arm as if he would cut it off. I dodged but still came away with a long cut on my outer left forearm. The fabric covering my mark fell to the ground. When Karrolei noticed it, he snickered.

"Branding yourselves now? I'll never understand your clan... I am growing tired of this game. Let us finish it. Shall we?" He moved so fast that I almost couldn't see him. I managed to protect my face, but I failed my body. I felt tiny stings and cuts all over my legs, arms, and torso. My strength was gone, and I was in too much pain. His attacks stopped and blood coated my body. My head felt light, and my knees buckled. Karrolei's hand caught me by the neck and lifted me up, feet dangling. His arm was charred black and stank of scorched skin. My dagger fell from my hand and clanged on the stone floor. I clawed at his hand as I tried to breathe.

"So, this is the Specter, a failed Genmari assassin. Strange that you would reveal your presence as you did. Creating panic and paranoia is not a Clan Ferrum tactic... No matter. Your little crusade is over." Karrolei's eyes began to glow a burning red as he prepared to sink my own blade into my stomach.

"Stop." The green smoke appeared without me thinking about it. It didn't stop him completely in time. The blade was embedded into my skin by a few inches, but I would live from that at least. Anger filled his eyes and they flashed.

"What affinity is this? What have you done to me?" His voice was low and threatening. I felt a small rush of confidence and I clung to it with everything I had.

"Put me down and let go." His arm shook violently but eventually my feet touched the ground. His hand shook as his fingers released my neck and the dagger. I pulled the blade from my stomach and took a step back. My vision swam and I blinked quickly. I knew that the mist would not hold him long. I pulled on all the energy I had left and sent it to my throat.

"You will not move from that spot. You will not call for help." His body slowly stopped shaking until he was statuesque. I sheathed my blades and he seethed at me.

"I will find you before you return to Autemia. You will die in this land." I tried to turn away, but the room swayed. I collapsed and coughed. Blood splattered on the floor as shots of pain exploded from my ribs. When I opened my eyes, I saw a fox moving toward me. He wrapped his arms around my torso and under my legs. He raised me up and turned quickly to the servant's corridor.

I glanced over my shoulder where the king stood and my heart quaked. His eyes blazed with a bright red light.

I remembered our escape in flashes. The fox, Silas, I realized, carried me down the corridor in a blurring sprint. There was the smell of food and the heat of roaring fires in a large kitchen. I was in a wagon being pulled by horses with two matching sets of terrified eyes staring down at me and I faintly squeezed the hands that held mine. There was a slamming door and Silas saying to find a healer that knew how to keep his mouth shut. Throughout it all, was pain, terrible, burning pain.

Chapter 25: Truths

I felt the pain before I was fully awake. My limbs were on fire and knives stabbed my right side with every breath. I gasped at the intensity of it and moaned when the pain doubled at my gasp. My eyes watered and a few tears escaped, running down my temples and wetting my hair.

"You're awake," Silas said. His voice was not kind. I was in his room at the Gold Armor Inn. I looked at him, confused by his tone. I tried to move but fiery pain surged through me. I looked down at my body. My chest and arms were nearly completely wrapped in bloodstained strips of cloth. A blanket covered my lower body, but I knew they looked the same. I closed my eyes and tried to take a deep breath. Another mistake. I coughed, racking my body with more pain, and blood trickled from my mouth. I tried to speak but no words came out. My throat felt like a desert. I swallowed with a wince and tried again.

"What happened?" My voice was hoarse, and it cracked.

"A disappointing display. I thought I had given you enough time. I thought you would be strong enough by the time we reached Karrolei. And yet... you failed. Such a disappointment." At the mention of his name, everything came flooding back: The ball, the Bloodied Men, the meeting, the king, and my utterly quick and brutal defeat. I wanted to cry. I had failed. I closed my eyes and thought about Silas' statement. I was a disappointment. I wasn't strong enough to face Karrolei. I didn't know... But... how did Silas even know we would need to reach the king?

"You knew that the king controlled the Bloodied Men?" I looked at Silas and found his mouth in a grim line. He looked up and sighed.

"Yes. I had my suspicions long ago but the letters from the raid confirmed it." I narrowed my eyes at him and gently shook my head.

"But the letters-"

"You never asked to see all of the letters." He didn't smirk but I knew he wanted to. I was at a loss. I had almost died. Why was he acting like this? Silas stood and walked to the window. He looked out and the sun's rays made his hair shine. It made my chest hurt.

"Why? Why would you keep that from me? Especially when I would find out anyway?" He didn't look at me when he spoke.

"Because you were weak then. I thought that letting you follow the breadcrumbs would be enough time for you to become stronger. I was, obviously, wrong. I thought I could help you realize your full potential, but you were too afraid." He sounded disgusted with me. His words tore a hole through my core. I felt angry and hurt and, after thinking back to how intimate we had been, used and betrayed and dirty. And yes, I had been afraid, but I didn't know that I couldn't defeat Karrolei. I was completely unprepared but I realized I could have had warning. I felt my eyes shine as I ground my teeth.

"You knew what Karrolei was," I said with a growl. He briefly raised a brow at me then turned back to the window.

"Knew that Karrolei was like you? Yes, I did. I had hoped that the years would have softened him. That too was not the case, however, I did expect you to do more damage than you did." My hands shook causing tremors of pain to radiate up my arms. Silas knew about everything, and he had been there, watching me fall. A few more tears fell down my face.

"Why didn't you help me?"

"You are a better fighter than I and you failed. Karrolei would have killed us both," Silas said flatly. I felt a part of me shatter. I had always been suspicious of Silas' motives, but I never expected this of him.

"So, you would have let me die?" My voice cracked again. Silas sat on the bed and gently placed his hand on my cheek. I jerked away from him, despite the pain, and clenched my jaw. He smiled softly at me. His voice changed then to the tone I had wanted to hear from the start. It was gentle and reassuring. He almost sounded loving. It made me sick now.

"Yes, I would have but you were resilient, and you survived. And now as you lay here in excruciating pain, I can see that you would love to hurt me. It shows me that there is still hope and that you can still prove useful. I still need you, Specter, just not as you are now. You will understand in time. Conveniently enough, you will have plenty of time to lay there and come to my side of things. You will nurture and strengthen that red, fiery power inside of you. I'll make sure of it... Now rest. We will leave tomorrow." He pressed a kiss on my forehead and left the room.

Tears welled in my eyes, and I cursed at myself. I would not let that devium have any of my tears. He didn't deserve them. He deserved to be cut to ribbons and left to rot.

"Specter?" I glanced around the room, but I didn't see anyone. There was a scraping sound from under the bed and Mouse appeared at my side. I widened my eyes at her.

"Were you under there the whole time?" I said, softly. She nodded. I must have looked terrible. She couldn't meet my eyes and looked like she was about to cry.

"I'll be all right. I'm just a little banged up." She snapped her eyes to mine.

"Banged up? When you got here last night, we didn't know if you would wake up. The healer said you wouldn't. He didn't know who you were, of course, but still. You are kind to me. You're the bravest and strongest woman I've ever heard of, let alone know. I don't want you to die... And Silas let this happen..." I smiled at her as her words made my heart feel a little lighter. I swallowed down the pain and reached for her hand. She flinched but then squeezed my fingers tightly.

"I'm awake. I will recover. As far as Silas is concerned..."

I would not be his tool. I would not let the darkness take over. The mark would stop it. I paused. The mark hadn't been enough to stop the darkness. Panic bubbled up from my core.

"Specter, what's wrong? What does he want you to do?"

"He wants to make me a monster." My voice cracked again, and I coughed up more blood. Tears of pain ran from my closed eyes again. Mouse ran from the bed to the table and brought back a cup. Water had never tasted so wonderful. I nodded at her in thanks.

"You won't let him make you a monster, will you?" I felt my eyes go cold as I stared at the ceiling. I didn't know what his plan was, but I wouldn't be a part of it. I wouldn't be his weapon.

"I'd die first." The weight of my statement filled the room. Mouse shifted uncomfortably and finally spoke.

"What are we going to do?" I furrowed my brow at her.

"We?" Her reply was swift and defensive.

"I'm not staying with him." I couldn't blame her, not after what she heard. I didn't really want her with him either. She was talented but she had been through enough already. I nodded and thought for a moment.

I glanced at my arm, where the mark lay hiding under bandages. There was only one thing we could do.

"First, I need you to bring me the most potent pain suppressor in all of Caneesho. Then, I need you to deliver a message."

Mouse made good on her end of the plan. She had left the room and reappeared with a strong smelling herb while the sun was still high. She instructed me to chew it and not let it out of my mouth until I was ready to be bedridden again. I nodded and she held it to my mouth. I fought the urge to gag and began to chew. The effects were almost immediate. It was still painful, and I felt lightheaded, but I was able to sit up after a few minutes.

I swung my legs to the floor and Mouse helped me stand. My chest was covered only by bandages, but my under-linens were still on. My thighs only had a few deep cuts on them, but each step sent a jolt of pain through my body. I ground my teeth on the herb and prayed it would continue to get stronger. Mouse helped me dress in a skirt, a large shirt, and my boots and she packed the rest of my things. She put the cloak around my shoulders and threw my bag over her shoulder.

"Where are the others?" I said.

"They left to gather supplies for the journey. They have to find a carriage or wagon for you to ride in too."

"When did they leave?"

"Just before I did. They said that they would return before supper, and they asked me to look after you." I hobbled to the door and Mouse dipped under my arm to help me. I smiled at her.

"Well, you certainly are, Mouse." She looked at her feet.

"Actually... my name is Umbra. Mouse is just a nickname the League gave me. I never really liked it..." Her words really struck a chord in me. I smiled again.

"You never seemed mousy to me. Let's go, Umbra."

We shuffled down the stairs with immense difficulty. My legs didn't want to support my weight which left me partially falling onto each step and pain ripping through me. When we reached the bottom, the exit to our right, I turned to Mouse with sweat glistening on my forehead.

"Have any more of that herb?" She shoved more into my mouth. I propped myself against the wall by the door and asked Umbra to get me a pen and paper from the innkeeper and then bring Tempest around. Umbra gulped but did as I asked.

As I finished the note, Umbra opened the door and looked pale.

"I never liked horses but yours is terrifying." I smiled softly.

"She just likes to be difficult. Do me a favor and cut a lock of my hair would you?" She nodded at me quizzically. I placed the blood red curl in the note and folded it tightly.

"What kind of note is this?" I chuckled at her and tried not to wince.

"You aren't surprised that I can write?" She shrugged.

"I think you can do anything." My heart melted. If she hadn't said so casually, I may have cried given the state I was in. I really wanted to prove her right.

"I'm trying."

Getting on Tempest was horrific. When I finally sat in the saddle, I turned and vomited from the pain. My body was covered in sweat, only making my cuts burn. I looked down at Umbra holding the note and she gave me more of the herb.

"Do you remember the knight that attacked me the night we met?"

"Edwin."

"Yes. Take that to him. Don't say who it's from. He'll know. Just tell him it is extremely urgent. Then I want you to meet me at The Sea's End. You know it?" She nodded and tucked the note in her pocket.

"Be careful," she said and bounded away.

"You too," I whispered and began the long, aching journey to the beach.

I fell off of Tempest into the sand when I tried to dismount. My body spasmed and tears streamed from my eyes. I vomited again. So much for the herb. As I slowly stood, I felt a stickiness on my arms and torso. Blood had started to stain my white shirt. I cursed and pulled my cloak tighter around me and hobbled inside after trying to hide the bloodied sand. The tavern was crowded but not nearly like the last time I had visited. People were singing and chatting and, of course, gossiping.

I paid the innkeeper for a room and added some extra coins for someone to stable my horse and bring food and drink to the room. Thank the gods there weren't any stairs. I was already faint, and I was terrified that blood was pooling at my feet. I went around the corner to the room.

It was small with a bed, a chest, a window, and a small table with a pitcher of water and a bowl. I stood in the middle of the room. I wasn't ready to sit or lay on the bed. I knew that I wouldn't get back up on my own. There was a knock on the door and a young boy brought in the food and drink. I tossed him a coin and told him that a girl without a pinky would be coming to join me. He nodded and left. I dropped my cloak to the floor and peeled off my shirt. I ground my teeth and cursed as my vision went blurry. I clung to the windowsill until the dizziness passed.

After a few breaths, I looked up. It was such a beautiful view of the sea. I opened the pane and softly inhaled the salty air. I had managed to keep my breathing shallow, but it was much harder with the ocean before me. As I watched the waves, the pain faded just a bit. I knew the pain was still there, but the ocean was so soothing. I was thankful for the reprieve.

I stared into the endless blue and remembered when my life was different. I longed for normalcy and what I thought was a simple thing: Acceptance. Then my life was burned to ashes, and I thought that I had to change. I became someone new, a force to be reckoned with because I wanted revenge. At least I thought I did. I remembered that it was actually Silas' idea. All of it was: The fighting, the killing, the revenge, the power. I didn't want that. The Specter did. I sighed and gripped the windowpane. What did I want?

The sun had fallen lower in the sky and the horizon started to shift away from blue. There was a light knock at the door and then Umbra entered, I could tell by her feather-light steps.

"Did you find him?"

"Not exactly," Umbra said, awkwardly. My body tensed as I caught the smell of books and spices.

"By the gods... What happened?" Aleron said as he entered the room. I glanced at him from over my shoulder.

"You're going to want to sit down, Princely. Umbra, can you wait for Edwin outside, please?"

Aleron rushed to me as the door latched. He quickly swept me up and laid me softly on the bed. His touch was so light, it was like I floated through the air. He removed my boots and then sat in a chair by my side, but I didn't see him move it there. I didn't think much of it. My head was starting to swim. I was finally able to look at him. His body was tense with a false calm. His messy black hair fell around his frantic eyes.

"I'm sitting. Now tell me what happened to you." I swallowed.

"I'm the Specter." He looked at me for a moment and his jaw tensed. I closed my eyes. I didn't want to see the anger or the disgust on his face. I had seen enough rejection today.

"I know." My eyes snapped open. His expression was soft. "I had my suspicions when I heard the story about the Specter in the woods. She matched your appearance and you both had the same weapons. I knew when I found you in Onisk, trying to learn more about the Bloodied Men. Honestly, it wasn't that hard to put together since I had already met you." He smiled at me but there was no smugness to it. It was a gentle, reassuring smile but I still wanted to cry.

"I tried so hard to keep it a secret from you. I thought that once you knew, you would have me arrested for being a caster." I felt silly after I said it aloud. How did I lie to myself about it not being obvious. His smile grew and he laughed. My heart leapt at the beautiful sound. He had a full, chesty laugh that was contagious. I began to giggle but pain erupted through my side, and I gasped. Aleron took my hand and pushed my hair away from my face. His lack of formality caught me off guard, but it felt wonderful. I closed my eyes and savored the feeling of his cool, soothing touch. I blamed it on the pain. Just a moment of weakness and a longing for compassion.

"Now tell me what happened to you." The moment was over. My mind whirled at the memory of the king.

"Karrolei happened," I said. All traces of humor fled from his face, and he sat straighter in his chair. He became the prince again.

"Explain what you mean." I swallowed nervously. I didn't want to tell him about his mother, but he deserved to know the truth.

"I found out that there was a meeting between Karrolei and the Bloodied Men. I thought that they were going to threaten him with war if he didn't recognize them, but I was wrong. He is behind everything. He plans to declare war. He wanted to ruin Rokellia because your family refused to give him more forces. Karrolei wanted to show you how ill-prepared you were for an attack. He had Ameris burned to destroy trade. He ruined the harvests. He said that... he killed your mother."

Aleron went completely stiff, and his eyes turned glassy as he looked through me. His hand began to shake, and his eyes started to glow an icy blue. My mouth fell open as every object in the room started to float into the air and blue lightning sparked around his hand. My heart thumped hard against my ribs.

He was like me. I felt relieved. I hadn't wanted to think about it, but I was so happy that I had someone besides Karrolei that was the same as me. I reached out and touched his face, overcome by awe and surprise. A million questions raced through my mind. What are we? Where did we come from? How many more of us are there? I stared into his shining eyes, but they still weren't looking at me. I swallowed down my questions and ran my thumb over his cheek.

"Aleron." He blinked a few times and his eyes cleared as the fierce glow faded until it was seemingly gone. The floating items softly landed in their places and the sparks disappeared. He sighed and I removed my hand from his face.

"Thank you... for telling me," he said. I squeezed his hand, and he gripped me tightly.

"You're welcome. I understand how you feel completely." We sat there in silence, looking anywhere but at each other. I knew he was remembering what he had lost just like I was. Finally, I continued the story.

"When I heard Karrolei's confession, I fell into the rage and tried to kill him. He did this to me. I didn't know that he would be so strong. I didn't know that he was... well I didn't know that anyone was like me..." Aleron slowly shook his head at me.

"How are you not dead? Karrolei is extremely powerful, even by our standards, and ruthless. Frankly, you got out lucky." My stomach churned as I tried to imagine something worse than this. I shivered as I remembered barely saving myself in time.

"It was my power. He called my affinity. I can control people's actions. I just told Karrolei to stop and... he did. I knew it wouldn't last long but I escaped." Aleron narrowed his eyes in thought.

"I have never heard of that kind of affinity. Interesting..."

"And the darkness? The bloodlust? Have you heard of that?" Aleron's face turned solemn, and he nodded.

"Yes, but this is an incredibly unique situation. My father would know more. Would you come with me to Rokellia? You would be safe from Karrolei. There is so much I can show you and we can figure out the rest together."

I looked at our clasped hands. My heart swelled with hope. There was safety, there were answers, and, most importantly, I wasn't alone anymore. It was the most complete I had felt since the morning of my birthday. I knew what I wanted. I wanted to discover everything I could about what I was. I realized that what I had always longed for wasn't acceptance from others because it was never enough and couldn't be enough. What I wanted was acceptance from myself.

Umbra slowly opened the door.

"Edwin is here. He's bought the healer, Specter."

"Thank you... Umbra? Please don't call me 'Specter' anymore." She smiled widely at me.

"What do I call you?" I smiled softly at her and looked at Aleron. His shoulders were tense, and his eyes were full of anticipation. I turned to the window and watched the cool beautiful sea swallow the raging sun.

"My name is Vespera."

The End.

The story isn't over...

Vespera's story continues in the next installment.

Coming Summer 2024

Acknowledgement

If you've made it this far- thank you. You have given me what I've always dreamed of: Acknowledgement of my work. I hoped you enjoyed the beginning of Vespera's story, but if not, at least you gave it a shot and that's really all I can ask for. Thank you.

This book has been 15 years in the making (no, I'm not exaggerating). It has gone through A LOT just like I have as a person and as a writer. I want to say thank you to the one person who was there for me for nearly all my various meltdowns and transformations over the years, barring only those he didn't know me for, my husband, Zak. I dedicated this book to our precious, feral boys and you. I want them to look back on this and see that it's okay to fail and break and get lost while trying to find your dream. But I want you to know that this only happened because of you supporting/hounding me the entire way. We parent by example. We fight for what we believe in and you always fight for me. I love you.

To all my smart, wonderful, beautiful friends who read this in its various stages throughout the years, thank you. And, yes, the second book is almost done. I swear.

Finally, thank you to the family that read the book. You know who you are. It means more than you'll ever know.